COVENANT: EXODUS

BOOK ONE OF THE COVENANT SERIES

JD TODD

Story Well Publishing
2637 Northgate Blvd
Fort Wayne, IN 46835
www.storywellpublishing.com

Publisher's Note: At Story Well we believe that every author deserves to have their voice heard, and by purchasing this book you have helped us continue to find new voices to bring to the world. Thank you for supporting us and our authors!

This is a work of fiction. Names, characters, places, and incidents are a product of the author's imagination. Locales and public names are sometimes used for atmospheric purposes. Any resemblance to actual people, living or dead, or to businesses, companies, events, institutions, or locales is completely coincidental.

Covenant: Exodus/ JD Todd. -- 1st ed.
ISBN 978-1-952876-00-4

This book is dedicated to my amazing kids and my beautiful wife Jessie. None of this is possible without all of you.

*Behold, I establish my covenant with you and your
descendants after you, and every living creature that is with
you, the birds, the cattle, and every beast of the earth with
you, as many as came out of the ark. I establish my covenant
with you, that never again shall all flesh be cut off by the
waters of a flood, and never again shall there be a flood to
destroy the earth.*

– Genesis 9: 9-11

Reimagining the Ancient World

Dr. Graham Reynolds(Archaeology Today: August 2018)

When I was asked to write this article, I must admit, my first reaction was one of disbelief. Indeed, there was a time when I was commonly published in any number of journals, but that was long ago. My more current research is not typically embraced by my peers, in fact, this very publication has, on numerous occasions, labeled my recent theories as pseudo-archeology at best, and flat-out idiocy at worst. One particular quote that has stuck with me stated, "Dr. Graham Reynolds has again shown us how dangerous information can be when it is manipulated to support wild theories with no regard for truth. His storied past seems to be leading to an asylum in his future." Eloquent. Recent events have, however, thrust my previously ridiculed opinion into the mainstream, and as I have never been one to hold a grudge, I agreed to write the following article and help boost the paltry readership of this once great journal (maybe I hold a slight grudge).

The point of this article, however, is not to focus on new events, as exciting as they indeed are, but instead to take a look far back into the history, or dare I say, prehistory of mankind. When thinking of ancient civilizations, we tend to believe that they were primitive compared to our technology-driven world. We picture half-dressed natives utilizing roughly formed tools to somehow carve out the greatest mysteries our planet has ever known. These were people that worshiped gods that we find to be strange or even silly, building structures that we see as impressive but basically useless. What most of us do not see is a civilization that possessed great knowledge of the stars. A society that knew things that we are only now beginning to understand. As humans, it is preferable for us to think of ourselves as far superior to these barbarians of ancient times, but what if we are not? What if we are now simply rediscovering truths that a great society in our ancient past had already unlocked, and what if they left us clues that allowed us to see their very existence?

For our first example, let us take a look at the Great Pyramids of Giza. Indeed, most anyone that has ever laid eyes on these massive structures has questioned how they were built. How did the Egyptians move stones of such incredible size without the help of modern day machinery? I believe that the question of how these stones were moved, although intriguing, is far less important than the question of why they were moved and who moved them in the first place. We have all been taught that it was the Egyptian Pharaohs, Khufu and Khafre, who had the monuments erected, utilizing a large slave labor force, as massive burial sites for themselves; giant testaments to their vanity, but most people are very interested to learn that no bodies were found inside of the pyramids. This seems like a very large oversight for a tomb. Not to mention the fact that there were also none of the requisite funerary relics found in every other Egyptian tomb of note. Every. Other. Egyptian. Tomb.

There is also the fact that the Egyptians never managed to build another pyramid with the same quality, or utilizing the same techniques, as the Great Pyramids; nor had they ever built anything of architectural substance prior. They continued to build pyramids, but never again could they create a masterpiece on the same scale. In fact, the proceeding pyramids seem to try to emulate the Giza Plateau, but they all fall very short, almost as though they are bad facsimiles built by someone striving to recreate the Great Pyramids but having no actual knowledge of how they were built in the first place. Bearing these facts in mind, as well as concrete scientific evidence that proves that the Sphinx, which has also always been attributed to Khufu, experienced significant erosion by rain which could only have occurred thousands and thousands of years before the time of the Egyptians and a different picture indeed begins to take shape. It is my belief that the Egyptians simply stumbled upon the already completed pyramids, claimed them as their own works, and had no idea what they had actually found. To them the pyramids appeared as great monuments, but what if they are indeed more than that? What if they serve an altogether forgotten purpose?

What that purpose could be, I have ideas but nothing concrete, and this is better served for another time, as this article is simply a way to get you thinking about the possibility that we do not know as much as we may think about the distant past. Prehistory is filled with mysteries that we simply cannot explain. The Nazca lines, a mystery that many people remain unfamiliar with, give us a puzzle of a different type. The Nazca plateau in southern Peru is an inhospitable place. As far as we can tell no human beings have ever called this place home, which is to be expected with less than a half hour of rain per decade on average. The plateau is rich in gypsum and each morning the dew causes the gypsum to act as an adhesive, gluing down the small pebbles of volcanic rock that cover the surface of the plateau. These pebbles also offer a different kind of protection to the grand artwork that is found here. As the sun warms the pebbles, they emit a protective layer of heat just above the surface of the earth that prevents the wind from disturbing what is without a doubt the largest canvas a human artist has ever used.

Viewed from the ground, the Nazca lines appear to be just that, lines drawn on the desert floor with little form or function, but when viewed from above, a tapestry unlike any other on earth can be seen. Hundreds of figures fill the plateau on a canvas that stretches tens of miles on each side: birds, whales, insects, monkeys, trapezoids, and rectangles are among the figures that stretch to the horizon. Each figure was constructed by digging a shallow rut into the earth in a continuous line. Scientists cannot date the lines definitively, so they have come to the conclusion that the lines were drawn sometime between 350 BC and 600 AD. This date range was reached by comparing pottery fragments found among the lines and radiocarbon dating of some of the materials found in them. The problem with these dates is that the materials and pottery shards could have easily been brought to Nazca at a later date. This is the scientific equivalent of finding a Coca-Cola bottle at the Great Pyramids and using that to determine when they were built. The lines could, in fact, be thousands of years older, this still remains a mystery.

The bigger mystery here, however, is the fact that the lines could have only been constructed as precisely as they were by viewing the project from above, from thousands of feet above to be exact. No natural formation of this height exists on the flat top of the plateau. There is no civilization, that we know of, that had the ability to fly in any way, shape or form, yet somehow the lines were drawn in the desert sand. Science has no convincing solution to this dilemma, nor do they have one for another mystery that Nazca holds. One of the figures represented atop the plateau is a spider, but not just any spider would suffice for the ancient artisans that used Nazca as their eternally enduring masterpiece.

Ricinulei, one of the rarest genus of spider known to exist, has only been found to reside in the most remote areas of the Amazon rainforest, and yet it has been depicted on the desert floor in the mountains of Peru. Professor Gerald S. Hawkins was the first to confirm that the spider depicted in the Nazca lines belonged to the Ricinulei genus, and this discovery has been confirmed by every other scientist to view it. How can anyone claim to know what type of spider it is that has been drawn in the sand? It is because Ricinulei has a particularly notable reproductive organ that extends from its right leg. After studying the lines, Professor Hawkins gave conclusive proof that the anatomy of the spider was one hundred percent mathematically correct, even though to view this particular appendage on the Ricinulei typically requires the use of a microscope.

The line drawers at Nazca duplicated this rare spider on a grand scale indeed. The spider stretches to a full length of over one hundred and fifty feet, although this is not the largest of the figures on the plain. A condor stretches nearly four hundred feet, the hummingbird is one hundred sixty-five feet long, and the lizard stretches over six hundred feet in length. Who were the line drawers? How did they have a knowledge of animals and insects that are only known to exist in geographic areas thousands of miles away across the treacherous Andes Mountains, and how did they monitor the progress of their creations? Perhaps the most important question of the line drawers of Nazca is why did they make the lines to begin with?

Many things in the ancient world remain an enigma, tantalizing us with a view of a past that we may not know even existed. Modern science would have us believe that it provides all of the answers to these unanswerable questions, although the facts clearly prove that it cannot. Throughout history, many advancements in scientific thought have been scoffed at and labeled as ridiculous and absurd, only to eventually be proved accurate. Copernicus was wise enough to wait until he was close to death before telling the world that it was not the earth that was at the center of our solar system, and most people of the time believed him to be a heretic. We now know he was right. Galileo was forced to live out his life on house arrest after refusing to abandon the beliefs that Copernicus had set forth.

It is hard to believe that, relatively speaking, not very long ago science would have us believe that the earth was flat, yet somehow the ancient Egyptians not only knew it to be round but had a more precise knowledge of the circumference of the Earth than Columbus did when he made his fateful voyage of 1492. Ancient history provides us with countless examples of how science can one minute be so self-assured as to persecute anyone that dares to disagree, only to adopt the very concepts that it persecuted at a later time, and it is my belief that this will hold true for exciting new theories emerging all over the world right now as well. It is easy to fall into the belief that science holds all the answers, and that we need to look nowhere else, but history has proven that often times science holds only one truth; the things that we believe now will be laughed at years from now, by people who believe they truly do have all of the answers.

The explosion remained unseen by all but one. The earth did not fall into violent upheaval. The most cataclysmic natural event in the history of the planet had just taken place and yet, no one had even heard a sound. Life was unaffected, for now.

Noahim paced back and forth in front of the table, its surface overflowing with ancient books and scrolls. He ran a hand through his short brown hair and across the stubble on his cheeks. His white robe, the sign of a Mul'Ki, flowed behind him as he tried to piece together what he had just witnessed. The Mul'Ki were advisors to kings, makers of the Law, and the only men who possessed the gift and could command the Ari Yet, or Old Magic. They were also readers of the skies, prophets, and healers. The Mul'Ki were so revered among the people that they had an almost god-like status. At the age of seventeen, Noahim had become the youngest high priest of the Mul'Ki in the history of Atla. That was eighteen years ago, and he had never before been faced with a problem like this one. It was the skies that had him so troubled today.

For the last thirteen days, the temperature in Atla had been increasing at an alarming rate and was now twice the normal temperature for spring. Noahim had been frantically searching the old teachings to find some clue as to what this could mean or what could be causing it, but thus far his search had proven fruitless. Then today he had witnessed an event that had shaken him to his very core.

He had been observing the sun through the Yevi, a device used to magnify distant objects and project them onto a surface to allow the Mul'Ki to study the skies safely and accurately. While observing the sun, which the Atlans called Ratam, Noahim had witnessed an explosion on a scale that was unimaginable. He guessed that the flair was hundreds of times larger than the earth itself. He had left the observatory and headed to the library to search for an answer in the old teachings.

Ratam was revered by the people as the giver of life, therefore countless books had been written on the subject, and Noahim knew that this would be no small task. He knew that he could not do this alone but he also could not risk telling the wrong person and inciting panic among the Mul'Ki, which would lead to panic among the people. He exited the temple of the Mul'Ki to search for someone that he could trust, someone that could help with this task. His first thought was of Jikar, his closest friend and trusted confidant. Unfortunately, Jikar was young, and did not possess enough knowledge on the old teachings to offer much help. Noahim held his hand up to shield his eyes from the blinding noon sun and took a second to collect his bearings, surveying the city that sprawled out around him.

The Temple of the Mul'Ki lay directly at the center of the city of Atla. The Temple was meant to serve three purposes. The first purpose it served was that of a library and research center for the Mul'Ki, the second was to display the technological achievements of the people of Atla, and the third was as a monument to the skies. The temple inspired awe in everyone that laid eyes upon it. It was a perfect circle that stood twelve stories. The first six stories were faced with gold, the top six with highly reflective glass. Even for Noahim, who had spent the majority of his life either being trained , living, or working in the temple, it was a breathtaking site. It was, without a doubt, an example of pure perfection.

A great amount of thought and effort had gone into planning the construction of the temple. The Mul'Ki had built in many different significant ratios, such as the circumference being a representation of the circumference of the earth. Noahim had once asked one of his instructors why they had believed that these ratios were significant enough to build the temple in this way and the response he was given surprised him.

"This way if all of the people of Atla were to perish, someday when others find the temple they may be able to decipher the significance of these numbers, and in that way they will know that they are not alone, that there have been those that came before them. It may also help those others to learn things about this world that they do not yet understand," his teacher had said. This greatly confused Noahim. He could not understand how it would be that all of Atla would perish, and who would these others be...but he was merely a boy when he confronted these questions and had quickly moved past them.

Noahim felt a familiar weight on his leg and reassuringly patted his ever-present companion Karok on his large feline head. "Have no fear, old friend," he reassured Karok, "I will figure this out." Karok's only response was to purr and press his head firmly into Noahim's hand. Karok was Noahim's RaSheen, which meant star companion. He was a black jaguar; the people called him BalaRa or born of the stars. Karok was jet black and twice as large as an average jaguar, weighing over five hundred pounds. Every Mul'Ki had a RaSheen, and many of them were big cats of some type, although never before had a BalaRa chosen a Mul'Ki.

Once a Mul'Ki had finished his training, he spent the next six months on a spiritual quest alone in the rainforest and during this time, his RaSheen chose him. That was the way that it had worked for tens of thousands of years in Atla...until Noahim was born. When Noahim was only three days old, Karok had appeared in Atla and settled in beside the door of his home. This event had caused quite an uproar with the people because seeing a BalaRa was extremely rare, and one had never ventured into the city before. Karok stayed at Noahim's door until his parents understood the meaning of the event and allowed the BalaRa to come into their home at which point he walked deliberately over to Noahim and lay beside him, choosing his Mul'Ki.

Because of the old teachings, the Mul'Ki understood how to communicate with animals, and, in this way, their RaSheen was an invaluable tool. The RaSheen perceived subtle clues in the world around them that humans could not sense and had saved the lives of many Mul'Ki on countless occasions. The RaSheen did not speak to the Mul'Ki; rather they communed with them, projecting their feelings into their chosen companion. Noahim and Karok shared a bond that was unlike any that a Mul'Ki and RaSheen had shared before. Noahim spoke to Karok, and in his own way, Karok spoke back. This morning Noahim could sense Karok's growing discontent.

Over two million people now lived in Atla. An intricate system of roads and water channels flowed in concentric circles outward from the temple. As Noahim looked into the market he noticed the surprising lack of people. On most days, the market would be a buzz of citizens trading goods, buying food, and playing games, but today it was almost totally empty. Even the familiar smell of baked goods and roasting meat was absent. "The heat must be keeping people away," he muttered to himself.

Karok nudged Noahim's leg, an effort to tell him to get moving. Noahim looked down, "I know...I know," he sighed, "I have to do something but where should I start?" For the first time since becoming high priest, Noahim was at a loss. He needed help and didn't know who to turn to. He didn't want to share the knowledge of the solar flare until he understood what they were dealing with. Karok, in his way, made a suggestion. "Yes, you're right I suppose, Jakon would be the most logical place to start," Noahim told Karok, "Any idea where he is?" and with that Karok bounded through the market, clearly knowing exactly where he could find Jakon.

Noahim ran to keep up, smiling at his always energetic companion. "Slow down, don't you know that it's hot out here for me?" he laughed, "And shouldn't you be hotter than I am? I'm not covered in fur after all!" But Karok kept up his breakneck pace and soon Noahim could no longer see him. It mattered little though because of the bond that he shared with his RaSheen; he could always sense right where he was. Noahim ran around the corner of the king's palace, narrowly avoiding the moat that surrounded it and leapt across the water. This was no small feat because the water was ten feet wide but Noahim cleared it with ease, landing lightly on the opposite bank. He reached a hand to his head and wiped the sweat from his brow, but it was replaced with more as soon as he put his hand back down.

The buildings were a blur as he ran by, making his way out of the city. Soon he was running beside the great TallaRa River. In early times, the Atlans had believed that the river was formed when the great Star Gods had arrived from the heavens and, upon landing, carved huge gouges in the earth as the ground slowed their descent; so they had named it TallaRa, meaning Path of the Stars. They had come to realize that its formation was due to the natural ebb and flow of the planet, erosion and earthquakes forming rivers, mountains, and valleys, but Noahim had still favored the ancients' version of events.

The forest began to grow thicker here, and Noahim knew that in no time at all he would be in the heart of the jungle. He sensed that he was closing in on Karok and increased his pace. Rounding a stand of trees, he came upon Karok standing in the center of a large clearing, a slight pant the only sign that he had exerted himself at all. Noahim slowed and saw that Kaylan, the golden jaguar that was Jakon's RaSheen, was standing at the edge of the clearing. Noahim, dripping with sweat approached Karok, "I don't know how you do it, old friend," he panted, "One day I'll be able to keep up with you." Karok nuzzled his hand and walked deliberately over to Kaylan. Karok towered over the other cat, who kept its gaze fastened steadily on the ground.

The RaSheen saw each other as equals, with the exception of Karok, and this behavior was exclusive to their dealings with him. He made a few guttural noises at Kaylan, and then stood silently, awaiting a response to his unheard question. Kaylan stared at the ground and slowly his lip curled into what could only be described as a sneer, and he growled twice. This seemed to satisfy Karok who bounded over to Noahim, once again pushing his legs, but this time in the direction of the jungle. "Alright, I am going, is that where Jakon is?" he asked the big cat. The only response he received was a more persuasive nudge.

Noahim walked into the jungle, parting the vast growth of vegetation with his hands and brushing the insects off his skin every few seconds. He came to another clearing, this one with a large pool of water in the center. This had always been his favorite place in all of Atla, and as a child, he had spent countless summer days basking in the sun of the clearing, although since becoming high priest he had not set foot here. The clearing was wonderfully preserved, the grass the deep green of emeralds and the softness of a lover's caress. The towering trees of the surrounding jungle seemed to make an impenetrable wall of natural solitude, and yet despite this dense fortress of vegetation, a constant breeze flowed through the clearing, cooling Noahim as he stood gazing at the beauty of the Jala'Kim, the pool of knowledge.

The Jala'Kim was built in the time of the ancients, carved from a single piece of marble. Despite the breeze that always flowed, the pool remained perfectly still, almost as though it were a sheet of glass reflecting the majesty of the heavens above it. Jakon sat beside the pool in his white robe, looking troubled. His long silver hair fell to one side of his head, presumably to keep it from touching the sacred water. It was believed by most in Atla that to touch the water of the Jala'Kim was instant death and even those who said they didn't believe dared not test this theory, although Noahim knew that they were wrong. When he was still a child, Noahim had spent many nights floating on the still surface of that water, gazing at the stars, knowing that somewhere in them his destiny would be found.

"I was expecting you," Jakon said without turning around.

"I assumed you would be...I need your help brother," Noahim said.

"You need more than my help Noah, much more, but I will do what I can to help you."

"I have witnessed an event...something that may help to explain this heat, but I fear that the worst is still to come..." Noahim said trailing off.

Jakon stood and slowly turned to face Noahim, "What is it that has you so troubled? What could possibly have the great Noahim asking the help of old Jakon?"

"Jakon please, we need to put our differences aside, I fear that our people are in danger," Noahim said, a touch of anger entering his voice.

"You fear our people are in danger?" Jakon accused, "Our

people were in danger the moment they chose a boy to do a man's job. You have no business as the high priest; I have been a Mul'Ki since before your great-grandparents were born. It is no wonder that you have run out of ideas."

"Jakon, I did not choose this post, nor did I desire it, but the people spoke and I accepted their wishes. And although I did not seek the position, becoming high priest has little to do with how long one has served as Mul'Ki, you of all people should know that!"

"I of all people," Jakon said his voice rising, "I of all people...," but he halted his rant as Karok strode from the jungle, his sinewy form looking more shadow than substance as he stalked towards the center of the clearing. Karok walked with his nose towards the ground, but his eyes never left Jakon, his head slowly bobbing right and left. Noahim watched as Karok lazily drew closer and thought that he had never witnessed anything more intimidating than the big cat. "Why have you allowed your RaSheen to enter the Jala'Kim? It is forbidden; I would like to think that our great leader knows this!"

Noahim held his hand out low by his side, and Karok came to him, nuzzling his head into his hand, reassuring him with his presence. "Karok is no ordinary RaSheen, I will remind you, and I am no ordinary Mul'Ki. Karok is the BalaRa, and I am your high priest. Perhaps you have forgotten this in your old age," he mocked.

"The BalaRa, bah! A ridiculous superstition left over from a forgotten time. The people used to believe in many silly stories; there is nothing special about you or that cat."

Karok growled menacingly, and Noahim felt his body tense as he prepared to spring towards Jakon. "Easy friend," Noahim said, "He is hardly worth your energy; he will die on his own soon enough."

"You speak to that animal as though he understands you...as though you share a bond different than other Mul'Ki with your RaSheen," Jakon spit, "You are a silly boy, and he is nothing but a beast..."

"Enough!" Noahim shouted, "I will have your respect Jakon.

Like it or not, I am your high priest. Karok's ability to understand me is hardly the issue, but you, my friend, should be glad that he does. Otherwise, he would have just made lunch of you."

"Fine, fine...I am but an old man," Jakon said, feigning defeat, "Tell me what it is you need my help with, and I will consent."

"I do not know how," Noahim said, "but I fear that Atla will soon be destroyed."

CHAPTER TWO

Erich Lawrence closed his eyes and tried to drown out the noise that threatened to overwhelm his senses and send him running in fear.

You're here to do a job, he told himself.

You can do this, he thought, although he really wasn't that sure he could.

Keeping his eyes closed he reached up and wiped the sweat from his brow. *It's just so hot*, he thought, *I can hardly breathe.* He pictured the rainforest all around him. He knew the jungle well. He had spent over three years in Indonesia exploring its depth, searching for the elusive treasure that everyone said he would never find.

Calm down.

Just breathe.

Get it together.

He continued to keep his eyes closed, willing himself to focus on the forest once again. It was peaceful, it was serene, and part of him felt like it was home. He had begun this journey twelve years ago at the age of seventeen. He never thought it would bring him to this place. It had all started when he decided that he wanted to join the priesthood. He would mission to the people of Asia, bringing the beauty of the Word of God to them. He had a plan, and everything had been going accordingly.

Everything had started on the streets of Chicago. Erich was an orphan, in and out of foster homes before finally running away at the age of fifteen. He had been living on the streets alone for more than three months when he had met Father Michael. Although Erich was wary at first, Father Michael's compassion and kindness had eventually won him over and he accepted a room at the church in exchange for cleaning and helping fix things that needed it. Two years later he decided that he wanted to be a priest and so he began his training. Father Michael had eventually accepted a mission in a small village in Sumatra, Indonesia. Sumatra, like much of Indonesia, was largely Muslim, and so when he learned of this mission Erich had begged to go along and complete his training there. They had arrived at the village outside of the town of Dumai and immediately began teaching the children about Jesus Christ and helping the local people build schools and churches. Everyone there loved Father Erich, as the children had taken to calling him even though he wasn't a priest yet. He was nineteen when he started working in that village, young and handsome he had quickly become popular with the local girls but he had taken a vow of celibacy, and he intended to keep it.

Then he fell in love.

Her name was Gema, and from the first moment she had passed by Erich in the village he couldn't take his eyes off her.

Gema was eighteen when she met Erich. She was instantly taken with him, his rugged good looks and compassionate ways seemed to draw her in. His blond hair and blue eyes seemed to captivate her, but it was his smile that made her fall in love. She knew that she could never have him, for many reasons. First he was a priest, and to tempt him would be a sin. Even if had hadn't been a priest Gema's father had arranged for her to be married to a man from the city, a man who's family had made a lot of money in the oil business and who had many connections to government officials. Forced, arranged marriage was somehow still a common practice in Indonesia. Still, she followed him everywhere, helping with the building projects or translating for him and teaching him the language.

Erich still remembered the first time that he had seen Gema.

She was walking by the church that he and some local boys were building, her long dark hair flowing behind her and she turned and smiled at him. Her eyes were dark pools of liquid serenity. She was tall for the village, five feet, seven inches and had a body that Erich decided was the reason people learned to paint and sculpt. She was beauty personified. Almost immediately Erich knew that he felt a strong connection to Gema, and more than once she caught his eyes lingering on her for just a little too long. Erich would quickly turn away, silently cursing himself for staring at her, as she looked toward the ground and smiled.

They began to spend all of their time together, and he soon realized that there was more to Gema than her looks. She was the most amazing person he had ever met. She reaffirmed his belief in God, because only God could create someone so miraculous. He still remembered the first time they touched. They were working alongside several children from the village, building a retaining wall along the eastern side of the church. Gema had asked Erich to hand her a trowel, and as she reached for it her hand closed around his. His heart stopped. He stood completely still, fearing to move and lose the feeling of her skin on his. She looked up into his eyes, and with a sharp intake of breath pulled her hand back and apologized. It was as though he knew what it meant to truly be alive for the first time in his life. An hour later, Erich watched as she sat on a bench taking a drink of water. She reached up to brush a stray strand of hair back behind her ear, and as she did, she turned and saw Erich staring at her. This time, he did not look away. He held her gaze, and she held his, and they both knew. This was love.

One day Father Michael had asked Erich to go into Dumai and get some things from the market there. Gema had accompanied him to help translate. The day had felt like something from a fairy tale. The walk to the city was more than two hours, they had never had this much time alone, but the two of them quickly fell into a comfortable familiarity, and they began to share things with one another. They spoke of their childhoods, growing up in very different worlds there was much to learn. They talked about their hopes and dreams. Erich told Gema that he loved helping the people in the village but he was uncertain if the priesthood was his true calling. He told her that he was beginning to feel that his life held something more than that in store, something incredible and important. She told him that she believed he could do anything at all. Then she told him how much she regretted that she was being forced to marry a man that she did not love. She had tried to tell her father this, but he would hear none of it. The family that Gema was marrying in to was the ticket out of the village for all of them, and her father had worked for a very long time to arrange the marriage.

After this they walked in silence for a bit before Erich stopped and grabbed Gema's hand, looking deeply into her eyes he said, "Gema, I hope I'm not out of line saying this, but it really isn't ok that your father would force you to marry a man that you don't love. You are a human being, a smart, caring, compassionate, beautiful woman. You deserve to be happy, but even more than that you deserve to decide what your life will be." The ghost of a smile pulled at the corner of her mouth and she squeezed his hands before letting go and turning her gaze to the ground. She said nothing, but Erich could tell that she silently cried for the next several minutes. He decided that he had pushed things too far and so they made the rest of the walk in silence.

When they reached the city they both seemed to cheer up. Compared to the slow and lazy life of the village Dumai may as well have been New York. Everywhere they turned their senses were assaulted. The two of them strode leisurely through the market, taking in all of the sights and sounds. Erich stopped at a vendor that was selling some type of frozen dessert and purchased one for the two of them to share. Gema laughed as the majority of the treat melted down Erich's hand and onto his shirt. He playfully touched her chin with the ice cream and laughed back as she promptly swooped it up with a finger and wiped the finger on his already smeared shirt.

They walked and talked, laughing and feeling truly free. At one point Erich was tugged backwards as Gema grabbed his hand to stop him while she looked at a booth that had caught her eye. Erich looked down at his hand in hers and swallowed, fearing to move because he didn't want her to let go. She didn't. They walked hand in hand as they got all of the items on the list, still holding hands and laughing as they left the city and headed back towards the village. By the time they were only half way home night had fallen. The jungle held many secrets, most of which came out at night. The sound of a branch snapping to the side of the path caused Gema to let out a small scream as she pushed closer to Erich. He reflexively placed his arms around her as they strained to see into the darkness, but the black of the jungle was all encompassing, the two of them could barely even see each other.

They stood silently, Erich's arms wrapped around her, her face buried in his chest. He breathed deeply, soaking in the scent of her hair, his breath coming more raggedly as his heart began to race. She turned her face toward his and said, "Your heart is beating so hard, are you scared?"

"No," he whispered, "I'm not scared..."

"Then what?"

"Gema," he said, pausing as he placed his hands on her face, "I love you. I have loved you from the very first moment I saw you. I knew it right then. I knew it when our hands touched when we were building the wall together. I knew it when I watched you show kindness to a small boy, I knew it when you told me your hopes and dreams, and I knew it when we kissed..."

Erich could see her smile even in the darkness and he felt a tear fall down over his hand, "When we kissed..." Gema said, "We have never..." but her words were cut off as Erich brought his lips to hers. They kissed passionately, deeply, losing themselves to the love that they both had felt for so long. Erich felt her hands reach under his shirt, then his skin was against hers. Her breath on his neck, their lips parting only long enough to whisper passionate 'I love you's' to one another.

This one moment stretched to eternity.

It was honest.

It was bliss.

It was perfection.

When it was over the two lay in the soft dirt of the jungle, their breathing beginning to return to normal. Erich's arm was behind Gema's head. She turned her eyes towards him and smiled. It was a smile filled with such profound sadness that Erich believed his heart would break. "What is it Gem?" He asked, "Didn't you want this?"

She sighed, "Erich I wanted this more than anything I have ever wanted in my life. This night was perfect. Even now as the sun begins to rise all I want is to stay here with you. Stay here in your arms. I have never felt this safe before, never felt this alive, but this cannot be. I have been promised to another...and you...you are a man of God."

"I will leave the priesthood, Father Michael will understand, and you do not have to marry someone simply because your father tells you too Gema."

"You do not understand how things work here. It is not that simple. The man I have been promised to is very powerful, I fear what he would do if I don't go through with this."

Erich began to argue but the sound of another breaking twig grabbed their attention. Erich turned just in time to see someone running away through the jungle. Gema sat up, covering her naked body with her arms as she scrambled to grab her shirt. Erich tried to quickly put his pants back on as he jumped to his feet yelling, "Hey! Hey come back here!"

He started to run after the person that had been spying on them but Gema grabbed his hand and said, "No please Erich, do not follow him. I saw the man that was running, he was an employee of my fiancé's. He must have seen us in the market and followed us here. He is on his way to tell him now, you must go!"

"Go?," Erich said, "I'm not going anywhere Gema, I'm in love with you! Let them come, we will tell them that you aren't marrying him. What's the worst that could happen?"

"He will kill you." Gema stated, "I am certain of this. He is a very powerful man, and he will not allow this insult to stand. He will come with men and he will kill you, please, you must leave..."

Erich looked around at the jungle, felt it closing in on him. Everything he had ever wanted was standing right in front of him. True love. The family he never had. Gema was everything, and now he was just supposed to walk away. "I won't leave you Gema. If this man is so dangerous I'll stay here, if nothing else to protect you."

"I am not the one that needs protection Erich. He won't hurt me. He is infatuated with me, he may even believe it is love, he will forgive me and we will still be married. My father will forgive me as well...but neither of them will forgive you. I am so sorry Erich," she said as a tear fell down her cheek, "but you must run, now! Do not go back to the village to collect your things, just leave, and go as far as you can from here. Please, I am begging you. I cannot be the reason that you lose your life."

Erich felt trapped. He understood enough about Indonesian culture to know that Gema was right, this man would be coming for him...but how could he leave? Where would he go? More than that what was the point of life if he had to live it without his one true love. He looked deep into Gema's eyes and saw the truth in them. There were no options. If he stayed he would be killed, and that would destroy her. He could not be the reason that she suffered. "I can't believe this," he said, "but I will go. I can't be the reason for your suffering. I love you, and I know that I always will."

"And I love you Erich, but you must go, now, and promise that you won't come back. I am to be married to another man, there will be nothing here for you but pain, and nothing for me but heartache. Now run, run as fast and as far as you can. Do not stop for anything."

Erich swallowed hard and put his hands on Gema's face. He whispered to her, "If it takes a million lifetimes I will find my way back to you." Then he kissed her softly, tears running down both of their faces. He turned and ran into the jungle. He ran for what seemed like hours, he had no idea where he was or where he was going. *What am I doing?*, he thought, *I can't just leave. I love her, and I know I'll never find another like her.* Erich stopped running and sat with his back against a tree, trying to make sense of his feelings. His eyes began to feel heavy as the emotions and the physical exertion of the day caught up to him. He closed his eyes, his head dropping to his chest and fell asleep.

Erich woke to someone shaking his shoulder, pleading with him, "Please Father Erich, you must wake up. Men are coming for you...please..."

He opened his eyes and for a moment could not remember where he was. Then it all came flooding back, the night with Gema, the man running through the woods, their goodbye, running and running, and then sitting against the tree. "I must have fallen asleep," Erich said, his eyes beginning to focus, "Paulus...is that you?"

"Yes, Father Erich, I have been tracking you for many hours. Men came to the village looking for you, many men. They are not happy, they are coming for you now, you left a very easy trail to follow. Now please, wake up, run!"

"Let them come." Erich said, "I'm not afraid. I'm not going to run anymore."

Paulus shook his head and turned to look out into the jungle, "I think you should be afraid, the men had guns."

As if on cue five men stepped from the jungle, four of them held small machine guns, the fifth didn't have a gun, but somehow looked the most dangerous of all. "Take the boy back to the village, make certain that he stays there, this does not concern him." He said to one of the men with the guns, who promptly grabbed Paulus and began pushing him through the jungle. Paulus protested loudly but the man paid no attention to it, shoving him roughly to keep him moving. Erich listened as Paulus's voice faded into the forest. The men all stood, staring at Erich, until the one without the gun spoke again, "Do you know who I am?"

"I have a pretty good idea..." Erich said with a half smile.

"So you know why I am here?" He asked.

Erich looked around at the men and slowly nodded.

"Good." Was all the man said as the man to his left hit Erich in the face with the butt of his rifle. Erich lost his grip on consciousness. When he woke he had no idea how long he had been knocked out, or where they were. The forest around them looked very different. The man stood in front of him, taking off his shirt as Erich sat on the ground, his hands tied behind his back. His ankles had also been tied together and his mouth had been taped shut. He stared at the man. "I hope this hurts," the man said as he landed a vicious kick to Erich's side. The pain was unbelievable, the wind was knocked from Erich, he tried to suck in breath but found it almost impossible because of the tape. The man kicked him again, and again, and then the other two joined in, raining down blows. The beating seemed to last for hours, although he had know way of knowing. He had slipped in and out of consciousness many times. Eventually the men seemed to wear themselves out. Erich could barely make out the shape of them, his eyes had swollen completely shut from the repeated blows. He couldn't move. He lay on the ground trying to breath through his broken nose, the tape still on his mouth.

"What should we do with him?" One of the men asked.

"Leave him, let the jungle claim him," came the chilling response.

Those were the last words that Erich heard before he drifted away into the blackness, knowing that he would never again see the sunrise...

That was seven years ago, and what a ride his life had been since. It had eventually led him to this point. The things that had happened to him in that rainforest are what inspired him to begin his quest. The quest that every person told him was foolish but that he had undertaken anyway, knowing that it was his destiny. He kept his eyes closed and continued to work to regain his composure. He pictured the clearing where he and Gema had their one magical night. He wiped more sweat from his brow. He could hear the people close by, talking. He could sense their anticipation. *This is it*, he thought to himself. *Just go for it.* He opened his eyes and stepped forward, out of the darkness and onto the brightly lit stage just as Jim Cochran, the museum's main investor, introduced him to the awaiting audience.

The auditorium erupted in a standing ovation. Erich smiled to himself as he walked to the podium. He knew that the results of his hard work and searching were just thirty feet behind him. He looked around at the huge auditorium. The balconies overcrowded with people. The aisles all clogged as photographers scrambled to get the best vantage point for the unveiling of what had been heralded as the greatest discovery in the history of the world, and yet, no one but Erich and the people that worked on the exhibit had yet set eyes on the discovery that had the whole world talking. It was hard to believe that this entire complex had been built just to house the things that he had found.

The new museum was just over two million square feet and had so many exhibits that Erich hadn't even seen them all. It would take people four or five days to see the entire place, but they would stay until they had. The waiting list just to get a ticket into the museum was already over one year long, tonight was the unveiling, and in just three days, the grand opening. He had not seen the entire museum because he was too busy making sure that the main exhibit was perfect. That and, of course, there was the book that he had written which would hit shelves tomorrow, the orders already in the tens of millions. Erich once again surveyed the crowd. *Is that the president of the United States?* he thought to himself, *man this is a big deal.* In his khakis, white t-shirt and hiking boots he was beginning to feel a little underdressed, but they had become sort of a trademark. He took one more deep breath and smiled at the raucous crowd, raising his arms in the universal signal for quiet.

They cheered even louder. He smiled again at everyone and reached for the microphone. The crowd began to grow quiet. He cleared his throat and brought the microphone to his mouth.

"It's good to see everyone here tonight," he said with a smile sounding only slightly nervous, "Apparently no one forwarded me the memo that this wasn't a casual dress type of function." The crowd laughed and applauded, and Erich gained some confidence. "It's hard for me to believe that just seven years ago I almost died in the rainforest in Indonesia, it's a great story, but if you want to hear it you'll have to buy my new book."

He paused while the crowd laughed and someone in the back shouted, "I thought everyone in the world already bought it," to more laughter and applause from the crowd.

Erich had such a way of disarming people, making them feel like they were friends as soon as they met him. The crowd was his, he could sense it. "I know that you didn't all get dressed up just to listen to me plug my book," he said, "This has been quite a journey for me. For a little while, I began to believe what everyone was saying, that this quest was foolish and that I was a complete, helpless idiot looking for something that didn't exist, and that had it existed wouldn't be anywhere close to where I was looking...but they were wrong." Erich paused for added dramatic effect and turned to look behind him. "Behind that curtain is the very thing that all of these people said I would never find, said didn't exist. Behind that curtain is something that man has searched for, for thousands of years. Behind that curtain is what you all came here to see, what people will come here for hundreds of years to see." He paused again, but this time, it was because his emotions had gotten the better of him. This journey was not without its casualties. He had lost love, lost friends, and almost lost his mind; but he had found the greatest treasure ever known.

"Ladies and gentleman, I give you......The Ark!"

CHAPTER THREE

The curtain behind Erich began to pull back as the crowd held their collective breath. The scene before them was nothing that they could have imagined, and even though the entire exhibit was designed by Erich, he still found himself in awe when he viewed it. The sheer size of the display was astonishing. The Ark stood directly in the center of the exhibit, and Erich knew that no one sitting in the audience was ready for what they were about to see. He still remembered the shock that he felt when he first laid eyes on the Ark in the jungle eighteen months ago.

For hundreds of years, artists have shown their interpretation of the Ark, and many of them were the same. The Ark had been imagined as a large barge-like boat, not meant for sailing but meant for surviving. Nothing could have prepared the people for the beauty of the real thing. The Ark was styled more like the great Phoenician boats of ancient history with high prows, a tall mast, and oars that were worked from inside the vessel. The prow of the boat was the elaborately carved head of a lion apparently in mid-roar. The Ark stood over one hundred feet tall, twelve hundred feet long and two hundred eighty feet wide in its center, narrowing at the prow and stern. There was surprisingly little damage done to the Ark, save the main mast which had snapped, and a gaping hole in the starboard side that was apparently from its final collision when it came to rest.

It was obvious that this boat had been meant to sail, to

navigate, not just to float around at the mercy of the wind and tides. The Ark Exhibit, which the members of the construction team had taken to calling the boat house, was almost as impressive as the Ark itself. When the Ark had been discovered, Erich and Jim had gone through several different ideas for how they would display the boat. Jim's first thought was to try and move the Ark to the U.S. and build a huge attraction there; although, once he saw the Ark he knew this would never work. After a few calls to the Indonesian government, and a few well-placed bribes, Jim had obtained the rights to purchase the land that the Ark sat on and began to look into ways to build domes around the existing structures and rainforest. This proved to be a difficult and expensive task, made even more expensive by Jim's insistence that the project was completed within two years from start to finish, and by Erich's insistence that great care was taken when constructing the domes to do as little damage to the surrounding rainforest as possible.

The entire project was done in the utmost secrecy, Jim using his newfound connections in the government to restrict the airspace over the construction site so the media was kept at bay. He also hired locals to guard the perimeter of the site twenty-four hours a day, which was quite a job because the site stretched over three miles on each side. By the time the project was done, the museum was housed in a series of connected glass domes. When viewed from above it was quite a breathtaking site, the largest of the domes, the one the Ark was housed in, sat in the center of six smaller domes. At its peak the "boat house" was over six hundred feet tall, the other exhibits were smaller, although each was still well over two hundred feet tall to accommodate the emergent trees breaking through the canopy of the forest. It was, in all effect, a giant terrarium, the largest indoor living rainforest ever created.

Lining the walkways, where people would now be able to get a closer look at the Ark were animal exhibits that housed everything from jaguars to giraffes. The exhibits were specifically designed to minimize the appearance of fences and to maximize the natural elements of the animals' homes. The hole in the Ark allowed visitors a look inside the massive structure, which was separated into four floors. The bottom two were divided into what appeared to be stables, animal housing and storage, and the top two floors were comprised of living quarters for the crew of the boat. There were animatronic animals living in the stables, appearing to eat and walk around their small enclosures. Through the hole, it was evident that there were several living quarters, although Erich knew there to be over three hundred separate living quarters on the Ark, each capable of housing four people comfortably.

On top of the Ark stood an animatronic man wearing a long robe and holding a staff, his long gray hair and beard hanging almost to his waist. The museum staff had, of course, named him Noah. Once the museum was officially open, there was a sound system that would feed details of Erich's discovery of the Ark, the exact dimensions of the gigantic vessel, and a story of what day to day life would have been like for the people and animals on the craft. Cochran had spared no expense when it came to the museum, and this exhibit was a testament to that fact. The museum had become one of the largest civilian construction projects ever undertaken and had taken just under eighteen months and hundreds of billions of dollars to complete. Under more normal circumstances, a building of this magnitude would have taken many years to complete, but Cochran had insisted on paying a premium for timeliness.

James Cochran had made his money the old-fashioned way, he had inherited it. His family had been one of the first in the United States to invest heavily in oil drilling and was well compensated for their venture. When he was born, Cochran was worth hundreds of millions, and he had done everything in his power to turn that money into billions. He was a savvy investor and ruthless businessman, taking chances on projects that others were either too scared or too ignorant to see the benefit in. His instincts had always proven right, never more so than with Erich Lawrence.

Erich Lawrence had come to see him when he was a lively twenty-three-year-old with a story that was out of this world. He told Cochran that he had spent the last few years in the jungles of Indonesia, first working in a small village on the island of Sumatra while learning to be a priest and then living in the jungle with an undiscovered tribe of natives. He had spent two years with the native people in that jungle and had learned their ways and their history. He told Cochran a story that the elder of the tribe had shared with him. It was the story of a great catastrophe that befell mankind and almost wiped humanity from the face of the earth. It was a story that most people had heard in one form or another, the story of the flood. This version was different.

The elder, who Erich told him was named Unta, told of a great society that had lived on an island continent. This society possessed skills and technology that many attributed to being recent inventions. They understood how to work metal, they had electricity, they had even mastered flight. They built magnificent structures and harnessed the powers of the Gods. Unta told him they were known as Sala'Ma, or the First People. Unta told Erich the following story:

There was another world underneath this one, where there lived man and animals. Everything was the same except the seasons were different there. This was the island of the Gods. It floated in the ocean, the Gods living with man, teaching them to build, and showing them the Law of civilization. The great God had become angry and vowed to destroy the earth, but man found out his plan and set upon to thwart it. They built many large boats and housed within them the seeds of humanity, taking plants and animals of their kind. They prepared for the day of the flood. One day the earth shook, and the stars fell from the heavens. The sun lost its course, and the land was overtaken by the water. The Sala'Ma set out to find a new island, one to rebuild their great society. They sailed for many months but could find no place that was proper for their new home. They found many people along the way, and taught them the Law. They taught them to build and to farm. They taught them to be great civilizations under the Law. After many years, the Sala'Ma found an island that they believed could be their home. Upon finding this island they took apart their boats and carried them into the mountains. Here in the jungle, they reconstructed their great vessels so that when the sky fell again they would be prepared. They gave an offering to the Gods and thanked them for helping them find their new home. They were the seeds of civilization.

Unta then told Erich that they had landed on one of the islands in Indonesia, although he did not know which one. He told Erich that all the people of the world had benefited from the first people. Erich left the village two months later and began to study the flood myths from around the world. He began to piece together in his mind what may have happened. He researched endlessly, finding what he believed, in the myths, to be the key to unlocking the mystery of the First People. He set out to try and find this lost piece of history but quickly realized that an undertaking like this was going to take something that he didn't have. Money. Erich had been searching the islands of Indonesia for a year when he determined that he just couldn't continue on his own. Then one day he read the story of a wealthy industrialist who made his money by taking bold chances on ventures that others found too risky or flat out ridiculous.

This man, whose name was James Cochran, had most recently financed a team of treasure hunters as they set out to find a legendary ship that was said to have been lost from the Spanish Armada. The ship was thought to not truly exist, but Cochran believed the men that came to speak to him and put up a considerable amount of his money to see their expedition through. Many people labeled him a fool and said that if he were going to just throw his money away that he should donate it to a worthy cause, but just six months into the expedition his men found the ship. It was the most lucrative maritime find in history. Cochran and his men had all made hundreds of millions of dollars. Erich knew that this was the man he needed to see.

He went to see Cochran at his office but was denied an audience with the man. He went the following day and was denied again. This proceeded for nineteen days until Cochran finally came out into the lobby of his building and said to Erich, "How many times am I going to have to turn you down, son?"

Erich's response was simple, "Every day until you say yes."

There was something different about the look in Erich's eyes and Cochran decided to meet with him. Erich told him his story and Cochran was sucked in by his overwhelming enthusiasm. "I know the Ark exists," Erich told him that first day, "I just can't prove it, but with your help, I will find it."

"Well, you've been looking for quite a while already," Jim said not looking convinced, "it seems like maybe it just isn't there, son. I haven't done much looking into it, but how big is Indonesia anyway?"

"Well sir," Erich said with the hint of a smile, "there are over 18,000 islands in the Indonesian archipelago stretching for over 3,000 miles. Just a few over 900 of those are permanently inhabited, and almost all of them are covered with dense rainforest. Other than the Amazon, Antarctica, and the Congo, it is the most unexplored region left on earth."

Jim was visibly stunned, "18,000 islands," he stammered, "how is that even possible?! This could take years son, and millions, hell, hundreds of millions of dollars."

Erich looked at him with steely determination and nodded his head, "You're right sir, it could take years...and I know that it could cost a small fortune, but just imagine...finding the boat that carried the survivors of a lost civilization! The boat that thousands of myths from all around the world talk about...just imagine what we could learn about our past...how much would that be worth?" Erich paused momentarily and swallowed, "I will find the ark, and when I do it will be the greatest discovery in the history of the world, and you will be right there beside me."

James Cochran smiled, and reached out his hand, "Well kid, you may just be crazier than me," he said, and with that, a partnership was born. Later that week, Cochran told the press that he was financing an expedition to find the lost Ark of Noah, although he decided that it would be best to keep the location a secret. Again, he was branded a fool, but he promised the world that Erich Lawrence would unearth the famed boat. Throughout the past few years, he had to convince Erich many times that he was on the right path and to see this through, and often times he had to convince himself, but true to his word, Erich Lawrence had delivered him the greatest treasure ever found.

Now Jim stood beside Erich on the stage and watched as the people in the auditorium got their first look at the Ark Exhibit. Everyone was speechless, the only sound in the room was that of each person's quick intake of breath and the relentless clicking of cameras. Jim put his arm around Erich and pulled him close to him, "You did it kid!" he whispered. Erich simply smiled, there were no words to describe this moment. Standing together on the stage they made an unlikely pair, Erich young and fit in his khakis and t-shirt and Jim, just shy of sixty, slightly overweight and dressed in an Armani tuxedo.

"We did it," Erich whispered back.

The crowd, finally regaining its senses erupted into cheers. The applause was deafening. Jim could see that everyone in the audience was eager to get their chance to get a closer look at the Ark Exhibit. This place, this museum, was the single greatest thing that he had ever done. He looked back over at Erich with a tear in his eye and sounding slightly choked up said, "We sure did kid......we sure did!"

CHAPTER FOUR

"So exactly what has you so troubled Noah?" asked Jakon.

"I have spent the last several days in the temple trying to find something in the old teachings that makes mention of an increase in temperature like what we are seeing, but have been unable to find anything," Noahim said, "but then today...today I was observing Ratam through the Yevi, and I saw something..."

"Saw what?" Jakon questioned, "If you want my help you must be more specific."

"I know Jakon, I just don't know exactly what it is that I saw," Noahim said.

"Well, what do you think it was then?" asked Jakon.

"I believe I saw some type of explosion on the surface of Ratam...something I have never seen before," said Noahim.

"Well, I have seen many of these occurrences on Ratam over the years," Jakon said, sounding unimpressed, "I suppose for one as young as you this may seem unusual, but Ratam is hardly a stable star."

Noahim stopped walking and turned to face Jakon, "I am familiar with the VegaRa," he said, speaking of the phenomenon of solar flares, "but this was unlike anything I have seen in the past or anything I have read about. Please do not mistake my youth for inexperience. I have studied the old teachings more than any Mul'Ki, including you old one."

"That is your problem Noah, you believe that all the answers can be found by reading the teachings of the ancients," Jakon scoffed, "but they were a misguided lot. They believed in the Gods, they worshiped the stars as more than what they are. You must have faith not in old doctrine, but in the science that we have proven."

"I believe in the Gods, I worship the stars," said Noahim quietly, "and I am your high priest. The ancients had more wisdom than you and I will ever know. Without them, none of us would have ever learned to be Mul'Ki."

"Learned to be Mul'Ki?" Jakon asked, "You more than anyone should know that you cannot learn to be Mul'Ki Noah, you just are or you are not." With that, Jakon turned and began walking again. Noahim walked beside him, simmering in his anger. Jakon had been a Mul'Ki for over three hundred years. When the last high priest had died, he was sure that he would be the people's choice as successor, but instead, it was Noahim that had been appointed high priest. Every high priest in the history of Atla had been over three hundred years old when they had been appointed, everyone until Noahim. The people had resoundingly chosen him, even though he had not completed his formal training.

Mul'Ki were born, this much was true, but they were not Mul'Ki from birth. At every birth in Atla, a Mul'Ki was present because he could sense whether the child had the gift or not. If the child possessed the gift, they would live with their parents until the age of five when they would be taken to live in the temple. There they would be raised by the Mul'Ki, each day being taught to harness their powers. They would be given lessons in the old teachings and learn to read the stars. It was a long process and many of the Mul'Ki were not fully trained until they were well over one hundred years old. Time seemed to flow differently for the Mul'Ki, and because of the gift, most Mul'Ki lived to be over six hundred years old.

Noahim, unlike every Mul'Ki before him, was able to command the Ari'Yet from the day he was born. His RaSheen chose him when he was only three days old, and that RaSheen was the legendary BalaRa. Noahim understood the stars in a way that no Mul'Ki in thousands of years had. He understood them as had the ancients, they spoke to him, much the same way his RaSheen spoke to him. Noahim was special, and most of Atla treated him as such. Jakon and some of his brethren, however, felt that Noahim was just a boy, a gifted boy, but a boy none the less. They felt that the BalaRa was nothing more than a fable, just a cat that came to stay by Noahim's side. The Mul'Ki in many ways despised Noahim and his God-like status among the people.

Before Noahim, all of the Mul'Ki were revered highly by the people, but once the BalaRa had chosen him people began to view him as something different. Many said that he was the fulfillment of old prophecy. That prophecy stated, "There will be one born with the gift so strong the BalaRa will seek them out when they are still a child. This one will command the true Ari'Yet. This one will drink from the Jala'Kim. This one will be the savior of Atla. This one will be the seed of humanity." The people still revered all of the Mul'Ki but Noahim was different to them. Jakon and some of his brethren had been upset by the people choosing Noahim as the high priest, they felt that he was not old enough to make the decisions a high priest must make.

"You know that the prophecy is just words?" Jakon asked, "There is nothing special about you boy. The people may have chosen you, but I did not. The people still believe in the old teachings, they are set in their ways and are too naïve to see that the ancients were foolish, primitive people."

"Jakon I know what you think of me," Noahim said, "I do not care that you and some of our brethren now choose to ignore the old teachings. I believe in the wisdom of the ancients. As for the prophecy, I have never said that I am the one of which it speaks, the people have said that. But know this......" Noahim paused and locked his eyes on Jakon's, focusing his Ari, or inner power, and cut off the flow of air to Jakon's lungs with a thought, "I will have your respect."

Noahim turned and walked away, leaving Jakon gasping for air outside of the temple. "When you are recovered, please come to

the garden. There is something there I want you to see," said Noahim, and he entered the temple of the Mul'Ki, Karok staying
outside and glaring menacingly at Jakon.

Noahim stood on the top of the temple in the garden of the
Mul'Ki. It was a beautiful place that was reserved only for the
brethren. The people were allowed to be in the temple at the request of a Mul'Ki, or with the permission of the high priest, and
the children that were being taught lived in the temple, but only
those that had completed their training were allowed in the garden. It was said to be a mystical place, a place of great power
unlike any other place on earth. There was a recreation of the
Jala'Kim raised on a platform in the center of the garden. A waterfall cascaded down the side of the pool and into a smaller pool
on ground level that held a multitude of koi, which the people
called Jala'Naset, meaning wisdom's guardian. The only other
place in all of Atla that the fish were found was in the Jala'Kim,
no one was sure how they had appeared in the pool in the garden,
no one but Noahim.

When he was still a young boy, at the age of seven, he had
caught several of the fish while swimming in the Jala'Kim and had
brought them to this pool. He had never told anyone that he had
touched the waters of the Jala'Kim, he wasn't sure what it had
meant. Legend told that to touch the water was death. Noahim
didn't know if the legend was wrong or if he was simply different.
Enough people already felt that he was different, he didn't need
to tell them about his journeys into the depths of the Jala'Kim.

The ground of the entire garden was covered in grass and
creeping vines. There were several trees that reached high into
the afternoon sky, two towering over fifty feet above Noahim's
head. They provided a great deal of shade around the area of the
pools, and this is where Noahim sat now. He looked around the
remainder of the garden. There were sculptures of the star gods
everywhere he turned. He knew their stories well. To his left, at
the foot of the pool, was the star god RaAlla, the great civilizer
who had brought peace to the people when they were still barbarians. In between the two tallest trees stood a statue carved in
white marble of a man with a long beard wearing a robe and holding a book above his head. Somehow the artist had captured the

essence of the man in his eyes, for the marble seemed to be alive there, to speak if one looked long enough.

The book had a single word on its cover, Dalanda, meaning Law. This statue was a tribute to Bradok, the Mul'Ki who had written the book of Law. It was this book that governed Atla. Bradok said that the gods had given him the laws in the book, that they wanted the people to have better lives and this is how they could accomplish it. Many of the Mul'Ki now believed that the laws were simply an invention from Bradok, that they were not divinely inspired and that they should be thrown out and replaced with all of the new knowledge. Noahim was not among them.

Noahim sat under the watchful eyes of the ancients, awaiting Jakon. He knew that Jakon despised him, but he was his high priest, and Noah did not believe that Jakon would disobey a direct order from him. Noahim was still contemplating what had happened outside of the temple. He had been furious with Jakon, furious with his obstinance. He had grown tired of Jakon and the other brethren throwing the prophecy in his face. He wanted to silence him, to show him that he possessed knowledge and skills that the others could only dream of, and when he looked into Jakon's eyes, he knew that a single thought would kill him. He had never felt that before, never felt the power so strong coursing through him.

Many Mul'Ki could do exceptional things, and Noahim was no different in that respect. Most could move objects with no more than a passing thought, and some could even create fire. Almost all of the Mul'Ki could control animals with their minds, utilizing them for their own purposes. The only animals that seemed to be immune to the power of the Mul'Ki were the RaSheen. No Mul'Ki that Noahim had ever heard of could control another human being. That was a new trick. As he was staring into the pool watching the Jala'Naset dart about he heard the door open behind him.

"How did you do that Noahim?" Jakon asked tensely, "How did you control my breath?"

"I do not know Jakon, I only know that when I looked into

your eyes, I knew that I could," Noahim answered.

"Liar!" Jakon shouted, "This is something you have learned from your precious ancients."

"No Jakon, it is not. I cannot explain to you how I did what I did, just that I knew I could, that is all. Shall we get to the business at hand then...."

"Yes, of course," Jakon said still sounding a little angry, "what is it you wish for me to see?"

Noahim stood and walked by Jakon, pausing long enough to put his hand on his shoulder, he allowed a thought to pass from him to his brother without words, *I am sorry Jakon*, and then went to a small pillar that stood at the base of the pool. There he retrieved a small purple and black flower that looked much like a lily. It was the most beautiful flower that had ever been created, and this was the first time that Noahim knew of that anyone had seen it. "The Ra'Naset has opened," Noahim said cautiously, "Do you have any idea what it means?"

Jakon stroked his long gray beard and peered intently at the flower, "I do not Noah, I am sorry..." he said, "I only know that it has never before opened in my lifetime."

The Ra'Naset, guardian of the stars, was said to be a mystical flower that had ties to RaAlla. The old teachings mentioned it very little, and always very cryptically. One passage from Song to the Gods stated When the Ra'Naset has displayed its beauty, RaAlla will dislodge from his place in the heavens. Noahim had read it over and over but had no idea what it could mean. RaAlla was a star in the constellation that the people called RaHasan. Noahim could see no way that RaAlla could dislodge from its place, but he had found that the old teachings were seldom straightforward and were often metaphors that were only deciphered after something had come to pass.

"I feel that it is of great importance, although I don't know why...," said Noahim.

"It is a flower, nothing more. Many things in nature have a cycle. The great comet of Kalon only passes once every 86 years, the cicadas only emerge from the ground every 16 years," Jakon said, sounding dismissive. "Perhaps this flower only blooms once every ten thousand years and that happens to be now."

"Then why would the ancients write about it? Why would they make a point to mention the Ra'Naset?"

"The same reason they saw fit to mention the BalaRa in a prophecy...because they were foolish old men who believed in fairy tales. If this is all that you have for me, I will be leaving now Noah."

"No, you will not be leaving Jakon, your high priest needs you, and it matters little if you think the work that I ask you to do is worth your time and efforts. You will do as I ask."

"Of course, high priest," Jakon answered sarcastically, "I did not mean to appear otherwise."

"Come with me to the Yevi."

Noahim and Jakon strode to the rooftop door of the garden and walked down the stairs to the Yevi one floor below. The Yevi sat on the twelfth floor of the building. This floor was dedicated to studying the heavens. Maps and charts covered the walls, outlining the knowledge that the Mul'Ki had achieved of the skies over millennia. The Mul'Ki had an obsession with the place that each star held in the sky. They understood precession, the slight wobble of the earth as it spun on its axis and had long ago learned where each star should be and when it should be there. Any variance in the skies was determined to foretell disaster.

Noahim walked over to the Yevi and turned it on. The back wall of the room lit up as the image of Ratam was projected upon it. "This is what I want you to see," Noahim said, "watch Ratam and tell me what you witness."

Jakon stood for a moment and searched the surface of Ratam, looking for whatever it was that Noahim wanted him to see. He saw the normal undulating surface of the star. It was a beautiful sight, the way the fire seemed to roll across its surface. Although Jakon had abandoned the old teachings he still held great respect for Ratam. "I see that the surface seems to be more active than normal, but that could be caused by any number of reasons. I also see the small VegaRa that are occurring, like I said before, nothing to be alarmed over," Jakon said.

"I too see the small VegaRa that are erupting. What would you say is the largest one that you have seen in all of your years studying Ratam?" Noahim questioned.

"I have often seen VegaRa that would be close to the diameter of our entire planet. Maybe some that are slightly larger. These are very small VegaRa Noah...,"

"I too have seen VegaRa that are close to the size of our planet, the explosion I saw this morning was close to half the size of Ratam, hundreds of times larger than our planet. Had you seen it you would not be so easy to dismiss it as an average event brother." Noahim stated.

"I fear that your eyes may have been playing tricks on you Noahim, there is no way that the explosion you saw was that large. Maybe the Yevi was not working properly, I do not know, but I know that you could not...," Jakon trailed off. He was staring at the projection of Ratam. Noahim turned to the projected image and saw what had made his fellow Mul'Ki fall silent. The entire surface of Ratam was in violent upheaval. Noahim saw that many of the explosions now taking place were as large as the one he had seen this morning.

"I trust now you see the problem," he said.

CHAPTER FIVE

After the insanity of last night, the museum seemed unnaturally quiet to Erich as he looked up at the Ark Exhibit. In just three days the doors would open to the public, and the world would begin a new dialogue on religion and mythology. Looking up at the Ark, Erich couldn't help but reflect on the last two years of his life, almost all of which had been spent right here in this boat. He knew that was about to change. In three days, the Ark would no longer be the place of solace that it had become for Erich. Instead, it would be the biggest tourist attraction in the world. He was beginning to feel the pangs of sadness over losing the Ark to the public. It had become the one place that he could escape the constant pain over the loss of Gema.

He had never forgotten her. He had even gone to find her after he had discovered the Ark, but the village wasn't there anymore, and no one seemed to know where the people had gone. He hadn't even been able to locate Father Michael. So he had come back to the museum, the place that now felt as close to home as any place on earth. He spent most of his time at the museum in the Ark Exhibit, often times, climbing up into the ship and walking through the living quarters. For the first year, he found a multitude of personal items belonging to the ship's crew and passengers and they had built exhibits to showcase them. The people of the Ark fascinated Erich. They had learned to work metal, a skill that was thought to be a much more recent development, and had mapped the skies to a frightening degree.

The people who built this boat had to have been a maritime nation, constantly exploring the earth, seeking out new lands and new people. A team of anthropologists hired by Jim were still trying to decipher the language that the books found in the Ark contained. It was painstaking work, and they had learned little information, although they had found that the Ark builders had been a star worshipping society and that they had a fixation with the constellation of Orion. In his studies of mythology Erich had learned this was a very common fixation for ancient people. Erich took another look up at "Noah" and then turned to find Jim.

He left the Ark Exhibit and turned left down the corridor that would lead him to the Garden exhibit, which the staff had nicknamed Eden. When he had found the Ark, it was apparent that the builders had plans to use it as a centerpiece for their new homeland. All around the jungle other finds had been made. Erich and his team had found the ruins of a large building made of stone, still partially intact, with inscriptions covering the surface of every wall. Some of the inscriptions were written in the same strange language as the books that the Ark held, while others were more like pictograms, hieroglyphics depicting ancient ceremonies and important events. The team named this site The Chapel. They had also found an area that appeared to have once been a garden, although the jungle had begun to reclaim this secret oasis. In the center of the garden area, the team had found a large marble pool, or what they assumed had been a pool, but the water had drained long ago.

It had seemed to Erich to be a spot of particular importance, although he didn't know why. One thing he wondered was where the people had acquired the marble and how they had moved such a large piece of it so far up the mountain. He walked briskly toward Eden hoping that he would run into someone from the staff that could help him find Jim.

Erich rounded a corner in the hallway and stopped to get his bearings. He looked at the map on the wall that showed the museum in its entirety. If he continued to the left, he would wind up in the Chapel Exhibit, to the right he would find the only exhibit in the place that wasn't a glass-domed rainforest, the Room of Records. It was here that all of the personal possessions of the Ark's crew were kept on display. The room was constantly being updated with translated journal pages and notes on the mathematics involved in the great maps that the Ark builders produced. Straight ahead of him was Eden, and beyond that, the offices of the museum staff. Today Erich assumed Jim would be checking up on the exhibits, so the office would be a last resort. The chapel was closest so he would try there.

When he arrived at the chapel, he found it empty. Not altogether surprising, but Erich had been hoping that Jim would be there. Erich had spent a considerable amount of time in the Chapel, mainly because the wall carvings fascinated him. He always felt that the carvings held information that was extremely valuable and that he would find the clue to deciphering the strange symbols if he searched long enough. He hadn't. Jim had never thought much of the Chapel, he didn't see it becoming one of the more popular exhibits at the museum, and he always felt that Erich overestimated its importance.

Garden it is, he thought. He left the Chapel and made his way toward the dome that housed the Garden Exhibit. As he arrived, he could smell the familiar earthen aroma of the jungle. The Garden was the second largest exhibit, but Erich had never been that fascinated by it. The marble pool was impressive, it was hard to imagine how the ancient people had managed to carve it so masterfully out of a single piece of block. It was even harder to imagine how they had transported the several-hundred-ton piece to their mountain residence; after all, no marble was found in the native land.

The scent of the jungle caused a memory of Gema to spark in Erich's mind, he opened the door to the dome and stepped across the threshold. The Garden had been beautifully designed, showcasing many rare species of flowers and birds that only existed in the rainforests of Indonesia. In the center of the room sat the giant marble pool surrounded on all sides by manicured beds of hundreds of different species of orchids. Behind the beds sat a waterfall that cascaded down through the jungle foliage from a height of over a hundred feet, starting its descent just above the jungle canopy.

The Garden had been set up as an aviary as well, and the birds that flew throughout the exhibit were sure to be a huge attraction for tourists. Erich was watching a Greater Bird-of-Paradise walk along the edge of the pool. Its feathers seemed to have every color of the rainbow; its tail feathers trailing far behind as it strutted down the side of the pool, casting darting glances towards the center of the marble behemoth. The birdsong and sound of the cascading waterfall mixed with the fluctuating rise and fall of the cicadas to create a symphony of jungle music. Every now and then Erich could hear the loud "kronk" sound of one of the rhinoceros hornbills that inhabited the treetops, quickly followed by an answering cry from its mate. It was late in the morning, had it been earlier, or evening, Erich knew that he would now also be hearing the loud calls of the gibbons that resided at the back of the Garden.

Erich walked to the edge of the pool, soaking in the jungle around him and sat on the edge. Obviously, the pool itself was off limits to the visitors of the museum, but being part owner had its advantages. Erich sat on the marble edge, facing the waterfall and placed his head in his hands. *Will I ever forget her?* He wondered. *Will it ever stop hurting?* He turned to face the pool and see if he had scared away the bird-of-paradise and was shocked to find that the pool had been filled with water. He searched the calm surface of the water, wondering what in the world Jim was thinking to risk damaging an artifact of this age by exposing it to water. Not to mention the fact that they weren't even sure that it had been a pool; everyone had just taken to calling it that because they could think of no other use for it.

Erich sat stunned, seeing the beauty of the forest reflected upon the glass-like sheet of water. He caught a glimpse of a small orange fish as the sun reflected off its scales. "You've got to be kidding me," he said aloud and turned to leave the exhibit. Not only was it filled with water, but had turned it into a gigantic koi pond. It seemed so disrespectful to Erich, who had always maintained a very protective nature over the discoveries that he had made in the rainforest. He had always felt that because he had found it, he had a responsibility to the people that had created all of this to protect it. He was the guardian of the Ark, and he didn't like what was being done in the Garden.

He stood to exit the exhibit but stopped at the door, taking one more deep breath of the jungle air and thought about Gema. There had been other women for Erich, but never another love. Every time that he found someone, they paled in comparison to his one true love. So, he closed his eyes and inhaled the jungle aroma, allowing the sensations to soak into his soul. He had thrown himself into the work here at the museum, into his discovery and writing his book, all in the hopes that something would repair the hole left by Gem, but nothing had. She had made the jungle his home, it appeared that it would stay that way forever.

Erich opened his eyes to leave and waited as they readjusted to the brightness around him. They refocused, and he saw to his surprise, a small black and purple flower sitting on a carved ledge above the pool. He was certain that he had never noticed it before so he went to take a closer look. As he approached the flower to get a better look, he saw that it seemed similar to a lily, although it was unlike any flower he had ever seen. The petals were a deep black and covering each petal were small purple dots. The dots are what had him so captivated; he couldn't help but think that there was a pattern to them, although he was sure they had to be random. Still, he couldn't shake the feeling that the pattern of the dots was something he had seen before. He took a deep breath and pushed the thought from his mind taking one last look at the Bird-of-Paradise as it took flight, spreading its beautiful wings and straining for a perch in the treetops, and walked out of the exhibit. Determined now, more than ever, to find Jim.

CHAPTER SIX

Noahim watched Jakon as he observed the image projected from the Yevi, hoping to find some clue to decipher what he was thinking. Jakon simply stared at the surface of Ratam, squinting his eyes as he scrutinized the image before him. Ratam appeared to be in great upheaval as large chunks of rolling fire were projected from its surface with each explosion. Noahim could almost hear the destruction as he watched the life-giver of the planet in what appeared to be a cosmic struggle for survival. "I have never before observed Ratam in this state of distress," Noahim said, still watching Jakon for some telltale sign of emotion. Jakon, for his part, was remaining utterly emotionless.

"This is a new event, as far as I know, Noah," Jakon stated slowly, seeming to choose each word carefully. "I too, have never observed this before. I have no idea what it could mean; although, I would think nothing good could come of this."

Noahim sat and absorbed Jakon's words. It was nice to know that Jakon also took this event seriously; Noahim had half expected him to remain unimpressed. Hopefully, seeing this would force Jakon to get past his emotions and help work for the good of the people. "I agree that this could only lead to something devastating," Noahim said, "I am glad that you see it too. I would like us to search through the old teachings and see if we can find anything that will help us decipher these events' meanings."

"The old teachings will provide us with nothing, unless you seek the cryptic riddles of fools, you should not look there. We need to alert the brethren so that we may work together to solve this problem."

"Absolutely not, we tell no one until we understand what it is we have seen here today. I know how you feel about the old teachings, Jakon, but I believe that they will hold the answer for this. I cannot do this alone, there are hundreds, if not thousands, of volumes devoted to Ratam. I fear that we do not have the time for me to go through them alone; that is why I asked for your help. At one point, you believed in the old teachings and studied them, so you will know which books we can ignore. Between your knowledge and my own, we can probably rule out at least half of the books in the library. We will go through the old teachings that remain, and once we have discovered the meaning of this event, we will then tell the brethren. Until then, not a word of this will be spoken."

"Noah, I understand that you have lived your short life based on the principles found in the old teachings," Jakon said, sounding almost kind, "and I also understand that you must feel some sort of need to verify their accuracy, thus proving the prophecy and legitimizing your appointment as high priest, but I cannot allow your blind faith in baseless nonsense to endanger our people. The answers that we seek will be found with us, not in the past. They will be found now!"

Noahim stared at Jakon, who was now on his feet pacing back and forth in front of the image of Ratam. Jakon looked invigorated, Noahim could sense a subtle fury growing within him. He had not expected Jakon to disregard him so blatantly. "Jakon, I have told you already that the prophecy holds no place in this!" Noahim said, "I understand that you have abandoned the old ways, but as a Mul'Ki you still must do what your high priest demands, and now I demand that you help me on this quest. If you feel that there are other brothers that could contribute to our search, name them now and I will consider it. I will concede on this point only. I am no longer asking for your help Jakon, I am demanding it!"

"You will demand nothing of me, boy!" Jakon shouted, "I have listened to your foolishness long enough, it ends today! Many of the brethren have grown tired of your bumbling youth and today I will seek them out. We will solve this problem without you. We will once and for all show the people that their precious prophecy is not worth even the parchment that it was scrawled upon! We will fix this. You are no Mul'Ki, I will see to it that everyone knows that!"

Noahim took a step back at the look of pure hatred burning in Jakon's eyes. Staring at his fellow Mul'Ki, he felt the certainty within himself that he could end Jakon's life with a single thought. He knew that he could do this, say that Jakon had died after seeing the image, probably the result of a heart weakened by age, and move to recruit a different brother to help aid his quest. He knew all these things were possible, yet he also knew he would not do them. He could not take the life of another, it was not his place to decide. He turned away from Jakon and walked to the wall of the temple. He stood looking out over the city, a city that he feared for and took a deep, steadying breath.

"Jakon, I am sorry," Noahim said, "I have underestimated you. I have underestimated your envy. I have always known that you feel I acquired the post that was meant for you, but it was not my choice to do so. I serve the people of Atla, and I have served them well. I know that you see before you a foolish child. I now know that you have completely abandoned the old ways. Science is now your God, but it is a foolish God indeed. How, Jakon, can you ridicule the ancients for their belief that they were right when you have the same belief of yourself? Do you not fear that one day your science will be proven as useless as you believe the old teachings to be? I have great pity for you brother because you have chosen to make me the demon responsible for all of your shortcomings. That demon is you. I once had faith that even though you despise me, you would seek to fulfill your duty as a Mul'Ki, that you would do as your high priest demands, and what is in the best interest of the people that we are sworn to protect. I guess that, in that way, I am a foolish boy. My heart has not yet witnessed enough betrayal to have lost the ability to trust in the goodness of people. You have opened my eyes brother. There is no goodness in you. That is why you were not chosen as high priest, because the people could see that. You may feel that because I was not taught as you were that that somehow makes me less of a Mul'Ki, but this also is untrue. I am a Mul'Ki, and I am the one chosen to be the high priest. I will no longer try and convince you that I am deserving of your respect. You say that there are many of our brethren that feel the same as you. I say today let their choice be known. I will gather of all the Mul'Ki at the Jala'Kim and we will see an end to this." With that, Noahim turned and walked away, leaving Jakon to stand alone in front of the angry image of Ratam.

Noahim walked down the spiral staircase that was at the center of the temple to the ground floor and went into his living quarters. He had lived in this same room from the day he turned five years old. The comforting familiarity helped to calm his rattled nerves. No one had ever done what he was about to do, but no one had ever had a need as great as his. He knew that at the heart of the discovery that he had made while observing Ratam, lay a terrible truth, but he had no idea what that truth was. Noahim walked over to the wall beside his desk and depressed a small black button.

This button sent power that had been harnessed from Ratam coursing through a series of circuits that would allow his voice to be heard throughout the entire temple. He could have simply sent a thought to all of his brothers, but some of those in training would not receive the message that way, so he instead said, "My fellow Mul'Ki," he began, "I wish to gather all of the brethren at the Jala'Kim, and all of the young men in training. I will be there in two hours, please assure that everyone is alerted and that everyone is there. I need to speak to you all about something that is of great importance to all of Atla. Seek out your brothers and tell them of the gathering."

Walking to his bed, Noahim sat down. The softness of the down mattress was inviting, he had not slept for more than three days, but he knew that this was not the time for rest. He looked over at the marble chest that sat in the corner of his room, knowing that inside were the robes that every other high priest had worn each day that they served as the head of the brethren. Noahim had always chosen to wear his simple white robes; today would be the first time that he wore the robe of the high priest. Noahim stared at the chest, and with a thought, it moved across the room until it was directly before him. He opened the chest and surveyed its contents.

The robes of the high priest were folded and sat at the bottom of the chest. Noahim still remembered the first time that he had seen Rashan, the man that was high priest when he was born, wearing these magnificent robes. Noahim had been no more than four years old and was playing in the yard in front of his home with Karok. Rashan had come to see the boy that the BalaRa had chosen. When he entered the yard, Noahim remembered knowing right away that the man must be the most important man in all of Atla even though he didn't know who he was.

The robes that Rashan wore had been made in the time of the ancients. The material used to make them was unknown and had the appearance of liquid silver. The robes seemed to flow like water over the shoulders of the high priest. The cuffs of the robes were black, with symbols representing the twelve star gods emblazoned on them in gold. The shimmering robes seemed to somehow catch all the light from Ratam, making it appear alive with energy. A black belt was cinched at Rashan's waist, the sparkling golden image of Ratam danced at its center. It was hard to imagine that any garment could capture the power of the high priest of the Mul'Ki, yet somehow the ancients had created robes that did just that.

Noahim continued to reflect on his first meeting with Rashan. "How are you little one?" Rashan asked as he came into the yard. Karok had sprung up and stood between Noahim and Rashan, determining if this strange man was a threat.

Karok growled menacingly at Rashan until Noahim said, "This man will not hurt me Karok, be calm." At this prompt from his master, the great cat settled down, walking over to Noahim and resting his giant head on the toddler's shoulder. Karok purred into Noahim's ear as the young boy stood staring up at the man. "Who are you?" Noahim asked.

"So, you can talk to him?" Rashan questioned.

"Karok and I understand each other, he's my best friend."

Rashan smiled, "That is very good, Noahim. My name is Rashan, and I am the high priest of the Mul'Ki. Do you know who the Mul'Ki are?"

"Yes," Noahim answered shyly, "many of them have come to see me. They ask me lots of questions, but I never know the answers. Some of them are nice and bring me candy, one even brought me this toy."

Rashan looked down and saw the toy that Noahim spoke of. It resembled a top, spinning there in the yard, except that this top was not spinning on the ground. It hovered just over a foot off of the ground spinning fast but remaining in place. Brilliant colors emanated from its core, casting patches of light much like a stain-glassed window all across the yard. Rashan continued to study the spinning object, "Do you know the name of the man that brought you this?"

"I think his name was Jakon, he was kind of funny. He told me that people would tell me I was special but that I shouldn't believe them. He said if I were special I could make this work. I can't remember what he called this thing, but all I can get it to do is spin around like this. I only do it because I like all of the pretty colors, and Karok likes to chase them sometimes," the boy said with a smile.

For a brief second, Noahim thought he saw a flash of anger in Rashan's eyes, but it disappeared so fast he was certain he imagined it, "Ah yes, Jakon," Rashan said, "I have known him for many years. It does not surprise me that he brought you this, Noahim, but I think you should know that this is not a toy."

"It's not?" Noahim said, sounding afraid that he had done something wrong.

"Do not be afraid, little one, you have done nothing wrong," Rashan reassured him, "This is a training tool of the Mul'Ki. It is called a Ra'dreda, it means star caster. Once the proper knowledge has been acquired by the Mul'Ki using this device, it can make the stars in the heavens appear here on earth."

"Wow, I hope I can learn to do that someday. Like I said, all I can do is make it spin around and light up. Someday can you teach me how to use it the right way?"

Rashan laughed, and Noahim had never heard a nicer sound in his life, "Oh Noahim if you only knew. There has never been a Mul'Ki that has been able to make the Ra'dreda spin and light up without years and years of training. If my memory serves me, the youngest man to ever make it do anything was me, when I was eighty-four years old."

"Eighty-four?" Noahim said, "That seems pretty old, I'm four. How old are you now?"

"Six hundred and ninety-one years old," Rashan said with a kind smile, "and you're right that is pretty old."

"So why can I make it spin and show colors...do you know?"

Rashan paused for a moment and looked deep into Noahim's eyes, "You can do this Noahim because, despite what Jakon told you, you are very special. Many people have waited a long time to see your birth, and I am one of them. I will teach you how to use the Ra'dreda soon, little one. I will teach you many things, but for now, I must go." Rashan then turned to Karok and said, "Keep him safe BalaRa, please, keep him safe."

It was less than a year after that first meeting with Rashan that Noahim had moved to the temple to live. Rashan had seen to all of his instruction himself, not trusting the other brethren to teach Noahim the ways of the ancients. The tension building between the Mul'Ki had been forming for years, some choosing to believe that they knew more than the ancients, and Rashan had not wanted Noahim corrupted by the views of these brothers. Noahim had been a fast learner and had an insatiable appetite for knowledge. By the time that he was ten, he was doing things that Rashan did not even know Mul'Ki were capable of.

Rashan had given Noahim a lot of space to learn on his own, he found that often the child understood the old teachings better than he did himself, and so it was he that was learning from Noahim. All the other Mul'Ki in training had very strict schedules, when they were in classes being instructed on star charts and learning the ways of the Mul'Ki, Noahim was off searching books in libraries or exploring the jungle with Karok. Rashan had followed Noahim once to the Jala'Kim when he was just a boy and watched from the woods as the boy stood on the edge of the pool and dove in. Rashan had almost burst from the trees, hoping to somehow save the child that he knew had to be dead, and yet before he had time to move Noahim had surfaced in the center of the pool laughing and splashing water towards Karok who was stalking along the pool seeming to implore his master to get out of the water.

A few weeks later, in a lesson, Rashan told Noahim of the power of the Jala'Kim and explained to him that anyone who touched the water would die. Noahim had looked surprised and said, "Has anyone ever touched the water of the Jala'Kim?"

"Many have touched the waters Noahim," Rashan said, "but none have lived. To touch the water of the pool of wisdom is death." Noahim said nothing and Rashan left it alone. He decided there was no point in telling the boy that he knew his secret. He knew that he was getting closer to death with each day and wanted to make sure to spend as much time with Noahim as he could. Rashan did not fear death because he knew what was in store on that great day, his only regret was that he had not had the joy of meeting this amazing child sooner. When Noahim was born the Mul'Ki were a fractured group, and Rashan was having a hard time keeping them together. Noahim's birth and the BalaRa's emergence had sparked confidence in the old teachings in some, but Rashan knew the time was coming that there would be no more compromise between the two groups.

Those believing the old teachings and those that sought to abandon them would eventually have to part ways, Rashan had known that for many years; although, he hoped that Noahim would somehow be able to stop this ever-growing rift. From the age of five, Rashan had raised Noahim, imparting on him all the wisdom he had learned over the last six centuries. At times, he had thought that he was expecting too much of the child, but Noahim always hungered to learn more.

The day that Rashan had died had been the worst day of Noahim's life. It was only minutes after his death that the people had resoundingly chosen Noahim as the new high priest, but for him, there was no joy that day. It was for that reason that Noahim had gone against tradition and chosen to never wear the robes of the high priest. Rashan was more than his high priest, he was like a father to Noahim. He had loved Rashan with all of his heart; he would not wear his robes. Now he sat staring at the robes of the man who raised him and lifted them out of the marble chest. He placed the robes and the belt on the bed and heard a noise as something hard struck the bottom of the chest. It was the

Ra'dreda that Jakon had given him all those years ago.

Noahim had no idea that Rashan had kept it. Just hours before his death, Rashan, like every high priest before him, had placed the robes of the high priest into the marble chest and sealed it so that no one but the new high priest could open it. Noahim had never opened the chest before today. He reached into the chest and pulled out the diamond-shaped glass Ra'dreda. He held it in his hand and focused his thoughts on it. Slowly it rose into the air and hovered just in front of his eyes. He concentrated his thoughts and made the room grow dark. Once the room was dark, he released a small thread of his Ari into the heart of the Ra'dreda and the entire room lit up like the night sky.

Noahim looked around, the diamond-shaped Ra'dreda spinning quickly in the middle of the room, and began to see the star gods take shape before him. The walls and ceiling of the room appeared to be the night sky, the stars and planets in their exact locations. He thought of Rashan and this final act of kindness to him. He felt overwhelmed knowing that Rashan had so much confidence in him that he had sealed a gift into the chest, something from a childhood that seemed so long ago. A tear escaped the corner of his eye and rolled down his cheek. Noahim allowed it to fall, feeling it trace a path around his chin and then succumb to gravity and hit the floor. He took a deep breath and withdrew his power from the Ra'dreda.

"Thank you, friend," he whispered to the air, "I wish you were here to fight this fight with me."

The room began to grow light as he walked to the spinning diamond and plucked it from the air. He placed the Ra'dreda back into the chest and after taking his white robes off, he folded and placed them on top of it. He closed the chest and picked up the robes of the high priest from the bed. As he put the robes on, he placed the belt around his waist and cinched it tight. He now understood that it had been destined for this to be the first day that anyone saw him in the robes of the high priest, they had been saved for this moment. He ran a hand through his hair and in his mind called to Karok. Within moments, the great cat stood at his side. Noahim held his hand down to allow Karok to nuzzle into it. "We have work to do, old friend.".

Karok let out a roar that seemed to shake the temple just as Namaah, Noahim's wife, came into the room. They had met shortly after Noahim was brought to the temple. Namaah's mother worked at the temple, cooking and cleaning and Namaah helped out and, in turn, received lessons from many of the brothers there. Noahim had not made a great first impression. He was six years old and had awoken in the middle of the night to Karok licking his face. "Ugh, get off me you dumb cat," Noahim had whispered, afraid that the other boys would be awoken by Karok's noisy tramping around the room. Karok playfully nipped his ear and then headed out the door.

"Karok," Noahim whispered angrily, "get back here! You're going to get me in trouble!"

Noahim had followed Karok out into the hallway where he stood, his huge black tail swishing back and forth. "Alright," Noahim whispered, "but if I get in trouble for this I'm not going to feed you for a week." Karok let out a soft mewl and took off running down the hallway, Noahim close on his heels. They ran down a long hallway and then took a flight of stairs up and Noahim knew that the cat was headed for the kitchen. He tried to catch Karok before he got there but had no such luck, the great cat had disappeared around a corner by the time Noahim was getting off the stairs.

Noahim ran as fast as he could, his heart pounding in his ears, and headed for the kitchen. He was just turning the last corner when he slammed into something that he hadn't seen in his race to intercept the rogue RaSheen. "Hey!" a small voice cried out, "Watch where you're going!"

Noahim stood up and began to pick pieces of what looked like food scraps off of his clothes. He saw Karok just feet in front of him eating the remains of what appeared to be a large steak, looking very pleased with himself. Noahim laughed, "Sorry about that, I didn't mean to run you over," he said looking up to see a frightened little girl in front of him, also covered with food and still clutching tight to the plate that she had been carrying. She was staring at Karok, looking like she couldn't decide if she should run or just die right there. "Don't worry," Noahim whispered, "Karok won't hurt you, he was just hungry. He's pretty big so he eats a lot."

"I'm not scared of your stupid cat," the little girl said, sounding defiant, "I'm just mad that you knocked me down and made me spill my food."

"I'm really sorry," Noahim said genuinely, "I can go get you more food in the kitchen. I'm Noahim, who are you?"

"I know who you are, *Noahim*," the little girl said, exaggerating his name, "everyone knows who *you* are."

"Oh, right, the prophecy," Noahim said, "well, I still don't know your name."

The small girl looked at Noahim and then punched him squarely in the arm. "Just watch where you're going, would you?" she said hotly, "you're not even supposed to be out right now."

"It's like I said," implored Noahim, "Karok just gets hung...." But he stopped talking because the little girl had already turned and ran the opposite direction down the hallway. Noahim looked down at Karok as he was finishing his impromptu meal, "Thanks a lot!" he said. Karok simply looked up at him and licked his lips. The two of them had made their way back to Noahim's room where he lay and thought about the small girl that still remained nameless. She had looked sad, well, she had looked mad, but Noahim sensed a sadness surrounding her. He was pretty good at telling that kind of stuff. The next day, he spent the first couple hours of the morning trying to find her. He eventually had found her in a hallway on the seventh-floor cleaning. "Hi," he said sheepishly, "I'm really sorry about last night."

"It's ok," she said, "sorry I punched you."

"That's alright," said Noahim, "I had just knocked you down, I deserved it, plus, it didn't hurt anyway."

"Ya right," she said with a smile, "I'm Namaah. My mom and I live here in the temple."

"It's nice to meet you Namaah," Noahim said, "Maybe we can play sometime. Do you like exploring the jungle?"

"I've never been into the jungle," Namaah said softly, "my mom says it's not safe."

"Well, you'll be safe with Karok and me," Noahim assured her, "We go in there all the time. There isn't an animal in all of Atla that isn't afraid of Karok," and with that, a great friendship was born. It wasn't until a year after Noahim had been selected as a high priest that he told Namaah his true feelings for her. She had felt the same, and they were married later that year. Namaah was his rock, she was always there when he needed someone to talk to. Today, she stood in the doorway of the room and stared at him, looking at a loss for words.

"You look amazing Noah," she said, "Simply amazing...."

"Thank you," Noahim said, "It was time."

"The two of you are quite a pair," Namaah said nodding toward Karok, "what is the special occasion?"

Noahim walked over and gently placed her face in his hands, drawing her towards him. He softly kissed her lips and pulled away, "I fear that today I will destroy the way that the Mul'Ki have always known."

CHAPTER SEVEN

Noahim strode through the jungle, making his way to the Jala'Kim. Karok remained by his side. The jungle heat, which had been oppressive earlier this morning, seemed to have little effect now that he wore the high priest's robe. He entered the clearing outside the Jala'Kim and saw all the other Mul'Ki's RaSheen, it was an impressive sight. Hundreds of tigers, jaguars, leopards, cheetahs, monkeys, a few small bears, and some deer-like animals were walking around the clearing or lying in the grass. Most of them stood when Noahim and Karok entered the clearing, and all of them averted their eyes when Karok turned his gaze to them. Noahim did not pause to take in this scene, he simply strode into the center of the clearing and made his way into the jungle on the other side.

The air around Noahim seemed to crackle with electricity, his face set into a mask of determination. Unlike the other RaSheen, Karok did not stop in the clearing to await the return of his master; instead, he continued to walk beside Noahim. The Mul'Ki were awaiting his arrival. He had heard whispered conversations as he approached through the jungle, no doubt the brothers speaking to one another trying to determine the cause of this unprecedented event. As Noahim walked into the clearing, everyone fell silent. They all watched as their leader, his silver robes reflecting the glorious light from Ratam, made his way to the center of the clearing.

Noahim made eye contact with no one, he did not want to lose his resolve. He felt the gaze of every man in the clearing focus on him as he walked directly to the edge of the pool and knelt down. He paused for a moment to ensure that each and every one of his brethren witnessed the event that was about to follow, and then cupped his hands and drank from the pool of knowledge. The water was sweet, and as it flowed into his mouth, Noahim's head began to swim. For a moment he feared that he had made a terrible mistake, but the sensation passed, and a strange feeling came over Noahim.

In his mind, he felt the nagging need to focus on what he desired most. He thought of the VegaRa that he and Jakon had witnessed. He then thought of the countless shelves full of books dedicated to the study of Ratam, and as he pictured those shelves, one book seemed to float away from the others and move closer to his eyes. The book remained in his mind's eye, spinning until he saw the simple title on the front, Ratam RaAva. He couldn't think of ever seeing this book in all his time at the temple, but he knew, without a doubt, this was where he would find his answers. He opened his eyes, stood, and faced his brethren.

Noahim surveyed the gathered Mul'Ki. Many of them were looking at him with a mixture of awe and fear, others looked confused, and some looked at him with what could only be described as contempt.

The jungle seemed to be still with anticipation. Noahim was the picture of power, standing before them in the high priest's robes, the BalaRa sitting at his side, watching the crowd with sharp feline eyes. "My brothers, I have a lot of work to do and very little time so I will speak plainly to you today. It is well known that there are many among us that no longer believe in the old ways," Noahim paused and stared directly at Jakon who simply smirked, "there has been a rift growing between us for hundreds of years. Our great high priest Rashan did his best to repair this rift, but I am here today to tell you that the time for compromise has ended. Ratam is in a state of great distress, and

I fear for the safety of all of Atla. Earlier today, I spoke to Jakon about these events, and he witnessed them with his own eyes. I sought out Jakon because I believed his experience and knowledge would be a great benefit to me in my search for answers, but I was wrong. Jakon refused to help me...refused to help his high priest." Noahim let these last words sink in and saw out of the corner of his eye that Jakon was leaning over and speaking to the brother standing at his right side. "I have always known that many of you believe that I am not worthy of this post. The people disagree! I have known all of you for almost my entire life, and many of you, I consider to be great friends. The people chose me because of the prophecy, a prophecy that some of you believe I do not fulfill, but I have just drunk the water of the Jala'Kim. The BalaRa sought me out at birth! I command the true Ari'Yet."

There was some stirring in the crowd now, and Jakon made his way forward, "This boy has done nothing special here today. We have all been taught since our birth that to touch the sacred pool is death, but how do we know this is not just another old superstition? The old teachings make mention of many that tried to drink from the pool and died, but tell me, has anyone tried in any of our lifetimes? The ancients were a foolish lot, many of us have grown to accept that. Is there no one here that will walk up and drink from the pool? Is there no one here that will show us all that this boy is not special?!"

Jakon looked at the men gathered and saw some squirming. *Old habits*, he thought, "Fine, then I will prove to all of you that this boy is not the fulfillment of prophecy," and he began to walk towards Noahim. As he drew closer, Karok stood to his full height and growled menacingly at Jakon. The BalaRa was making it clear that no one would approach his master on this day. "He proclaims the virtues of the ancients and yet at the same time defies them by allowing his RaSheen entrance to this sacred ground! Tell your beast to stand down!"

Noahim leveled his gaze at Jakon, "Karok is no beast brother. I tell you now that to drink from this pool is death, you will not survive, but if it is your wish, I will tell the BalaRa to stand down."

"Stop!" yelled a voice from somewhere in the middle of the

gathered men, "Jakon I cannot allow you to do this." The voice belonged to one of the youngest Mul'Ki, a man named Zackara. He had only finished his training this month and become a Mul'Ki at the age of ninety-one. While training, he had grown a particular attachment to Jakon and had become his constant companion. Jakon relished the role of mentor and had filled Zackara's head with his view of the ancients. Zackara was now making his way to the center of the gathering, "I will drink from the pool," he said calmly, "I have been taught much from the great Jakon, and I believe that he is right and that nothing will happen to anyone that drinks from the pool, but if he were to die, the people would suffer greatly for that loss. I will prove to all of you that Jakon is the true high priest."

Zackara walked to the edge of the pool and sat on his knees. He looked into the water and could see the Ra'Naset darting among the water. He cupped his hands and slowly lowered them toward the water. The crowd stood silently watching, the jungle seemed to hold its breath with the brethren. Noahim placed a hand on Zackara's shoulder and quietly said, "This has only one result brother, I beg you not to do this."

Zackara shrugged his hand off his shoulder and glared at Noahim, "Jakon was the true high priest, the only result this has is to prove to everyone here that you are not special!" and with that, he plunged his hands into the cold water of the Jala'Kim. The moment that his hands touched the surface of the water there was a sound, unlike anything that Noahim had ever heard. It was not a loud noise, but the power that it held was obvious to all around, it seemed to somehow be the sound of lightning. Zackara fell to his side, dead before he hit the ground. Noahim glared at Jakon, who looked to be in shock.

"We have no more time for this, brothers!" Noahim shouted, "I am here today to tell you that all of Atla is in great danger. We must work together to find a solution, but I will have no more petty arguments slowing me down. Jakon says that many of you feel that I am not a true high priest, that some may even think that I am not a true Mul'Ki. I no longer wish to prove anything to you. Today, each of you will make your stand! Today, you will choose your side! You can choose to come with me, back to the temple, and help me find a solution to the problem, or you can choose to go with Jakon. Where you go, I do not care, but you will not be allowed in the temple from this day forward. The ancients had great wisdom, and we have not even begun to understand them or their teachings. Some of you believe that we now have knowledge that is superior to that of the old ways, that our science can replace the old teachings. I say that you are fools! I say to all of you today that you must choose!"

Noahim stood in front of the crowd, the silver robes flowing around him, the golden image of Ratam at his waist appeared to be alive. He took one last look at all of his brothers and said, "I have no more time to discuss this. I am going back to the temple to try and save us all. I am thankful for all of you that choose to come with me, ours is the path of life. To the rest of you, the brothers that choose to follow Jakon...I will allow you until nightfall to remove your belongings from the living quarters in the temple. You will not be allowed entrance to the libraries or the observation rooms. I care little where it is that you go. You have chosen your path, and that path leads to death. This is all that I have to say, brothers. Make your choice!"

Noahim strode through the men, a few here and there patted his shoulder, most simply stared. At one point a man, no doubt a follower of Jakon, tried to block Noahim's path, but one roar from Karok and he thought better of it. Noahim and Karok entered the jungle side by side, leaving the hundreds of men in their white robes standing in the clearing.

The silence hung in the clearing until well after Noah and Karok were lost to the jungle. The men all seemed too stunned to speak, but then, as though an invisible veil had been lifted, they all began talking at once, their voices rising into a cacophony of sound. The scene became chaotic as the men began to shout at one another.

"What disaster is he talking about?" shouted an old man near the center of the gathering.

"Who does he think he is...telling us that we must choose a side?" An angry voice from the back shouted.

"I agree with him," a dark-skinned man with a shock of gray

hair was saying loudly to the man beside him, "this has been going on for far too long. I wish he had told us what this great danger is, but no matter I believe that Noahim is the fulfillment of the prophecy. He is the one...and I will follow my high priest.

"How could anyone agree with him," a younger man was now shouting, "he comes here and tells us nothing other than that we are in danger and then demands that we blindly obey him or what...we are no longer Mul'Ki? He does not have that kind of power..."

"He has all the power," another voice growled, "Do you not see that is the problem. The people and their blind faith in the prophecy and in this boy have given him far too much control."

"Noah never asked for that," a young blond-haired man shouted, "it is not power that he seeks, he seeks the..."

"How can you say he does not seek power when he just told us all that we must follow him or leave the temple?" exclaimed another.

"He wants us to follow the teachings of the ancients," a very old man said, his voice barely able to be heard above the shouts of other men, "it has nothing to do with following Noahim. He simply wants us to continue to abide by the teachings that have ruled us for millennia. There is wisdom in the teachings of the ancients, I for one believe that."

"Enough!" shouted a commanding voice from somewhere near the center of the fray as men began to move out of the way, making room for the man who shouted. Jakon emerged at the center of the newly formed clearing in the middle of the gathered Mul'Ki and turned a furrowed gaze on the men now backing away from him. "Enough of this. Noahim may be young and ill-prepared for his post, but he is right about one thing...the time for petty bickering has passed."

Jakon paused again, drawing in a deep breath and pulling himself up to his full height. He surveyed the men around him, searching their faces for any clue as to what they were feeling. Jakon knew that many of his brethren would leave the temple and that when they did he would become their leader. For the past several years there had been many hushed meetings with some of the other Mul'Ki about how to accomplish just this task, re-moving Noahim from power...and now that foolish boy's arrogance had done it for them. Jakon knew that Noahim had underestimated the growing discontent among his brothers, and now as he looked around the clearing he could sense that many of the men simply needed a small push to join him.

"Today you have all witnessed an unprecedented event," he said as he continued to look around the gathering, "today a man has let his arrogance dictate the future of Atla, and we cannot...we must not allow this to stand. The people believe that Noahim is the fulfillment of prophecy and today he came here and drank from the Jala'Kim to show you that he is indeed the one."

Murmurs ran throughout the clearing at this, and a man in the back shouted, "That is right! Noahim is the one, and today he proved that fact. It is on your head that Zackara is dead Jakon! He drank from the Jala'Kim to try and prove what you have been saying since the day that Noah was born...that he is not special, that he is not the one, but he is, and today he proved it!"

Jakon smiled at this, looking at the man with what appeared to be pity, "I am not standing here today to argue with anyone about whether Noahim is the fulfillment of prophecy or not..." he said, all trace of anger was now gone from his voice, he sounded almost fatherly, "I am here instead to say that it does not matter if he is. We have placed our future in the hands of men from the past for far too long. So, I ask you now, as did your great high priest, which side do you choose? Do you choose to continue believing and abiding by the teachings of old fools...of superstitious zeal-ots...or do you choose to align yourself with the living?"

Jakon could sense the tides turning in his favor, "Let me ask you this...was it the ancients that harnessed the power of Ratam and brought light to the darkness of night?"

"No, it was us," a man standing right in front of Jakon said tim-idly.

"That is right, it was us," Jakon said smiling, his voice taking on more strength as he swept his arms out to the men, "And was it the ancients who built the Temple of the Mul'Ki, the very tem-ple that Noahim intends to take away from us?"

"No, it was us!" several men shouted back at once.

"And was it the ancients that mapped the entirety of our world? Did the ancients protect the people of Atla when invaders came from other shores?" Jakon shouted now, his eyes blazing.

"It was us!" the shout was returned, many of the men thrusting their fists high into the sky as they yelled.

Jakon stood, a look of intensity burning in his eyes, "That is right, it was us. We did all of those things and so much more. The problem that Noahim spoke of, I witnessed today with my own eyes. Ratam is in a state of great distress. I agree with him that it may well be a sign of impending doom, but I do not agree with him on how we will solve this. The answers will not be found with the ancients...they will be found with us!" At this, the crowd roared. Jakon scanned the gathered men and smiled. He could see that there were still a handful of men that did not agree with him, but no matter, he would deal with them later. A new day had dawned in Atla, today they would throw off the shackles of the ways of the ancients and embrace their true power, for Jakon knew that only then would they find the answers that they sought.

CHAPTER EIGHT

Erich stormed through the hallway, determined to find Jim and give him a piece of his mind about his treatment of the pool in the garden. He was hoping that today would be a time for both of them to talk about the gala last night and finalize plans for the grand opening, but he could not bear to think that such a priceless artifact was potentially being damaged just to give a few tourists something pretty to look at. Erich walked into the outer office of Jim's two-room office suite and saw Carolyn, Jim's receptionist seated behind the desk. She broke into a smile, "Erich, it's so great to see you."

"Thanks, Carolyn," Erich stated, trying his best not to let his temper seep through, "Have you seen Jim?"

Carolyn paused, looking Erich over, seeming to sense his urgency with the question, and possibly sensing his underlying anger, "Jim is in a meeting right now, Erich," she stated, "Sorry but he really can't be bothered, could I get you some coffee? I'd love to catch up."

"Coffee won't be necessary," Erich said as he stalked across the room towards the large double mahogany doors that led to Jim's office, "And don't worry, it won't be a bother at all..." he said with a grin.

Carolyn tried to stop him, but Erich was already halfway across the outer office and made it to the doors with plenty of time to spare. Erich pushed the doors hard from the center, causing both doors to swing open together. As he entered the office, he took in the entire scene, Jim was seated behind his massive desk, papers littering every available inch of its surface. He held his head in his hands and seemed to be at a total loss for words. His clothes were disheveled, his tie loosened, and the top two buttons of his shirt undone. The noise from the doors being thrown open brought him out of his apparent stupor and he locked eyes with Erich, and in that instant, the anger that Erich had been feeling over the exhibit vanished. Over the past three years, Jim had become like a father to Erich, and every time he saw him he couldn't help but smile. Jim looked relieved and smiled back, "Quite an entrance son," he said smiling, "meet Mr. Paul Manado and Mr. Nagato, his attorney."

Manado, Erich thought silently, *why did that name sound so familiar?* The two men sat with their backs to Erich but upon Jim's introduction they both stood and turned, and Erich couldn't believe his eyes. "P...Paulus...," he whispered, stumbling on the name.

"Hello Father Erich," Paulus said with a smile, "It has been far too long, I hope life finds you well." Paulus extended his hand and smiled and at that moment Erich was transported back eight years in time, back to the village where he had met his love, back to Paulus being marched through the woods by an armed man. He rushed to Paulus and embraced him. Erich then held him at arm's length as if to be able to take it all in. The last time he had seen Paulus, he had been a scrawny boy of fourteen, now a man stood before him.

"Paulus, it's so amazing to see you," Erich beamed, "How have you been? How is everyone in the village? I tried to come back a couple of years ago, but the village was gone...I think about you all so much..."

"The village fell apart shortly after you left, Father Erich, I will explain more to you at a later time when we are alone. For now, there is a matter that requires immediate attention."

Erich looked confused, he looked first at Paulus, then at Jim, and finally at the man sitting to the right of Paulus, Mr. Nagato. He seemed very unhappy and he sat very still with his hands clasped together tightly on his lap. His black suit was impeccably pressed for someone who had obviously made the trek to the museum at some point this morning, and he showed no effects of the heat in the office. "So, you two know each other, huh?" Jim asked, a wry smile cracking his face, "well then maybe we can hurry up and get this nonsense over with, what do you say?"

"Mr. Cochran," Mr. Nagato finally spoke, his words clipped into a staccato beat, "I assure you that my client and I did not travel to your museum for nonsense. We have very real concerns regarding the compensation of his people. Your museum is on his people's ancestral homeland, and the governing entity that you purchased it from, unfortunately for you, had no right to sell it, as it did not belong to them."

Erich looked stunned, "Paulus, what is going on?" he implored, "Your ancestral homeland? This place is hundreds of miles away from your home, hell, this isn't even the same island Paulus...I don't understand..."

"You are right...you do not understand, and therefore you should refrain from speaking on the subject. You knew that I, like yourself, was an orphan. A few years after you left, my grandfather came and found me, he showed me my true family history. This place belonged to my ancestors, these are their things that you have put on display for profit. This place is rightfully mine."

Erich was reeling now, "Paulus please, drop the father, it's just Erich, I'm no priest. I didn't mean to upset you or insult you. That's wonderful that your grandfather was able to find you. I have no reason to believe that you would lie to us about this being your ancestors' home, what is it that you want? I'm sure we can work something out..."

"Now hold on just a minute Erich," Jim interjected, "I understand that you know this fella from somewhere in your past, but I'm not about to give up any part of this place without rock solid proof and an order from a judge telling me I have to."

The four men sat silent, tensely staring at each other. No one spoke for over a minute until Erich cleared his throat and spoke, "Look, Jim, I know that Paulus wouldn't mislead me. I have known from the time he was young what type of man he would become. Paulus, I'm a wealthy man because of the discovery I made here. I would be happy to give you everything I have, just say the word and it's yours."

Paulus looked back and forth between Jim and Erich, "Fath...Erich," he said, catching himself, "I do not want your money. I want the museum to stop operating. I want my ancestors to have peace in knowing that they are not being exploited. I want my people now to come here and live in this place, among the remnants of our once great past."

"Your people now?" Erich questioned.

"Yes," Paulus stated, sounding more confident with each word, "I now lead my people, the descendants of the Sala-Ma. I have sought all of them out, I have located and brought together all of my people, and I would like this to be our home, this is where we belong. You do not understand the importance of what you have found here."

The Sala-Ma. The words hit Erich like a sledgehammer, driving the wind from his lungs. He had never before heard anyone speak of the Sala-Ma outside of that jungle village where Unta had found him and saved his life. He searched his memory, trying to recall any time that anyone in the village that he had lived in with Paulus had mentioned the Sala-Ma but could think of none. *Who had told Paulus of the Sala-Ma? Was there any way that this could be true, could Paulus be a descendant of the mystical people that had built everything that surrounded them now?* Erich was just about to ask Paulus how he had learned of his descendants when Jim spoke.

"So, let me get this straight," Jim said, eyeing Paulus carefully, "You want me to give you the keys to my museum."

"Yes," Paulus said.

Jim broke into a big smile and let out a soft chuckle, "Well look here pal, I don't know what your lawyer friend there has convinced you of, but there is no way in hell that will ever happen. I don't care what kind of proof you have. Ever heard of Disney World, well its worth tens of billions on paper and it isn't one-tenth the attraction that this place is. No way I'm just gonna give you my museum. You're kind of crazy, I like that, most people think I'm a little crazy myself. As long as you can give me proof that this land belonged to your ancestors I will give you and your people fair market value for the land, hell, I'll even give you a percentage of the profits from the museum from now until we close, but that's gonna be it, partner."

"I'm sorry to have to burst your rather egotistical bubble, Mr. Cochran," Mr. Nagato stated, not looking the least bit sorry, "This is a cease and desist order maintaining that effective immediately you must stop business at this museum until this matter goes before a judge." Mr. Nagato handed Jim a folded piece of paper which he took slowly, skepticism apparent on his face, and began to read, his face turning white as he read the letter. Without taking his eyes from the paper, he pressed the intercom button on his phone and said, "Carolyn, get Doug down here right away. I need him to look at a document."

CHAPTER NINE

Noahim made his way to the temple, determined to find the book that he had seen in his mind. The heat of midday was oppressive and very few people were about in the central square, even those who were simply waved or nodded in acknowledgment to their high priest. No one in Atla, save the Mul'Ki, had any idea of the importance of the event that had just transpired, although Noahim knew that they soon would. As soon as the people began to see some of the Mul'Ki moving their possessions from the temple, they would know that things had changed. Noahim imagined there would be little else that people would talk about for the next several days, but he didn't have time to worry about the people's reaction to what he had just done. He simply needed to find Ratam RaAva.

As Noahim entered the library and scanned the seemingly endless rows of books, his task felt overwhelming. He had no idea where to begin, no idea where to turn. Letting his eyes lose focus he turned his thoughts inward, and instead of focusing on the problem, he focused on the solution. This book would not be found here in the library; he knew this was a fruitless search. Noahim had looked over all the books on Ratam that the library housed after witnessing the Vega Ra. As Noahim sat and pondered what to do next, the sound of approaching footsteps caught his attention.

He had no need to turn and see who was heading towards him, he could recognize the distinctive sound of his wife's footsteps as she crossed from the marble flooring of the hallway to the soft, carpeted library. He sat with his head in his hands trying to remember any mention that Rashan may have made about this book. He felt the air at his back stir slightly as Namaah approached. She stood silently, gently rubbing the tension from shoulders that, to Noahim, seemed to carry the weight of the entire world. "Noah..." she said softly, "I have been worried. I still do not know what you meant by saying that you were going to destroy the ways of the Mul'Ki, but I can feel how much stress you are under...I am worried about you."

"Namaah, I have much to tell you, but you must trust me that right now I do not have the time. I need to find a book... a book that I have never heard mention of, nor seen anywhere in all of my time at the temple. This book may very well be the key to saving everyone."

"I have no idea what could be so urgent about this book Noah, but I know that you would not be searching for the book if it were not important." Namaah paused briefly before continuing, "And I also know that you will tell me what has transpired between you and your brethren when you feel you have the time. What book is it that you seek?"

"I need to find a book entitled Ratam RaAva, but I don't even know where to begin looking for it."

"Ratam RaAva...," Namaah said, looking somewhat shocked, "Where did you learn of this book?"

" Today, at the gathering of my brethren, I chose to drink from the sacred pool to solidify my place as the fulfillment of prophecy. When the water touched my lips, I had a feeling unlike any other. At first, I was convinced I had made a terrible mistake, but soon felt as though the pool could somehow help answer questions that I have been plagued with... and if these questions remain unanswered, I fear that our way of life is over."

"Noah...I know where you can find Ratam RaAva."

Noahim could not speak. He stared for a moment at his wife,

"How could you possibly know where I could find this book?"

"The day before Rashan died he sent for me. I did not know him well, but he had always been very kind to me," Namaah paused for a moment, remembering how hard her childhood had been, "Many of the Mul'Ki did not treat my mother or I very well. In their eyes, we were beneath them and there was no reason to show us kindness. My mother worked very hard in the temple but the pay was little and we often had to go without food. In fact, the night that we met I was on my way back to our quarters after sneaking into the kitchen and stealing some scraps. The noise that was made when I dropped the food alerted the kitchen master, and when he found the mess in the hallway he came to our quarters and took me directly to Rashan. I was petrified, I knew that the high priest would surely kick my mother and I out of the temple. The kitchen master explained to Rashan how I had been found stealing food. Rashan looked at me and told the man to leave the two of us alone. I still remember the smug look on that man's face as he turned to leave. The door shut and I was expecting Rashan to grow angry and tell me how horrible what I had done was, and how the food in the kitchen was for Mul'Ki and the boys in training, not for cleaning women and their urchin children, but he did not yell. He simply asked me why I had been stealing the food. I told him it was because I was so hungry and had nothing to eat, even though I knew that he wouldn't care. He smiled at me and told me to stay where I was for a moment. He left the room and came back several minutes later carrying a large tray that was overflowing with food. Fresh fruit, cheese, bread, dried meats... more food than I had ever seen and simply said, 'Do you think that this will suffice for the evening, for you and your mother? I am sorry, but it is all that I can come up with on such short notice.' I could not believe my eyes. All of this food for my mother and I...I looked at Rashan and saw the kindness in his eyes. I smiled, and with tears in my own eyes told him how it was more food than we had ever had before. I reached down to grab the tray to carry it back to our quarters but he grabbed my hand and gave it a small squeeze saying, 'There is no need for you to burden yourself with this large tray, I will carry it back for you, just lead the way.' He talked to me all the way back to my room, telling me that the job my mother and I did was just as important as any other job in the entire temple. He told me that he would like very much for me to tell him if anyone was mistreating us, and as we approached my quarters he said, 'I know that you have been helping your mother with the cleaning and I want you to know that this cannot happen anymore. Tomorrow I will bring some women from the town to be your teachers. I can see a great intelligence in your eyes Namaah, and I want to make sure that we don't waste your potential. I know that someday you will do great things for Atla. And you can be assured that you and your mother will never want for food again.' For the next several years, I saw very little of Rashan, but he did check in on me every now and again to make sure that I was keeping up with schooling. Then one day, out of the blue, a page came to my room and told me that Rashan was requesting to speak to me. I was very happy to go and thank him for everything that he had done for me, I had no idea that he was sick and I was shocked when I got to his quarters and found him lying on his bed looking very close to death. He motioned me over to his bedside and I knelt beside him and took one of his hands. He smiled at me and said, 'I have watched you for all these years Namaah, watched you change from a small child into the beautiful woman that you are now. I have watched the friendship that has grown between you and Noahim and it has pleased me greatly to know that he has a friend as kind and genuine as you. I fear that I will not be here much longer, my days are coming to an end. I wanted to tell you how proud I am of you, but more than that I want to entrust you with something that is very special to me. What I am about to give you could someday prove to be the key to the very survival of Atla, please do whatever it takes to keep it safe.' And then he placed a book into my hands. I looked into his eyes and promised him that I would keep it safe, and I have. I have always wondered if it was just his illness that made him place special meaning to the book or if it would truly prove to be as important as he said. I can give you Ratam RaAva Noah, I have done my job of keeping it safe."

Namaah turned and without another word left the library. Noah watched as she walked through the doorway, and allowed himself a moment to reflect on everything that had transpired today. He knew that calling the gathering had changed the very fate of Atla, but he had also believed that it was an absolute necessity. For far too many years, the fracture amongst the brethren had been growing, and Noah knew that if Atla was to survive from whatever dangers were coming, they could no longer afford to be divided. While Noahim was prepared for the gathering and what would come, he was not prepared for what would happen when he drank from the Jala'Kim. The thought had never crossed his mind that it would show him what he needed to find...and if that was not enough, somehow, years ago, Rashan had entrusted that very book with the woman that would become his wife.

Had Rashan known what would happen? Had he known that this great danger would befall Atla? Had he known that I would divide the Mul'Ki?

Noah stared out of the window of the and pondered all of these thoughts. Lost to himself, he failed to hear Namaah approach, and so when she gently touched his arm, he startled back to the present and smiled at her. She handed Noah the small, plain book. Noahim held it and stared at the faded leather cover and the gold leaf that spelled Ratam RaAva. Many of the letters no longer possessed any leaf in them, just an impression from when the cover was originally tooled. Noahim could hardly believe that this tiny book was even long enough to possess any information that could be useful, but he was out of ideas and had to believe that Rashan had a purpose for entrusting this book to Namaah. Noahim absentmindedly traced his finger along the gilded letters, and in that moment, something felt vaguely familiar about the book, although he couldn't quite place what it was.

He was absolutely sure that he had never before seen or even heard mention of this particular book, and yet that feeling of familiarity still persisted, like a fly buzzing around inside of his head, not allowing him to completely dismiss it. Namaah sat at his side, Karok at his feet, and yet at that moment, Noahim felt very alone. He wished that Rashan was still with him, wished that he could guide him through this journey. He turned and looked up into Namaah's beautiful and loving eyes, "Have you read this book?" he asked.

"No Noah, "she whispered, "I cannot read it."

"Cannot read it? Did Rashan give you that instruction?"

"Open the book Noah, then you will understand."

Noah sensed her sadness but did not understand, so he slowly opened the book. It had been written in an ancient language, one that Noah had never before seen. All at once, Noah understood why the book seemed so familiar, and why Namaah had appeared shocked and saddened that Noah believed he would find answers in this book.

"I always thought that maybe, at the end, Rashan had lost some of his mental ability," Namaah said, "I have witnessed that happen to many men and women that sit at death's edge. As soon as I got home from my meeting with him I opened the book and saw that it had been written in a language that I had never before seen, so I took it to Hazan, the old scribe, and asked him if he had ever before laid eyes on the language of this book. He studied the book for a good long time Noah, and finally handed it back and said that he could state with certainty that he, nor anyone else in all of Atla, had ever before seen this language. He then told me that he was the most gifted translator Atla had ever known, and that he had deciphered over four hundred ancient languages in his nine hundred years on the planet, but that this was beyond even his talents. I am so sorry Noah, I know that you believed you would find answers here...."

Noah looked at the first page of the book, at the strange, almost alien symbols and then turned to the second page. He felt Namaah's hand tighten on his leg, as she readied herself to be his support in this time of need, and then he turned to her and smiled. "Everything I need to know, I now believe, will be found in this book," Noah stated.

Namaah looked dazed as she wiped a tear from the corner of her eye. She sat up, looking deep into his eyes, searching for his meaning. "Noah, I do not understand how you believe this could help...you may as well throw this book away, it has no meaning to anyone in this world."

At this, Noah laughed out loud, throwing his head back. Karok, annoyed at being disturbed, lifted his large head and let out a loud chuff to express his displeasure. "Sorry old friend," Noah said to the cat, "I will try harder not to disturb your sleep." Namaah was confused by Noah's sudden change in demeanor, it was as if he had gained some new understanding from the book, but Namaah knew this could not be the case. She feared that he was succumbing to the pressure of his post and to his own exhaustion, as he had been getting very little sleep for the past several weeks.

"Namaah, you need not worry," he said with a smile that melted her heart, a smile of pure relief and joy. "There are some things that I have never shared with anyone about the powers that I possess, and I will now share one of those things with you. For some reason, I have always had an understanding of language, a great and deep understanding. Things that take others years, even centuries, to understand, I can understand with only a glance. This book is no different. When I first held the book, I had a sense that it was familiar to me, although I did not know why, but now I understand. The title of this book, Ratam RaAva, seems to be in our language, but it is not. It is also in the same strange ancient language that fills the rest of this book. This book was written long ago by Bradok and then translated by scribes and priests millennia later, for the language that he had written it in had been lost. I am sure that you, along with most everyone in Atla, can recite most of the words in this book from your memory."

Noah smiled knowingly at Namaah, whose confusion was only deepening, "Noah, you surprise me every day. I do not understand what you mean, you have an understanding of language, but I believe you. You never cease to amaze me, but I am sure that I have never before read this book, in this matter, you are mistaken."

Noah nodded his head, "Namaah, I agree that you have never before read this book as it was intended to be read. I learned long ago that many of the ancient languages had been translated very poorly, and these translations often led to a complete lack of understanding of the original text. I have countless examples of this but now is not the time. Bradok spent many years writing this book, and the priests and scribes spent much longer struggling to decipher its meaning. At any means, the translation was completed, and when it was done, they presented it to the people of Atla so that all could share in its beauty. Only they didn't leave the title as Ratam RaAva, for they knew, like I have now discovered, that even though this appeared to be in our language it was not. They translated the title to Song to the Gods."

Noah paused, allowing this to sink in. Song to the Gods was one of the most famous books in all of Atla. From the time children were born until as adults they perished, this book was read. It was considered part one of the "Holy Books" of the ancients. There were three "Holy Books": Song to the Gods, The Fall, and The Law. Although most people would say that Song to the Gods was the least important of the three books, many would also say that it was the most beautiful, and the most tragic.

It was a story of how the Gods had become angry at their creation because they were disobedient, and so, as punishment, the Gods sought to destroy the earth, but RaAlla had decided that he did not agree with the other Gods, so he came to earth to warn the Atlans of the impending disaster. He told the high priest of the Mul'Ki at that time, a man named Razac, that he needed to prepare for the coming disaster. RaAlla told of how the other Gods had decided that man had become evil and so they were sending a time of great trials to the earth. There would be earthquakes and volcanic eruptions, and all of the world would be plunged into the icy waters of a flood. RaAlla told Razac to build a temple to the gods and to go to the temple and sing a song of praise so that the Gods could hear the people's remorse and know that they would try harder to please them. Razac quickly began working on the temple, but his efforts were too late. The earthquakes came, followed by the volcanic eruptions, and finally by the floods. Razac had told many of the people to head towards the high mountain ranges of the lands to the north. Many of the people set off in giant vessels, containing plants and animals and stores of food, they did not know how long they would need to be away.

The people begged Razac to accompany them, but he said that he must stay and finish his work on the temple, that he must sing to the Gods so that they could all avoid tragedy and someday return to their homes. Some of the people agreed and reluctantly left without their high priest while many others stayed and helped Razac work on the temple. Shortly after, the people set out for the mountain ranges and the catastrophes began. The ground shook, and the waters rose. Everyone in Atla that had not left for the mountains perished, and even many of those on their way to the mountains perished in the storms. It was a dark and uncertain time, but eventually the earth calmed, the waters receded, and the people of Atla made a new home.

That was where they were now, in this home in the mountains, and where they had been for thousands of years. The first thing the people did when they got to this new land was build a temple identical to the one that Razac had been trying to complete when the tragedy struck. The people sang to the Gods at least once a week, every week, in the new temple, and this way they hoped to always keep the Gods appeased, and avoid another catastrophe. RaAlla vowed from that day forward to never again set foot on earth. He then promised the Atlans that they would find him in the sky each night, and by this, they would know that they would be safe.

"Noah," Namaah said, "If this book is simply Song to the Gods then how will it be at all useful?"

Noah sat and thought about how to say what he now understood, "Namaah, it is now evident to me, just from reading the first page of Ratam RaAva that the true meaning of this book has never been understood. The title does not actually translate into our language, but I can tell you that it does not mean Song to the Gods. The true meaning is hard to explain, but a closer translation would be The Gods' Noise, although even that is insufficient to describe what is meant by the title. I know the words in Song to the Gods by heart, and these words are not the same. I now know that I must understand the true meaning of this book if I am to save Atla...."

CHAPTER TEN

Erich stared at Jim, wondering if there was any way that this could be true, could Paulus have somehow managed to acquire something from the government forcing them to stop business at the museum, and if so, what would the repercussions be if they did not follow the instructions? Erich knew Jim had to be furious right now, although he wasn't saying anything, apparently intent on waiting for Doug, the head of the legal department for the museum to arrive. The silence in the room was becoming oppressive as the parties simply stared at one another, until Paulus finally broke the silence, "Erich, I would like to talk to you in private for a moment if I could."

"I don't know about that right now Paulus, I'm also a part owner of this museum so your lawsuit is going to make it tough for you and me to catch up on old times. If you have something to say to me you can wait until my attorney arrives. I guarantee that we can make this right to your people, we can give you all that you deserve, you don't have to do it like this Paulus, you don't have to try and take the entire museum from us."

"Erich, please, we need to talk, there are matters of great concern to you that I must bring to your attention..." Paulus began to say, but Erich cut him off, his voice beginning to grow angry.

"Matters of great concern? This museum, the ark, everything

you see around you, this is my life, there are no matters of greater concern to me than this place."

Paulus began to look uncomfortable as Erich continued to grow angrier. "E...E...Erich just listen to me, please," Paulus stammered, "You need to hear what I have to say, it's about Gema." The words hit Erich like a punch to the solar plexus. Before he even had time to respond, the doors opened again and Doug Fisk came walking in.

Doug had worked with Jim since the beginning, starting out as a paralegal as he put himself through law school. He proved to be a tireless worker, quickly gaining Jim's respect, and upon passing the bar at the age of twenty-eight was made the head of the legal department for Jim's entire company. That was twenty-five years ago, although to look at Doug you would assume it was forty. He had aged hard due to a combination of too much scotch, too many cigarettes, and too little sleep. He was around five-foot-eight and now carried around a decent sized belly with him. He had lost the majority of his hair about twelve years ago, although what was left he was desperately clinging to, spending the better part of an hour each morning applying various chemical regrowth treatments and finally styling it in a sweeping comb-over that managed to cover less than five percent of his bald, shining head.

Doug had perpetual dark circles under his eyes, probably caused by his penchant for working ninety-plus hours each week, and in the last four years or so had developed a nasty ulcer so he commonly carried around a bottle of Pepto-Bismol and an economy size bottle of Tums antacids. As soon as he walked into the room, Erich could see the wheels in Doug's mind begin to turn, for everything that he lacked in looks he made up for in brains and tenacity. He seemed to be sizing Mr. Nagato up as he walked by him and stepped to Jim's right side. "What can I do for you, Jim?" He asked, his voice somehow managing to sound even more exhausted than he looked. Although with the new exhibit opening and all of the dignitaries and celebrities that were staying at the hotels and the museum this weekend, it was expected that he was overworked.

Jim didn't say anything, he simply handed the cease and desist order to Doug and continued to stare at the mounds of paperwork on his desk. Doug looked at the document, unimpressed at first, but concern was mounting on his features as he continued to peruse the court order. "How did you get this?" Doug asked, speaking directly to Mr. Nagato, who gave a tight-lipped smile before answering the question.

"An order like this is not difficult to obtain when the government knows that they sold land that was not theirs to sell," he said smugly, "the government wants to avoid embarrassment and my client wants this museum," he paused to allow this to sink in, "it's as simple as that really."

Doug looked ashen, even more so than usual, as he turned to Jim and leaned down to whisper in his ear. Erich could not hear what Doug was saying, although after sitting in on countless meetings with Doug and Jim he knew that this was part of the routine. Doug would lean down and quietly tell Jim what the situation really was and advise him on his response, at which time Jim would typically ignore the advice and say something slightly offensive to the other party involved. This was not one of those times. As Doug whispered his advice, Jim's head slowly sank down, his face growing paler with each second. Jim looked at Doug and Nagato, and then to Paulus and Erich, and couldn't find any words, he seemed to be at the edge of tears. Doug took a step back and simply stared at Nagato. Jim tried to swallow the lump in his throat and then spoke, all the bravado that typically accompanied his voice now gone, "And you're sure Doug?" he asked, to which Doug simply shook his head yes, "I don't believe this..." he trailed off.

Jim slowly stood up and made his way to the door, opening it. He did not walk through the doors, instead he stood off to one side and addressed Paulus and Mr. Nagato, "Look boys, Doug here is the best in the business, and I trust him with my life," Jim drawled, "but I'm going to have to make a couple of phone calls to the people running this rock before we go any further. I would put you up in a room in one of the hotels while we figure this out, but they're all sold out...in case you didn't know, this was gonna be a pretty big weekend. Anyway, I'll make a couple calls, and we can reconvene here in the morning, 8:00 AM sharp, now get the hell out of my office."

Mr. Nagato smiled, although Erich was not focused on him, he was looking at Paulus, who did not look to be the slightest bit pleased with himself. "So, you will cancel the grand opening of the museum?" Paulus asked, no longer the confident leader of his people that he had seemed just moments before.

"You fellas haven't really given me much of a choice now have ya?" spat Jim, "I'm going to make some calls and see if I can't change some minds to allow me to at least open the place, I mean hell, do you have any idea how much money I've spent on this, how many people are here for it, how excited the world is to see this?"

"None of that is my concern Mr. Cochran," Paulus said, "my only concern is that these doors do not open, period." With that, Paulus and Nagato walked out of the office; although before they left, Paulus walked over to Erich and grasped his arm, pulling him close so that he would be able to hear the whispered words he was about to say. "Meet me in the garden in one hour, come by yourself, I will explain myself to you then," he said in a whisper that was audible to no one but Erich. Erich watched them leave, a sense of disbelief threatening to overwhelm him. His past and his present had come together in a violent collision and left him confused and disoriented.

"That's some nice friend you got there son," Jim said to Erich, "glad I could help bring you two back together."

CHAPTER ELEVEN

Namaah watched as Noahim poured over Ratam RaAva, he had worked on translating the unknown language since the moment she had handed him the book, that was nine hours ago. Namaah had not left Noah's side, but she still had no idea what he was finding, although several times he had made exclamations to himself about a new understanding of passages in the book. He had a copy of Song to the Gods, the lone copy of Ratam RaAva, and a book that had started as blank pages but was now nearly filled with notes and passages written in Noah's small, precise handwriting.

Noah turned the last page in the Ratam RaAva and stared at the closed book, at his notebook filled with the information he had gleaned from its pages, and finally turned his bloodshot eyes to Namaah. "If this book is true," he whispered, "it will shake Atla to its very core." He then put his head in his hands and began to try and understand the information that he had spent the last several hours acquiring.

"What does it say, Noah?" Namaah asked.

Noah thought for a moment about how best to frame these next words. While he paused Karok appeared, and Noah held his hand to his side, feeling the familiar and comforting weight of Karok's massive feline muzzle fill his palm, a deep rumbling purr emanating from somewhere within the giant cat. Noah looked at

Karok, his ever-present companion and indeed his closest friend and smiled. "You're right old friend, things will get worse, much worse, before they get any better. Namaah, what I have found in this book, I believe, is proof that the scribes and the priests that translated the original text purposefully and willfully molded the words that Bradok had written in an attempt to gain even greater power and control over the people of Atla. If you remember when the three books were presented to the people, Atla was in a time of great turmoil. After the great floods the people were fragmented and each group began to acquire their own way of life. The devastation was on a scale that we cannot imagine, from books I have read in the past at its peak there were more than one hundred million people living in Atla, and after the floods only about twenty thousand still remained, and they were spread far across the globe, in bands of anywhere from one hundred to one thousand. Much was lost; art, language, agriculture, technology, but more than any of these things, what was lost was information. For thousands of years, these survivors eked out a living from the land they had found when fleeing the ever-rising water, and I am sure that at first, they held fast to the culture of Atla. I am sure that they did the best they could to preserve the knowledge they had acquired, to somehow hold onto the very essence of Atla, but their numbers were simply too few to accomplish such a lofty goal."

Noahim paused for a moment, unsure of how much information to share even with Namaah, for he knew that the truth of this may shake even her solid foundation, but he also knew that he could not hide anything from the woman that he loved. "As time passed, almost everything was lost, and that is when the dark times descended on Atla. Written language was lost, which accounts for all of the dead languages, like the one that Ratam RaAva was written in, and science and technology become fuel for myths. In some places men of science still existed for a time after the floods, but so many had stayed with Razac, determined to finish the temple and stop the impending disaster, and with none of the tools that they had become reliant on they were not able to pass along the information that they had gained through hundreds of thousands of years of careful study. Eventually, all of these men died, and with them died the knowledge of a time when man had truly begun to understand the world around us. Some of them tried to pass along this knowledge, but could find no successful way to make those around them, who were more often than not simple farmers, understand the complex topics that they were speaking of. So a man named Thanenbaum, who was the greatest scientist of his day, decided to pass along the information through unique means....he turned the science that he was speaking of into myth."

Noah watched Namaah for a reaction, but it was clear that she did not understand what he was saying. He felt the desperate need to make her understand his true meaning but simply could not find the words. He decided to try a new approach, "I know this is not making sense, let's pretend that you have information that only you possess and that no one around has the ability to understand, what would be the best way to ensure that this information is not lost to all future generations when you die?"

Noah waited for a response that he was not sure he would get. "I am not clear what you mean Noah..." Namaah said softly.

"Alright, if we look at Atla today, at the children of our land, what is it that they know better than anything else? Do they understand the complexities of the night sky?"

"I would not think that very many of the children grasp the significance of astronomy if that is what you are asking..." Namaah said uncertainly.

"Exactly!" Noah exclaimed, as if now everything should make perfect sense, "They have no idea how we can understand that the phase of the moon or a certain star's placement would have any impact on life in Atla, but even though they do not understand this they all possess the necessary information for understanding."

Namaah sat, confused and slightly disappointed with herself because she could tell by the smile on Noah's face that he was sure he had made it so clear that she would understand his meaning, and suddenly, unexpectedly, she did understand. "They do not understand the significance, but they know the old tales, like the TallaRa River being formed by the Star Gods as they fell to earth...and the need to sing songs to appease the Gods to avoid catastrophe."

"Exactly. The information has been passed down to them through the old tales, hidden within myth and legend are small nuggets of science that are conveyed to the next generation. In fact, some myths contain complex mathematical sequences in them that we are just now beginning to understand, such as..." but the statement would not be completed as the building around them reeled from an explosion somewhere on the floors below.

CHAPTER TWELVE

Noah leapt from his chair and grabbed Namaah's hand, urging her towards the door. His worst fears were coming to life, he was too late to save the people, they would all be destroyed because of his ineptitude. The building shook again, and Noah heard a crash as part of the ceiling in the library collapsed. They had just cleared the door when he sent a thought to Karok, *Get her to safety!* He did not need to wait for a response from his RaSheen. He ran back into the room and saw that the back half of it was now nothing more than a giant gaping hole, letting in the blackness of the night and the hellish glow of the fire from somewhere above them.

Noah had no idea what had caught fire, but he knew they had to move quickly because the earthquakes were just beginning, if what he had just read in Ratam RaAva was correct, no one was safe anywhere. Noah slid to a stop at the desk he had spent the last day working at, grabbed the three and books and fled for the door. He could still hear Namaah screaming his name, but Karok let him know that they were indeed on their way out of the temple. He knew that there was no way the elevators in the building would still be functioning, the shockwave that had rippled through the building would have been enough to arm the safety sensors in them and render them useless for now. He headed towards the stairs and began the long journey down all twelve flights of them.

Noah knew that more of his brethren must be in the building still, and he could not stand the thought of leaving them to perish, so he sought them out with his mind. He sensed that the two floors directly below were empty, but there was definitely some-one on the ninth floor, and many others fleeing from the floors below. In his mind he saw the men fleeing, saw the panic of the scene that must by now be gripping all of Atla, as the citizens would certainly be reeling from the effects of the earthquake, scrambling from their homes and seeking a place of safety that Noah knew did not exist. He rushed to the ninth floor and saw two of the youngest Mul'Ki there, struggling to move a large beam that had collapsed.

He could not see why the men were trying to lift the beam, but he knew that for them to be there, in the midst of the chaos struggling to dislodge it that there must be someone trapped be-neath it. He yelled at the men, "Get back!" and focused all of his Ari on the task of moving the gigantic beam. The beam shot into the air, with a force that made the other Mul'Ki recoil in what ap-peared to be fear and surprised even Noah. Then, with a small flick of his hand, it was sent hurtling against the back wall of the temple some seventy feet away, as though it was nothing more than a twig that had gotten in his way. He saw the man, lying still in a pool of blood. He could not see his face but beside him sat a small golden lion tamarin, looking longingly at Noah, seeming to plead with him for his Mul'Ki to be rescued. Noah knew this RaSheen well. His name was Nuni, and he was the smallest of the companions that anyone had ever seen He was also Noah's best friend Jikar's rasheen.

Noahim and Jikar had entered into the temple at around the same time some twenty-nine years ago, at the age of five, and had quickly become friends, as there were no other boys within fif-teen years of their age in the temple at the time. Rashan had feared that Noah's training being done differently would ostra-cize him from the other Mul'Ki, many of whom already held resentment towards Noahim for the uproar he had caused with the people, so he allowed Jikar to sometimes train with Noahim. The decision had proven to be a very wise one indeed. Jikar, also always very advanced for his age, helped to push Noah to reach greater heights than he could have done on his own, but more importantly, he provided a true friend that Noahim could count on. Noahim still remembered the day that had cemented their friendship forever.

Noah was seven, and he and Karok had been playing beside the Talla'Ra River, Noah using his Ari to send small flat stones skipping far out into the water. He would focus and using only his mind lift a small stone, let it float in the air in front of him and then with a thought send it skipping away. Karok found this to be particularly entrancing, as he paced back and forth between Noah and the water, often looking as though he wanted to jump into the river after the stones. Noah was laughing at his RaSheen as a group of older boys came walking over to the river. One of them, a boy named Tarrin, had always been extremely mean to Noah, resenting what he saw as special treatment of the boy from the high priest. Noah saw him approach and tried to quickly get up and walk away, but Tarrin grabbed him by the shoulder and pulled him around to face him.

"Where you off to so quickly Noahim?" Tarrin said, drawing out the last part of Noah's name, "Why don't you show us what you and your dumb cat are doing down here by the river?"

Karok let out a low growl as he stood to his full height and most of the boys took a wary step back, "Don't worry about him Karok," Noah said trying to sound brave, "he's just jealous of us that's all."

"Jealous," the older boy laughed, "of you... you skinny little weakling.... What in the world would I be jealous of? No, I just thought that it looked like you were hoping to go for a swim but needed some help..." Tarrin said as he quickly lifted Noah off of the ground, holding him over his head as he began walking to the river. This was apparently all that Karok could stand and the giant cat leapt up and loosed a roar as he started to charge towards Tarrin.

There were very strict rules for using your Ari against another of the boys in training, and Noah had to assume that the same would go for using your RaSheen, although since he was the only Mul'Ki in Atla's history to have a RaSheen during his training, there was no such written rule. Still, Noah thought he should err on the side of caution, and so he quickly shouted, "No Karok, stay back, I will be fine." At this, the older boys grew bolder and really began laughing. Karok was not happy about this direction from his small companion, growling and pacing rapidly as he tried to decide if he should listen to Noahim, or attack the boy that was holding him.

Tarrin shouted out, "Listen to the little weakling, acting like that animal can understand his words, what a stupid little..." but his final words were cut off as a rock came flying from somewhere beside them and struck Tarrin hard, squarely in the temple. He fell to one knee, and looking around sputtered, "You aren't allowed to use your Ari on other students, I'll have kicked out of here for that..."

"He didn't," replied a small voice belonging to seven-year-old Jikar. "Leave my friend alone or else I will sic Karok on you." As Jikar finished speaking Karok came to stand beside him, towering over the tiny child, and chuffed at the boys.

"You can't do that," Tarrin said, not sounding sure of himself at all as he rubbed the growing lump on the side of his head, a small trickle of blood beginning to flow, "It's against the rules."

"It might be against the rules for Noah to do it," said Jikar, loading another stone into the sling he held at his side, "But there's no rule saying I can't tell Karok to eat you...and like you were just saying, no one would believe that an animal would understand me anyway. So, I guess I will count to three. One..." he said beginning to swing the sling over his head.

Noah was now standing beside Jikar, staring at his friend in amazement. These boys had tormented Noah so many times, and now Jikar was set to send them running. Jikar stood swinging the sling above his head, the whistling sound growing louder as the rock inside gained momentum, "Two...."

Tarrin and his friends stood staring at Jikar and Noah, seething, until finally Tarrin had enough and started walking towards Jikar shouting, "How dare you threaten me, I will have your..."

But Tarrin never finished his statement as Jikar said, "Three..." and let loose another stone, this one hitting Tarrin square in the stomach and doubling him over. Jikar smiled as Noah held in a laugh, but he wasn't done yet. He looked at the other boys, all clenching their fists but clearly not sure what to do, and then at Karok and said matter-of-factly, "Okay Karok, you can eat them now..." and Karok roared and took off after the older boys. All of them ran in different directions, running into each other in their frantic bid to get away. Noah and Jikar lay on the grass beside the river holding their sides from laughter as Karok came bounding back to them, something black hanging from his mouth. Noah reached up to grab whatever it was saying, "What in the world is that..." but as his hands closed around it he knew that it was a small piece of Tarrin's robe that Karok had torn off. This brought out another bout of great laughter from the boys as Karok jumped around them playfully. After that day, the older boys had never bothered Noah again, although from time to time he did see Tarrin staring at him menacingly from a distance.

Noah came back to the present, and as he approached, Nuni jumped onto his shoullder and pulled at the collar of his robe. Again, the past overwhelmed him as Noah was reminded of the day that Nuni had chosen Jikar. When the people chose Noah to be the high priest, Jikar had not yet finished his training. In fact, neither had Noah, but because Karok had sought him out at birth, and so he, therefore, had a RaSheen, he was considered to be a Mul'Ki. Jikar, on the other hand, had no RaSheen, and still had fifty to seventy years of training to complete before he would be a Mul'Ki, but Noah could not imagine leading the brotherhood without his most trusted friend at his side; so, just days after he had been chosen he secretly sent Jikar on a quest to find his RaSheen. Eighteen days later, Jikar had returned with the small golden tamarin perched on his shoulder and a smile plastered across his face as Noah welcomed him back as a true Mul'Ki. This decision had not sat well with many of the other Mul'Ki. They had voiced their opinion that Jikar was far too young to be a Mul'Ki and that allowing someone to go on the quest for a RaSheen before their training was complete was dangerous and irresponsible, and not a decision that someone ready for the post of high priest would have made.

Noahim ignored them all. He reasoned that if Jikar were not

ready to be a Mul'Ki, no RaSheen would have sought him out in the forest. If he was not ready, he would have returned empty-handed and continued his studies. Noah believed all of this to be true and so allowed the complaints to fall on deaf ears, chalking them up to jealousy over his post, his youth, and his immense talents.

The sight of his friend's body now lying bloody and broken in the temple almost overcame him with grief. Nuni leapt from Noah's shoulder and jumped around and around, squealing in fear. To Noah, this sight was a relief because had the man already been dead, his RaSheen would also have perished, so even though it was evident that Jikar was in desperate need of help, he was alive. Noah had to get him to safety, had to try to heal him. "Go, now!" Noah commanded of the other two men, and they both turned and ran towards the stairs, Noah bending down and scooping up Jikar in his arms, whispering into his ear, "Do not leave me, brother, we have much work to do." Jikar's eyelids flickered and flashed open for a brief second taking in the destruction around them and seeing that it was Noah that was carrying him, and a small smile found his face, "Looks like you were right," he said as he closed his eyes.

Noah struggled towards the door, but with the added weight of carrying Jikar it was now much slower going, and the air was becoming thick with smoke, forcing its way into Noah's lungs each time he took a breath, making each step more and more difficult. Noah was on the stairs, knowing that he had only moments before Jikar succumbed to his injuries, his blood was now flowing freely from a wound in his head, spilling down Noah's arms and making his tenuous grip on the young man even shakier. Noah would not fail him. He moved as fast as he dared down the steps, willing himself to fight through the burning in his lungs.

Another jolt to the building almost made him lose his footing, and confusion began to creep into his mind. It had not felt like an earthquake; it had felt as though the building above him had been rocked by an explosion. Noahim thought of the labs where many of the Mul'Ki had been conducting various experiments and determined that something that one of them had been working on must have been quite volatile and whatever the substance may have been must have caused the explosion. He could hear groans as the temple fought to keep itself upright, could make out the sounds of cracking beams and shattering glass, and the thunderous roar of various sections of the roof collapsing in on him.

Noahim could feel that he was slowing down now, but he fought on. *How much farther could it be?* he thought, *three more floors...four...can I make it?* Noahim began to question if he would ever see Namaah again, her smiling face swimming at the corners of his mind as the spots that marked the inevitable blackout began to creep into his field of vision, but he moved onward. He stumbled, falling to one knee, and could not find the strength to regain his feet. He knew if he left Jikar here on the stairs to die that he would indeed find his way out, but he also knew that was not an option.

*This is where I die...and with me all hope for Atla...*he silently thought, "I am sorry that I have failed you Namaah," he choked out of his burning lungs, although the sound was barely audible above the now deafening roar of the fire and the symphony of destruction all around him, "I am so sorry..." he whispered as he fell to his other knee, still clutching tightly to Jikar. Just then the door in front of him burst open and what appeared to be a living shadow tore into the stairway. Noah was on the very edge of consciousness, too consumed with the smoke to make sense of the blackness that moved into the room with him, until the shadow let out a roar that seemed to dwarf the noise of the fire.

Karok leapt to Noah, pushing against his hands with all of his might, lifting him to his feet. The great cat used his teeth to grab the belt at Noah's waist and led him to the doorway, and the three, Noah, Jikar, and Karok spilled out of the stairway into the luxurious grass that surrounded the temple's east entrance. The cool night air filled Noah's lungs as he lay on his side, gulping in the air as someone dying of dehydration would gulp water at first chance, Jikar's warm blood still spilling out around him. Slowly he regained his senses, searching the faces for Namaah, knowing that Karok would never have come back for him had she not already been safe.

The scene unfolding before Noah seemed to make no sense. Indeed there was a measure of chaos, but after an earthquake of this magnitude, the entire population should be fleeing for cover, or at the very least the people would have gathered at the temple awaiting Noah's advice on what to do, but only a few people surrounded Noah, many sitting in the grass trying to regain their senses in the same way that he just had, others tending to men that had been wounded, but most simply staring at the temple as it burned behind him. Noah had no time to look at that now though, his mind quickly returning to the matter at hand. Jikar had lost so much blood on their trek down the stairs, and Noah had no idea how much he had lost under the column before he had found him. He crawled over to him, his lungs still aching from the smoke and placed two fingers on his throat, searching for a pulse.

Seemingly from nowhere, Nuni jumped onto Noah's shoulder. Noah abandoned the search for a pulse now knowing that Jikar must still be alive, no matter how tenuous his grip on life was, and quickly went to work assessing his injuries. Right away, Noah saw the wound on his head. It sat just above his right temple, his blond hair had been matted with blood, and Noah tried to move the hair aside to see just how bad the injury was. As his hands found the wound, his heart sank. The skull beneath the wound had been crushed, there was a depression in his friend's head that by his estimate was at least half an inch deep and about the size of an orange. Atla had healers, but none that would arrive in time, and even if they did this was an injury beyond any abilities that he seen.

Others had gathered around, watching the tragedy on the ground play out before them. Noah was out of ideas; he closed his eyes and placed his hand over the wound and whispered the words, "RaTam Naset NaAva Noir." He had no idea where the words had come from or why he had spoken them, but he knew they were important. Noahim sat with his eyes closed, his hand pressed to his friend's broken body, afraid to open them and see that Jikar had left them, see Nuni also lying dead at the side of his Mul'Ki. From the expectant silence of the crowd came a quick intake of breath, and in that moment, Noah felt a strange warmth emanating from his hands, felt the power of his Ari surge through his body.

He opened his eyes and saw that the wound in Jikar's head was lessening, that the depression was gone and that the skin was somehow closing itself together, ebbing the flow of blood. Nuni lay on Jikar's chest, eyes closed, but alive, and suddenly a slight rise in Jikar's chest could be seen, followed by a ragged exhalation of breath. Noah just stared at his hands, at the light that seemed to come from within him somehow. It was true that many Mul'Ki possessed healing powers, although Noah had never before heard of anyone being able to repair a wound so severe, and he had never known that he possessed these powers. He risked glancing away from his hands and lifted his gaze upwards, and there standing above him was Namaah, a look of complete and utter awe filled her beautiful face.

"You always do surprise me, Noah. Always."

Noah's only response was to give her a small smile and return his gaze to Jikar, who seemed to be stirring now, unbelievably struggling to sit up. "Stay lying down brother," Noah said softly, "your injuries are severe." Jikar took in the scene, confused by the destruction around them.

"What happened Noah?" he managed to get out, although his voice was little more than a rasping sound of breath, most likely due to a combination of the blood loss and smoke inhalation. "I remember the earthquake, but nothing after that, and I feel fine, a little shaky, but whole..."

"You wouldn't be fine at all," said Antin, one of the Mul'Ki that had been trying to free Jikar when Noahim had found them, "Your skull had been crushed by a column that had fallen on you; somehow Noahim healed you...I...I have never seen anything like it. That glow, the wound coming back together...the power that must have required Noah. I do not..." but before he could finish Noahim cut him off.

"We have no time to discuss this now, the people must be panicking because of the magnitude of the earthquake. We know that special precautions were made during construction of the temple and a quake that could damage a structure this sound must have destroyed half the city...or more..." Noah trailed off.

"That's just it," said Hezel, one of the oldest Mul'Ki in all of Atla, "There was no earthquake, I do not know what happened here, but I can assure you it was no earthquake, I was on the first floor when the building rocked and I ran out of the building and towards the center of town so that I could try and keep the people calm, but there was no damage anywhere. It was as if no one else had felt the blow...I turned back to see the temple ablaze, and collapsing...we need to move farther away, I fear we are not safe this close to the temple."

Noah stared at Hezel in disbelief, "No other damage, this makes no sense...but you are right. First, we move away to safety and then we will do our best to make sense of these events." Noah bent down to Jikar, "Do you feel that you can walk?" he asked.

"Yes," Jikar stated, "I am certain of it, I feel fine Noah, great really..."

Noah began to walk away from the temple, leading the gathering of Mul'Ki and the younger men that were still in training away from the building. Namaah made her way up beside him and grabbed his hand, and he felt the comforting weight of Karok as he leaned some of his massive frame against Noah's left leg as they walked. Noah gave Namaah's hand a squeeze and placed his hand on Karok's head, "Thank you Karok," he said softly, "you saved my life again." Karok's only response was to nuzzle his head into Noah's palm, as he had done since Noah was a small boy. Noah was looking off in the distance, struggling to see if he could make out any damage to other areas of Atla when he tripped over something, looked down and saw the body of a small mountain lion lying dead in the grass at his feet. He stopped moving and looked around, spotting several other RaSheen lying dead in the grass. None of them appeared to have any injuries, which could only mean that their Mul'Ki had perished in the blaze that was now consuming the temple. He counted eight dead RaSheen in the field, and including Zackara, who had died drinking from the Jala'Kim, that made nine.

Noahim knew of no other time in the history of Atla, except during the wars in the early years, that so many had been lost so quickly. He hoped he made the right decision forcing the other priests to make a decision on which path they would follow. He had no idea how many men had left to follow Jakon. Around him, there were maybe twenty Mul'Ki, not counting the eight that he now knew to be dead. That left over four hundred to still be accounted for. Certainly not that many had sided with Jakon...certainly more than just these twenty men saw the truth of the situation. Noahim began to think he had made a grave error, but his thought was cut short when another explosion rocked the night sky. He turned around just in time to see a new ball of flame engulf the upper floor of the temple.

This latest explosion was too much for the building to handle, it swayed for a moment, briefly righting itself, before toppling to the ground, its gold and glass amplifying the light from the fire that Noah knew would consume the entire building by morning. Noah just stared at the destruction. His thoughts moved to all of the books that he had never had a chance to read, to all of the knowledge that would now be lost forever. He thought back to the conversation he was having with Namaah when all of this had started and began to understand how those early survivors must have felt knowing that they possessed knowledge that would die with them and struggling to find a way to pass it on. A flash of light in the distance to his left caught Noah's attention, and he turned in time to see another fireball screaming towards the battered, defeated temple. They were a fair distance off but silhouetted against the night sky by the glow of the flames Noah could just make out Jakon's long beard. Even more than that, he could feel the weight of his glare on him, his burning hatred trying to consume him, as his conjured fireballs consumed the temple.

CHAPTER THIRTEEN

Erich walked through the empty hallways, his footfalls bouncing off of the tile, reverberating in the silence. He had no idea why he was going to meet Paulus. Paulus, who had been his friend, had looked up to him, no longer. Now Paulus was the enemy, the man trying to take away everything. *There is nothing he can say to me...nothing that will make any of this make sense,* he thought, *he could have come to me...why did he do it this way...why am I even going to talk to him? Jim would have my ass if he knew I was meeting with the man that had just served the museum with a cease and desist order without legal counsel,* but he knew why he was going to see Paulus.

Gema.

Even the thought of her name filled Erich with such conflicting emotions, the joy that the memories of their short time together brought, followed by the crushing despair of having lost her. As he walked, he allowed himself to reflect on all of the good times that they had shared together. He remembered one particular day that had been key to him falling for that amazing woman. Erich had been teaching a small group of boys the gospel that morning, and they had taken a break to play a game of soccer. The boys were all ten or eleven and, as is often the case at that age, not entirely compassionate with one another. One small boy, Josef, had been born with a disorder similar to multiple sclerosis, so he had trouble walking and his back arched in an odd way, which led to the other boys never really wanting to play with him or be particularly kind to him. As the boys chose teams, they very purposefully left Josef out of the game and quickly scrambled to start playing before Erich had a chance to tell them to be nice and allow Josef on one of the teams. Erich had turned in time to see Josef hobbling towards the forest at the edge of the village, tears brimming in his eyes, but before he could go and talk to him, a bunch of shouting from the soccer game drew his attention.

Two of the other boys were now rolling in the dirt kicking and punching at one another, screaming about cheating. Erich ran towards them and broke them up, holding them at arm's length as they continued to try and hit one another. Erich calmly spoke to them about the importance of non-violence, and about how Jesus would have told them to turn the other cheek. Once he had the boys calmed down and they were back to their game, he turned to find Josef but could not see him anywhere, and that was when he spotted them. Gema and Josef were walking hand in hand back from the forest. Gema was talking to Josef and the look that Josef had on his face said it all. Here he was, the boy that no one wanted, walking and holding hands with the most beautiful girl in the whole village. Erich had never before seen a look of such happiness on Josef's face.

Josef continued to beam as they strode directly into the center of where the other boys were playing their game, walking toward a bench on the other side of the village. As Gema and Josef walked, Erich saw that the other boys had stopped playing the game and were staring open-mouthed at this unlikely pair. Once they reached the bench, Gema helped Josef sit down and then leaned in towards him to say goodbye, as she did she quickly glanced at the other boys staring at her and smiled before turning back to Josef and giving him a kiss. Josef's light brown face went cherry red as Gema stood up and walked back through the group of boys who now couldn't decide who to stare at, Gema or Josef. Josef simply sat on the bench wearing the world's biggest smile. Erich had never even told Gema that he had witnessed this act of kindness, he had never told her that because of what she chose to do that day, the other boys began including Josef in everything they did; he became a sort of hero to them. That one small act of compassion had changed the little boy's life forever, and not a lot of people could understand what Josef had felt that day, but Erich could completely relate to the fact that one kiss from Gema and your world was never the same again.

If Paulus had information on Gema, Erich needed to know what it was. That was all he was going for; he had no interest in the apologies he was sure would come from Paulus when he arrived at the garden. Erich looked up and realized that with his mind preoccupied he had walked right past the garden, so he turned around and headed back down the hallway, pausing outside of the door to steel his resolve to decline the forthcoming apology, and entered the forest beyond.

Paulus sat on the edge of the pool gazing down into the mirror-still water. Erich walked up behind him, noticing the golden fish dance and dart through the depths of the pool. He hadn't noticed earlier today, probably due to his anger that the pool had been filled, that no matter how close the fish swam to the surface of the pool, the waters remained still. It was quite an entrancing effect; at one point, a very large golden fish seemed to skim the surface with its back, and still, not even a ripple broke the mirror sheen of the water. Erich had stopped walking, trying to see if somehow the light or the refraction of the water was making it seem as though the fish were closer than they were, but he was sure that their closeness to the surface should be causing at least some small stirring in the water. *How is the pool remaining so still?* he thought as he took a step closer to the edge, leaning down to break the surface of the water with his hand, wondering if even this violation would cause the ripple that he knew it had to.

Just as his fingers where about to break the surface, a hand shot out and grabbed him by the wrist, "I would not do that brother..." whispered Paulus, who had moved from his position sitting on the wall and now stood beside Erich. Erich was so startled that he almost lost his balance and fell into the pool, Paulus steadying him with a hand on his shoulder.

"Shit....," Erich said under his breath, "I forgot you were even in here. I got caught up watching the fish swimming in the pool and couldn't understand how they could be so close to the surface without disturbing it in the slightest, it must be some kind of optical illusion...." Erich stopped talking and shook his head to try and clear his mind, screw the damn fish and the damn pond, he was here to find out what the hell Paulus was doing and what information he had about Gema. "Forget it, not important. What do you want Paulus? Aside from ruining my life that is..."

Paulus stared into Erich's eyes, and Erich was struck by the sadness he saw there. The man had just seemingly won a pretty large victory for his people today so sadness is not what Erich was expecting. "Erich, I have no idea where to even begin....so much has happened since you left the village. I need you to know that my desire is not to hurt you, nor do I desire personal gain, this is bigger than both of us..."

Erich raised a hand in an attempt to cut Paulus off, "Whether it is your desire or not this will hurt me, Paulus, it already has. Everything was taken from me the day I was forced to leave the village, I left at the time what I believed to be my calling...every friend I had on the planet...my love...and now this is all I have, this place, my legacy, and you want to take it away from me...don't tell me that you aren't trying to hurt me..."

"Erich, I know this makes no sense to you but you do not understand the truth of your own discovery and the dangers that go along with it. This boat is not what you think it is, this place is not what you think it is, the people that once called this place home are not who you believe them to be..." Paulus seemed to hesitate, just for a moment, almost as though he was unsure how much to tell Erich, "There may be information hidden somewhere at this site...information that in the wrong hands would be disastrous..."

"What are you talking about Paulus? The danger here would be not sharing this amazing information with the rest of the world; some of the scientific discoveries that we are just now beginning to translate will change the way that we look at the past, and possibly the way that we live in the future. If the translations are correct, it appears that these people possessed an amazing ability to harness energy from the world around them. Clean, free, renewable energy and that's just the start, there are hundreds of books that we have found throughout the site, the vast majority of which appear to be scientific in nature. I can't even begin to imagine what these books have to teach all of us and..."

Paulus cut Erich off, his voice rising slightly and his eyes taking on a hard edge that Erich had not seen before, "You say the vast majority of these books seem to be scientific in nature....so you have found other books that are not about science?" Paulus questioned, "What are these other books about?"

Erich took a deep breath and tried to see the young boy he had once mentored in the man that stood before him, "I don't know Paulus, it's tough to say what the books are about. Like I said, the translation process has proven extremely difficult. I know that they have found a couple of books that appear to be historical, and maybe a few that seem to either be religious or mythological, but there is no telling when they will actually be translated."

"I would like to see the books of mythology that have been discovered," Paulus said sounding excited, "Can you arrange that Erich?"

"You're kidding right?" Erich deadpanned, "You come here and shit all over everything I've spent the last six years working for and now you want me to pull some strings and get you access to a couple of books?"

Paulus visibly shrank from Erich's words. He sat down on the edge of the pool as a peel of thunder roared from outside the dome. Erich began to hear the pitter-patter of rain falling on the roof, a howler monkey somewhere in the exhibit let out a shriek as lightning tore through the sky and thunder again rolled across the rainforest. Paulus took a deep breath and began to speak softly, "Erich... as I said, I asked you to come here so I could explain myself, I will take the opportunity to do that now. I know how much this discovery has meant to you, and how this journey has changed your life, but I think you will be surprised to find out that yours was not the only life that was changed when you decided to embark on this quest. Shortly after Mr. Cochran made the announcement that you would be searching the various islands of Indonesia looking for the Ark, some men visited my village. They came asking questions about you, about where you had stayed when you were in the village, who you talked to the most, and what information you could have been given about the Ark."

"That doesn't really surprise me, Paulus, a lot of people were trying to figure out where I was looking. They wanted to try and discover the boat first, claim it for themselves. It got so bad that we had to pay people to go out and spread bad information about where we were looking and hire a team of military personnel to go with us on the search. Look, I'm sorry that you had some people come and try to feel you out for answers, but that doesn't excuse what you are doing Paulus..."

"Erich, please...," Paulus said raising a hand, asking to let him finish. He waited as the thunder and rain escalated, the sound was now so loud as the rain hit the glass dome and the thunder rent the air around them that Paulus was certain the dome would soon give way and collapse under the might of Mother Nature. He slowly looked up to reassure himself that they were safe under the dome and continued speaking, "No one had any information of course. At this point, it had been at least two years since you wandered out into the jungle, to tell you the truth, we were all very certain that you had died. I had, after all, spent many weeks searching for you after you left. The men told us that you had indeed survived and that you had become a bit of a celebrity because you claimed to know where you could find the Ark from the story of Noah. No one in the village could believe it, we were all so relieved that you had not died, Gema most of all..." Paulus paused, allowing this statement to sink in before continuing, "The men were nice enough at first, seemingly just interested in you and your life with us in the village. They tried to ply us with food and tobacco, the way most westerners do, but once they realized that they would not be getting the answers they sought, they resorted to other tactics... they started on Father Michael. I guess they believed that if anyone in the village knew where you learned the information, it would be the man that you served under, and they probably also felt that everyone in the village would want to see no harm fall to the man that had taught them so many things. The men brought Father Michael to the center of the village. They told us that if we didn't tell them right away where you got your information they would hurt him. We begged them to believe us that we did not know, but there was no reasoning with them, they beat him to death in front of all of us..."

Paulus paused again, this time because the memories were too much for him to bear. He looked up and noticed that all of the anger had left Erich's eyes and had been replaced with a sadness that seemed so deep it might swallow them both.

Erich spoke, his voice heavy and cracking with emotion, "I had no idea that I had caused harm to the village, I am so sorry Paulus, is...."

Paulus again raised a hand and cut Erich off, *the worst is yet to come*, thought Paulus, and he prepared himself for the retelling of the rest of the story. "I ran to Father Michael, pushing the men away from him and falling to the ground, I tried to give him the breath of life, but he was indeed gone. The men stood mocking me. One man, who I had heard called Malik, and who seemed to be their leader, pushed me aside with a muddy combat boot and called out to everyone in the village, 'Another will die every ten minutes until I have the answers I seek' he shouted at us. Hatred and evil burned in his eyes. We all stood still for what felt like hours, until slowly Malik looked down at his watch and then back at the expectant crowd of villagers and smiled, 'so be it' he said as he grinned and pulled one of the younger girls from the crowd, a girl named Nadya, she was only ten years old..."

"I remember Nadya," Erich said softly, tears coming to his eyes, "Paulus this is too much, I can't take this, I had no idea that this had happened. I understand why you would want to come and take something from me, and I don't blame you, just tell me if Gema was hurt, please...."

Erich sounded and looked like a man totally defeated. "I take no pleasure in this brother, but you must understand what we are up against, please let me finish and then I will answer any questions you still have. As Malik pulled Nadya from the crowd I knew that I could no longer just stand by and watch. Even though I knew the men would kill me, I jumped up and pulled the small knife I carry with me to carve wood and jabbed at Malik with all my might. I was trying to stab him in the neck, but he brought up an arm and blocked my assault, my blade skipped across his cheek. He grabbed my arm and twisted it, forcing me to my knees in front of him. I saw a thin red line of blood bloom on his cheek and thought that even though I was going to die, at least I had wounded him. He continued to twist my arm to the point where I knew it would break, and then he reached behind his back, and when his hand came forward again it held a large black pistol. He looked around at everyone that was gathered and screamed 'this is not what I want, you have chosen this path. I only seek information, but because you refuse to give me what I need, your fate will be the same as this foolish boys' and he placed the cold barrel of the gun to my head. I wanted to close my eyes. To break down and cry and beg him not to end my life, but I knew that I had at least saved Nadya for the time being, and I refused to give him the satisfaction of seeing me cower before him, so I stared directly into his eyes as he glared down at me. It seemed like everything was moving in slow motion, I saw a single drop of blood fall from his cheek as his finger tightened on the trigger. I wondered what dying would feel like, wondered if heaven was real, wondered if I had been good enough to go there. I thought about all of the people that I love, my father, my friends, even you Erich, and I knew the trigger would relent any second, but before he ended my life a scream rose from the jungle. Gunshots rang out, I threw myself to the ground and Malik and his men dove for cover, not knowing where the shots were coming from. I felt rough hands on my shoulder, tried to shove them away, but a voice spoke quielty in my ear, cutting through the chaos and a peacee settled throughout me, as I heard these words, 'I am Unta, I am here to help you, I need you to stand up and take me to your sister, no harm will come to either of you, I doubt these men will give you such an offer.'"

Erich had so many questions rolling around inside of his mind he could hardly decide which one to ask first, "Unta...and your sister...I didn't know that you had a sister..."

"Neither did I and that is exactly what I told Unta. He looked shocked and simply said, 'so they never told you...I should have

guessed.   Paulus...your sister is Gema, take me to her now.'
Gema...my sister....and how did he this man know my name? I
began to ask him, but he held told me that all of my questions
would be answered eventually but first, we had to find Gema, he
called her...the key." Paulus paused as more thunder rocked the
forest outside of the dome.

"I knew that I would get no further answers from this strange
man until we found Gema, and even though I did not understand
what was going on I feared that at any moment the world would
return to normal, so I hurried towards Gema's house, although I
did not know if she would be there, she was so often in the forest
with..." Paulus had stopped himself before he said the name of
who Gema was usually in the forest with and Erich felt a hot dagger of pain stab through his heart. Paulus could see the pain on
his friend's face and seemed to be taking a long time to frame his
words more carefully.

Erich spoke up, "Paulus, I was never naïve enough to believe
that Gema would not find love after I left, and in fact I am glad to
know that she did, although," he said with a hint of a smile, "I
don't think that I need to know his name."
Paulus looked at Erich with a small smile, "It is not what you think
Erich, but you are right, a name can wait until later. We found
Gema at her house, and Unta quickly spirited all of us away into
the jungle, taking us to the village of his people. He did not stop
to get anyone else, and although I feared for the rest of the village,
I felt that going with this man and that getting Gema to safety was
of the utmost importance. So we ran, stumbling, trying to keep
up with this ancient man who moved like a shadow across the
jungle floor. We ran hour after hour, straight through the night,
stopping only briefly for food and water, and so that Gema and I
could rest. When we finally reached his village, the day was just
breaking, the warm orange glow of the sun lightening the sky in
the distance. We stood with our hands on our knees struggling
to normalize our breathing. Unta stood and looked at us, a smile
on his face, breathing no harder than if he had simply walked to
the river for some water, and said 'Come children, I will give you
the answers that you undoubtedly seek but be prepared, there

will be much joy in the village when we enter, much joy that the two of you are finally home.' I couldn't imagine what he meant but as soon as we entered the village, I could see that he was right. People poured out of every home, many of them crying and touching Gema and I's arms, caressing our faces, speaking in an unfamiliar language. I couldn't understand what they were saying, but they were obviously overjoyed that we had made it to the village. Unta took us to the center of the village, where there was a large round communal home. He stopped in the doorway of the home and turned to face the other villagers and spoke to them in their native language, at which time they all cheered and then turned to go back to their homes. I asked him what he said to them, and he said, "The truth," and he walked into the building. We followed him inside and Unta spoke the following words, 'I am sure that you are wondering why we have brought you here, why we saved only your lives at the village, for rest assured that we have dealt with Malik before, and everyone in your village is now dead. These questions will be answered, but first, you must know who you really are. When you were both but small children, you lived with all of us, the ancestors of the Sala'ma. Your father was our chieftain, the wisest man in a thousand years to lead our people, and the protector of a great secret. Fifteen years ago, Malik came to our village, looking to speak to your father about this secret. Malik would stop at nothing to get what he wanted, first killing your mother in front of your father and then coming after the two of you. I escaped with the two of you into the forest and fled as fast as I could. I knew that the village would never again be safe for either of you and so I ran for days through the jungle. I stopped only long enough to eat and drink and left no trace of my journey for Malik to follow. Eventually, I found a small village and left you with the priest there. He apparently convinced different families to adopt you both. I am not sure why he chose to keep the truth about you being siblings from the two of you, but I assume he had his reasons. I returned to my village to find it burned to the ground, less than one hundred people had survived. Our chieftain was dead, and the key... was gone. We all decided that we needed to stay close enough to your new village to keep an eye on you, yet far enough away to never again attract the attention of Malik. We succeeded in doing just that until the day that I found Erich near death in a clearing in the forest.'"

CHAPTER FOURTEEN

Tarrin stood on the hillside looking out into the city, brushing a strand of his long brown hair out of his eyes and tucking it behind his ear. *What have we done?* He thought to himself. It had been over a week since the attack on the temple, and still, Tarrin found it difficult to think back to that night. Everything had happened so fast...the gathering...Noah and his ultimatum...Jakon and his impassioned response. Tarrin had agreed with Jakon, although now he had begun to wonder if that had simply been because of his already strong dislike for Noahim. From the first day that Noah had come to live with the other boys in training, Tarrin had resented the boy. The one. So smug...so arrogant...after all, did they not all have the gift, were they not all special in that regard?

Tarrin had heard the older men speak of the times before Noah was born when the citizens respected all of the Mul'Ki equally, but that had indeed all changed the day that the Bala'Ra had sought him out and fulfilled the first part of the prophecy, and now Noah had drunk from the Jala'Kim. At that moment, he had shown that he was the one the prophecy spoke of, and yet Jakon had insisted that it did not matter. He insisted that the prophecy was as useless as the man himself...still, Tarrin could not avoid the gnawing feeling in the back of his mind that what they were doing was wrong. They had destroyed the temple, attacked their own brethren, even killed many Mul'Ki that night. *How could killing gifted men be the answer?* he thought.

Some of the men that had perished that night had been friends of Tarrin's, men that he had grown up with, men whose only crimes had been following the orders of their high priest. "What has you so troubled son?" a voice spoke into the silence of the morning, and Tarrin spun quickly around, his breath catching in his chest as Jakon approached, Kaylan slinking at his side. "Tell me your troubles, and I will do my best to help."

"I am fearful Jakon," Tarrin said slowly, "Fearful that we have done the wrong thing. Attacking the temple...men died at our hands..."

Jakon pursed his lips and nodded his head slowly, taking a moment before responding. "I too lost friends that night Tarrin, men that I had known for centuries, men that I served beside. I feel the loss as deeply as anyone...but make no mistake, this was not our doing. Noahim forced our hand. The moment he banned anyone that does not agree with his way of thinking from the temple, he sealed his own fate. His ego has run unchecked for far too long. Let me ask you this...does it seem to you that someone worthy of the post of high priest of the Mul'Ki would so greatly fear a differing of opinion from his own that he would cast out anyone who dares think for themselves?"

"No, it does not..."

"Exactly, by his own actions he proved to be unworthy...proved that he needed to be removed."

"I agree with that, but why destroy the temple...why kill those that chose not to agree with us...are we not guilty of the same pride and arrogance as Noahim then?" Tarrin asked cautiously. For a moment, he thought he saw what looked like a flash of anger blaze across Jakon's eyes, but it was gone before he could be certain and replaced again with that kind smile.

"The temple needed to be destroyed to send the message to the people of Atla that a new day is upon us," Jakon said, his voice growing a harder edge to it now, "No longer will we be slaves to the old teachings, slaves to the whim of the non-gifted. No longer will we allow those that cannot even wield the Ari'Yet to decide who the high priest of the Mul'Ki is. We are the Mul'Ki, we shall decide who leads us. The people had their chance, and they chose to put a boy in charge of the greatest order of men that has ever lived...but no more. We are not here to serve them...indeed they are here to serve us...and I intend to remind them of our great power. The gifted that were lost when we destroyed the temple were a necessary sacrifice, a means to an end. Have you not noticed that the people now look at all of us the same way that they once looked at their precious Noahim?"

Tarrin thought before answering, "I have noticed that the people now regard us differently, although it seems to me that it is not the same way that they look at Noah..."

"In what way?" Jakon asked in a low voice.

"Well...," Tarrin said nervously, his eyes shifting as to not make direct eye contact with Jakon, "when the people look at Noahim it is with a mixture of awe and respect. When they look at us now...at this new order of the Mul'Ki...I see only fear."

Jakon smiled triumphantly, "Fear is respect, young one, but understand I care not if men that are below me respect me. I only care that they do as they are told, which is why we must show the people that we are to be feared because if they are scared, they can be controlled."

Tarrin nodded as he tried to take in what Jakon was saying, "But why must we control the people?"

"Ahhh...," Jakon said smiling, "that is the most important question you have asked thus far. We must control the people to protect our way of life. Atla is an amazing place, but it is not because of the millions of citizens that live here that we have achieved so much...no, it is because of us...the Mul'Ki...and yet it is a non-gifted man that serves as our king. It is the non-gifted that force the brethren into serving them in their menial tasks. All the while, we should be being served by these very people so that we can focus our energies on more important pursuits. How far could Atla have come if the majority of our time was not spent dealing with daily trials and tribulations of the non-gifted? Just think of how much we could do if we were free from the tasks of ordinary men...and in the end, these same men will benefit from our greatness, their lives will be improved by their very service to us."

Tarrin looked unsure, but Jakon sensed that he was close to seeing his point of view, "Tarrin, I know that this is difficult. What I am asking of you is not an easy task, but greatness comes at a cost. You can be great Tarrin, I want you to be my second in command. I need someone like you, someone young...someone hungry who can help me rally the other Mul'Ki when the time comes for war, and believe me that time will come."

"War?" Tarrin said tentatively, "War with who?"

"War with Noah and the people that choose to follow him. It is not my desire, but can you not see that his blind adherence to the old teachings make him a danger to everything that we are working towards? He will always maintain that we should serve the people, that ordinary men are our equals. He will always believe that all of the answers lie in the past...but they do not. I have witnessed with my own eyes the upheaval of Ratam, and I agree with Noahim on one point, that trouble may be coming...but I believe that his insistence on following the teachings of the ancients will mean the destruction of everything that we have created. If we are to stop this impending disaster, we need to have every Mul'Ki searching for the solutions here...and now...we must not be distracted by the old ways. That is why we must continue to portray a strong and unified front. We must continue to inspire fear in those that look upon us...this fear may well be the only thing that prevents a war..."

Tarrin was nodding now, "I understand Jakon. It is not going to be easy, but I believe that you are right, that for the good of everyone we must proceed with this plan. I do not, however, understand how I could possibly be your second in command. I am not even Mul'Ki, I have no RaSheen, the older men will not listen to me."

"Then you make them listen!" Jakon said loudly, his eyes flashing again, "and as for you not having a RaSheen, I was thinking we could do something about that..." Jakon stepped aside and from behind him a small orange and black tiger strode into the clearing. Tarrin watched in awe as the cat walked over to him, sniffing the air around him and crouching low to the ground, muscles rippling beneath its beautiful coat. "This is Tora..."

Tarrin simply stared with wide eyes, "She is beautiful," he said in a whisper, "but how can she possibly be my RaSheen? I have not undertaken the quest; how will she choose me?"

"The bond can be forged in many ways," Jakon said with the slightest hint of a smile, "if there is one thing that the ancients were good at it was hiding information from us, but I have begun to unravel many of the old teachings, and to glean the hidden knowledge and the power within. I now know how to force the bond of the RaSheen, so go and gather as many of the young and uninitiated men as you can find, bring them to me at the Jala'Kim. Today we will begin to build our army...an army that you will lead, Tarrin...an army that will strike fear into the hearts of all that even hear a whisper of it..."

CHAPTER FIFTEEN

"This is all almost too much to take Paulus. You and Gema being brother and sister, ancestors of the Sala'Ma, Unta being your
grandfather, the man that saved my life in the forest, the man that
started me on my quest to find the Ark, and on top of all of that,
I find out that my decision to search for the Ark, to make the information public, meant the death of everyone in the village and
put you and Gema in constant danger....."

"Gema and I were already in great danger Erich," Paulus said
softly, placing his hand on Erich's shoulder, "We just didn't know
it yet. Malik has never stopped searching for us, for the secret
that my father possessed, and he never will, which is why I am
here. I need your help, Erich."

"My help?" Erich said sounding stunned, "I thought you were
here to stop the museum from opening..."

Paulus smiled a little, "I have not been totally honest with you
Erich, but I am getting there. I told you that you do not know
what you found, and that much is true, you did not find the vessel
that carried the Sala'Ma to their new home."

Erich looked confused, "Of course I did Paulus, it is..."

Paulus cut Erich off, holding a hand up, "Erich, I know that
much of this will be confusing at first, but believe me, it is true.

You did find a boat that belonged to members of the Sala'Ma. However, Unta and I believe that the boat that you found was not the one that the legend spoke of, it was not the one that held the seeds of civilization. Before the catastrophe befell the Sala'Ma, there was a division among their people, on one side there was a man named Noahim that stood for good, and on the other Jakon, who stood for evil. It is too much to explain right now, and much of it you would probably not believe anyway, but please believe me when I say that the boat you found did not belong to Noahim."

"Who cares who the boat belonged to," Erich said shortly, "What does any of this have to do with anything?"

"Malik is a descendant of Jakon, and I of Noah," Paulus said, "That is why he seeks us out, he was trying to find this place before you did, and he will be here soon to claim what he believes is his."

"And what is that?" Erich asked, looking skeptical.

"The secret that my father had, the secret that he believes will give him unlimited power," Paulus said, sounding serious although Erich knew that he must be joking.

"Unlimited power..." Erich said coldly, "What in the hell are you talking about Paulus, none of this makes any sense, plus the security around this place is intense, he'd never get in anyway."

Paulus stared at Erich for a brief moment, holding his gaze, and then looked down into the pool of water and began to speak again, "This pool, it is called the Jala'Kim, it means Pool of Wisdom in the language of the Sala'Ma. Well, this isn't the actual pool, this is a model of it that Jakon made here, in this jungle that was his new home, after his powers started to fade. It is said that anyone that drinks from it, or even touches the water will die instantly, except for the one that the prophecy speaks of..."

"Prophecy... powers...," Erich said incredulously, "I don't think I can take much more of this Paulus..."

Thunder continued to roll outside the protection of the domed jungle, although Erich didn't think the storm would last much longer, it felt like this one would be quick and violent. The silence between Paulus and Erich grew thick, the jungle seemed to push in around them. Paulus spoke slowly, calmly, purposefully, "Malik will be here soon; he will kill everyone that stands in his way. He believes the secret that he has sought for so many years is on that boat; it is not. We must make everyone leave the museum now, or there will be more death than you can imagine."

"Even if I believed you, getting everyone to leave the museum will be pretty tough," Erich said with a sigh, "You heard Jim. He doesn't plan on acting on your cease and desist order until tomorrow at the earliest, and even then, it will take a long time to get everyone out of here. There are thousands of people here for the grand opening, not to mention the staff..."

"You need to convince him that it is for the best that he has everyone leave right away, it's the only hope."

"I have to be honest with you Paulus," Erich said with a hint of sadness in his voice, "Your story seems crazy to me but it does explain how Unta happened to find me dying in the jungle, they must have followed me after I left the village because they were watching you and Gema. But the rest of it, prophecy and killers on the loose searching for some secret from an ancient society, it sounds like a movie or something. Give me one good reason why I should believe you..."

Paulus stifled a small laugh, "My story is too outlandish for the man who found Noah's Ark..."

"Well," Erich said, smiling a touch himself now, "if what you said is true it looks like I found Jakon's Ark, and Noah's Ark is still out there somewhere."

A flash of lightning lit the jungle surrounding them, and with it, Erich saw a look of determination set across his young friend's face, "That is right Erich, Noah's Ark is still out there somewhere, and that's exactly what I need you to help me find."

"You want me to help you find this other boat...why do you need to find it, and how would I be able to help?"

"Why would I believe that you couldn't help me find it? You found this place...and that is something that Unta's people had tried to find for thousands of years. You found it in two. I know that you can help me find where Noahim and his people rebuilt their civilization. As for why...Malik will stop at nothing to find it, and if he does, the world may never be the same."

Erich rubbed his forehead with his fingers and scrunched up

his face, shaking his head in disbelief, "The world may never be the same...for God's sake, Paulus listen to yourself, you sound like a damn lunatic."

Paulus smiled a small knowing smile, "I know what I must sound like Erich, and I assume it is what most people thought you sounded like before you found all of this," Paulus motioned in a circle around him, "but now I am asking you to trust in something bigger than yourself, we must find these other boats, they contain knowledge that must be kept from Malik at all costs."

"What kind of knowledge?" Erich asked skeptically.

Paulus sighed, "Erich, we really do not have time to go into everything, but basically Noahim, Jakon, and some other men at that time possessed powers that we would consider magic, or at least something akin to magic. They could make things levitate, telepathy, the ability to communicate with animals, extend their own lives into hundreds of years...the list goes on and on. Noah believed that these...powers, for lack of a better word, existed for the betterment of mankind, Jakon believed they made him a god. At least, that is what he believed by the end of his life. Jakon did not believe that human life was valuable in the least, save for any value that someone may be able to provide him, and Malik shares that view. The good news for us is that Malik does not possess the same powers as Jakon, who knows what he would be capable of he did."

"And the boat comes in where..."

"The boat is believed to hold the secrets to unlocking these powers. As Unta tells it, Noahim was different than anyone that had come before him, although he isn't sure exactly what was different about him, he was the fulfillment of a prophecy, or at least, most of the people at the time believed he was. It was said that he had a book that would unlock the key to limitless power, and the legend states that he hid it in the city that would become the new home for his people. The secret my father possessed was a book that will help lead us to the lost city of the Sala'Ma."

Erich couldn't believe what he was hearing, "You are definitely losing me now Paulus. How did you get the book that your father was protecting, and if Unta had that book and knew about all of this Noahim and Jakon stuff, why didn't he tell me about it?

Why did he lead me to the Ark that is here under this dome?"

"The book that my father was protecting was found as soon as Malik and his thugs left the village after they killed my father and many others. Unta has possessed the book ever since, but it has been of little use until recently because it was written in a dead language that no one could translate, now Unta has found someone that is able to translate the book, and with it, a wealth of information that had been lost, has been found. This is where we learned of Noahim and Jakon, and of the rift between the Sala'Ma people and the great catastrophe that befell them."

Erich stood up beside the pool and began to pace, unable to sit still any longer, "Well that makes a little more sense I suppose. Still...if this book tells you how to find the lost city I still don't understand why you need me."

"The book doesn't tell us where the city is," Paulus said, "It just gives us a starting point. Look, Erich, the truth is, you found Jakon's Ark when no one else could, and I believe you can help us find this lost city."

Erich looked at him, doubt filling his mind. "Look, Paulus, what you are saying may be true...I don't know what I believe. In one way, it does help explain quite a bit about how the people that built the ark that I found seemed to be so advanced, in truth, sometimes I think they were more advanced than we are now, but it just seems off. I just don't understand what happened recently that would have allowed the book to be translated..."

Paulus looked at Erich for a long moment, again seeming to weigh if he should share some secret info with him. Erich wanted to say more but held back, he couldn't explain it, but he felt as though something of importance was about to happen. As though the jungle itself could sense his anticipation, it all became very quiet, the rain ceased beating on the dome, the song of the birds and even the constant drone of the many forest insects faded to nothing. An uncomfortable silence grew as Paulus continued to determine just how much he should say. Finally, taking a deep, steadying breath and returning his gaze to Erich he said, "What happened recently is that Unta showed the book to...Gema's child..."

CHAPTER SIXTEEN

Noahim sat in silence, his eyes closed, his breathing a slow, practiced rhythm. The sounds of the forest intertwined with his exhalations to form an almost eerie melody. He felt the first rays of the morning sun break through the canopy and fall upon his upturned face. In these moments of deep reflection and concentration, it was as though he felt everything and nothing all at once. He heard the sound of the monkeys chattering to each other hundreds of feet above him in the canopy, the buzz of mosquitos and other insects, the songs of the many different birds of the great forest filled the air. He was so in tune with the world around him, he could hear the sound of a droplet of water as it made its way across the surface of a leaf high above him, could see its journey as gravity pulled it towards the ground. The droplet began to trace the veins of the leaf as it slowly slid toward its downturned tip. It held there briefly as if it were fighting against the very laws of nature and then succumbed to the relentless pull of the earth below as it began its two-hundred-foot free-fall to the surface.

Noahim felt all of it, and with his eyes still closed, slowly raised his right hand, palm down, and held it in front of his body, waiting expectantly for the rogue droplet of water to land. He counted in his head, *three...two...one...* and as he knew it would, the droplet alighted on his skin. He smiled. It had taken years of study and practice for him to be able to achieve this state of oneness with the universe, and he had been ignoring his own need to connect with the world around him far too much lately. It was easy to become distracted by the constant needs of others, but today, he knew that a decision had to be made, and his mind must be clear before he could make such a difficult choice.

Noahim sensed a small rabbit at the edge of the clearing and connected with its mind. His mind filled with the emotions of the rabbit. The rabbit felt everything in much the same way as did Noah today, it was frozen by indecision...hide, fight, or flee. Noah knew the rabbit would flee. Put distance between itself and this unknown danger, find a new, safer place. This was also what Noahim had decided to do. It had been two months since the attack on the library, and every day since had been consumed by preparations to flee Atla.

The people seemed split on what to do. Many of them, at first, wanted to side with Noah, to accept that their way of life was soon to end, but once they were faced with the real preparations for leaving the place they had always called home, many of them joined Jakon. It also did not help Noah's case that most of the Mul'Ki had joined with Jakon as they sought to create a new society, where Jakon and his magical brethren would rule over the others. Only a handful of Mul'Ki had decided to stay with Noah, a fact that, at first, had surprised him, but that he now realized he should have seen coming. So many of the Mul'Ki were jealous of Noahim's status among the people, or at least the status that he used to enjoy. Now, most of the people of Atla thought that he was a fool that had lost his mind as he told them all of their inevitable doom and set about with preparations to flee from this place with his followers.

Noahim again tried to keep his mind clear and think of nothing, and everything, at the same time. His mind reached back out to the rabbit, and as if sensing this intrusion into its thoughts, the rabbit finally gave into its urge and fled as fast as it could away from the clearing. Noah sighed and opened his eyes and looked out at the Jala'Kim, his mind was as clear as it was going to get. In the past two months, much had been accomplished, but much more still needed to be done.

Noah, his Mul'Ki, and the people of Atla that had decided to stay with their high priest had spent the last two months building four large ships and provisioning supplies for them. The ships were truly massive, although Noah worried that they would not be big enough. Noah had no idea how soon they needed to be ready for the coming floods, but come they would, and it was his job to make sure that the people would be ready. Noah now divided his time equally between using his magic to help the people build the boats, teaching the other Mul'Ki to harness their Ari more powerfully so that when the time came to sail the boats they would be able to help control their path, and trying to determine what other hidden messages might be found in Ratam Ra'Ava. Although he didn't have nearly as much time to do this as he wanted. For now, studying the book would have to wait so that they could finish preparing for the floods.

As Noah walked through the jungle, Karok came to meet him on the path, nuzzling his large head into his hand. Noah looked down and smiled, "Am I a fool, old friend?" he asked. Karok simply leaned his weight into Noah, as he so often did as a way to show his support. Noah left the forest behind and headed towards the sea where they were constructing the boats. The construction site of the boats was at the bottom of a large hill that swept down from the forest edge. As Noahim approached, the magnitude of the site left him somewhat awestruck.

Over four hundred men worked on the boats, some, on scaffolding that was built beside the large vessels, used pitch to seal the hulls of the giant ships, while others worked on rigging on the decks, and still, others were busy readying the gigantic sails. Noah knew that inside the boats, countless others were busy finishing the living quarters, stables and storage areas. Beside the construction site was a large garden area where many women and children, and some of the elderly men that could no longer handle the heavy lifting, worked to prepare food for the voyage for the citizens as well as the animals that would be taken on the trip with them. There were also areas where fish and other meats were being dried and cured for the voyage, as well as flour being ground from manioc root and corn and fruit being preserved in jars. The men and women that had chosen to stay with Noahim, while few in number, had all worked tirelessly to prepare for the impending disaster.

As Noah stood and surveyed the people, Jikar came running up to him, looking somewhat nervous. "Noah, I am glad you are here," he exclaimed, "there is something that you need to see in the Jaguar."

Noah had wanted to go and talk to Namaah, to see how her preparations with the people were coming, but he could tell that Jikar was deeply troubled so Namaah would have to wait. "Of course, brother," Noah said, "Lead the way."

The Jaguar was what they called the largest of the four boats, each being named after the animal that emblazoned its bow: The Lion, The Cheetah, The Leopard, and The Jaguar. Jikar turned quickly and headed towards the Jaguar, which, aside from being the largest of the boats and the one that Noah would oversee on the voyage, also held the new libraries of the Mul'Ki. After Jakon had attacked Noah and the other Mul'Ki in the temple, Noah had set out to find every book of the ancient teachings that was still available in Atla; luckily, the library was not the only repository of the ancient texts. Long ago, the Mul'Ki had made a habit of keeping copies of many of the most important books in multiple sites throughout Atla so that not all of their amassed knowledge could be destroyed at once. Rashan had shared this knowledge with Noah, but no one else, and Noah was certain that had Jakon known of these hidden libraries he would have set out to destroy them. Once again, Noah was thankful for the foresight of the ancients for they had been able to recover hundreds of books from these hidden libraries, and along with the books that they were able to salvage from the temple, begin to rebuild a library of the ancient teachings.

The library was located on the deck of the Jaguar, its placement on the boat serving multiple purposes. The first was that because of all the books and equipment they had salvaged from the temple, they needed a large area and Noah had not wanted to compromise living quarter space because they were short on room already. The second being that by putting it on the deck they were able to add several large windows so that they could use devices like the Yevi. This way, the Mul'Ki could maintain a watchful eye on the skies. Noahim had not had the time that he wished to continue to study Ratam RaAva but he had learned enough from the book to know that they would indeed need to remain attentive to the stars.

As Jikar and Noah entered the library, they were greeted by Thomas, the oldest of the Mul'Ki, who had chosen to remain and help Noah. Thomas was 790 years old, his skin was heavily wrinkled and a deep shade of brown, his hair and beard gray and unruly, but his brown eyes sparkled with the energy and intensity of a much younger man. As he approached, he absently ran a hand through his wild hair, trying very unsuccessfully to smooth it down into place. "Noah, I am glad we found you, there is something you must see," he said breathlessly, as though he had spent the last several minutes doing strenuous manual labor.

"What has you so troubled old one?" Noah asked.

Thomas looked at Noah, then at Jikar and back to Noah, seemingly struggling with where to start, "I was going over some observations that were made last night and thought that I noticed an error in the data that was collected. It seemed that Phillip had incorrectly identified the placement of RaAlla, so I went to speak to him about it, but he insisted he had been accurate... that he had taken the utmost care in his report because you told all of us this task was of the highest importance," Thomas paused for a moment, "Noah, I checked back into the records and for the last three days RaAlla has appeared slightly out of place in the night sky. It is almost imperceptible, but somehow RaAlla has moved from where tens of thousands of years of study teach us it should be."

Noahim walked to the charts spread out on the table and began to look at them, to see this information with his own eyes. He absent-mindedly put his right hand down at his side and Karok was there, nuzzling into his hand, reassuring him. If the data that had been recorded was correct, and Noah had to assume that it was, for he had made it very clear to all of the Mul'Ki that their very survival may depend on this information, then Thomas was right. RaAlla was not where it should be. Noah was finally beginning to understand the prophecy he had spoken to Jakon about months ago. *When the Ra'Naset has displayed its beauty, RaAlla will dislodge from his place in the heavens.*

At the time when the Ra'Naset had opened, and Noah had read the prophecy, it hadn't made sense to him. How could a star dislodge from its place? After studying the words in Ratam RaAva and realizing what the ancients had endured and what they had been trying to prevent, he now realized that it was not RaAlla that would be moving. The prophecy simply meant that if RaAlla was not where history told them it should be...catastrophe was upon them. Somehow Atla had shifted ever so slightly, its place on earth now different than it had been in the past, making RaAlla's placement in the stars different as well. Noahim took one final look at the charts, rubbed the top of Karok's massive head and turning to face the other men in the room, took a deep breath. "Brothers," he said, his voice barely more than a whisper, "it begins."

CHAPTER SEVENTEEN

Erich just stared at Paulus, his mouth opening and closing slightly, as though he were trying to say something but had forgotten how to speak. Paulus allowed his old friend time to gather his thoughts and simply stood silently, looking out into the jungle beyond the giant glass dome. "Her child..." Erich finally said slowly.

"Yes, her child Erich. Gema..."

"Stop. I don't want to know," Erich blurted out loudly, angrily.

"Erich there are things I need to tell..." but before Paulus could finish the sentence there was a strange popping sound from above and the lights in the garden went dark. A series of pops and clunks rang out as lights, pumps, AC units, air filtration, irrigation systems, electrified fences for the animal exhibits, and many other electrical systems all began to shut down.

It was still daylight outside of the dome, although the storm clouds had yet to dissipate so the light that came in from the outside was feeble. Erich and Paulus looked at each other and then around the exhibit, "The power goes out a lot with all of the storms, I'm sure it's nothing to worry about," Erich said, although he didn't sound entirely confident, "I'm sure the backup power will be on any second," and with another soft clunk and whir the emergency generators turned on and soft red lights began to turn on throughout the exhibit. "See..." Erich said with a small smile, "Now..." but he was cut off again, this time by the clear sound of gunfire erupting in the hallway outside of the garden. "That sounded like gunshots," Erich said, surprise filling his voice.

"That's because it was," said Paulus matter-of-factly, pushing Erich to the side and heading towards the door, "Malik is here...." As if in response, more gunfire and screams filled the hallways outside the garden. Paulus strode toward the door, placing his hand behind his back and pulling out a large black pistol. Erich stared in disbelief as Paulus reached into his front pocket and pulled out a small black cylinder and began to thread it onto the end of the pistol.

"Is that a silencer?" Erich asked.

"A suppressor...yes."

"What the hell did you bring that for?"

More gunfire sounded from out in the hallway, "Do you really need to ask that Erich?" Paulus asked, "We need to try and get out of here, are there any back entrances to the exhibits?"

"Well ya, there are maintenance tunnels and staff doors all over the place, but they won't do us any good now. Only the main exhibit doors are operational on emergency power. So, I guess we have to go out that way," Erich said as he pointed towards the front door that led to the source of all of the gunfire and screaming. They both walked slowly toward the door, straining to try and hear anything that was happening in the hallway. Erich began to make his way towards the small window in the door, hoping to glance out into the hallway and see if their path was clear, but before he could do that Paulus reached out an arm and stopped him.

"Wait, brother," Paulus whispered, "do not show yourself, we have no hope of making it out there, Malik will have too many men with him, and they will be well armed. We need to get away, but before we do I need you to take me to wherever it is that you store the books that you have found in the ark, we need to take them with us..."

Erich squinted his eyes and placed two fingers to his right temple, trying to rub out the headache that was growing there. "Look,

Paulus, there is no way out of this exhibit but through that door until the power comes back on. And as far as the documents, they are held in many different places depending on the stage of recovery that they are in. Without knowing what you are looking for, I have no idea where to begin, and even if I did, I don't know how we could get there if these men are as dangerous as you say. I know the books may be important to your people, but right now I think we have bigger problems."

Paulus exhaled deeply, and a look of determination came over him, "These books aren't just important to my people, they are of the utmost importance to all of humanity..." Paulus paused, seemingly weighing some valuable piece of information that he wasn't sure if he could give Erich. "Erich, some of what you are about to see will make little to no sense, and may, at first, seem frightening, or unbelievable, but we have no time to discuss it right now. I am going to get us out of here, but first I need to find a book, a book that would have this symbol on its cover."

Paulus took a deep breath and removed his shirt. Paulus's bronzed body was so muscular that it appeared to be hewn from stone and his friend's entire body was covered with a series of tattoos, strange symbols that looked oddly familiar to Erich, although he was certain that he had never seen them before. Bright blues, reds, greens, and yellows mixed with the deepest, darkest black covered almost every inch of the skin under Paulus's shirt. As Erich tried to rectify the image before him with the boy he had once known, Paulus rolled his shoulders, the muscles across his chest and arms rippled and bulged, the tattoos seeming to come alive. Paulus looked directly into Erich's eyes, and at that moment, Erich saw that he was indeed not the boy that he had known all those years ago in the jungle, he had changed. He was the leader of his people.

Paulus stared directly into Erich's eyes with a look of determination, "This is the symbol that will be on the book, can you take me to it?" and with that, Paulus turned around and stood tall, allowing Erich to soak in the singular image emblazoned across his entire back. Paulus had never been able to see the tattoo on his back, he would not allow it to be photographed and knew that trying to look at in a mirror would not do it justice, but even though he had never laid eyes on the symbol, he knew that its beauty was startling. Until this moment the only people that had seen the tattoo were Unta, Gema, and Adhi, the man who had labored for close to three months to craft the incredible work of art on Paulus's back, but Paulus knew the effect that it had on people. He knew the power that lay within the symbol.

Erich could not tear his eyes from the symbol on his friend's back. Emblazoned in the most brilliant shades of orange, red and yellow and stretching from the base of his neck to the small of his back was a stylized image of what Erich knew instantly to be the sun. The surface of the tattooed sun seemed to ripple in waves, and Erich sensed a power radiating from the symbol, but more than that, he again felt a sense of familiarity when he looked at it. Erich was beginning to lose himself in the beauty of the symbol, forgetting all about the danger looming just outside the door of the garden. The world had begun to dim somewhat, the sights and the sounds seeming farther away as he stared at the tattoo. Erich found his breathing growing steady... rhythmic...his mind clearing as the symbol before him became his entire focus. The image of the sun seemed to burn itself into every fiber of his being, the fear that he had known only seconds ago evaporated. He continued his deep, steady breathing and closed his eyes.

In that instant, everything became clear, the world came rushing back to him. The sounds of the storm, the jungle, and the calamity in the hallway assaulted his ears. The earthen smell of the forest filled his nostrils. He felt the humidity and stillness of the air. A crack of thunder roared through the late afternoon sky and shook the dome above them. Erich opened his eyes, and Paulus was standing in front of him, putting his shirt back on, covering the kaleidoscope of tattoos. "I saw that symbol on one of the first books that we recovered," Erich said, "I know exactly where it is, we need to get to the Ark."

Paulus gave Erich a wry smile, "I never lost faith in you, Erich, I knew that you could find it. Can you get us to the Ark exhibit through the service tunnels?"

"I can get us there, but like I said before, the only doors that work on emergency power are the front doors to the exhibits.

The staff doors will only open from the other side, they are designed to allow people out in an emergency situation, but not in."

A loud noise that sounded as though it came from just outside the door to the garden drew Paulus's attention momentarily. "I will take care of that, just take us to the door, Erich, please. We have no more time...they are here."

Erich could sense that Paulus had a plan, so he quickly turned and walked toward the waterfall at the back of the exhibit. Paulus followed closely behind keeping an eye on the door at the front of the exhibit. They could both hear shouting from the other side of the door, it was in a language that Erich did not recognize, although with the sounds of the storm, the animals in the dome, and the door between them he couldn't really hear it well enough to know if it was a language that he knew. Gunshots rang out as someone began shooting at the door, the sound muffled by the thick metal. Erich knew that the door wouldn't hold out a barrage like that for long, these doors were designed to help regulate the jungle within, not as a means of security against a group of heavily armed lunatics.

As they ran, Erich heard a sharp sound, almost like a hand clap behind him, he turned just in time to see Paulus lower the silenced Glock. "They were starting to make some headway blasting through the window, I can't hurt them from here, but the bullet striking the window from this side should give them pause enough to allow us to make it to the door." Erich just hoped it would be enough time.

As they approached the waterfall, it became clear to Paulus where they were going, "The door is behind the fall isn't it?" he asked, sounding genuinely impressed.

Erich continued to run but said through his ragged breathing, "Ya, Jim and I wanted everything to be as hidden as possible, so we used a lot of the existing natural features, or created features that look natural to hide any maintenance doors, ventilation shafts, air exchangers...you name it. We wanted it to remain a jungle to the visitors." Erich swung to the left of the fall and quickly darted behind it, Paulus following behind him. In the darkness behind the fall, it was nearly impossible to see the flat, featureless, gray, metal door, although Erich knew exactly where it was. "It's here, Paulus," he said reaching out and helping guide his friend to the door, "I really hope you have a plan."

Paulus stared forward, and raised his hands, his palms facing the door. Erich watched as his friend closed his eyes and his brow furrowed slightly, a small bead of sweat ran down Paulus's forehead. Erich was about to say something about the need to hurry, but just before the words escaped his mouth, a small movement caught his eye. He turned his eyes towards the door just in time to see it shudder again, seemingly pulling at the restraints that held it in place. He let his gaze again settle on Paulus, who stood at rigid attention, the muscles on his forearms quivered with exertion as he pressed against an invisible force. Erich watched as the crease in his brow deepened. Paulus made a quick pushing movement with his hands, and the door was torn off of its support and thrown a good ten feet down the hallway behind it.

Erich simply stared at Paulus, a mixture of fear and awe clouded his features, "What the..." but before he could finish the statement Paulus cut him off, the urgency and exhaustion in his voice making his words sound frantic.

"There is no time now Erich, quickly take me to the book so that we can leave with our lives...."

CHAPTER EIGHTEEN

Noahim turned and ran from the library, flying onto the main deck of the Jaguar he searched with his mind for the rest of the Mul'Ki. *Brothers, the time has come, get the people to safety inside the boats. Get whatever provisions you can, it will begin soon*, he spoke directly into their minds. He ran to the edge of the Jaguar and looked out over the site of the other three boats. Even though none of the other Mul'Ki spoke back to him, in his mind, he could see that his message had been received, people had begun to run throughout the site, gathering what they could. Everywhere he looked, men and women helped gather the children and animals and load them into the boats.

Noahim smiled a weary smile, he knew that many in Atla would meet their end soon, and it saddened him, but they had made their choice. He had done his best to convince them, but Jakon had proven a persuasive enemy. Jakon had convinced the people that Noah was a fool that believed in everything the ancients said, because if he did not believe the old teachings, then he had to admit that he was nothing special. Jakon told them that they would all build an empire of great power, where they would each live lives of luxury and ease, but the more he heard word of Jakon's new teachings, the more he became convinced that Jakon only valued the Mul'Ki. He believed that anyone without the gift was not of his concern. He sought to create a world where those that could command their Ari were served by those who could not.

Noah still could not figure out how so many of the citizens of Atla had been taken by these lies, but he could no longer spend time worrying about those that had made their choice. Although many would die, Noahim took solace in the fact that Atla would not die with them, the people that were coming with Noah would preserve what Atla truly was. Just as the ancients had, they would find a new home, they would rebuild, they would pass on the knowledge that the Atlans had spent millennia acquiring, and Noah would find a way to prevent this from ever happening again. Of this, he was sure.

As he looked out over the site, an almost imperceptible tremor rose through the planks of the ship. All at once, the forest erupted into a deafening cacophony of sound as birds by the thousands took flight. The skies became black as the birds all flew out to sea, leaving Atla behind. Watching the birds fly away, Noahim knew that it could not be a good sign. Just then, he saw Karok bounding toward him, the hair raised along his neck. Karok came skidding to a stop at his side as Noah looked around at everyone working on the boats and the ground. No one else had seemed to notice anything and they all continued to finish the work they were doing. *Did I imagine it?* Noahim thought to himself, and in answer, Karok let loose a low, quiet growl. It had not been imagined, it was beginning right now. Noah looked out and realized that he had to get down to the people, get them to hurry, get them inside these boats. He began to run towards the side of the giant vessel, turning his head to look at the men working all along the boat he shouted, "There is no more time, put down your tools, get to safety inside the boat, help anyone that needs to be helped, tell everyone you see, it is starting! And pray to Ratam that we are ready!"

The men all stared at him, stunned, as he flew across the deck of the ark, Karok pounding beside him. As Karok veered towards the stairs that led to the outside, Noah continued to run full speed towards the ship's edge. "Noah," shouted an older man that had been working on the rigging, "Stop!" The man had begun to run towards Noah with his arms outstretched, as though he intended to grab him. Noah saw the man running towards him and simply held out a hand towards him, the man was knocked from his feet and slid backward on the deck, coming to rest in a heap of sail fabric.

Looking over his shoulder at the bewildered man, Noahim smiled and without saying a word launched himself over the railing of the deck. Karok let loose a roar that shook the ground as he continued his full speed descent towards the Ark's entrance. Noah couldn't believe the speed that the ground was hurtling towards him at, he had never jumped from anywhere near this high, the deck was well over a hundred feet above the ground, although he knew that he would be safe. Even so, the sight of the ground rushing to meet him in a crushing embrace was an unsettling one. About five yards above the ground he held his hands out to his sides and lifted his palms, and his descent ceased. He alighted safely on the ground without missing a step and continued to run towards the people shouting, "Everyone get to the safety of the Arks, it begins!"

People began to turn and look at Noah as he ran towards them, but instead of reacting, they just stared, dumbstruck. *Why aren't they moving?* he thought to himself. In answer to his unasked question, Karok burst from the entrance of the Ark and again let loose an ear-shattering roar. This seemed to get the attention of the people and everyone began to run, scooping up children and provisions as they went. A mad rush was being made for the entrance of the Ark. Noah continued to shout, rounding the corner of the Jaguar and coming into full sight of the rest of the Arks.

Ten other Mul'Ki ran towards him, their robes flapping behind them, their RaSheen clearly agitated at their sides. The animal companions had obviously sensed what many of the men had not. Noahim did not know how much time they had, but he knew that the tremor he had felt while on the boat had been a warning. "We must act quickly brothers, get these people to safety, tell me quickly how the situation is progressing."

The first man to speak was Hazul. He was middle-aged for a Mul'Ki, around three hundred years old, and the black hair at his temples had just begun to turn gray. "We have everyone moving as fast as we can," he said somewhat hesitantly, "but there is a problem at the Lion."

Noahim squinted his eyes looking towards the far end of the clearing. The Lion was the final ship in the clearing, and it had been decided that it would house most of the largest animals. Noah hoped the problem was not with the animals, he did not want to deal with any angry elephants right now. "What is the problem?" he asked as he started towards the large ship.

"For some reason, we cannot get the door to open," Hazul said rapidly, "It...it is as though it has been sealed with magic. I have tried everything within my power to open the door, but it is impossible."

"Why would the door be sealed with magic?" Noahim said, beginning to run towards the far end of the clearing.

Hazul looked around nervously, "I was hoping you would know that, high priest."

Noahim was certain that the humid conditions of the jungle and the rushed nature of building the arks were responsible for the door being stuck, and not anything magical. "Has anyone been able to get inside?"

"Not yet, as far as we know, there is no one on the boat, although the animals and all the provisions are already on it."

Noahim looked forward and saw the Lion looming into view. All the boats were impressive, but there was something about the figure at the stern of this one, the proud lion in mid-roar that gave Noah pause every time he saw it. He looked around at all of the people and shouted, "Please, everyone back away from the boat, I am going to attempt to free the door."

Noahim closed his eyes and held his hands out in front of him, preparing to release the flow of energy he was storing up into the door of the great ship. He opened his eyes and drew a slight breath, readying the flow of energy, but before he released it, movement along the back of the Lion caught his attention. He hesitated, fearing that the power he was about to release into the door could cause the person injury and shouted to them, "Please step back from the ship, you are not safe where you are."

The voice that came back to him was filled with such hatred and malice that chills ran up his spine, "I would not worry about my safety boy, it is you and these misguided fools that have chosen to throw their lot with yours that are not safe." Jakon spit as he strode towards Noah and the others.

Noahim had not laid eyes on Jakon since the night of the attack when he saw him in the glow of the fireball that he had sent to destroy the temple. He looked even more menacing today. His white Mul'Ki robes had been replaced by robes of bright red and gold that flowed for many feet behind him. In his left hand, he carried a long, elaborately carved staff made from what appeared to be mahogany. The top of the staff had been carved into a likeness of his RaSheen Kaylan, the golden jaguar, who strode beside him now.

Trailing just slightly behind them was a party of no less than forty former Mul'Ki, all of who had traded their white robes for robes of black, the darkest black that Noah had ever before seen, cinched at the waist with a belt the color of Jakon's robes. Each of the men in black also carried a staff in one hand. As they approached, Jakon shouted a guttural command and they came to a halt, each man then lifted his staff and pulled from each end. The staffs split in the middle and pulled apart, each becoming a sword with a length of roughly three feet. The weapons looked as though they had been fashioned from black glass and had streaks of red that flowed throughout their length, giving them the appearance that they were wet with blood. The men stood at rigid attention, swords drawn and eyes trained on Noahim and his people as they awaited their next order from Jakon.

A hush had fallen over the people, Noahim and his ten Mul'Ki stood and faced the imposing war party. Kaylan and the other RaSheen began to move toward Noah and his men. Noah could not imagine a more intimidating site, forty large cats striding forward fearlessly as the men stood behind them, a wall of black and red, swords glistening in the sunlight. It was then that he noticed that all of the RaSheen that were with these men were large cats. It was true that the majority of RaSheen were cats, but there were many men who had joined with Jakon who's companions had been deer, monkeys, bears, and many types of other animals. It appeared that the war party had been selected based on what type of RaSheen they had. Noahim couldn't help but think it was a good choice, the effect was quite chilling.

Noah also noticed that almost all of the men in the war party were not Mul'Ki, or at least they had not been at the time of the fateful gathering. The army seemed to be comprised of all young men who had not completed their training and so, therefore, did not have RaSheen when they left the temple, but that was not the case any longer. The great cats continued to make their way towards Noah's group, and Noah could not help but wonder how all of these men had been able to go on the quest and find their RaSheen so quickly, and how all of them had found large cats. It seemed too much for coincidence...and then Noah noticed Tarrin standing at the front of the army, a look of malice in his eyes. *What has happened that all of these men would turn to the ways of evil so quickly?* Noah thought.

As the cats stalked forward Jakon began to speak, drawing Noahim out of his thoughts, "Fools and followers of this useless boy, I have come here with a message and I will not mince words...I gave you all the chance to come and join me, to join the new Atla, you declined. For far too long we have been beholden to ancient teachings, the helpless and hapless musings of fools...," Jakon paused for a minute and spread his arms in front of him, motioning to the site of the arks, "and now this boy tells you that a disaster is coming and that he is your savior." Jakon said the last word as though he had taken a bite of rotten meat. "He is not..." Jakon's voice lowered, becoming little more than a whisper, "I am now giving you another chance. Come. Join me, and together we will throw off the shackles of these foolish men...together we will spread out and conquer the rest of the world...together we will be unstoppable."

Noahim stared at Jakon, "Conquer the world?" he asked. "That is your wish, to conquer the world? What is your intention, to force other people to obey your new ideals?"

Jakon laughed loudly, "If need be, yes...I will force them. Do you honestly believe that you have not been forced to live the way that you do? The ancients have provided us with rule upon rule, and for what? What has it ever gotten us? Take you, Noah, you have more power than most men can even imagine but what is it that you do with that power? You spend your days seeking solutions to ancient riddles or settling the petty bickerings of men that are far beneath you," Jakon waved his arms to motion to the people scattered around the clearing, "we are gods, Noah...you and I...and the other Mul'Ki. Gods. We should be treated as such."

Noahim looked at Jakon with a mixture of sorrow, anger, and pity on his face, "We are no gods brother, that much I can assure you. We are men...gifted men...but men none-the-less, and now you want to use these gifts to conquer and enslave? The gifts that we possess should be used for the betterment of mankind. The ancients knew that...I know that...these men that stand beside me know that...and I know that there was a time when all of you knew it as well," he said motioning to Jakon and his army of Mul'Ki.

The air between the two groups of men was thick with anticipation. Jakon stared, sneering at Noahim. As the men faced off, Kaylan began to slink towards Noahim, his head hanging low and slightly angled, a low growl began to emanate from his throat. Without warning, Karok sprung from Noah's side, and with a roar, lashed out with his front leg at the smaller cat. Kaylan threw himself to the side in an attempt to avoid the massive paw and its razor-sharp claws. He was fast, but not fast enough, and Karok's claws sliced into his right front leg, gouging so deep into the muscle and bone that the leg was almost amputated. Jakon fell to one knee as the pain from his RaSheen's wound overtook him. He gasped and looked towards his wounded companion just as Karok sprang towards the old man, mouth opened wide in a roar.

"Enough!" shouted Noahim, "There will be no more bloodshed here today, Karok." Karok stopped short of striking Jakon and turned to Noahim, hunger and bloodlust in his eyes. Noahim shook his head at the big cat and turned his gaze to Kaylan, who was now laying on the ground, a pool of blood, growing larger by the second, welling around him. Noah held out his hand and let his Ari flow into Jakon's RaSheen. The wound on the cat began to close, the muscle and skin coming back together. Once again, Noah was shocked to find himself able to perform such a complex healing. Jakon was beginning to come to his feet again now, hatred burning in his eyes as he looked from Noah to Karok. He was about to say something but appeared to think better of it, deciding to wait and allow Noah to finish healing his companion, knowing that he did not possess the skill required to repair such a terrible injury. In fact, he wasn't sure that anyone else, but Noah, could have repaired the wound.

As the men all stood silently watching the healing take place, Noah spoke again in a quiet voice, "Jakon...brothers...I want no harm to come to any of you. I know that there is good in all of you, even if you are misguided, you can find your way back. Please help us, together we can save Atla!"

Jakon simply shook his head in disgust, "The only thing to save Atla from Noahim," he paused and watched Noah put his hand down, his job of healing Kaylan completed, "is you..." and then Jakon held up his hand and concentrated all of his power. Noahim was lifted twenty feet into the air, his body hurtled backward. He had no time to react, he watched as four of Jakon's men with swords advanced on Karok, saw ten others opening the door to the Lion and entering the ship, and saw Jakon smiling as he nodded his head towards Noah as if to say, look behind you. Noah turned and saw the side of the Jaguar rushing with impossible speed towards him as he slammed into the ship, falling to the ground in a heap, darkness overcoming him.

CHAPTER NINETEEN

Erich and Paulus ran as fast as they could through the service tunnels, the only thing lighting the way was the red hued emergency lights. *It's ok, I know these tunnels, they don't*, he thought, *plus they have no idea where we are going.* Even though he knew that he was right, the thoughts did little to reassure him. As if reading his mind, Paulus spoke, "They will be expecting us to find the easiest route out of the building, not to go deeper into the museum, it will buy us some much-needed time to regroup and form an escape plan. I need to somehow reach Nagato, to let him know to rendezvous at the ark, but I have no cell phone coverage in these tunnels..." he said as he ran looking down at the black iPhone in his hand.

"Mr. Nagato," Erich said incredulously, "I don't think your lawsuit should be top priority right now Paulus."

"Nagato is not my lawyer," Paulus said between ragged breaths, "he is a greatly feared warrior, very skilled in battle and strategy, and he can help us escape. The lawsuit was a ruse to get us access to you Erich, to get your attention."

Erich shook his head, *well it definitely worked*, he thought. "The Ark exhibit is just ahead, it's the next door on our right. Speaking of doors what the hell happened back there Paulus, how did you do that to the door?"

"Erich, I will explain everything once we are safely out of here, but now is not the time. As soon as we get to the exhibit, we need to get the book and then get out of this museum."

"Ok Paulus, I get it...." Erich said as his hand groped for the emergency exit lever on the back of the door. He found it and pulled, the door hissed and slid back into the wall opening in the far back corner of the Ark exhibit. The Ark itself towered above them. They both stopped as they neared it, Paulus looking up in sheer awe.

"It is more beautiful than I could ever have imagined," he said, his tone a mixture of reverence and excitement. "Go and get the book, I will call Nagato and tell him to meet us here. If I can't get ahold of him, we will need to leave without him, although that is a last resort."

Erich continued to sprint past Paulus, running towards the open entrance of the boat. "Follow me, the cell coverage gets better the higher up you get. Sometimes the dome can cause interference."

"Where is it that you are going, Erich?" Paulus shouted as he ran to catch up.

Erich's only response was to turn with a slight smile and point straight up. Paulus watched as Erich reached the gaping black hole that was the door to the great ship. He slowed a half step before bolting into the interior, shouting back to Paulus, "Be careful, there are a ton of animatronics down here, and wires everywhere. Look where you're running and try to keep up." They ran recklessly over the wires and props of the exhibit, but Erich had no fear of falling, he knew this place better than he knew anywhere. Behind him, he could hear Paulus trying to communicate to Nagato on his phone, but it sounded like he still didn't have a strong enough signal to be heard.

Paulus simply repeated the word Ark four times and put the phone back into his pocket, picking up his pace to try to catch back up to Erich. As they reached a sloping ramp that headed up, Paulus was again awed by the sheer size of the vessel that they stood in. From the point where they stood now, roughly in the center of the boat, it was impossible to see either end. Everything just faded into blackness. The only time that he could make out how high the Ark rose above them was when a flash of lightning would momentarily light the interior. Erich was now leaping from the ramp to a ladder that seemed to rise the rest of the way to the deck. As he pulled himself onto the ladder, he took a moment to turn towards Paulus, "It's not an easy jump, but it's the fastest way to the top," he said, "when you hit the edge of the ramp, push as hard as you can. If you don't make it to the ladder it's only about a ten-foot fall, it will hurt, but it shouldn't break anything. I'll see you at the top!"

Erich began climbing as fast as he could, pausing just long enough to watch Paulus effortlessly make the jump to the ladder, *well maybe it's not as hard as I thought*, he thought to himself as he continued to climb. His heartbeat pounded behind his ears, his hands were slick with sweat that seemed to cascade out of all his pores at once. His senses were all on high alert as the adrenaline coursed through his body. He couldn't help but get a sick satisfaction from their current situation. He had spent a lot of time risking his life in the jungles of Indonesia, and it had been a long time without a real adventure.

He paused at the top of the ladder and let one hand slide from the rungs and grasp a small handle on the door directly above his head. He twisted the handle and pushed and the door swung outwards, the stale jungle air rushed over his skin and the pale late afternoon light flowed around him. He pulled himself out of the hatch and climbed onto the observation deck of the Ark. He had no need to get his bearings and began to run towards the building in the center of the ship. He heard Paulus once again trying to raise Nagato on his phone, it sounded as though this time he was successful.

"Come now!" he shouted into his phone, "we are on the top of the ship, Erich knows where the book is, he is taking me to it now. I have no idea how far behind Malik and his men are. Bring as many weapons as you can carry." He again pocketed the phone and ran to catch up.

Erich reached the door to the first building and ran inside. It was a small wooden structure with glass running the length of one side, allowing whoever was inside an unobstructed view of the sea and the sky on that side of the craft when it was sailing. Paulus followed through the door. Once inside, he saw Erich kneeling in front of a series of cabinets. He grasped the handle of the third cabinet and pulled. Paulus could not get a good look inside of the cabinet, but Erich let out a shout, "Got it!" he exclaimed as he turned from the cabinet. Paulus caught a glimpse of a small object in his hand.

"Is that the book?" he asked breathlessly.

"Ya, it's the one," Erich answered, "This was the first artifact I found on this boat. I wanted to keep something special, something that belonged to just me and the Ark and this was it. That's why it isn't under lock and key in the exhibit hall or in one of the labs where they are working on translating the language that all of these books are written in. The first time I laid eyes on this book, I could sense it was something special. I lost so much to find this ship, I just wanted to keep this one thing."

Erich and Paulus stood on the massive deck of the ship, the lightning from the storm outside still flickering. Erich reached out and handed the book to Paulus, who stared at the golden image of the sun emblazoned across the cover of the ancient tome. He continued to stare down at the book in his hands and slowly raised his eyes towards Erich "We may have just saved the world."

CHAPTER TWENTY

Noahim lay on his back... he was sore everywhere. He felt as though he had fallen down a never-ending flight of stairs. He heard the whispered sound of voices around him, felt the comforting weight of Karok pressed up against his side. He couldn't remember the last time that he had felt this tired. The journey from Atla had been far more difficult than he had imagined, and the seemingly never-ending problems that required his constant attention had grown tiresome. It seemed as though trivial matters were constantly distracting him from his real work, determining what had happened that day so many months ago when, as the handful of citizens that had survived had taken to saying, the sky fell.

Thinking back to that fateful day always threatened to plunge Noah into a great sadness. The loss of life was inconceivable. Almost all of the citizens of Atla had perished that day, Noah had been able to save less than a thousand men, women, and children. The survivors, along with Noah and the twenty-four Mul'Ki that remained with him, had escaped the disaster on three of the four large arks that they had been building in the months leading up to the disaster. Noah was told that Jakon and all the rest of the Mul'Ki had confiscated the final ark, the one they called The Lion...and loaded themselves and enough provisions for several months aboard it just in time to escape. Noah himself had not witnessed this event as he had been unconscious. In fact, that attack had left Noah close to death, and unconscious for many of the first few days of their journey.

Jikar had told Noah that after the attack, the scene had quickly escalated into complete and utter chaos. The men that came with Jakon, their former brothers, had set out to attack Karok. Jikar had described that bloody battle to Noah in detail, although he hadn't needed to. For the first several weeks of the journey, all that anyone could speak of was the great Battle of Karok. Apparently, even though he had been set upon by no less than ten men and twenty RaSheen, Karok had fought furiously and killed seven of the men, ten of the RaSheen, and injured the majority of the rest of them before turning his wrath toward Jakon. Jakon, sensing that he had underestimated the power of the BalaRa decided that running was a much better option than fighting. After Jikar had first told Noahim how Jakon had left the battle, he did not believe him and made him tell, and retell, the story several more times before becoming convinced. Jakon and his men had run aboard the Lion and, according to Jikar and all the other witnesses from that day, when Karok ran towards the loading ramp of the boat, Jakon stood on the deck and shouted an incantation, lifting the boat high into the air as it rocketed away from the site. It was less than one day later when the catastrophe began. When the sky fell.

Since that day, Noah and the other survivors had not seen Jakon and his people, nor anyone else for that matter. The flood was even worse than Noah had expected, it had been sudden and violent. Noah had learned from Ratam Ra'Ava that the ancients had suffered a similar fate, and thanks to the warnings in that book, he had at least been able to escape with enough people to rebuild Atla...if they could ever find land again that is. Noah and the others had been sailing in the Arks for months and had yet to see any land anywhere, although Noah believed that was because at this time they really didn't know where they were. All of the star charts and maps that the Atlans had been making for centuries were rendered useless because of the disaster, but Noah held out faith that there were other people that had been spared, other lands that had not been flooded, and they would find them.

Dwelling on the past would offer no solace, so he opened his eyes and without looking around spoke to the other two men in the room. "What is it that you have come seeking friends?"

There was a short pause and then one of the men spoke, "Noah, we are sorry to bother you, we know that you need your rest, but there is...something that you need to come and see."

Noah inhaled deeply and tried to keep his voice even and calm, "Whatever it is, I am sure that one of the other Mul'Ki can attend to it. Please ask Hazul or Thomas, and I will see to anything they cannot in the morning." He made a dismissive gesture with his hand, but the men did not leave. They simply stood, looking at the ground, shifting uncomfortably on their feet. Noah let out his breath and pushed himself up from the bed, "as you wish, show me what you must."

The men shared a glance between one another, turned and walked through the door, Noahim following behind. As they left his room, Noah glanced down the long hallway lined with living quarters for hundreds of people. The gentle, rhythmic rocking of the large vessel helped calm his nerves. Many of the people had a difficult time adjusting to the constant movement, but Noah had found that he had a deep love for the sea. There was something oddly comforting to him about the rocking of the giant boat, the sound of the waves lapping at the sides, the rush of wind when he stood on the deck, the breathtaking view as the water seemed to stretch to eternity in all directions. Yes, Noah loved the sea, although by now he longed to find a new home for the Atlans. The close quarters and the lack of privacy and provisions often made for tense situations.

As they walked through the hallway and towards the stairs that led to the main deck, Noah soaked in the sounds all around him. He heard men and women laughing, people singing, far in the distance he could hear the sounds of a baby crying, he knew that it must be one of the three children that had been born since their journey began on the Ark. Those small children had each been a miracle, and an affirmation of the fact that the Atlans would survive, that life would survive. As they walked, he focused his mind, searching out the mind of Jikar. *Please brother, he whispered into Jikar's mind, meet me on the observation deck outside of the library, something has some of the citizens in a distressed state, and I fear that I am too tired to offer them the peace of mind that they need.*

He felt a response resonate from Jikar and smiled, hopefully, this wouldn't take long and he could be back in bed with Namaah before she even realized he had left. As they climbed the stairs, Noah felt Karok press into his leg and so he reached his hand down to scratch the great cat behind the ears. While Noah had found the sea to be a wondrous place, Karok was decidedly more displeased with their current situation. The big cat had no room to run and stretch his legs, he could not hunt for game or sport, and ever since Noahim had been a small boy swimming through the waters of the Jala'Kim at night he had known of Karok's distaste for water. "We will find a new home soon old friend," he murmured to his companion, "this I promise you."

"What was that high priest?" one of the men said without turning around.

"Nothing," Noah said back, "It was nothing. Where are you taking me?"

The man turned around and gave Noah a half smile, "It isn't much farther, trust me, I think you will find that we have not wasted your time." It was then that Noah realized that one of the men was Joshua, the father of one of the new infants on board the Ark. Joshua was a skilled carpenter, having helped to design much of the layout of the Arks, and tirelessly working to improve conditions aboard the ships. Noah had not spent a lot of time with the man, but the time that he had spent with him had shown him that Joshua was a hard worker, a good man that could be trusted. And most importantly Joshua did not seem the type to wake the high priest for a trivial matter. *Maybe this will prove to be an endeavor worthy of the loss of a couple hours of sleep*, he thought to himself.

As they were about to reach the top of the stairs an energetic voice from below called out, "Slow down up there! What's your hurry, I am sure the water can wait!"

Noahim turned and saw Jikar bounding up the stairs behind them, his RaSheen, Nuni, sat perched on his shoulder. As Jikar approached, he smiled at Noah and patted his shoulder. As he did, his RaSheen jumped from his shoulder directly atop Karok's massive back. The big cat swung his head around and bared his teeth at the tiny monkey but allowed the smaller animal to ride on his back, although not without emitting a low growl to voice his displeasure. "Come now Karok," Noahim said with a smile, "I can hardly believe that you can even feel an animal that small."

Karok pushed hard into Noah's legs in response almost tripping him. Jikar and Noah both laughed as they came to the top of the stairs. The men had already opened the door to the observation deck and walked out, the smell of the sea enveloped Noah as his eyes began to adjust to the darkness. The sky was clear tonight; the stars burned brightly in their new-found homes in the sky. Noah still found it disorienting to see stars that he did not recognize in the night sky above him. He would often search out the familiar constellations and formations that had ruled the night skies for his entire life thus far, but it seemed these formations were here to stay. As they crossed the deck Jikar spoke up to the men leading the way, "So what in the world has you two so worked up that you went and risked the wrath of the high priest, or more accurately, the wrath of the high priest's wife to get him to come up here?"

The only answer to his question was the creaking of the masts and the steady thumping of the waves. "Well?" Jikar said, doing his best to sound exasperated, although Noah could tell that he was simply having fun with the men, "Are either of you going to answer me or am I going to have to...." But he was cut off as Noah walked directly in front of him staring at the horizon. Jikar turned to follow his gaze and could barely believe what he saw, "Is that land?" he whispered.

Noahim just continued to walk towards the edge of the ark, staring into the distance. Jikar followed him as the two men that had led them to the deck smiled at one another. Jikar looked around and saw several groups of other men standing on the deck in various spots all staring towards that dark smear on the horizon. It was difficult to tell because of the darkness, but there was definitely a large area far away that seemed to blot out the stars behind it. Noahim turned toward Jikar, a smile spreading across his face, "Go and wake the others, all of them! Tell them to come to the deck now!" Jikar and Noah embraced, the feeling of relief washing over them both. Even Karok bounded around the deck like a kitten, chasing Nuni, as the little monkey tried desperately to reach the safety of Jikar's shoulder. Noah looked around and saw the other men on the deck celebrating and breathed out a sigh of relief. Soon they would be on dry land again, the only question was what that land would hold for them.

CHAPTER TWENTY-ONE

Erich and Paulus had just gotten to the main door of the Ark when they heard the sound of a door opening at the front of the exhibit. Erich held his hand up for Paulus to stop moving and placed a finger over his lips. They both stood completely still, their bodies flattened against the inside wall of the Ark and listened. The constant drone of the insects within the dome pulsated through the still air as they continued to listen for any sign of danger. Paulus moved closer to Erich and whispered, "It could be Nagato, he is supposed to be meeting us here..."

"It could be," Erich whispered back, "or it could be Malik and his thugs. We shouldn't take any chances...wait here, I'm gonna go check it out." And before Paulus could object, Erich had slipped through the door and into the surrounding jungle. Paulus watched as Erich made his way along a line of giant trees that stretched out of sight above him. He kept to the shadows, silently stepping over roots and bundles of wires that stretched through the underbrush. Paulus was surprised that Erich could move so silently, then again, he realized that Erich had lived with Unta for quite some time, and had learned their ways. Not to mention that he had spent the better part of his life exploring the jungles in one fashion or another.

So Paulus stood in the darkened interior of the Ark and waited for a sign from Erich. He looked down at the book in his hand abd couldn't believe that after all this time, and all of the death and destruction that this book had caused, he was holding it. He ran his hand along the patterns of the sun and couldn't help but wonder what the book would reveal to them, what secrets it held. He opened the cover and by the faint light coming from outside the Ark could barely make out the strange symbols within. He turned to the next page but only found more of the strange symbols. Paulus continued to stare at the symbols so intently that when Erich placed a hand on his shoulder he almost shouted in surprise.

Erich whispered, "Three men are positioned just inside the door to the exhibit, although from your description of him, none of them appear to be Malik. I get the feeling they are either waiting for him to get here...or waiting for us, either way, it doesn't look good. They each are pretty heavily armed. From what I could see, they each have a couple of guns, a mix of pistols and automatics, and possibly some concussion grenades. We need to be careful getting out of here, I don't think we can risk the noise of your little trick with the door being ripped off the hinges again. What do you think we should do?"

Before Paulus could answer, they heard the door at the front of the exhibit hiss open again. A voice rang out through the stillness of the exhibit, "Enough of this game. I have come to collect what is rightfully mine. The book belonged to my ancestors, and I want it. I am not leaving without it. I know that you are both in here somewhere, and I know that you are outmanned and outgunned. So, come out and show yourselves. Give me what I want and end this, now!"

Paulus stared into the darkness towards the front of the exhibit and whispered to Erich, "It is Malik. Our only hope is to escape through the service tunnels, we can...", but a woman's scream cut him off.

"That was Gema, I am certain of it...," Paulus whispered.

Before Paulus could finish, Erich bolted through the opening and ran towards the front of the exhibit, shouting as he went, "Gema!" Paulus took the book from his hand and hastily hid it beside the door of the ark before running after Erich. They both ran towards the entrance of the exhibit, towards the sound of the screaming. As they came to the entrance, the scene that unfolded before them made no sense to Erich. The three guards stood, their guns raised and pointing in the direction of Erich and Paulus. Malik stood in the center of the men holding tightly to Gema's upper arm and pushing the barrel of a pistol into the side of her head. She stood silently staring at the ground. Erich slid to a stop, his eyes transfixed on the woman that he loved, the woman he had lost so many years ago.

"Wait..." he pleaded, "Just stop. We can work this out, please don't hurt her..."

His words seemed to amuse Malik, who simply sneered at him as he pushed Gema to the ground. "Your pleas mean nothing to me...give me the book or she dies...I don't need her; I only need the child..." Malik said motioning over his shoulder to a guard that Erich hadn't noticed until that moment.

The guard stepped forward into the light, roughly dragging someone with him. It took Erich a moment to comprehend what he was seeing. Standing beside the man was a small girl, she couldn't have been more than 7 or 8 years old, her jet black hair was pulled into a ponytail. She was wearing blue jeans and dirty pink t shirt. She lifted her face to meet Erich's gaze, and as she did Erich's breath caught. She was in every way a smaller version of Gema, save one. Blazing blue eyes stared at Erich from under a furrowed brow. The girl did not look scared, she looked angry.

"Paulus," Erich said slowly without taking his eyes from the child, "Give them the book."

Paulus made no move to hand the book to Malik, "Erich, this book is beyond dangerous. If you understood what Malik had planned, you would not want it anywhere near him."

"I don't care, Paulus," Erich said, his voice growing louder, "Give him the book. I don't care what he does with it. We can't just stand here and watch him hurt them, give him the book."

"Even if I give him the book, he will still kill them, and then he will kill us. The only reason we are still alive is that he doesn't know where the book is..." Paulus said evenly, staring at Malik the entire time, a look of pure hatred burned in his eyes.

"If you tell me where the book is, I will only kill the two of you," Malik said evenly. "The girl is necessary to our plans; her mother is not. If you cooperate now, I will spare her life. If you choose to keep playing this game I will kill her in front of you both, then I will kill you. I have no particular desire to hurt her, but I also will not hesitate."

Erich looked back and forth between Paulus and Malik. For the first time, he and Gema looked at one another. He could see her pain and fear and it broke his heart, but he also saw a spark of hope in her eyes. He looked back to Malik and tried to keep his voice steady when he spoke, "The book is in the Ark. It must be by the front door, that's the only place he would have had time to stash it."

Malik turned to his companions and quickly nodded his head towards the Ark. Two of the men that had been holding guns toward Erich and Paulus, split off from the group and ran towards the opening of the great ship. Paulus looked at Erich with a sadness that was indescribable and then turned his eyes towards the ground. "How did you find them?" he asked.

Malik seemed to weigh the question for a moment before responding, "I am a very powerful man," he said, "When I want to find something, I find it."

"You are not as powerful as you think..." Paulus said.

"I am more powerful than you can even imagine." He said sneering.

"Look, you will have your book, what do you still need them for?" Erich asked, motioning to Gema and the girl. *If I just keep him talking long enough to find a way to get them to safety...*he thought, but nothing came to his mind. He felt confident that he could overtake Malik or the gunman that held the girl before they could react, but he knew he could not take both. And with no way to communicate an attack plan with Paulus, he had to look for a different way.

"From what I understand, somehow this girl," Malik said pointing his gun, "is the only person who will be able to read this book...so that is why I need her. I assume that keeping her mother around will be good insurance for getting her to do whatever it is

I need." Paulus looked shocked that Malik knew that the child could read the ancient language. Malik saw the look of confusion on his face and smiled slightly, "Ah yes, Paulus, my people are everywhere. One of my men..." but before he could finish Malik was cut off by the reappearance of his men arriving back from the Ark. He quickly spoke in a language that Erich had not heard before and handed Malik the book. Malik's eyes shone with a sick excitement as he held the book. He raised his eyes to Paulus, a look of pure malevolence sparkled in them, and raised his gun, pointing it directly at Paulus's face, "And now that I have what I came for, it is time for us to part ways..."

The corner of his mouth turned up slightly as he readied to pull the trigger. At that moment, a number of things happened all at once. Erich launched himself at Malik, hitting him in the stomach and knocking him off balance. The gun fired as they tumbled in a heap to the ground. As soon as Paulus realized what Erich was doing, he pulled the gun he had tucked into his waistband and took aim at the men holding Gema and the girl, but there was no shot that he could take that didn't endanger them. Paulus turned his attention to Erich and Malik, seeing if there was any way that he could help his friend. As he watched, a shot rang out from the entrance, the bullet passed so close to his ear that he could feel the wind from it. Paulus dove into the forest behind him, taking cover from the men shooting at him.

The door to the exhibit opened, and Nagato came running into the center of the scene, a pistol held in each of his hands. He took only a second to assess the situation before landing a flying kick to the face of one of the guards. The man fell hard to the ground, Nagato launching himself over him and firing with both pistols at the man holding Gema. The man shook from the impact of the bullets striking his chest and fell backward. A shot rang out from behind Nagato, the bullet caught him in the shoulder and spun him around as he dove to the ground for cover. Paulus turned to see Malik standing above Erich pointing his pistol at him.

Paulus raised his gun and fired at Malik until the clip ran out. Malik dove for the door shouting, "Mateo, Ahmed, go!" Paulus looked up just in time to see Malik and two of his men make it through the door with Gema and her daughter. He started to run towards the door to go after them, but another of Malik's men opened fire with the small machine gun he was holding. Bullets tore through the trees around Paulus who again dove to the ground. The shooting stopped momentarily, Paulus assumed, so that the man could put another clip into the gun. He risked a glance up just in time to see Erich sneaking up behind the man. Paulus wanted to draw the man's attention so that Erich could get to him safely, so he stood and ran from his cover just long enough for the man to see him.

Erich saw Paulus dart from cover and knew that it was a diversion for his sake. He wouldn't waste the moment. He closed the gap between him and the machine gun-wielding thug and struck out hard, delivering a sweeping kick to the man's kneecap. The kick caught the man off guard, and he fell to the ground, the gun clattering from his hands. Erich jumped on top of the man, trying to pin him down. He delivered a hard punch to the man's nose, but it had little effect, the man was clearly a well-trained fighter. Erich swung his fist hard again, but the man easily blocked the blow and brought an elbow up, smashing it into Erich's chin. Erich fell backward off of the man, scrambling to regain his footing and jumped back towards him.

The big man took a step towards Erich, his massive arms flexing as he opened and closed his fists. He took another step and then froze as a bullet struck the floor in front of his foot. Erich whipped around to find Paulus pointing the machine gun at the man's face. The big man looked between all of them with contempt and spit out a mouthful of blood, mumbling under his breath in the unknown language. "Move again," Paulus said menacingly, "and I'll shoot. Where are they taking the woman and child?" The man simply stared straight at Paulus, a look of hatred burning in his eyes. Paulus moved the gun a fraction of an inch and pulled the trigger, the bullet grazed the man's ear. "Where are they taking the woman and child?" he asked again, his voice quieter but more intense.

The big man looked between Paulus, Erich, and Nagato and gave a half smile. Erich saw his jaw muscles flex and before they knew what was going on the man's eyes rolled up into his head, and he fell to the ground convulsing. "Shit!" Erich yelled, "he must have some type of suicide pill in his mouth, we need to try and save him, he might be our only chance to find them..."

"He is already dead my friend," Paulus whispered, "it is too late."

CHAPTER TWENTY-TWO

Namaah inhaled the salty air and opened her eyes. In front of her, Noahim stood on a cliff overlooking the sea, the waves gently rocking the three boats that were anchored several hundred yards offshore. Even from so far away, the ships still looked larger than any she had seen before. Karok sat at Noah's side, both of them seemed to be scanning the horizon intently. Namaah knew that Noah was searching for any sign of Jakon and the other Mul'Ki that had fled Atla on the Lion. Although there had been no sign of the other ship in the three years since the catastrophe, Noahim had remained concerned that Jakon was coming.

Namaah had done her best to convince Noah that they were safe now, at least from Jakon, but it was to no avail. As she approached her husband, she could hear him talking quietly to Karok, although the noise from the wind and the surf blocked the words sufficiently that she was unable to make them out. He sensed her approach and turned towards her, a smile growing on his face. Karok stood up and took a few steps towards Namaah, brushing lightly against her leg as he passed. "I fear that it is almost time for us to leave," Noah said as he put his arms around her, "We have been here long enough, we must continue our search for a new home."

Namaah had expected as much, Noah had said after a short time on the new land that it would not work as a permanent home for the survivors of Atla, but he had decided that before they continued on their journey, they should search for other survivors of the great catastrophe. They had found several scattered groups across this land, groups that before the flood may have lived in relative harmony but since that time had fallen into chaos and discord as the remaining survivors fought over the limited amount of land and food. Before the flood, this had been a prosperous land, but the tidal waves had destroyed their homes and killed the majority of the animals that were used for meat. The remaining people and animals were driven higher and higher into the mountains as the waters continued to rise, their resources becoming harder to find as they climbed.

When Noah and his people had found the first of these survivors they were attacked, but there was little risk of them hurting any of the Atlan survivors, Noah and the other Mul'Ki made sure of that. The people were in awe of the power that Noah commanded as he displayed for them his ability to lift large objects, objects that not even a hundred men could have lifted, without touching them. Noah had quickly begun to understand the strange language that the natives spoke, teaching them to grow crops and herd animals the way that the Atlans did, and replenishing their own supplies in the process, but they knew that the time would come when they would have to press on and find their new home.

Namaah put her arms around Noah's neck and looked deeply into his eyes, "I know that you feel we must continue to search for a new home, but why Noah?" she asked, "Why is this place not as good as any other?"

"This place is too exposed. It took us only a matter of a week to find the people that lived here. Jakon will be coming, we cannot risk him finding us before we can complete our mission," he said, "I know that some of you think that I am crazy and that he will not be coming after us, but believe me, Jakon will never stop."

Namaah sighed and shook her head, "And this mission that you speak of, what exactly is our mission...other than to find a suitable place to settle down and have children?"

"Namaah, there is nothing that I desire more than to have a child with you," Noah said softly, "but our mission right now is more important than that. The Ratam Ra'Ava gave instructions that we need to build the machines to produce the Gods' Noise. Only the machines can prevent the sky from falling again. And it is not enough just to build the machines, we must build them in the right places. This is not the right place, I had hoped that it was, but it is not."

"And how will you know when we find the right place, Noah?" she asked.

Noah looked at his wife, and smiled slightly, returning his gaze to the sea. He stared out into the turbulent water for several moments before finally answering, "There are many things hidden within Ratam Ra'Ava, similar to a code. Complex mathematical equations weaved into the tapestry of the myth that, when worked out correctly, point to times and places or give us maps of the stars that we can then use to navigate to these places. The problem is that ever since the day that the sky fell, the maps of the stars are useless. We now look up into a foreign sky, a sky devoid of all of the stars and planets that we have spent millennia mapping out, so aside from having to decode Ratam Ra'Ava, I also need to somehow decipher this new placement of the stars, or rather, our new place on the planet."

Namaah seemed to weigh this information, looking towards the skies and back to Noah before asking, "What exactly do these machines do, Noah?"

"I am not altogether sure how the machines work, there is still much that I am trying to work out in Ratam Ra'Ava, as well as in other ancient texts that are mentioned within those pages...but from what I have gathered thus far it appears that the machines, once activated, somehow prevent the earth from shifting the way that it did when the sky fell..."

"How will the machines accomplish this task...and if they are known to prevent the sky from falling why have they not been built before now?"

Noah smiled slightly and shook his head, "I have to admit that I do not understand at all yet how the machines will accomplish this, although I am fairly certain that only the one that the prophecy speaks of can activate them when the time comes. As for why they have not been built before now...for that, I believe, I do have an answer. I am fairly certain that Ratam Ra'Ava was written to help protect and convey the information about the machines at a time when the Mul'Ki were uncertain about the future of Atla...but after the catastrophe, the myths that were passed down were changed in some ways. The code seems to be stripped from the version that we, and all the other people of Atla, were taught as children. At first, I assumed that this was because the original version of the book was simply mistranslated, but the farther that I have dug into Ratam Ra'Ava, the more certain I have become that the information hidden within was purposefully manipulated..."

"Who would have done this, and why?" Namaah asked.

"The Mul'Ki have always been the only men that translate ancient texts, so it would seem that at some point after this book was written, a group of Mul'Ki decided they needed to keep some of this information hidden. At first, I could think of no reason that they would have wanted to hide the information that could have saved the people of Atla...but recently I discovered what I believe to be that very reason...Ratam Ra'Ava does more than just give instructions on how and where to build the machines, it also has hidden within its pages information on how to master the True Ari'Yet...."

The statement seemed to hang in the air for several moments, and Noah began to wonder what his wife was thinking, until she simply asked, "What is the True Ari'Yet?"

"Power without limitations," Noah replied. "For someone that wields the True Ari'Yet, virtually nothing would be impossible. I believe that when the men that were translating this book stumbled upon hidden references to the True Ari'Yet, they feared that much power would corrupt any man that was able to master it, and so they made the decision to erase the references. The machines and the True Ari'Yet are linked together, so to destroy the information about the True Ari'Yet also meant destroying the information about the machines. It is possible that they believed that because there had already been a catastrophe, the machines were no longer needed. They may not have recognized that the catastrophes have been happening since the dawn of time, that is something that I understand after reading the original text, but I have an understanding of language that they may not have had. It is also possible that they fully knew that by destroying the hidden messages that they were setting the stage for another catastrophe, but felt that preventing anyone from commanding the True Ari'Yet must be done by any means necessary...I do not profess to understand their motives, but I am certain that the information within the text was taken out purposefully."

"So, you believe that the intent of these men was to protect the people of Atla by burying the truth?"

"I believe that, regardless of their intent, millions of people died as a result of their actions...and not just people in Atla, but people all across the planet. The machines could have prevented the sky from falling, but these men chose to put their own agendas ahead of the interest of the people. They chose to..."

"Noah, I think that it is dangerous to blame all of these deaths on those men. It is obvious that they believed that the information on how to master the True Ari'Yet was too dangerous to allow it to fall into the wrong hands. Think about what would happen if Jakon were able to control it, what would you do to prevent that from happening?"

Noah seemed to consider this for only a second before responding, a hard edge to his voice, "I would not lie to the people. How many other things did these men lie about? How much of our beliefs are based on their distorted and manipulated view of the past? How do we know that their motives were pure?"

"I guess that is something that we will never know Noah, but I choose to believe that these were great men that would have only done this for the good of the people of Atla."

Noah took a deep breath, "I want to believe that as well Namaah, I truly do...and I cannot begin to imagine what would happen if someone like Jakon were to wield the power of the True Ari'Yet, so in that way, while I may not agree with their methods, I can at least understand why they chose to do what they did...but I cannot help but wonder..." he trailed off as he looked away from

Namaah momentarily.

She placed her hand softly on his cheek, turning his face so that she could look into his eyes. She saw the concern radiating from them, but she held his gaze. She tried to convey so much through that touch...her belief that everything would be better, her belief that they would find a new home, but most of all her unfaltering belief in him, "You cannot help but wonder what, Noah?" she asked.

He stared into her eyes, and with her touch felt a calm wash over him. He sighed and said, "I cannot help but wonder what other things they hid from us."

CHAPTER TWENTY-THREE

Erich sat with his head in his hands trying to make sense of the last few hours of his life. After Malik and his men had escaped, Erich, Paulus, and Nagato had set out to find Jim. With everything that he had been through today, Erich wouldn't be able to handle it if something bad had happened to Jim. Luckily, they had found him in his office. Once the power had gone out, he had remained holed up inside. With the storm, and the fact that his office was so far away from the exhibits, he hadn't even heard any of the gunshots; until security had come to the office to tell him that there was a situation, he hadn't known anything was wrong at all.

"Ok, so let me see if I got this all straight. You two," he said pointing to Paulus and Nagato, "came here with some bullcrap story, telling me that your ancestors built this Ark to keep me from opening the museum so that some lunatic, that also thinks his ancestors built this place, wouldn't get his hands on an ancient book written in a language that only an eight-year-old girl can read...does that about sum it up?"

"You forgot the part about Paulus being one of the X-men or something, and ripping a security door off the hinges with his mind..." Erich said without looking up, "but ya, other than that, I think you nailed it."

Jim sat back in his chair shaking his head, "Well I gotta say, I have heard some crazy shit in my day, but this is definitely the craziest, and considering I'm the guy who just built a museum for Noah's freaking ark that's really saying something. Do we have any idea how that maniac and his thugs got past our security? I mean, we paid millions for the security system and have a whole team of people in place and backup measure after backup measure. How the hell did they get in?"

"I think the more important question here," Erich said, "Is why now...why after all that time would they just come and attack?"

"Clearly, something moved up their timetable, information they didn't have before...they must have found that we had the ability to read the ancient text," Paulus said, an audible sadness in his voice, "and they decided that with the information we now possessed, and the museum on the cusp of opening, they had to act fast."

"Or they had someone in your village," Erich said flatly, "someone watching you, listening, waiting...and once they learned of your plan to come here and get the book they decided that they didn't have any more time. Maybe someone in your camp let them know exactly what was going on, forced their hand, caused them to kidnap Gema and the girl, and come and attack us."

Erich was looking heatedly at Paulus now, his anger clear. "Her name is Sophia," Paulus began,.

"What?" Erich said.

"The girl, Gema's daugher, my niece, her name is Sophia. I just thought you should know so that you don't have to keep calling her the girl. As for a spy in my village, someone siding with Malik, not a chance. I know everyone too well...there is no one that would endanger Gema or Sophia, or the entire world for that matter."

Paulus shifted uncomfortably, looking like he wanted to say something but hesitating. "Just say what you need to say, Paulus," Erich said, "We don't have any time to waste."

"Mr. Cochran, we need your help," Paulus said, "We must go after Malik. He has my sister and my niece, and I cannot begin to describe their importance. The book that Malik stole tonight is only part of what he needs to complete his plans, but the book may lead him to the rest."

"And where is the rest of what he needs?" Jim asked slowly, "And what do you want me to do for you fellas?"

"I am not totally sure, but I believe the rest of what he needs is wherever Noah ended his journey," Paulus said, "we will need money and supplies to get what we need to try and beat him to wherever that is, that is where you can help us. You have the means to get us anything that we could need. Malik has the book and basically unlimited resources, but with your help, maybe we still stand a chance of catching up to him and saving Gema and Sophia...and the rest of the world."

Erich stood up, "I don't really care about the rest of the world, I still don't know how much of that I believe, but I will find Gema and Sophia. I will save them."

"You're damn right you will son," Jim said, "Whatever I can do to help is at your disposal Erich...name it and it's yours."

Nagato cleared his throat and stood up, wrapping a bandage around his upper arm where he had been shot. "There is still a problem," he said in a clipped tone, "We lost the book so we have no idea where they are going. There is no amount of money that can change that."

"Maybe not," Erich said walking towards the man, "But I found this place when no one else could. I can find where Noah and his people ended up too. If we can beat Malik there and find whatever it is he needs, we could use it to trade for Gema and Sophia's safety."

Nagato still looked unconvinced and was about to say something, but Paulus spoke first, "Erich is right. With his help, we may be able to get there before Malik; we must stop him at all costs. Mr. Cochran, I am sorry for our deception and promise that we will be forthcoming with all of you from this point forward."

Jim looked at Paulus and squinted, "Look, fellas, I don't like being lied to...," he paused while he collected his thoughts, "but I suppose if you had told me the real story I wouldn't have believed you anyway. Erich is like a son to me, and I will do anything in my power to help him. If he says he trusts you, then I will trust you too, but let me be clear...do not lie to me again. Now, what do we need?"

Erich looked at Paulus and then Nagato before speaking, "We are gonna need a helicopter and a small team to go with us. I had a small team on the Sulawesi mission, led by a special forces, Rambo-type, Alex Mitchell, I need them...but tell Mitchell just one other guy this time, a big team makes it too dangerous. And get whatever supplies they say we need." Erich paused and watched as Jim sent messages on his phone, "I want us to be ready to go as soon as possible. Jim, you arrange the chopper, I'll get ahold of Mitchell and get you a list of supplies."

"I will get word to my people to have them send some of our bravest warriors to accompany us," Paulus said standing up and walking towards the door, getting out his cell phone as he did so to make a call.

Erich jumped up and grabbed his arm, pulling him close with a look of warning in his eyes, "Sorry Paulus, but you can't contact anyone about this mission, it's just too risky. Let's just get Mitchell's team here, them and us, that's it."

Jim looked between all of them and shook his head, "That's all fine and good, I can have the helicopter and the team assembled and here within 48 hours, but...exactly where the hell are we going?" They all sat in silence, Nagato stared at the ground, Paulus at Erich. Erich held his gaze as he thought about the question that Jim had posed, and realized he had absolutely no idea where they would go, but he would figure this out. He had to, he wasn't about to lose Gema again.

"Paulus," Erich said, "Do you know what it is that Malik is hoping to find when he translates the book and finds where Noah and his people went?"

"The book that my father died to protect, the one that Sophia was the first to be able to translate, spoke of the book that we found on Jakon's ark." Paulus paused for a moment before continuing, "It said that the book would contain information that would lead to the seed of humanity, and with the seed would be a way to unlock the true Ari'Yet."

"What is the true Ari'Yet?" Erich interrupted.

"It is from the ancient Sala'ma language, the closest Sophia could get to translating it is true magic. My people, and more importantly their ancestors before them, had learned to channel the energies of themselves, and the energies of the world. They used this energy to do amazing things..."

Again, Erich interrupted him, "Things like using their minds to rip doors off walls?"

Paulus laughed lightly, "Things much greater than that, I have only begun to understand how to wield the Ari'Yet, but yes, it is what I used to move the door. There is a prophecy that the book spoke of many times, it said, 'There will be one born with the gift so strong that the BalaRa will come seek them out when they are still a child. This one will command the true Ari'Yet. This one will drink from the Jala'Kim. This one will be the savior of Atla. This one will be the seed of humanity."

Erich looked puzzled, "There are phrases within that prophecy that are very similar to the myth that Unta told me about the Sala'Ma. I have never heard of the Bala'Ra though, any idea what that is?"

Paulus shook his head, "Unfortunately no, we do not have any idea what the prophecy is referring to. But the point here is that the secrets of the Ari'Yet cannot fall into Malik's hands. I have only begun to learn the secrets; what you saw with the door was nothing compared to what the Ari'Yet is capable of. We must find him and stop him... at all costs."

Erich walked to the far side of the office and stared out the window at the rainforest beyond, contemplating the question he knew they all were thinking. Where were they going? He knew that everyone was looking to him, but he had absolutely no idea where to even start. Erich thought back to the journey he took to find the Ark. He had relied heavily on the myths that he learned from Unta and from other tribes in the area, but he had also enlisted the help of Graham Reynolds, a man that had written countless books focusing on the evidence, mythological and empirical, that a global flood had indeed happened at some point in human history. Graham had spent much of his life focused on finding the remnants of a great lost civilization, and when Erich had told him that he believed he would find that civilization in Indonesia, Graham had been extremely skeptical, but he had nonetheless helped Erich in every way that he could.

"I need to go make a phone call," Erich said abruptly, spinning away from the window and walking back towards the center of the room he grabbed the cell phone out of his pocket, noticing for the first time that the screen had shattered at some point during the events of the last few hours. He pushed the button on the side of the phone and behind the spiderweb of cracks, the screen came to life. Erich breathed a sigh of relief as the familiar icons of his home screen came into view. He quickly tapped the contacts icon and scrolled through the list, settling on Graham's name he tapped the screen again and held the phone to his ear.

"Erich Lawrence!" the voice on the other end of the phone exclaimed in a strong English accent, "I assumed you were far too busy this week for phone calls, or I would have called and congratulated you, the museum opening is all that anyone can talk about!"

Erich smiled at the sound of his friend's voice. During his search for the Ark, Graham had been a great resource to him, but more importantly, he had been a great friend. Graham knew, more than most people, the feeling of self-doubt that arose from all the world calling you crazy. In fact, prior to Erich's discovery of the Ark, Graham had been labeled a conspiracy theorist at best, and a nutjob at worst. The mainstream scientific community had laughed at his ideas and research, calling his theories pseudo-science, and then came the Ark.

Everything changed for Graham with the credit that Erich gave him for assisting in finding the Ark. The scientific community still scoffed at his ideas and theories but to the general public, he was a superstar. Since the discovery of the Ark, Graham's books had consistently remained at the top of the New York Times bestseller list. He had made countless guest appearances on news programs and talk shows to lend his expertise to the Ark coverage and had filmed several documentaries outlining some of his theories on the great flood catastrophe and on the origin of humanity in general. No matter how much the scientific community refuted Graham's claims, the general public would not be swayed.

"Actually Graham," Erich said, "The museum opening has been postponed..."

"Postponed!" Graham interjected, "what in the world could be so important that it would postpone the opening of the single greatest attraction in history?"

"I can't talk about it over the phone, but I need your help. Where are you now and how long would it take you to get to Sulawesi?" Erich asked.

"Well as luck would have it I just landed about an hour ago on the island, I am headed towards the museum now, did you think I would miss the opening?"

"I heard you were scuba diving off the coast of Japan somewhere, so I just assumed you wouldn't be able to make it. Please come right away, come to the main security gate and have them call Jim, they will bring you to us."

"I will be right there," Graham said sounding worried, "I hope everything is all right."

Erich paused for a moment before answering, "So do I Graham...so do I."

CHAPTER TWENTY-FOUR
_____

Graham sat staring between Erich, Jim, Paulus, and Nagato. He was dumbfounded. The story that he had just been told was unbelievable, and yet he knew that Erich would never make any of it up. "So, what exactly would you have me do?" Graham asked as he surveyed the room, running a hand through his wavy gray hair.

"No one knows more about the great flood than you," Erich said emphatically, "or the people that survived it. We have to find where Noah and his people ended up. I don't even know where to begin looking. There are thousands of islands in Indonesia, and we don't have time to search them all. Is there anything that you have come across in your research that could give us a clue into where these people may have ended up?"

Graham could hear the desperation in his friend's voice. "I have a theory...and much of what I have learned tonight seems to substantiate my beliefs. I have believed for many years that humanity owes a great debt of gratitude to a civilization from our past...a past that we have forgotten about. I began to formulate this theory very early on in my research of the great flood myths from around the world...there were just too many similarities between the myths that I was finding from every corner of the globe. And then when Erich found the Ark, it became clear that the people that had built and sailed that vessel were not from any civilization that we knew about. That is really when my theory began to take shape, and now after hearing more from you, Paulus, about the Ari'Yet and the strange abilities that the Sala'Ma possessed I feel almost certain that I was on the right track..."

"And that track was...?" Erich asked.

"That the people that built the Ark are the same people that I have been trying to track down through my research...the great lost civilization...Atlantis..." Graham said excitedly.

"Atlantis...," Erich deadpanned, "the island that sank to the bottom of the ocean..."

Graham had expected this reaction, in fact, he was quite used to people thinking that his theories were a bit insane, "Yes and no...I believe that the people that built your Ark are the survivors of Atlantis. I do not believe that Atlantis sank to the bottom of the ocean, I believe that it is indeed covered by water, but it does not lie at the bottom of any ocean."

"How could it be covered with water and not at the bottom of the ocean, where is it?" Paulus asked.

"Antarctica... a land below this one...where everything is the same, except the seasons are different." He paused long enough to make his point, "Just like the myth that Unta told Erich that led him here said, an island below this one. Antarctica...covered in water...just frozen water."

"So, you think this lost civilization has just been on Antarctica this whole time and no one has found it yet? How is that possible?" Jim asked sounding skeptical.

"Because Antarctica is the least explored area of the world. There are no permanent residents of Antarctica, and as far as mainstream science would have us believe, there never have been. So, take into consideration the lack of people looking, the inhospitable environment, and the fact that the continent is covered in ice that, in some places, reaches two miles thick...it seems to me that it is the perfect place to find this great lost civilization." Graham said talking more and more excitedly as he continued.

"But if the environment is so inhospitable how did this ancient civilization thrive?" Paulus asked.

"Simple," Graham said, sounding surprised that everyone had not already come to this conclusion for themselves, "because it didn't use to be that way. Did you know that Antarctica is a desert that averages less than 8 inches of precipitation per year, and that..."

"Who cares!" Erich interjected forcefully, "I don't really care about this civilization right now Graham, I'm sorry to be short, but we need to rescue Gema and Sophia, and right now it seems that the only way to do that is to find whatever it is that Malik is looking for before he gets there. So, unless you are suggesting that we go to Antarctica, I think we need to move on."

"You are right Erich, you will have to forgive me. I tend to get overly excited when I talk about this, and tonight has me more excited than normal. I know that finding your friends is the only important thing right now, and I do not think that we should be looking in Antarctica. I think that's where these people began their journey, but not where they ended up. I believe that we will find what we are looking for deep in the Amazon rainforest."

"The Amazon?!" Jim exclaimed, "South America? Why would these other people have settled so far from where the group that sailed this boat ended up? Doesn't it make more sense that they are on one of these islands out here somewhere? Plus, where would you even begin to look in the Amazon?"

"Jim please," Erich said as he looked around at the group assembled with him. Jim was clearly agitated, he was a man that was not used to losing, and tonight had been one loss after another. To his left sat Paulus and Nagato. Nagato appeared almost eager, a hunger behind his eyes. Erich watched as Nagato fed bullets into a clip in his hand and then shoved the clip into his 9mm Glock, tucking it back into his waistband. Paulus looked lost. He had, of course, lost his sister and his niece today, and Erich knew that fact weighed heavily on him, but he also knew that Paulus had more on his mind than just Gema and Sophia. Paulus was the leader of his people, and he believed that it was his responsibility to protect this secret of his ancestors, thereby protecting the world. Erich knew that he would have to make sure that Paulus did not jeopardize Gema or her daughter in his quest to save the world. "My first instinct is to continue to search out here in

Indonesia as well, but I want to hear Graham out..."

Graham took a moment and looked into Erich's eyes and hoped that he could somehow see the truth in them, "I believe that your Noah left us a trail of breadcrumbs to follow, we just have to know where to look. Erich, you know that I have dedicated my life for the past forty years to trying to establish the truth behind a great lost civilization. I began by pouring over every book of mythology from every civilization that I could get my hands on, which I have to say was a lot more difficult at that time since there was no internet," he said with a laugh, pulling a small Moleskin notebook out of his pocket and holding it up. The black leather cover was cracked and worn, the seam almost bursting with the overstuffed content between its pages, "All of the most important of these myths, along with so many other things I have discovered on my own journeys are in this journal. Decades of research and explanation all leading to one conclusion...Atlantis was no fantasy."

Graham paused, looking around the group, noticing that every eye was now on him, "As I said, my fascination started with mythology. Much like you Erich, I was intrigued by the fact that nearly every civilization that has ever existed on this planet has a deluge myth. My journey began when I first read The Golden Baugh, the comparative mythology book compiled by the great James Frazer. The Golden Baugh led me to his incredible work on The Great Flood, and that is when I realized that a global flood must have actually happened. While doing my own research on flood mythology, I began to take note of a great many societies that also possessed what can be called civilizing god myths. These myths all speak of great men or Gods that came from the sea, taught the people laws, agriculture, and architecture, and possessed technology and knowledge that far surpassed that of any other culture of those time periods. They built structures that are still around, and still unexplained. Your Noah and his people left a very clear line of mythology in their wake, from the stories of Oannes from Babylonian and Sumerian myth to Quetzacoatl in Mexico and Central America and those of Virococha in South America, and tales of the same from China, Indonesia, Australia,

Native Americans, Inuits in Alaska...the list goes on and on. All of them involving a similar description of these gods that came from the sea, brought order to chaos, and then returned to the sea. We are basically following the path of these civilizing gods...the path of the pyramid builders. Not to mention the fact that we have to assume from the information we have gotten from Paulus that Noah would have wanted to stay far away from this other Ark, and being across the ocean and the Andes mountains I feel would have been very attractive to these people. There are also rumors of a lost city in the jungles surrounding the Amazon River that the locals have spoken of for centuries. I have actually been gathering information about this very lost city for the last several years and was about to embark on a journey to find it myself."

"I've read your research Graham, and I know that you believe that the survivors of Atlantis ended up in South America, but I don't see how you can be so sure that they are the same people we are looking for," Erich said.

"The fact is that nothing in life is certain Erich," Graham began, "but I think it makes total sense. I had never understood the fact that you found the Ark on Sulawesi, it seemed to fly in the face of all of my own theories...and yet now you have told me how this great civilization was fractured, and we have to assume that as this Noah searched for a new home he would have helped those small groups of survivors that he encountered across the globe, leading to the stories of the gods. Think of how Noah and the others with him would have seemed to these people. Not only did they possess great knowledge, but also great power. A power that could have helped to build the pyramids in Egypt, Asia, and Central America. A way to explain the unexplainable...the reason that we cannot understand how the pyramids were built is that they were built by men that had gifts beyond our own. It would be like someone 10,000 years ago trying to understand how we put a man on the moon...we would simply appear to be gods."

"Let's just say that we believe you," Jim drawled, "do you have any actual idea where we would be going?"

"I know a basic region, but it is still going to be an incredibly difficult journey," Graham said shaking his head.

Erich looked between all of the people seated around him and back to Graham, "How sure are you on this Graham?"

Graham held Erich's intense gaze and, trying to sound surer of himself than he was, simply said, "Very."

Erich nodded his head, "People's lives are at stake, so you better be."

CHAPTER TWENTY-FIVE

Noahim stared out over the water, wondering if they would ever find a home. It had been many years since the disaster, and they seemed no closer now. They had been to many lands, always finding roughly the same thing; men and women living in terrible conditions, warring over what few resources remained. In each case, the Atlans had taught the people agriculture, architecture, and the laws according to the Book of Law. After years of searching for the proper place, Noah and the Mul'Ki, along with the help of the natives, had constructed one of the massive machines that Ratam Ra'Ava had called for. They now searched for a new place to call home, the place where they would build the final machine.

As Noah stood surveying the water before him, a pair of arms slid around his waist, and he felt Namaah press into him from behind. She lay her head down on him and squeezed and he felt her slightly rounded belly press into his back. He turned and kissed her forehead, "Are you feeling well this morning?" he asked her, the concern clear in his voice.

Namaah smiled at him as she held her hands on her growing stomach, "Yes Noah, I am fine, just as I am every time that you ask."

From the moment they had realized that Namaah was pregnant, Noah's entire life had changed. He would soon have a child, and that carried even more responsibility than being the high priest of the Mul'Ki. He knew that he must protect Namaah and their child at all costs. It had been many years since they had seen Jakon and the other Mul'Ki that had left with him. In fact, Noah was not even certain that they were still alive, but he knew that he must remain vigilant. He had let his guard down once before, and it almost cost all of them their lives. That would not happen again.

Once they had survived the first few years after the disaster, Noah truly began to believe that they were safe. In those first few years, they faced dangers that Noah could not have imagined. Earthquakes, volcanic eruptions, massive flooding, and some of the most extreme weather that the planet had ever seen. One day it would be warm and calm out and the next so cold that exposed skin became instantly damaged. It had seemed that it would never end, but it had. Eventually, the planet began to stabilize, the weather returned to normal, the seas began the long slow process of receding back, and the Atlans continued to search for a new home and the right place to build the machines. It was on this search that Jakon and his men had found them.

Noah and Jikar had been hiking through the jungle for most of the morning, checking out a place that Jikar thought may work for building the first machine. Jikar could not read the Ratam Ra'Ava and many of the ideas expressed within those pages, especially those regarding the machines, were very difficult for Noah to convey. Even so, Jikar tried his best to help Noah find locations that would work for building the machines. On this day, he was taking Noah back to a place that he had stumbled upon while searching for food with some of the natives of the land. "It is just up ahead Noah," Jikar said, turning to smile at his friend, "I wish I understood more what it is that we are looking for...hopefully this place will be what you need. I think we can all agree that it would be nice to build these machines so that we can finally find a new land to call our home, to rebuild Atla, and to get off of these boats!"

Noahim smiled and answered, "The boats are beginning to smell a little bit...and Karok would definitely be much happier once we never have to set foot on them again." In response, the big cat let out a soft roar and picked up his pace, running up ahead through the jungle. "I wish that I could explain what it is that we are looking for, but I cannot. There are many words from the Ratam Ra'Ava that simply have no equivalent in our language."

Jikar stopped walking for a moment as they came to a divergence in the path they were following, "I know that you would not be taking so much time and care with this search if it were not important," he said thoughtfully, "and I do not imagine that you enjoy having to tell Namaah that her desire to have a child must continue to wait." At this, he laughed lightly and pushed his friend playfully on the arm.

The two men and their RaSheen continued walking down the path, moving deeper into the jungle. Noah surveyed the land around them. It was very different from Atla, the trees here were much smaller, and there were many animals that Noah had never before seen. As they walked, he reflected on all that they had been through since the disaster and wondered if he was doing the right thing. Some of the citizens had questioned the need to build the machines, but Noah had convinced them that it was necessary for their continued survival. He just hoped he was right. Jikar spoke, bringing him out of his contemplation, "So this is it, will this work?" he said, spreading his arms out and motioning to the surrounding area.

Noah looked out over a clearing cut in the middle of the forest. It seemed almost perfectly circular, and Noah could not even imagine what could have caused it. In the center of the clearing was a small pond, the water so smooth that it reflected the majesty of the sky above it in perfect detail. He scanned the area and understood why Jikar had thought that this would be a promising location to build the machine, but it was not. Noah had known this from before they had set out on the walk, he had realized several days ago that they would not find the right place to build the machine in this land, but had wanted to stay for just a little longer. They had developed wonderful friendships with so many of the native people of this land and Noah hated to leave. He knew that the time had come for them to move on, he just had not told anyone else yet, allowing them to enjoy their last few days in this place.

"Jikar, this place is wondrous indeed," Noah said, "but I fear that I have not been honest with you. We will not find the place we seek in this land...I only wanted to..." but before Noah could finish Jikar cut him off.

"I know Noah," he said smiling, "you are a good man. I realized yesterday when we spoke that you knew we had to leave. I only wanted to show you this place because I thought it might remind you of the Jala'Kim like it had me. You are my best friend Noah, I can tell when you are trying to hide something from me, and you do not need to do that anymore. I believe in you...I believe in what we are doing...and I will always support your decisions, no matter how difficult they are."

Noah placed a hand on his friend's shoulder and squeezed, "Thank you Jikar," he said, "you are truly a great friend." The two men stood there for several minutes in silence as they stared at the beautiful scene before them. Movement from the far side of the jungle caught Noah's eye and he turned to see Karok burst from the trees, running full speed towards them. "What is it Karok?" Noahim asked aloud, sensing the danger. As if in response to the question, Karok took two huge bounding steps and launched himself over Noah's shoulder landing on the other side of his Mul'Ki and let loose a roar so intense that it almost took his breath away.

Noah and Jikar spun around to see what Karok had sensed and what met them turned Noah's blood to ice. From the jungle thirty men strode, each dressed in robes of the darkest black, their feline RaSheen by their sides. In the center stood Jakon, dressed in his robes of red and gold. Tarrin stood at his side, a small tiger crouched as if to pounce stood beside him. Jikar and Noah continued to search the surrounding jungle, trying to gauge the danger they were in. As the men approached, Jakon stopped and held up his staff. Upon seeing this, all of the other men stopped as well. Every eye was on Noahim, who stood completely still, trying to take in the gravity of the situation. Karok stood tensed in front of Noah, every muscle in his body quivered. Noah could feel his bloodlust, he was not afraid, he longed to tear into the men, the men that had betrayed all of them. Men that had destroyed the temple, tried to kill Noah on multiple occasions, and stolen a boat that was meant to house almost one thousand citizens of Atla.

Jakon spoke first, "Listen to me, and listen well, boy... This will be the last offer you ever receive in this life," he sneered, "I have come to collect what is rightfully mine...the knowledge that you possess about the True Ari'Yet. I am the true high priest; I have united the brotherhood. It is you that tore us down, you are the one that destroyed our way of life, not me...and yet it is you that has the key to seemingly unlimited power. How is it that you can control the breathing of another Mul'Ki, or fix wounds that are beyond even the most talented of healers? How is it that you are able to drink from the Jala'Kim, that you can communicate intimately with your RaSheen, that you can lift things with your mind that are greater than what all of the rest of us could if we combined our powers...I believe the answer is in that book that you risked your life for...the Ratam Ra'Ava."

The final words chilled Noahim, for part of what Jakon said was correct. In the Ratam Ra'Ava Noah had found the information needed to build the machines along with information that helped him understand his gift, to harness it in a way that no one had before. He was still trying to understand the full breadth of what he had learned, and in fact, often times he had no idea how he had performed a feat of great magic and power, it just seemed to happen when the need arose. Ratam Ra'Ava did not possess the key to unlocking the true Ari'Yet, but it did give knowledge that could start Jakon on that path. Noah knew that if Jakon could find a way to translate the pages he would learn that there were three other books that he would need if he were to unlock the True Ari'Yet. Noah had located one of them within the books that he had found in the secret libraries on Atla but had had no luck finding the others. Jakon did not know of these other books, and Noah had no intention of allowing him to find out about them.

Noah turned his attention to Jakon's soldiers, and he could not help but feel disheartened. Many of these men had been his friends...his brothers...and now here they stood ready to go to war with him for a lunatic that had gone mad with power. Noah could not even imagine what Jakon would be capable of if he unlocked more of his gift, but he knew he never wanted to find out.

"Jakon you are wrong," Noah said, meeting Jakon's hate-filled gaze, "It is not the Ratam Ra'Ava that allows me to do these things. The book is merely instructions on how to carry about tasks that you would find menial, nothing more. The reason that I can perform acts that no else can is simple..." Noah paused and turned his eyes to the rest of the group stepping towards them, bringing himself even with Karok, who stood up from his crouched, tensed position to walk to Noah's side. "I am the one...I am the fulfillment of the prophecy...I command the true Ari'Yet, and no matter what you try, you never will." He said these last words as forcefully as he could, watching the reaction in Jakon's eyes.

Jakon grew even angrier, some of his men began to shout things at Noah and draw their swords. He raised a hand, silencing them and began to stride toward Noah and Karok, Kaylan at his side. Noah could not help but notice that the big cat kept a wary eye on Karok, there was no doubt that he had not forgotten their last encounter, which would have left him crippled at best, and dead at worst if not for Noah. As the pair approached, Noah felt his sense of dread lessening. The shouting of the men began to fade away. He could sense everything around him, every insect, every animal, every other person. He had never felt anything like it before, it was as though all of the energy of the world flowed through him.

The power he felt from it was incredible. Noahim knew that if he were to harness that energy he could destroy all of these men...he tried to touch the power...and then suddenly it was gone. He was back in the clearing watching as Jakon advanced with Kaylan. He turned to see Jikar readying himself to fight. He held his hand up and whispered to his friend, "Relax my friend, there will be no bloodshed here today, we are outnumbered. We must try to appease Jakon, for the sake of our families and friends."

Jikar visibly relaxed but did not take his eyes from Jakon. Noahim turned his focus back to Jakon, "I want no harm to come to any of you on this day Jakon. Tell me how we can resolve this peacefully."

Jakon laughed out loud, "Peacefully," he spat, "the time for peace is gone, boy. We have no fear of you, no fear of your handful of the gifted. We have come to collect the book, that is all. Give it to me and you can take your pathetic band of followers and continue on your way. Withhold it and I will destroy you, and all of them, and claim it for myself all the same. The choice is yours, oh great high priest..."

Noah felt as though he were trapped. It was clear that Jakon had increased his own power somehow during their voyage, Noah could feel the energy surging forth from his foe. He searched his mind for answers, but none came. "The rest of my war party is at your ships now, waiting for a single word from me to destroy everyone there. You know there is no way that you can protect them from here. Your wife, your friends, your brothers...will all be killed. I am a patient man Noah, but that patience has worn out. You have evaded me for far too long. Give me what I came for or I will send my men the signal and everything you care about will be lost."

Noah knew that Jakon was telling the truth, and he knew that the handful of Mul'Ki that he had left behind would be no match for the hundreds of men that Jakon must have there waiting. Noah looked around, defeated. There was but one answer. "You win Jakon, I will give you the book. I am not willing to risk harm befalling any of my people, so I will not give it to you until every one of your men is back on board your ship, and all of my people are on ours. I want your word that once I give you the book, you will leave this place, you will go in the opposite direction of wherever I take my people, and you will let us be."

Jakon sneered, seeming to consider Noah's words, "My men will board the ship now, and once I have the book, I will let you and your people leave unharmed. I do not consent to give you solace forever though...but I will let you be for now. Where is the book?"

"You will have it once I know my people are safe. Do not test me on this Jakon, you will not find the book without my help." Noah said matter-of-factly. Jakon held Noah's gaze intensely, seeming to weigh Noah's words. As he did, Tarrin approached on his right side and whispered something in his ear. Noah saw Tarrin's eyes flash to settle on Jikar momentarily, before he stepped back and took his place slightly behind Jakon.

"Hello Tarrin, I see that you have managed to find a companion..." Noah said, a note of question in his voice. It appeared to Noah as though Tarrin had been purposefully avoiding his gaze but at these words, Tarrin turned his eyes toward Noah, and in them, Noah saw hatred burning.

"Yes Noah, this is my RaSheen, Nala. Jakon, in his wisdom, knew that I was ready to be Mul'Ki. She has been with me since before the fall of Atla...the fall that you caused, I might add." Tarrin said, his voice sounded more confident than he looked, his eyes shifting between Noah, Karok, and Jikar the entire time he spoke.

"Tarrin, why are you doing this? Is your hatred of me so strong that you would do what you know is wrong?" Noah asked.

Tarrin's eyes took on a fierce edge as he responded, his voice rising in anger, "This is not now, nor has it ever been about you Noah. This is about what is best for the Mul'Ki, and what is best for the people..."

"What is best for the Mul'Ki was for you to destroy the temple? What is best for the people was for you to convince them that I was wrong and that they were safe...and then when the catastrophe was upon Atla, simply abandon them all to die?" Noah said angrily.

"Enough!" shouted Jakon, eliciting a growl from Karok, "We have not come here to debate with you, boy. You will bring me Ratam Ra'Ava now. There will be no more talking."

Noah surveyed the entire clearing, Jikar standing tall beside him, Nuni perched on his shoulder...Karok tensed, never taking his eyes from Jakon and Kaylan...men and their RaSheen lining the forest edge...Tarrin bristling as Nala slinked around his legs...and Jakon and his golden jaguar standing, the menacing staff in his hand, his robes swirling in the wind. "So be it." He said and turned to leave. They walked through the jungle, Jikar and Noah leading the way, Jakon and his men following behind at a distance.

Jikar reached out to Noah in his mind and spoke, *Do you really think we can trust him?* He said.

I believe we have no choice, he thought back.

After several minutes, the village came into view. Namaah ran towards them, "Noah," she said breathlessly, "There are hundreds of men here, Jakon's men. They have not said anything to us yet, just stood silently watching. They are..." Noah cut her off.

"Jakon is right behind us," he whispered, "I must give him Ratam Ra'Ava. It is the only way." She looked deep into his eyes and could sense his concern, but Namaah trusted Noahim with all of her heart. She knew that if this were what he thought was best, it would be.

"What should I do Noah?" she asked.

"Tell the people to prepare to leave, Jakon's men will be leaving now, we will need to leave by morning. He has agreed to grant us safe passage, but I fear not for very long." Noah said. Namaah ran back towards the village, to spread the word to their people that the time had come to leave. As Noah and Jikar approached Jakon's men, Noah noticed that many of them had begun to draw their weapons. Jakon must have noticed this movement as well, he held his hand up, and the men stayed their hands. With another flick of his wrist, the men turned on their heel and began to march in a line towards the beach where Noah could now see The Lion was moored.

"My men will board our ship now, and then you will give me the book, or I will destroy everyone here," Jakon said.

"Once your men have left this shore, you shall have it, but it will not help you Jakon," Noah said, "You will never have command of the true Ari'Yet because you are not the one..."

Jakon spun on Noah, splitting the lion-headed staff in two as he did, a long black, glass-like blade glittered in the sunlight. He brought the blade to Noah's neck and drew his face close to him, whispering violently, "Do not mistake my willingness to leave here today without harming you and your people as weakness. I have more power than you can imagine and one day I will be the one that ends your life. Get me the book now or I will destroy you..." As he spoke, Noah saw two men running towards he and Jakon, he tried to shout to them to stop but he could not move because of the blade that Jakon held to his throat. He turned to touch his Ari but for some reason, he could not. He was helpless.

The two men were Mul'Ki that had come with Noah, Thomas and Hazul. Noah could see their RaSheen running beside them. Hazul yelled out to Jakon, "Release him Jakon, or you will...." But his words would never be finished. In a flash Jakon spun, swinging his blade with all his might, catching both men across their throats. The scent of blood filled the air, and Noah watched in horror as the men's heads were cleaved from their bodies. The RaSheen that had been running beside them crashed to the ground, as the life force from all of them was extinguished. Jakon turned to Noah, madness in his eyes. "The book...now!" he shouted.

Noah could not believe his eyes. Jakon had just killed two of his men as easily as he would slaughter a chicken for a meal. The men's bodies lay in a growing pool of blood, Noah felt as though he would be sick. Karok stood beside him, growling menacingly. Jikar and the other Mul'Ki surveyed the scene and looked to Noah, asking silently how they should proceed from here. Noah simply shook his head and turned to get the book.

"Noah," Namaah said, bringing him out of his memories, "Were you thinking about him again?"

"Yes," Noah whispered, the rhythmic rocking of the boat on the waves helping to calm him, "I still fear that he will return every day, and if he has learned to command the true Ari'Yet I have no idea how we would stop him."

Namaah shook her head, "Noah, you are the one. Only you can command the true Ari'Yet, I believe those men perished long ago searching out new lands to rule. We needn't worry about them right now; our only concern is finding a place to raise this child."

Noah looked deeply into Namaah's eyes, wishing that it was that simple, he cupped her face in his hands and brought his lips to hers, whispering, "We will find our home...this I promise."

CHAPTER TWENTY-SIX

Erich stood alone in the hallway outside of Jim's office, his eyes squeezed tightly shut. *What now?* He thought to himself. His life had completely changed in the last twenty-four hours, and not in any of the ways that he had expected it to. He had known that with the opening of the museum finally here, his life would never be the same again...but he had been preparing himself for a new life of talk show interviews, book signings, and endlessly attending events as a special guest once the public was finally allowed to visit the Ark. And now, none of that mattered.

He had found Gema. In that brief moment, in her eyes he thought he had glimpsed something...was it love...and now she was gone. Erich took a deep, shuddering breath and tried to reign his racing thoughts back in. He knew that the only thing that mattered now was finding Gema and her daughter and rescuing them from Malik, and to do that he would need the help of all of the people on the other side of the door. Inside the office, Graham, Jim, Paulus, and Nagato were busy working out exactly where they should start the journey and what they would need for provisions. The other members of the team were scheduled to arrive late this evening, and once everyone was assembled, they would all be boarding a helicopter and heading to the most dangerous place on earth, the Amazon rainforest.

Erich knew that Jim had already spent a considerable amount of time on the phone lining up many of the supplies and speaking with Mitchell. Even with everything that was going on, Erich couldn't help but feel excited to see Alex Mitchell again. The two had shared so many incredible experiences, in fact, after the discovery of the Ark, Erich had tried to hire Mitchell as his head of security, had offered a small fortune, but Mitchell had turned it down, saying, "Come on, you know I'm not cut out for a desk job...I need some danger in my life," and now Erich couldn't help thinking that this definitely qualified as some danger.

As Erich entered the room, he heard Graham discussing what the party would need to take with them, "Listen, I understand that you want to ensure that we are well-provisioned but the fact is, the smaller and lighter this team is the better. Trust me, this is not my first foray into the Hell Verde..."

"Hell Verde?" Jim interjected, "What does that mean?"

"The Green Hell," replied Graham matter-of-factly, "It is a name given to the Amazon by many explorers throughout the years, the first I heard use of it was in the book Exploration Fawcett about Percy Fawcett's early journeys into the jungle...before he was lost to it."

"Lost to it?" questioned Jim.

"Fawcett explored more of the rainforest than anyone before him, and none since has reached deeper into its depth and come out to tell the tale. Originally, he was simply trying to explore the unknown regions and make maps of them, but eventually, he became obsessed with finding a lost city that he called "Z." He kept much of his research and knowledge hidden from everyone though, being paranoid that at some point someone would beat him to his goal. I actually have relied heavily on his various journals in my own quest to find a lost civilization. He was a legend. On all of his journeys men died or went mad, succumbing to the relentless pressure of the Amazon, but Fawcett seemed almost god-like in his ability to handle not only the most grueling physical tasks but also the mental torture of an extended journey into the jungle. He..."

"Died or went mad?" Jim interrupted, "what the hell could be that bad about the place? I haven't spent much time out here in the jungle...and I know that it's tough terrain, but that sounds a little extreme to me..."

Graham's brow furrowed as he began to speak, "I have not spent as much time in the rainforest here in Indonesia as any of you, but I have spent a lot of time in the Amazon, and I can tell you it is unlike any other place on earth. The dangers that lurk within it are too many to list. To start with, one might think that because it is a rainforest, food would be found in abundance. I know from speaking to Erich that many times here in Indonesia that is the case...but in the Amazon, hunger is a way of life. There is little to hunt because most of the animals reside high in the trees, more than a hundred feet above the forest floor and the canopy is so dense that there is also very little vegetation that grows. This is one of the reasons that so many scholars believe that there could never have been an advanced civilization in the Amazon...they call it a false paradise."

"False paradise?" questioned Paulus.

"Yes," replied Graham, "it means that although it would at first glance appear to be a place abundant in life and food it is actually a deadly environment where many of the plants and animals have developed incredible defense mechanisms. It is this very system of belief that led to the mass slaughter of so many tribes at the hands of the early conquistadors. It was believed that all of the groups that inhabited this land were simply primitive sub-humans, and because they had no culture, there was no moral dilemma in slaughtering them. And while it is true that some of the tribes in the region appear to be quite vicious, there are also many signs of advanced civilization that have been found by multiple people, Fawcett included. For instance, there have been pottery shards found that appear to be of finer craftsmanship than anything made in Ancient Greece or Rome, and date to about the same time period. Cave paintings have been found that depict complex ritual and religious ceremonies. And let's not forget that there are some tribes that have such an incredible knowledge of the healing properties of the forest around them, that they make Western medicine look barbaric by contrast."

"What's your point?" Erich stated flatly, not looking overly impressed.

"My point, my dear boy," Graham said, "is that clearly there is enough sustenance to be found in the jungle to support large societies, if one only knows where to look."

Erich looked around at the group as he asked, "And how do we know where the right place to look is?"

"Simple," stated Graham, "we take someone with us who already knows where everything is. I have found on my own journeys, that someone from the region, someone that knows not only the secrets to finding food but also the hidden dangers of the forest can be the difference between life and death."

"So, it sounds like you already have someone in mind?" asked Jim, scowling slightly.

Graham slowly nodded his head, "Two people as a matter of fact. Twins. They have accompanied me throughout three journeys deep into the jungle. I met them after coming in contact with a previously unknown tribe in the Bolivian region of the rainforest. They have a deeper connection with the jungle than anyone I have ever before seen...and in my own forays into Hell Verde I have never seen their equal in knowledge of natural remedies. Just as important, they are also familiar with several of the tribes in the area which will also lessen our risk. That will, of course, be of limited use as we near our goal, seeing that we will be traversing to an area where none have explored before, or at least have not made it back to tell us about it, and so, therefore, the tribes we may encounter will more than likely be unknown to the twins as well."

Erich looked skeptically at Graham, his brow furrowed, "Really, how dangerous are these tribes? I mean, shouldn't we be far more worried about food and predators?"

"I think that we would be wise to give all the dangers of the jungle equal respect...but just so you know, the tribes of the Amazon are often exceedingly dangerous. There are still many tribes that have never had contact with other people, and so they often view intruders into their lands as a threat that must be dealt with extremely harshly. In fact, in Exploration Fawcett, Colonel Fawcett details numerous encounters with hostile native tribes where his group was attacked, archers raining six-foot-long arrows down from the canopy in one instance. In another, his group was surrounded by over three hundred men all armed with either a spear, a bow and a quiver of arrows, or a blowgun with darts that had no doubt been dipped in one of the countlessly available lethal poisons of the region. In each of these cases, he was able to escape, but most have not been that lucky."

Erich cut him off sounding dismissive, "Well ya, but you said Fawcett was exploring a hundred years ago, I'm sure it's changed a lot since then. How realistic is it that there are still dangerous tribes lurking around the jungle?"

Graham laughed and smiled as he replied, "Well Erich, the current estimates are that there are still close to one hundred uncontacted tribes in this forest...so I would say the deeper we venture, the more likely we are to run into trouble. And let's not forget that we are not the only people searching for a lost civilization in this jungle, and what has happened to most all that have embarked on this quest. There are many people, to who, finding Z is an insatiable desire. Many of these obsessive men, Fawcett among them, have ventured into the jungle never to be seen again. In fact, since Fawcett's own disappearance, which many say could only have come from being kidnapped or killed by natives as the man seemed to be immune to almost all other dangers of the jungle, more than one hundred of the men that have ventured into the jungle searching for answers as to what happened to Fawcett and his men have never been seen again, and that doesn't include the men that have gone missing or died searching for Z as well. It seems as though the jungle guards Z as its most precious secret and almost all that attempt to find it remain in the jungle forever. And just so you don't start thinking that I am just being overly cautious or caught up in the past, you should know that I, myself, have had several very close calls, and have heard others talk about many more. In fact, one of the men that I spoke with, James Lynch, was kidnapped by a hostile tribe in 1996 when he was searching for clues to what happened to Fawcett. His party was set upon and kidnapped, and after being held captive for a couple days, it was made clear to him that the men intended to kill his son, James Jr. So, James, thinking of some of the things that he had read about Fawcett and how he narrowly escaped many times from hostile tribes, quickly began to gesture to the chief. He offered the tribe the men's boats and all of their supplies if they would free them. It worked, and the men were freed, but like I said...they are in the vast minority. Most that have gone in search of Fawcett or Z are simply never heard from again. I, myself, have not even embarked on my actual journey to Z, although I have been getting closer to being ready to begin that adventure. I have been waiting until I had amassed every piece of information I could from mythology, other explorer's accounts, satellite imagery, and what I have been learning from tribes throughout the Amazon region for the past decade. The plan was already in place to leave in about two months' time, at the end of the rainy season, but I feel that now is as good a time as any. I am certain that the twins will join us, and will prove to be one of our most valuable resources."

The group looked to be in a state of shock. Clearly, hearing the tales of all of these men that had lost their lives journeying to the same place they were now planning to go, had them shaken. Jim, feeling the need to try and make some headway in this spoke up, "So what will y'all need, how many men, how many boats, all of that stuff? Mitchell is compiling a list as well, but I need to do something, I'm not used to just sittin around."

"Boats will be of no use," Graham said, "We will be traveling inland, away from the river for much of the journey, and even when we are close to the river, it is so treacherous...all but impassable. We will be better off traveling on foot, and the fewer men, the better. We should keep the party to ten men at the very most."

"I think we are making a mistake by not taking more people," Nagato said, "if these tribes are as dangerous as you describe, the more men we have, the better off we will be."

"I understand thinking that way," said Graham thoughtfully, "but you are wrong. The more men and more supplies we have, the bigger threat we will seem to these tribes. Not to mention, we will be louder. A smaller group can remain undetected much easier...especially one in which all of the members of the group have experience moving through the jungle."

"Then I guess that rules me out..." Jim said, looking slightly sullen.

Erich crossed the room and placed his hand on Jim's shoulder as he spoke to him, "Jim, you are like a father to me, and I could never let you go with us, it will just be too dangerous. Plus, we will need someone here that has a basic idea of where we are going and can send help if we need it...assuming we can find a way to communicate..."

Jim smiled, "I know I'm not in the best shape," he said patting his stomach, "and so I'd probably just slow ya down anyway, but you can take the sat phone and, hopefully, if you have an emergency it will work."

"It won't." Graham said matter-of-factly, "I have tried all of the various sat carriers and none work in the area of the Amazon that we are traveling to, but we can take it just in case. I will get you a list of the supplies that I would like to see us leave with to go along with the security team's request. The Amazon is a place unlike any other on this planet. Erich, I know that your time in the Indonesian rainforest was trying, and that good men and women lost their lives due to the dangers that you faced, but please know this...around every corner of Hell Verde, death awaits...so we must never let our guard down. Our survival will rely on our ability to function as a team, to trust one another, so if any of you have doubts about this mission, the time to speak is right now."

Erich looked at the men in the office. Graham looked eager, Erich could think of no one he would rather have to guide them. He looked to Jim who gave him a small reassuring smile and nodded his head almost imperceptibly. Nagato simply stood and racked a round into the chamber of his pistol. Finally, he looked at Paulus and, in his eyes, saw an intensity and resolve that could only be matched by his own. Erich took a breath and nodded, "Alright, then let's go."

CHAPTER TWENTY-SEVEN

The waves pounded relentlessly as the boat rocked in the violent sea. Tarrin sat alone with Nala looking out over the crashing, white-capped waves as the rain pounded down. He stroked the top of the tiger's head as she purred gently beneath him. He could feel her sense of contentment, and deeply wished that he felt the same way, but his mind seemed as turbulent as the storm-tossed waters tonight. Once again, they were on the hunt for Noahim and the other survivors of Atla. Jakon had learned many things from the book that he had sought for so long, the Ratam Ra'Ava, but he had not, as of yet, been able to touch the True Ari'Yet.

Limitless power, Tarrin thought to himself. *That was the goal of all this misery...of all this death. How much longer will we be on this boat, searching for something that I am no longer certain Jakon could, or even should, ever wield?*

Jakon had been more than fair to Tarrin, that much was certainly true, in fact, he had become his second in command...leading his large army of brutal men throughout the lands that they encountered...searching for the remaining clues to unlock the True Ari'Yet, and conquering all that they encountered along the way. Jakon's army had grown to an incalculable number and was comprised of the most vicious men from each civilization that they had conquered. Not to mention that it was led by Tarrin and a multitude of other gifted men, each of whom had benefited greatly from the things that Jakon had learned in Ratam Ra'Ava.

Tarrin still struggled to believe that he was able to wield the amount of power that he now could, and yet, even though his own power had been increased tenfold since they had left Atla, it paled in comparison to that of Jakon. Tarrin closed his eyes and succumbed to the rocking of the great boat, allowing himself a brief moment of rest. His hand slid from Nala's head as his body sagged and his mind was lost to dreams.

He looked across a bloody battlefield, men lay everywhere, dead or dying. A cloying smoke hung to everything from fires that dotted the landscape. Tarrin knew that these fires had largely been set to destroy the bodies of the fallen due to the smell of burning flesh that permeated the air. All around him lay the charred and smoking bodies of the fallen's RaSheen. He watched as another man, a Mul'Ki that he had known for many years, lifted a giant boulder into the air and used his Ari to send it towards a group of oncoming soldiers on horseback. The men had all been shouting war cries as they held their swords above their heads, charging toward Tarrin and the other Mul'Ki that stood beside him. They had looked fearless and brutal but upon seeing the giant rock hurtling through the sky, their bravery faded quickly. The men broke rank and turned their horses, trying to escape what was an inevitable fate. The boulder smashed into the group, the bodies of the men and horses did not slow down the magically propelled projectile.

Men and horses were turned to a mist of blood as they were bowled over. Tarrin turned to the man beside him that was responsible for the carnage and saw a look of what could only be described as elation on his face. The man's face wore a triumphant smile, and he seemed to be on the verge of laughter as he soaked in the destruction. The look gave Tarrin a sickened feeling in his stomach, but as he watched, a shout from their left drew his attention and he turned just in time to see a group of several hundred archers all unleash their arrows at the same time, all pointing toward Tarrin and his men. Tarrin watched as the arrows climbed into the sky, crested and began to fall back to earth towards him and his brethren. As the arrows fell, a feeling of great anger permeated his soul. These men would take their lives in any way they could, just as Jakon had warned them. Lesser men always feared the gifted, feared what they did not and could not understand.

The other Mul'Ki had yet to notice the barrage of arrows heading toward them. Tarrin held out a hand and concentrated his Ari. The arrows slowed and seemed to stand momentarily still in the sky. Men around the battlefield began to take note of the striking scene. Hundreds of arrows, many of them having been lit on fire before they were shot to maximize the damage they would cause, now hung motionless, mere feet away from the group of the gifted that had been wreaking havoc on the men. Tarrin stood with his hand out, his red robe flowing in the wind, Nala slinking around his legs. He looked toward the battlefield and met eyes with the man that seemed to be leading the other army, the corner of Tarrin's mouth lifted ever so slightly, and he pulled his hand back as if readying to throw a punch and then thrust his hand forward. The arrows spun in place and headed back towards to the archers at an impossible speed. The battlefield had fallen silent as everyone stood and watched the event.

The arrows all found their mark as men fell, one after another. When it was over, not a single one of the hundreds of archers still stood, all had been struck dead by their very own weapons. Tarrin turned his eyes back toward the battlefield and watched as the men from the opposing army began to place their swords onto the ground, taking on a supplicating gesture, clearly indicating that the battle was over. Jakon approached, unseen, on Tarrin's right side and said, "Well done my son."

Tarrin was shocked by the sudden appearance of Jakon, "Thank you, Jakon," Tarrin said, "These men were fearsome warriors, but are obviously no match for us. Now that they have surrendered they should greatly increase our armies might."

Jakon seemed to weigh the words before responding, "Which man is their leader?" he asked, a trace of venom in his voice.

Tarrin looked across the field at the men and saw the

commander, the only man not kneeling in subjugation, and pointed to him warily. Jakon seemed to appraise the man for a moment and then, with a flick of his wrist, the man was thrown backward toward a rocky cliff face. Tarrin turned to stare at Jakon. In the past, they had always allowed those that surrendered to join their forces. Jakon simply stared, a look of hatred on his face, as the man smashed into the rock face and crumpled. "Kill them all," he said flatly, "make an example of them. Let the most vicious of your men have free reign over the women and children."

Tarrin could not believe what Jakon was saying. He felt as though he could not give this order. Killing in battle was one thing, it was you or those that stood against you that would die, but killing men that had surrendered, women and children...that just did not make sense. Once again, the scene dissolved and Tarrin found himself alone in a dark place. He could not tell where he was, he could see nothing. As he stood in the darkness, a light appeared far in the distance, small and weak. It seemed to bob up and down as though it were floating unsteadily in the sky. Little by little it grew larger...closer...Tarrin began to realize that the light was not floating, it was a small orb of light that floated inches above someone's hand, and as the person walked toward Tarrin, the light bobbed with each footfall.

The darkness was such that even as the figure grew closer, Tarrin could not make out who it was. The darkness was complete. A brief flicker of green light to the right-hand side of the figure was all of the information that Tarrin needed. It was Noahim and Karok that approached him now. "Stop," Tarrin called out, his voice cracking slightly, "Come no closer to me, Noahim."

The light did not stop advancing towards him, and Noah's voice spoke calmly, "Do not fear Tarrin, I have not come to harm you, only to speak to you...to answer your questions..."

Tarrin laughed, "What questions do I have that you can answer?"

Noahim still continued to stride forward. Tarrin could now make out his face clearly and had begun to be able to see the outline of Karok, dark and sinister. "Whatever questions you may have..."

"Where is Nala?" Tarrin said, his voice growing stronger from the anger he felt at not having his RaSheen, "that is the only question I have."

"How should I know that?" Noahim said, and it almost sounded to Tarrin as though he were mocking him, "you created this place...this is your dream...and yet you ask me where your companion is. I have no idea where she is Tarrin, although I do know that she is no RaSheen. A RaSheen is earned by a Mul'Ki, not given..."

"Your RaSheen was not earned." Tarrin said coldly, "You were but a baby when the BalaRa sought you out."

"Ah, this is true," said Noah, "but that would be an altogether different case, I believe. I am the one, Tarrin. The savior of Atla. The seed of civilization."

"If you are the one then why is Atla destroyed?"

"Atla is not destroyed...at least not so long as the things that we believed in live on. That is how I am to save Atla, by preserving our culture...our ways. Atla is not a place. It is who we are. It is our teachings, our history, even our gift." Noahim paused for a moment, "Atla was not destroyed when the sky fell. Yes, many died, and needlessly I believe, for if Jakon and your lot had helped me, we could have saved so many...but alas, it was not the way. Be assured that Atla lives on...with me and my people. You and Jakon and the others that serve your goals, you are the true threat to the destruction of Atla."

"Enough," Tarrin said, his voice growing heated with anger, "You said yourself that this is my dream, I will not be spoken to in this way. This is nothing but a figment of my own imagination. Leave now, Noah."

Noahim actually laughed at this, "Oh this is indeed your dream Tarrin, but I am no figment. I am very real, and I possess power that you and Jakon will never understand. I came here today because I believe that you have questions, I want to help answer them... understanding is the key to everything...so again I ask you, what is your question?"

"If you are not a figment tell me something that I would not know in my own mind...tell me where you and your people are."

Again, Noahim smiled, "We are safe. We are in a place far away from you where we are building a new Atla...it's not too late for you Tarrin...not too late for any of you. You can rejoin the side of light. You know the question that you want to ask...ask it now..."

Tarrin stared at Noahim, and could no longer decide what was real and what was not. None of this made any sense, and although Tarrin did indeed know that he was dreaming, he could not escape the feeling that this was indeed somehow Noahim's actual consciousness speaking to him. This was something that many Mul'Ki could do, invade the dreams of others to influence their behavior, although it was not typically acceptable to practice this particular brand of magic on another Mul'Ki, and there were none that Tarrin knew of that could accomplish this task without being within eyesight of the person that they wanted to influence. Clearly, Noah was many thousands of miles away, at least that is what Tarrin had assumed. It made no sense that this was anything more than a dream, but he knew this to be the truth. Noahim had sought him out...was speaking to him now. The thought made Tarrin desperate to wake.

"I can think of only one question that you could answer for me, Noahim," Tarrin said coldly, "How can Jakon unlock the True Ari'Yet?"

Noahim shook his head, his mouth turning down slightly in a frown and said softly, "Tarrin you disappoint me...this is not the real question that burns in your soul. Can you not stop posturing for even a moment and admit your own self-doubt? Just earlier this evening you sat and wondered if Jakon wielding unlimited power would be a good thing. Do not think me so foolish as to believe that this is the question that plagues you. I know that you are unsure of your mission...unsure if it would be wise to continue to help your power-hungry master in obtaining the key to limitless power. This is how I know that it is not too late for you. And the question that I came here to answer was one that you asked of Jakon in this very dream...it is the same question that you ask every night in your dreams..."

Tarrin swallowed hard, his eyes widening. The feeling of unreality of the moment had gone, and now, this all felt too real...he felt like his entire being was an exposed nerve. Nothing in his life had prepared him for this feeling of vulnerability, and in this dream state that now seemed to be the most real thing he had ever experienced, he spoke the question that he asked in his every dream. His voice weak and cracking, he said simply, "What is it that we have become?"

Noahim locked eyes with Tarrin, and said, "You have become..."

But the words would not be finished. Tarrin awoke to his shoulder being violently shaken, the echoes of a voice raised in alarm repeating his name swam through the muddled thoughts of his mind. "Tarrin!" Jakon was saying, his voice growing louder, "Tarrin, wake now!"

Tarrin blinked his eyes and shook his head as if to physically shake the words of Noah from him, "Noahim has visited me in my dream..." he said, not meeting Jakon's eyes.

"Impossible," Jakon scoffed, "There is no Mul'Ki that can invade the dreams of another without being able to view that person with their own eyes. I am sure it felt real, but it was only a dream. Nothing more..."

"I am not so certain," Tarrin said, looking up, "It felt like no dream that I have ever had. He told me things, said they were building a new Atla...."

Jakon sat up a little straighter with this news, "Where?" he said hungrily.

"He simply said far away." Tarrin hesitated, feeling embarrassed and not wanting to share any of his doubt with Jakon, the man who had given him so much...had found his RaSheen...had made him his second in command. "He said that he had the answer to the question that plagues me..." he trailed off.

Jakon looked appraisingly at Tarrin, "And what question is that?"

Tarrin took a deep breath and said, "What have we become?"

Jakon seemed momentarily caught off guard before asking, "What do you mean?"

Tarrin swallowed, resolving himself to say what had been plaguing him, "I mean that we have changed...you have changed.

After the last battle, we slaughtered all of those people that had surrendered...women...children...their screams still haunt me. How can we commit these horrific crimes and still be fighting for what is right?"

Jakon looked almost wounded, and when he spoke there was no trace of anger in his voice, only pain, "I know this is not the way that we have done things in the past, but our mercy has clearly been a mistake. We have allowed the men and women that we have conquered to continue living, and, in fact, have given them a better life by teaching them our ways and giving them the advantages that come from living in a society governed by the gifted, but our mercy has allowed other men to believe that they should attempt to fight for their freedom. This has led to more death than I care to imagine. How many have died each time we conquer a new land?"

Tarrin thought momentarily before answering, "It is impossible to know, but typically, many thousands die before surrender is considered an option."

"Exactly, and how many will die after this, once word begins to spread that if you resist the Army of the Gods you will be destroyed? Not just your soldiers, not just those that directly oppose us, but every man, woman, and child will be destroyed. Their blood will fill the streets, their homes will be burned, their fields will be rendered useless for generations to come. Their very memory will be erased as we lay waste to all that stand in our way. How much resistance do you think we will face then?"

"So, you mean to kill anyone and everyone that does not willingly submit to us?" Tarrin asked.

"Yes." Jakon said with finality, "By doing so, we will save many more than we kill. You will see that what seems to you the brutal path is actually the merciful one..."

Tarrin weighed each word as Jakon spoke and slowly began to nod his head, "I see now the truth of what you speak. These few lives sacrificed will save countless others." His eyes welled with tears now as he stared at Jakon, feeling so much remorse for his doubt in this great man, "I am sorry that I have doubted you...sorry that I have been weak."

Jakon placed a hand on top of Tarrin's hand and spoke

affectionately, "And what is our cause?"

"To use the gift to set back the natural order of this world. If the gifted rule, everyone benefits. It was our subjugation that led to the destruction of Atla, and once we rule all of this world, we can ensure that nothing like that ever happens again. The death that was caused when the sky fell is more than a million of our armies could ever cause, and so those that seek to oppose us...oppose life. I now see this. I am so sorry that I doubted you Jakon. You are the one that united the brotherhood, that led us from our bonds of slavery. You are the one that discovered how to forge the bond between RaSheen and Mul'Ki. You are the one that took the gift to heights that none has ever before known. I will never doubt you again..."

Jakon smiled and nodded his head, "You are too kind, Tarrin," he said with a laugh, "I am but an old man who has the help of the most gifted men in this world. Together we will put an end to all of the misery of this earth. The Ratam Ra'Ava taught me that the sky has fallen before, it will fall again, and when it does once again, millions and millions will be killed. We will find a way to stop it, to build our order, to protect life. Do you now know the answer to your question? What have we become?"

Tarrin stood and placed his hand atop Nala's head. When he spoke, there was no longer any trace of hesitation or weakness in his voice. His voice was strong and confident as he said, "We are the protectors of life...and all that stand and fight against us are commanded by death himself. We shall send them all to meet their master. We have become the Army of the Gods."

CHAPTER TWENTY-EIGHT

Erich surveyed his team. Sitting on a fallen log to his left were Paulus, Nagato, and the two men that Graham had recruited, the twins Sanjaya and Natal, who seemed to be perfect facsimiles of one another. The twins were short, standing just over five feet five inches, with close-cropped black hair and deep brown eyes. Their skin was a caramel color, and their build was slight but muscular. Adding to the difficulty of telling them apart, they both wore dark cargo pants and no shirts. Erich had spent many moments since they had arrived trying to discern some difference between them but had no luck so far. Graham simply addressed them as the twins whenever he spoke, leading Erich to believe that he also couldn't actually tell them apart.

The twins understood some English, although neither of them spoke it well, so most of their communication was either nonverbal or done through Graham, who had picked up enough of their language to help facilitate communication within the group. Erich was amazed at how soundlessly the two of them could slip through the jungle. He had been trained in the art of stealth and combat at Unta's village, but this was on a different level. In the jungle, they were living shadows. Erich had to assume that skill could come in handy if they ever met up with Malik and his men.

Standing at the perimeter of the area where they now stood,

machine gun cradled in his arm, an unlit cigar sticking out of his mouth, was the man that accompanied Mitchell that simply went by the name Rock. Erich thought that it was an appropriate moniker, seeing as the man basically looked like a boulder with eyes and stubble. Rock was close to six feet tall. Erich guessed that he weighed three hundred pounds. Rock's neck was the size of a small tree, and his arms and legs were at least triple that. He was a barrel-chested man with a craggy face that had several scars slashing across it, the most noticeable of which started on his left cheek and traveled across his eye, ending at his hairline. His hair was little more than a grayish-black fuzz that lined his head, and most of his face, and his small eyes shone brightly with intelligence. It had surprised Erich on a number of occasions how agile the big man was. He could keep up with any of them, other than Paulus and the twins.

Graham stood talking with Mitchell, gesturing wildly. Erich smiled slightly at the look of mild annoyance on Mitchell's face. He was very familiar with Graham's passion and knew that to the uninitiated it could be a bit much. When Alex Mitchell had arrived Erich had to stifle a laugh at the look of confusion on the rest of the teams face when he introduced first Rock, who everyone had assumed was Mitchell, and then Alex. *I guess when I said special forces Rambo type they thought I was talking about looks, not skill set*, Erich mused inwardly.

Alex Mitchell was indeed every bit the skilled and fearless warrior that Sly Stallone's John Rambo had been, although most people would never have assumed that on first glance. Mitchell was about five feet eight inches tall, and couldn't have been more than 150 pounds with long black hair pulled into a pony tail. Tribal tattoos covered most of the dark skin of her arms and shoulders. Her black tank top hugged the curves of her body tightly and Erich had more than once caught Paulus staring at the beautiful woman as they made there way through the jungle, and he couldn't blame him, after all she was stunning, but they all learned quickly that she was also a leader that could be trusted to get them through anything safely.

They had been in the jungle for just over two weeks and were now trying to reach a tribe that Graham had spent many years cultivating a relationship with. Graham got out his map, checked it over and estimated that they were about three miles northeast of the tribe. As they hiked, Graham began filling the group in about his first encounter with the tribe, telling them all how they had nearly killed him and his entire party, but luckily, he had come prepared with gifts. A shout from up ahead stopped Graham's reminiscing, and the group watched as the twins, who had run off ahead as they often did, came running back into view shouting something.

"Igapo!" one of the twins was saying, Erich thought it might be Natal, but he wasn't really sure.

"What does that mean?" asked Paulus.

"It means we might be in for a bit of a delay..." Graham said trying to look past the twins but seeing only jungle ahead.

"What is an igapo?" Erich asked, "Are they dangerous?"

"Teeth or poison?" Nagato murmed looking around nervously.

Graham chuckled slightly, "Igapo is basically a swamp. Hopefully, it's not too big, and we can just hike around it without losing too much time."

"Why isn't it on the map?" Mitchell asked, looking down at the iPad in her hand.

"They usually come from the rainy season, so many are unknown, although sometimes they are large enough that they are permanent wetlands, and the rainy season only serves to make them bigger."

This seemed to satisfy Mitchell as she grunted her acceptance and they continued walking. Once the igapo came into view, Erich was stunned by its size. It stretched miles on each side, so far, in fact, that he couldn't make out the edge of it. They could see the opposite bank far away in the distance, it looked to be only about a mile, maybe two, wide. All throughout the center of the swamp were dead trees stretching high into the sky. "Holy shit," Rock said, "that's one big mud puddle. So now what, doc?"

Graham looked all around the igapo and ran a hand through his shock of gray hair, "I have no idea. I guess we go around."

"No way," Mitchell said, "We can't even see how far it stretches, and once we get around we'll have to come just as far back to get on the path to the tribe, plus, not sure if you've noticed yet, but the bugs are even worse here. I think traveling around this thing could add days and get us eaten alive by these damn bugs. Let's make rafts and cross it. I'm sure the twins can help us if they know what we're trying to do, they seem pretty resourceful."

"You haven't seen anything of their resourcefulness yet," Graham muttered before calling out to the twins, "Sanjaya, Natal...precisamos de barcos..." he said in Portuguese.

The twins looked out at the igapo and shook their heads slightly, clearly not agreeing with Graham's request.

"They don't want to help?" Erich asked, "or they don't understand?"

"They understand," Graham said looking at the men and then out at the water, "I told them we need boats, but from their reaction, I would say they don't fancy it as a good plan. Many tribes consider igapos to be places of evil spirits, although they could just be worried because, often, caimans make these swamps their homes. Especially if the igapos are not seasonal, and judging by the fact that the trees all throughout this one have died, I would say that this one is here to stay, and not seasonal, so the chances of some pretty large permanent residents are high. I have to agree with the twins that crossing seems dangerous."

Mitchell spoke emphatically, "This whole damn mission is dangerous, everything out here seems to want us dead, and let's not forget that the other people's lives rely on our ability to figure out where we are going and get there fast. I can't take the time of a detour, especially when we don't even know how long of a detour we will be taking. We have some big guns, they could easily take out a caiman...we have to cross, it's the only way."

The twins had been following the conversation and simply turned and ran back into the jungle without a word to anyone. Erich watched them go, trying to discern what this behavior meant, but before he had time to ask if this meant that the twins were or were not going to help them, something large and green flew from the jungle and landed with a thunk several yards away from where the group stood. It was a piece of bamboo that had been cut down from the surrounding jungle. "I guess this means they're in," Rock said with a smile, lumbering off to help cut down the bamboo. In short order, the twins and Rock had collected enough bamboo to construct two large square platforms using the bamboo and nylon rope that Mitchell had placed in each pack, and had fashioned several poles to help push and navigate the raft through the water. Because the rainy season was over, Graham had been fairly certain that the water would not be too deep, and they would be able to just push themselves across. It had taken about four hours to complete construction of the boats which meant that it would be dark well before they reached the other side.

"Maybe we should set up camp and cross in the morning?" Paulus said, eyeing the water nervously.

"We have spotlights, Paulus," Mitchell said, "It will actually make seeing anything lurking in the water even easier in the dark because we will see their eyes from plenty far away. Plus, if there are caimans in these waters we are probably at greater risk setting up camp this close to the swamp, seeing as how they are nocturnal and all. I think our best bet is to just get across this damn thing as quickly as we can and then get away from it. We should be able to cross it fairly quickly and then make headway through the forest until we feel safe."

"Let's just get going," Erich said, scanning the edges of the water for any sign of the deadly black caimans, "we're burning daylight."

"Ooh-Rah!" Rock said biting down on the unlit cigar and patting Erich on the back.

"Indeed," Graham said with a small smile, stepping out onto the first raft. Rock followed behind him, then Paulus stepped on followed by one of the twins. Erich stepped out onto the other raft, Nagato and the other twin followed him as Mitchell stayed on shore and began to hand Erich bag after bag of gear. He then handed the other half of the bags to Rock. They had decided that it would be best for each boat to have one security member, to keep a lookout for predators, and one of the twins who would do the majority of the steering, since they had the only experience piloting crafts such as these, and Mitchell had wanted to split the provisions so that they weren't placing everything on one raft in case anything happened.

"Get us there safe, Natal..." Erich said with a smile.

"Sanjaya." The twin corrected with a small smile.

"Dammit," Erich whispered to Mitchell, "I really thought I had it that time."

Mitchell snorted a laugh and yelled loudly, "Move out!" The twins' poles worked in synchronization as they pushed the rafts out into the dark water and away from the safety of shore. The first hour was very uneventful. The two rafts glided through the water, the twins expertly navigating. They were almost two-thirds of the way across when the sun set and darkness began to claim the swamp as its own, although far in the distance, a slight orange glow still hung to the horizon. Erich watched as Mitchell flicked on the spotlight and began making large sweeping movements through the water in front of the rafts. He turned to see Rock doing the same thing on the other boat, which was about fifteen feet to Erich's left. Erich could hear Rock and Graham talking. They were discussing the tribe they were going to see, Graham filling him in on all of their customs. It seemed to Erich that Rock was developing a particular fondness for Graham and his rather eccentric ideas, although he liked to give him a hard time about them. Erich was pulled from the two men's conversation by Mitchell shouting, "Three o'clock, two hundred yards out, got something in the water."

Rock swung his beam to the coordinates to give more power to Mitchell's light and two eyes glittered like jewels in the darkness. "Caiman," she said, "and by the looks of it, a damn big one. Can you steer away from it Sanjaya?"

The twin nodded and shouted something to his brother, and they both began the process of pushing to reroute slightly to the left. Erich looked back towards the glowing eyes, but they were gone, "Shit," Mitchell said under her breath, "He's gone under. Rock, arm up, I'll keep sweeping with the light until we find him again. You better take the safety off."

Everyone on the boats was in a state of full alert, Erich could feel his heartbeat quicken. They had seen a couple of caimans so far on the trip, and Erich hated the thought of seeing one of the giant black lizards up close and personal. He knew from stories that Graham and Mitchell told that they were incredibly deadly. His thoughts were cut off by the sound of automatic weapon fire. The muzzle flash lit up the night as Rock held down the trigger on the machine gun. The bullets ripped into the water only twenty yards in front of the boat. Ripples were flowing outward in ever-growing circles, the machine gun fire was trained at the center of the ripples.

"Cease fire!" Mitchell shouted loudly, to be heard over the chatter of the gun.

Rock immediately stopped firing, the silence was somehow louder than the gun had been as they all stared at the water. Erich turned to look at Rock who still held the gun at the ready, stock pressed firmly to his chest, head tilted with one eye closed as he looked down the barrel that smoke slowly spiraled up from, "Come on..." Rock said around the cigar, still holding the gun at the ready. Something moved under the water, and Rock squeezed the trigger once again, but just as he did the light flashed off of a large green lily pad as it floated to the surface, and Rock let off the trigger and laughed roughly, "Well, I think I got that one. Maybe next time..." The world exploded as something huge slammed into the bottom of Erich's raft and all of them were lifted several feet into the air. Erich looked for one horrifying moment at the other raft and then darkness engulfed him. He hit the water and watched as Mitchell, Paulus, and Sanjaya all went flying in different directions. Erich kept his eyes opened wide as he hit the blackness of the water, searching for the sinewy shape of the caiman in the darkness. During the assault, the light must have been knocked from Mitchell's hand, and as it sank to the bottom of the swamp a massive form was illuminated in the water.

At first, Erich thought he was looking at a small submarine, which made no sense at all. He kicked hard and found that he was standing in only about five feet of water, as his head broke the surface he stared all around, seeing the others also surfacing. Rock was swinging the gun wildly. Clearly, no one knew what was happening. "Get a light over here," Erich shouted. "I saw something in front of me..."

"Get the gear!" Mitchell shouted.

"Screw that Mitch," Rock growled as Nagato swung the other light in the direction of the capsized boat, "You all need to get to shore as fast as you can. There's something big in there with you."

Mitchell looked around, straining to see what Rock was talking about. The longer they sat in this water, the more danger they were in. She turned to see the raft floating several yards away, useless and broken as though it had been made of twigs. "How the hell did a caiman do this?" she said to no one in particular.

"It wasn't a caiman," Erich said looking around in wild desperation, "Your light lit it up as it fell through the water, it was huge and sort of round, or oval shaped. I didn't get a great look, but it almost looked like a submarine...could it be Malik?"

"How the hell would he get a sub into this thing, plus it's only about five feet deep, I don't think it would work." Mitchell said, "I don't know what it was, but it wasn't a sub."

"Whatever it is," Rock said sounding nervous, "It's still in there, and it's huge, so I say swim like hell towards the shore. I've got your six. Get Sanjaya up here to help pole this and make us move faster, I don't think he weighs enough to upset the balance of our raft."

"Good thinking," Mitchell said and turned to to see Sanjaya being pulled aboard the raft by his doppleganger brother. As he climbed onto the raft, Mitchell caught a glimpse of a large fragment of bamboo sticking out of Sanjaya's thigh, and the reality of this new situation hit her, "Not good," she whispered and turned to find Erich and Paulus, "Look guys, Sanjaya took a pretty big piece of bamboo to the thigh, that blood is gonna bring every caiman in the whole damn swamp. We better get to ground and fast. Stay together, we may be able to make ourselves look large enough to give them pause before attacking us. Rock is a good shot, but if they come after us, he won't be able to shoot them without risking hitting us, so that's not much of an option. I think our only chance here is to make it to shore...fast."

Erich and Paulus both nodded at him, and they turned as a group, sank back into the water, and began paddling and kicking as fast as they could. "Cover us!" Mitchell shouted as the group swam, staying as close together as they could. Erich couldn't help but think that this might be a bad idea. All of the noise would just bring the caimans right to them, a buffet for the prehistoric beasts, but he had no experience with them, and so he deferred to Mitchell's judgment, who Erich knew had spent time in this jungle on various missions.

As they swam, Erich did his best to continue searching the water, struggling in vain to see what had attacked them. The light continued to pass over the group, scanning the dark waters, but nothing was seen. Suddenly Erich felt a surge of water from behind him, as though something large was readying to pass him. He tried to shout to Mitchell and Paulus, but it was too late. As he opened his mouth, something huge and rock solid slammed into him from behind, pushing him down into the darkness.

His mouth filled with muck as he was pushed into the bottom of the swamp. He tried to turn and swim back to the surface, but the weight that was on him was too much to fight against. His hands scrabbled behind his back, desperately striving for purchase but were met with only slippery skin stretched across muscle. It was not the scaly skin of a caiman, but something smooth, slick, and utterly enormous. Erich could not even imagine what the thing was, but as he struggled, he knew that this was it. His vision began to blur as his lungs burned and his brain screamed at him to take a breath. Erich wanted nothing more than to give in and suck in the water, filling his lungs and ending the pain, the fear, the struggle...but he thought of Gema...of her little girl...and knew that he could not relent. The water all around him began to glow, and Erich realized that the raft must be close, must be shining a light down now. He struggled to turn and try to see what had him pinned, but what he saw seemed to be a moving rock bathed in the weak light from the raft. His lungs were on fire, he knew that any second he would involuntarily give in to his body's demands to take a breath and would drown. He fought this...he had to live. As he turned forward, he was shocked to see Mitchell's face mere inches from his own. She placed a hand firmly on each cheek and began moving her mouth closer to Erich's face.

Erich didn't understand what was happening...thought he was

hallucinating or already dead but as Mitchell's lips met his he understood and was prepared for the blast of air from her. His head cleared slightly and the incredible burning in his lungs relented, Mitchell held up a finger, surfaced, and came back with another life-giving breath. Mitchell pointed at Erich and then balled herself up, pulling her arms and legs tight to her body. Erich understood and did the same, and as he did Mitchell swam away quickly. The area around Erich suddenly was filled with bullets trailing through the water. He could just barely make out the muffled firing of the machine gun, although he guessed they must just be yards away now because the light was so bright. All around him bullets flew, and as he held his arms and legs in, afraid that he would be shot himself, the pressure on him relented slightly. A new sound, a much deeper boom came from above, and the water became cloudy with a dark substance that Erich realized was blood from the gigantic creature. Another blast boomed through the water, and he felt the creature shudder. Felt it sway, saw hands reaching towards him as Mitchell came back into view. Muffled shouting reached his ears, and he heard splashes as others must have jumped into the water.

Suddenly the weight on his back was gone, and he was being pulled towards the surface. He broke the surface of the water, and gasped in a breath, the sounds of the world returning to him as spasms racked his body and he continued to take deep, heaving, ragged breaths. A small cheer rose from the boat as he felt hands pull him onto the raft. "No...room...for...my...weight...," he said between convulsive breaths.

"Nagato is coming with Paulus and me, and we gotta go fast because this much blood is definitely gonna bring the cavalry," Mitchell said as she and the two men began swimming as fast as they could. Erich was on back, looking up into the starlit sky, realizing this was the first time that he had seen stars for at least a week, and tried to understand what had happened.

"What was it that attacked?" Erich asked, his voice hoarse but growing steadier.

Rock answered, "A hippo...," he growled, not taking his eyes off of the water in front of them. He was still watching intently as Graham now manned the light, sweeping it back and forth, allowing it to fall over the group of swimmers in the center of each arc. The twins worked in unison, propelling the raft as quickly as they could.

"A hippo?" he said slowly.

"Yep...a hippo," Rock repeated.

"I told you it couldn't be a hippo," Graham said sounding frustrated, "there are no hippos in the Amazon, or anywhere in South America for that matter."

"Well, then that one must have been lost." Rock said, "Cause that fat bastard was a hippo. The Newark zoo has a few, I know what I saw."

"And how would a hippo have gotten into the Brazilian rainforest?" Graham mocked.

Rock seemed to think about it for a moment before responding with a simple two-word answer, "Pablo Escobar."

"Pablo...Escobar...," Graham spluttered, "What the bloody hell are you talking about?!"

"I think Graham is right," Erich said slowly, trying to diffuse the situation. "Pretty sure there are no hippos in this area of the world. Either way, thanks for taking out whatever it was; you saved my life, Rock."

Rock grunted and shook his head, "Let's talk about it when we get to shore, for now, I need to make sure that no more hippos that shouldn't be here try and kill another member of my group, so I'd like to stay focused."

With that, everyone grew very silent. Rock did not seem like the right guy to argue too much with. Erich had his eyes trained on the group of swimmers, he watched as Mitchell made landfall first, pulling herself up out of the water and taking a few steps quickly onto the shore, she pulled a large black pistol from somewhere behind her back and began searching the surrounding water for signs of trouble. Paulus and Nagato climbed out close behind her, both men visibly drained. The raft was only a few moments behind, and Rock continued to search the shore, Graham shining the light throughout the water. As the raft ran up onto the shore, Graham stumbled and fell backward, casting the light high into the treetops that rimmed the igapo. As the light flashed through the trees, Erich was sure that he saw two sets of eyes high in the canopy staring down at them, but the light fell away. He stared at the spot, trying to discern any shape or outline.

He squinted up, shaking his head and thinking to himself that it must have been a monkey, or a trick of the light glancing off a wet leaf...but it sure looked like something...or someone was watching them. As he sat staring he felt a solid hand land roughly on his shoulder, "Glad we got you through that, Padre," Rock said, "Things got a little hairy back there. I guess Mitch was so sure you weren't gonna make it that she decided to let her true feelings come out. It was a beautiful moment...really glad I was there for the start of you two's love story..."

Erich grinned as Mitchell walked up and rolled her eyes, "I could do worse..." she said.

"You have done worse," Rock barked, "Anyway, let's get the hell away from this water, there might be another hippo."

"For the last time," Graham said sighing, "there are no hippos in South America."

Before Rock could respond Mitchell said quickly, "Well there was at least one, I saw her up close and personal."

"I just don't know how that could be...," said Graham.

"I already told you," Rock said with a smile, enjoying riling the Englishman up, "Pablo Escobar."

"What in the devil are you talking about?" Graham asked.

"In the eighties, at the height of his cocaine empire, 'ol Don Pablo had a herd of African hippos brought to his compound in Brazil. When the feds finally captured him, the place was left to rot, hippos and all, only it seems like the Amazon is a perfect place for African hippos and they got busy...well...getting busy. Four hippos turned into over two hundred, and then a couple of them broke through a fence and those couple of hippos turned into a couple hundred more. Something about the weather here makes them super horny I guess, cause they just pop 'em out like bunnies," Rock said with a laugh, "They've been spotted all over the place, several hundred miles from Escobar's old compound. Farmers see 'em, kids see 'em in ponds, they've even attacked a few people and killed some livestock. The government here doesn't know what to do, cause now there are natural born wild hippos living in the Amazon. No one knows how to handle it."

Graham looked floored. He stood with his mouth gaping and didn't seem to know if he should believe Rock's story or not. After several seconds of silence, he spoke, "And how do you know all of this?"

"I like to read National Geographic when I drop off timber," Rock said with a smile, "They've had several articles about the hippos...it's quite a fascinating study in invasive species." He said this last part in a horrible imitation of Graham's accent.

"Drop off timber?" Graham asked.

"Ya...what do you Brits call it...go to the loo?" Rock said.

Realization crossed Graham's face as he said, "That's disgusting."

Everyone laughed now as Mitchell said, "Disgusting or not, looks like we've got another thing to watch out for. Guess we better avoid igapos, or whatever they're called, from now on."

"I thought it was just what we needed to break the monotony," Rock said, "get the old blood pumping. Plus, I've wanted to shoot that .470 nitro express ever since I first saw it...kicks like a son of a bitch but took that hippo out like it was a squirrel."

"Well, we lost over half of our supplies," Mitchell said shaking her head, "including our food and ammo, so I think monotony would be a good thing. Now let's just hope that this tribe has some info that makes all of this worth it."

CHAPTER TWENTY-NINE

Jikar sat in front of the Jala'Kim, thinking back to how far they had come...wondering what the future truly held for them. He and Noah were both fathers now, Noah with Namaah of course, and Jikar with a native woman that he had met shortly after they arrived in this new land. This place was by far the most treacherous they had been to, and Jikar often wondered if that wasn't part of what made Noah so certain that it was the right place for them to finally make their home. It would indeed be difficult for Jakon and his men to find them, and even more difficult to get to them if they ever were able to discover where this place was. *Jakon.* Even the thought of the name made Jikar flushed with anger. The growing legends surrounding Jakon had spread to almost every land that Noahim and his men had visited. An Army of Gods...that's what the people said about him. Jikar knew the truth though, Jakon was no god.

Jikar reflected back to a conversation he had with Noahim while they were still searching for this place. Jikar had been growing weary of their constant searching and had begun to wonder if Noahim had simply lost his nerve and was so fearful of Jakon that they would never settle into a new home. It was on a particularly stormy day at sea that Jikar had brought his concerns to his best friend. "Noah," Jikar said, entering into Noah's chambers, "do you have a moment to speak?"

Noah looked up from the book that he was making notes in, "Of course Jikar, come...sit down," he said motioning to the bed beside his desk where Karok lay sprawled.

Jikar looked at Karok and back to Noah, "It is ok Noah, I will stand. I just need to know how much longer this journey will take us."

Noah scowled slightly as he spoke, "Jikar, we have been over this many times. We cannot stop searching until we have found the correct place for both machines. Not to mention the fact that we must find a place that is safely hidden from Jakon and his men."

"Why did you not just kill him, Noah? I know that your power far exceeds his, why is it that you allowed him to live...we would be free of that fear if it was not for your mercy."

Noahim considered the words, "It was not for mercy that I let Jakon live. Jakon has many fervent followers, men who believe that he is the true and rightful ruler of all of the world. Had I killed Jakon do you not think that one of those men would have taken up his mantle? There would be no peace in that. I must try to appeal to the humanity left in Jakon, only if he renounces his ways will we have peace. To kill him would simply make a martyr of him, and his followers would grow ever more devoted."

"Then if you will not kill Jakon, why do we not just find a new home that is safely away from him now? We could abandon the search for the site of the second machine and search instead for the place that will be safe from him. Surely, we have done our part. Our people have suffered for many years on these boats. We deserve a home."

"Our people do deserve a home Jikar...but that home will not protect them from the sky falling again, and the machines will. It is our duty to preserve life. I understand what needs to be done. I am sorry that it causes all of us discomfort, but it is temporary."

Jikar looked like he wanted to say something else but hesitated before blurting out, "Are you afraid of Jakon, Noah? Afraid that he is more powerful than you?"

Noah turned away from Jikar and waited to answer. "What if

I am?" he asked, "What would that mean to you?"

"It would mean that you are not the one. How could you be the one and still be fearful that someone's power exceeds your own?" Jikar answered.

Noah looked back at his friend and held his gaze, "The prophecy states that the one will be able to control the True Ari'Yet, ultimate power. I do not control this power, so I am not the one...at least not yet. I believe that we are defined by more than just prophecy."

Jikar and Noah sat in silence for several moments listening to the sounds of the waves crashing into the boat, "I have always believed in you Noah...have always supported and trusted you. If you have been worried that you are not the one, I feel that I deserved to know this. We all have put much faith in you."

"I know this Jikar, I was ashamed to tell you that I had doubts. You have always been so certain of me, so certain of the prophecy. I also feared the others would cease to follow us if they knew of my doubts...but know that I did not intend to hurt or deceive you. I do believe that when the time comes, I will be able to harness the True Ari'Yet. After all," he said pointing at Karok, "The BalaRa did seek me out...and I have drunk from the Jala'Kim...it is why I continue to search the Ratam Ra'Ava...to unlock the True Ari'Yet...to save us all..."

Jikar looked at his friend, studied him, and placed a hand on his shoulder. "I do believe that you are the one, Noahim, I always have."

A noise behind him brought him back from his memories, and he sprung to his feet, sword in hand as he spun to face the threat. Karok stood on the edge of the clearing, a quizzical look on his face, and Noah strode from the jungle and into the clearing, smiling as he saw his friend. "I thought I may find you here," he said.

"I still cannot believe that we built all of this," Jikar said sweeping his hand around to encompass the surrounding city that lay within the protected walls of the jungle.

"It is amazing," Noah said, "but come with me now. I am about to place the final stone on the machine, I want you to be there with me, to lend your gift to mine. I can do it alone, but I prefer to do this together. The final step of our journey. I could have accomplished none of this without you."

Jikar smiled and slid his sword back into the scabbard at his side, "Do you really think that the machine will help you unlock the True Ari'Yet?" he asked.

Noah considered for just a moment before answering, "I think it may...yes. There are many things that still remain clouded in mystery about the machines, but I do believe that they may indeed be the key."

"Then let us go, old friend!" Jikar said and slapped Noah on the back, "today is indeed a day of celebration." And he turned and walked into the jungle, Nuni on his shoulder.

"Come Bala'Ra," he said to Karok, "Let us go see if I am indeed the one."

CHAPTER THIRTY

They had been in the jungle for almost a month, at least Erich thought it had been almost a month, the days were beginning to run together, it felt much longer. Erich thought that the nickname, Hell Verde, was well deserved. It had been a torturous time so far, and they weren't certain how much closer they were now than when they had first arrived. They walked day in and day out through a perpetual dawn on a planet with a green sun, bathing everything in its eerie glow. The last seven days had been particularly difficult as they ventured further away from the river in search of a tribe that Graham was hoping to speak with. Erich really had no idea whether it was smart to chase after this tribe or not, but they didn't really have any options. At this point, the only thing they could do was hope to get to that city before Malik.

The group had been set up in their current camp for three days, enjoying a brief rest from constant hiking while Graham and Mitchell had gone to talk to the tribe. Graham hadn't wanted everyone to go because he had not wanted the tribe to be intimated by the large group, plus it would have taken much longer to travel with everyone and all of their gear. Graham and Mitchell had arrived back around two hours ago, but so far had stood by themselves talking animatedly and looking at several maps. As they sat and waited, Erich felt the constant pang of hunger gnawing at him. They had grown used to being hungry, in fact, Erich was certain that had it not been for the twins, the group would have already starved to death. They had brought enough provisions for what should have been around sixty days but had run out of that food over a week ago, most of what they brought having been lost in the igapo. At first, Erich thought it would be no big deal for the group to hunt, but there were not very many animals that came within shooting distance, most choosing to stay well-hidden in the canopy. Erich had caught quick glimpses here and there of the animals in their lofty perches, but hunting was not a viable option for sustaining the group.

Luckily the twins had ways of providing more than enough for everyone. They would set snares each night when they made camp, and each morning would have a variety of small rodents. They were also incredible archers and could take out parrots as they flew over the group, which to no one's surprise, tasted a lot like chicken. The twins' knowledge of the jungle was astounding. They created salves for wounds and insect bites, a powder that they called tok-tok that, when burned, acted as a powerful insect repellent; although, the group used it sparingly because the smell was strong and they did not want to attract the attention of any hostile tribes in the area.

Erich watched now as the twins stood over a campfire stirring a mixture of chopped cassava and some type of large catfish they had caught this morning with their bare hands. The two men animatedly told stories and laughed as they cooked. Erich looked around at the rest of the group. Paulus was meditating, a standard practice these days. Nagato was trying to find a way to make the electronic devices they had charge, the solar chargers that they used did very little in the heart of the jungle, and Rock simply sat at a makeshift table cleaning the guns, and checking and cataloging their ammo. Erich couldn't help but notice that other than the twins, and Mitchell, the group was beginning to look a little rough. Each had lost some weight, the results the most prominent on Rock, who Erich could only assume typically subsisted on around five thousand calories a day. His clothes hung loosely from his body, and his skin seemed almost loose around his muscles. Erich was certain he didn't look much better. He could feel the effects of a month without bathing and shaving and knew that he was covered in a layer of mud and bug bites. The twins, on the other hand, looked almost the same as they did on day one, except their clothes were dirtier, and the large bloody rip in Sanjaya's pant leg from the bamboo sliver. Amazingly enough, the wound had been completely healed by plants the twins found throughout the jungle.

Erich decided that he'd had enough of waiting for Graham and Mitchell to let him know what had happened so he stood up and walked over toward them, "So...," he said, letting his voice trail off, the word almost as much of an accusation as a question.

"So...what?" Graham asked distractedly, continuing to look down at the map.

"So, what did you guys found out?" Erich asked heatedly, "You've been back for two hours and haven't said a damn word to anyone!"

Graham looked up and gave a quick shake of his head, almost as though he was just noticing Erich for the first time, "We made it to the village and began speaking to the shaman there, he told us that there had been tales of a forbidden city hidden deep within the jungle, a place where animals guarded a terrible secret. He said that no one ever returned that had gone searching for it. He said it was a place of the deepest magic..."

"That's got to be the place then, right?!" Erich said, his excitement growing.

"It would appear so, yes," Graham said, pausing momentarily, "however, he could only give us a very general direction. He warned us not to go look for it, he said the animals that protected the place were far too dangerous. I tried to get him to explain what he meant by saying that the animals protect the city, but he would only say that there the animals did not behave in the same way they did in the rest of the forest...."

"The Mul'Ki could commune with animals, they each had a special animal companion, this is definitely where we must go." Paulus said, "Which way are we heading? We should leave at once."

"Wait, there's more that he told us," Graham said slowly, glancing at Erich with a worried look, "The shaman told us that the men of his village patrol the forest, always on the lookout for intruders that mean to do them harm. Apparently, these scouts are meant only to follow intruders and report back if they see anything. They only engage if threatened. Five days ago, they followed another, much larger group that passed by about twenty miles south of here. He said that it was many men with big weapons, they made a lot of noise as they progressed through the forest. The men had a woman and a child with them..."

"Gema..." Erich said softly, "We need to leave right away, it was only five days ago, and they are going to move much slower than us. If we cut diagonally, we could set out to make up the twenty miles to the south and the extra mileage that they would be ahead of us from the five days. How far do you think that they could get each day Mitchell?"

Mitchell weighed the question for a moment, "A group that size with terrain like this, I would say six...maybe eight miles. The undergrowth isn't bad here because the canopy is so thick, so they don't have to hack through as much. The biggest thing that would slow them down is the sheer size of the group, and the fact that they have to be on the lookout for dangerous animals, among other things."

Paulus looked between all of the men, "Erich, we must not try to intercept Malik's group," he said, a look of certainty on his face, "we must try to make it to this city that the shaman spoke of. That is the most important part of our mission; if we focus on beating Malik and his men to the lost city we can explore the ruins and hopefully find the book..."

"And then what?" Erich said, his face going scarlet with anger, "leave Gema and Sophia to die?! I am going to save them, do whatever the hell you want Paulus..."

Mitchell spoke up now, "Paulus, there is no way in hell that we are going to the city. We go after the others. If we stop them from reaching the city so be it, but this is a search and rescue mission, first and foremost."

"Then where are we going?" Paulus said, "Can anyone even tell me that?"

"Listen to me Paulus," Erich said, "for the first time since we walked into this hell, we have real information on where Gema and Sophia are, and we're going to find them. Any delay could mean that they die. This is your family for God's sake! How could you be suggesting anything else?"

Paulus began shaking his head, pacing back and forth, "I love them both more than you know Erich, but this is bigger than all of us! And as I have said, we still have no idea where we are actually going. Our goal should be to find the city, that has been the plan all along; we should see it through."

Mitchell placed a hand up to silence the rebuttal that was already coming from Erich, "Guys, listen, please...everyone's nerves are shot. It's hot as hell, we are overworked and underfed, these damn bugs are eating us alive, and Paulus is right, we don't know where we are going...but the fact is, we have our first solid lead on the ruins and on the other group. You all know my feelings on which lead to follow but I don't speak for everyone. Just be aware, we better choose which way we are going and fast...we can't keep arguing. So, what's it gonna be?"

"We go after Gema and Sophia," Erich said firmly, "Nothing else matters."

Paulus looked at Erich, his eyes full of regret before saying, "We must find the ruins, once we have done that we will find the others, they are headed there anyway..."

Nagato simply nodded his ascent with Paulus and looked at the ground, unable to meet Erich's eyes.

Rock looked between everyone and with a small smile said, "I say we go find these bastards and get the kid and her mom back...I've been dying for some real action out here."

Everyone turned to look at Graham who shook his head, his eyebrows raised and said, "I don't know what we should do, I understand the logic of both plans. It is possible that if we arrive at the city first, we could find what these men are seeking and use it to barter for the captives' release. If they have so many more men than us, taking them on here in the jungle may be a foolish...and deadly...proposition. I just wish we would get a sign..."

As if on cue, a large black panther panther strode out of the jungle. Other than Rock pulling his gun up and taking aim at the intruder, no one moved. The cat was huge, at least three times as big as the largest one Erich had ever seen. Paulus spoke, "Please, put your weapon down, no one make any sudden movements." The cat seemed to take no notice of anyone in the clearing except for Erich. Its muscles rippled beneath its velvet black coat as it stalked forward, keeping its large green eyes focused on Erich.

"I shoot on three," Rock said in a guttural whisper, his finger tightening around the trigger, "One...Two..."

"No," Erich hissed, "don't shoot."

Rock's eyes flicked back and forth between the cat and their group, he felt the resistance of the trigger, knew that it was almost to the break-over point, knew that he only had to apply a hair's breadth more pressure and he would light the giant cat up...but he paused, enraptured by the scene in front of him. "Dammit," he whispered between clenched teeth, lowering his gun slightly and relaxing his finger on the trigger, "You better not be wrong Erich..." he whispered, leaving the threat hanging in the air.

The cat made its way closer and closer, finally stopping mere inches from Erich. He could feel the heat radiating from its gigantic body. Erich stood as still as he possibly could, his heart pounding in his chest, his skin icy with sweat. A low purring sound was emanating from the cat as it stood staring up at Erich, and then, without any warning, the great beast tensed its legs and pushed up, placing a giant paw on each of Erich's shoulders, their faces mere inches apart. Erich didn't dare to even breathe. In all of the world, at this moment the only thing that existed was himself and the jaguar. The cat seemed to peer directly into his eyes and let out a great exhalation, the warm, moist air filling Erich's face. He knew that he should be terrified right now, yet for some reason he felt himself relaxing, the tension in his body ebbing away. Erich released the oxygen he had been holding in a long steady breath and closed his eyes.

The great cat seemed to accept this gesture as confirmation that this was the man it was looking for and simply dropped back to the ground, nuzzling its head into Erich's hand. The cat stood beside Erich, surveying everyone else in the clearing. No one made a sound until Rock, lowering the gun again, slowly spoke the words on everyone's mind, "What...the...hell...was that?"

CHAPTER THIRTY-ONE

"So that just happened...," Erich said looking around at his group, which now included the giant jaguar. Since the cat had arrived, it was all that the group could talk about. Paulus and Nagato seemed especially worked up.

"Raja," Nagato said, motioning toward the large cat, "Raja Bintang!"

"What does that mean?" asked Mitchell.

"It means star king," Erich said slowly, "at least I think that's what it means, but that doesn't make a lot of sense to me. Nagato must be referencing some myth of his people. A lot of the tribes are very superstitious, there are many legends about big cats throughout Indonesia. I'm assuming that black jaguars would hold a special significance because of their great rarity, and this one in particular, because of its size. I mean, I have some experience with big cats...jaguars are not typically very big, and this one is huge...prehistoric in size."

As Mitchell and Erich continued to talk, Paulus walked over and added, "The Raja Bintang is a legendary beast from the teachings of the Sala'Ma..." Paulus began, "The legend tells of a great black cat that can communicate with men and is truly the king of all beasts. It is said that all other animals will obey the Raja

Bintang. He is said to be as black as night, born from the stars to rule over the beasts of this world. Some men in the village believed they had found the Raja Bintang several years ago in the jungles surrounding the place where Unta had taken Gema and I after Malik came."

"What do you think he is doing here?" Mitchell asked, nervously eyeing the cat, "What in the world could make him just hang out here beside you? I mean he's acting like a damn dog for God's sake."

Paulus looked at the great cat, his face a mixture of fear and awe, "I honestly have no idea," he said, "to tell you the truth, I always assumed the legend was just that...a legend. I never thought that the Raja Bintang actually existed. To see this with my own eyes, to have confirmation of one of the great Sala'Ma legends...it is an overwhelming feeling."

"Legend or no legend, the cat is making me nervous," Mitchell said.

Erich looked down at their new companion, who was now acting somewhat agitated, stalking back and forth in front of him. "I feel like he wants something...and I know that sounds crazy, but these last few weeks have taught me that anything is possible." The cat looked up at Erich, seeming to understand what he said and bounded several steps ahead into the jungle, disappearing into the brush and then quickly coming back out. The great cat stood there, making a chuffing sound and looking directly at Erich, then once again, ducking into the cover of the forest.

"I think it wants you to follow," Paulus said matter-of-factly.

"So, what, you can communicate with animals now too?" Erich said.

"Maybe he's just seen an episode or two of Lassie...it isn't that hard to figure out that it wants us to follow," Rock said and paused, "I can't believe I just said that..."

Erich turned and looked at Mitchell, who simply shrugged her shoulders, clearly at a loss. "Following the cat doesn't seem to be any crazier than anything else we are doing out here, what do you think Doc?" Mitchell said turning her attention to Graham.

Graham shook his head and rolled his eyes at the nickname that Rock and Mitchell had given him, "For the last time, stop calling me Doc," he said with feigned exasperation. "And I suppose you are right, this whole venture is predicated on the belief that mythology often has a basis in tangible, real-world events so it makes as much sense to follow this legendary beast as it does to be out here in the first place."

"What he said," Rock boomed out, standing up and slapping Erich on the back, which earned a wince from Erich as he rolled his shoulder and rubbed the spot where Rock's giant palm had landed, "Let's move out, but I think we need to quit calling it the cat, or legendary beast, or whatever else, how bout we give it a name."

Mitchell looked at Rock and shook her head, "A name?"

"Ya, a name," Rock said, "I find it kind of creepy to have to say let's follow the cat, or the beast, makes me think we've all gone a little, as Graham and his English brothers might say, bonkers. I think a name would give her a proper place, let her know she's part of the group..."

"Part of the group?" Mitchell asked, "And she? How do you know it's a she?"

"Well, you see..." Rock began, "a boy has a..."

"Okay Rock...we get it," Erich interrupted, saving the group from the obviously crass biology lesson Rock had in store, "and I have to admit, I kind of agree. I like the idea of being able to refer to her by name. It will definitely make me feel less crazy for following a strange, giant jaguar into the Amazon rainforest hoping that it will help lead us to the love of my life before a group of psychopathic murderers find the key to limitless power in a lost city built by the survivors of Atlantis..."

This earned a small chuckle from the group. "Fine," Mitchell said eyeing the cat as it stalked beside the darkened forest. "Although, if this cat's a girl doesn't that mean it isn't the Star King from your legend?"

Paulus thought about it for a moment, "I suppose a king should have his queen, plus, if the Raja Bintang is real then it obviously came from somewhere so a female of the species would be a necessity, right?"

This seemed to settle the matter with the group, and the cat, seemingly sensing the moment, leapt into the center of the team and let out a deafening roar. The jungle immediately fell silent as they all stared at the feline figure crouched low to the ground, eyeing all of them with a fierce intelligence. Nagato walked and placed a hand on Erich's shoulder, looking directly into his eyes and nodded, saying only two words, a small knowing smile on his lips, "Raja Bintang..." he said, watching as the cat stalked towards the jungle.

"Alright then," Erich muttered walking towards the spot that the cat had disappeared, "Lead the way, Raja." He paused momentarily, catching Nagato's eye, who nodded approvingly, apparently pleased with the name that Erich had chosen for their new companion. Knowing there was no more time for hesitation, Erich plunged into the darkness of the jungle beyond. Paulus and Nagato following, with Graham, Mitchell, and Rock bringing up the rear, and the twins already lost to the shadows.

CHAPTER THIRTY-TWO

That is why I have told you that you must be careful when you are practicing your swordsmanship Rashan," Noah said to the young man at this side. As he spoke, he allowed a small trickle of his Ari to flow into the wound of the other young man, who was lying on the ground bleeding from a large gash on his upper arm, where he had been struck with a sword. The wound began to glow slightly as the skin pulled closer together.

"Well if he would have protected himself it would not be a problem," Rashan said as he smiled up at Noah, running a hand through his messy shoulder-length hair, "but I will try harder to be careful in the future father."

"Please be sure that you do. I would not want your mother to find out you almost cut off your best friend's arm." Noah said playfully.

"Almost cut off my arm," the boy on the ground said, "Ha! He is just lucky that I slipped in the mud. His sword is no match for mine."

"You may be right, Amare," Noahim said to the boy, "but even so, your father would not be happy with me if you lost an arm."

"This is true!" a voice from behind them shouted as Jikar came into view, "Although, I think I have to agree with my son Noah, he is slightly better with a sword than yours."

Noah and Jikar embraced as they laughed, walking away from their sons and allowing them to continue their training. It had been fifteen years since they had found their home here in the jungle. Many decades had passed since the survivors had left Atla, and much had been accomplished in that time, searching for the proper place to build the machines that would make the God's Noise.

The construction of the first machine had taken over four years to complete, and when it was finished, it had taken Noah and the other Mul'Ki another two years to construct the myths that they would use to pass down the information that was needed to operate the machine. Noah and the others had left that land a little over twenty-five years ago, traveling and seeking out this new home they had made for themselves in the jungle. Building the second and final machine here in this new land was far more difficult, and had taken much longer due to Noah's insistence that the machine not be nearly as visible as the first. The first machine had been placed in a way that all would see it, and it would become legendary, but this one needed to be less conspicuous.

To accomplish this feat, the Atlans dug deep into the earth and buried all but the very top of the machine. It was a painstaking process. The machine was incredibly large, so the sheer volume of earth that had to be removed was staggering, and then came the task of disposing of the dirt once they had dug it out. A pile of earth the same size as the machine would have been no less noticeable so the Atlans had to move the dirt, creating a small ridge that also served as a defense around their new home. Defense was needed from people but also from some of the more troublesome new animals that they had encountered since arriving, namely the giant black lizards that lurked in the depths and on the shore of the great river. The Atlans had tangled with this particular beast many times since arriving.

Life in this new jungle home had become good for the survivors of Atla, and Noahim hoped that it would stay this way forever. Along with building the machine, the Atlans had also worked to create a new Atla. The first project that many of the men had decided to work on was to create a replica of the Jala'Kim. It had taken much time, but the final result was such an exact match to the original that sometimes when Noah sat and meditated in front of this new Jala'Kim it was as if he were in the old Atla again.

The six remaining Mul'Ki along with Noahim had also begun to train more children in the ways of Mul'Ki, although the training here was much different than it had been in Atla. In the past, the Mul'Ki had always chosen the children that they sensed the gift in, but here in this new home, Noah had decided to teach every child in the ways of the Mul'Ki. There were so few Mul'Ki left, and he feared that their ways would be lost, so he made the decision that each child of Atla would be taught in the ways of the ancients. Some of the children exhibited subtle signs of the gift; the ability to communicate on a base level with animals, harnessing enough energy to heal small wounds or move small objects. Although, none of them were able to do very much with their gift, with the exception of Noahim's son Rashan and Jikar's son Amare, who both had proven from a very young age to be incredibly gifted. Even Karok had found a mate in this new home, and just three months ago she had her first litter of kittens, all of them jet black, and all of them twice as large as a normal jaguar.

As Noahim walked and thought of his son and the amazing gifts that he seemed to possess, another thought crossed his mind. It was a thought that had been weighing on him heavily for some time now. For a Mul'Ki, age was dependent on power, most of the men aged like everyone else until they were in their mid-twenties, and at that point the aging process would slow to a crawl, and depending on the strength of the gift in the Mul'Ki, it could be hundreds of years before they would progress much in age. It was rumored that Bradok had been over three thousand years old when he finally succumbed to death. This was one of the reasons that the Mul'Ki had been able to learn so much about the stars and their relationships to events here on earth. It was also why it was rare for a Mul'Ki to take a wife, or at least it had been until the flood.

In the past, the Mul'Ki were too busy seeing to the needs of the people, studying the texts from the ancients, and conducting experiments to further scientific and technological advancement to worry about love, not to mention that falling in love was never an easy task for someone who would outlive their chosen mate by hundreds of years. However, now that there were so few Atlans remaining, it seemed imperative that each of the Mul'Ki marry and have children. It was hoped that they would have a greater chance of bearing gifted children. Noahim had always known that his love for Namaah was destined to destroy him, for she would surely pass on well before him. They had been gone from Atla for so long and Noah knew that Namaah should be showing her age by now, should, in fact, be a woman entering the twilight of her life, but she was not. She was as young and radiant as ever.

Noah was not the only one that noticed this either. Jikar had pointed out that all of the other men and women from Atla had aged significantly throughout the journey, only Namaah and the Mul'Ki seemed unaffected. The citizens attributed this to some part of Noah's gift, further confirmation that he was the one, but he was not so certain. He had tried for many years before leaving Atla to discover some ancient teaching that would allow him to grow old with Namaah but had never found anything alluding to such magic. So, he had resigned himself long ago to the truth that he would grow old alone, and yet somehow Namaah did not age like the others. Noah had even asked her about it, but she simply said, "Remember my mother? She looked young for her age as well!" And that had been the end of it.

As they walked, Karok bounded from the jungle, nearly knocking Noahim over. "Calm down old friend, what is your hurry...," Noah said, trailing off. He sensed the danger before he saw it and spun around in time to see Jakon lift his hand, paralyzing Noah and Jikar in place, holding them with his Ari. "Hello Noah," Jakon said calmly, "I am here for the remaining portion of the book, the pages that you removed. No more tricks, no more games. Give me what I came here for. Before you say no...," Jakon turned and shouted something over his shoulder, and two men came from the jungle, one of them was Tarrin, holding Namaah in between their arms. "I will not hesitate, Noah, I believe that you know that."

CHAPTER THIRTY-THREE

As they trudged through the jungle following the giant black cat, Erich listened with slight amusement to the conversation now taking place between Rock and Graham. "So, what makes you so sure that the people we are looking for escaped from this great flood? I mean hell, the whole idea of a flood that covered the entire earth seems pretty crazy to me...," Rock said, breathing heavily from the exertion of carrying the large packs of equipment through the dense jungle.

"Well," Graham began, "Erich found Noah's bloody Ark, I would think that is proof enough, but since you don't seem convinced, I will see what I can do to change your mind. For starters, I find it hard to believe that all the myths of a global flood would exist if the basis of the story weren't rooted in some universal truth or memory."

Rock didn't seem impressed by this statement in the slightest, "Ya I know, there are quite a few stories about it, but stories don't mean it's true..."

"Quite a few does not begin to describe the number of Great Flood myths, or their striking similarities," Graham said in his clipped English tone. "There are over one thousand verified, and independent, myths involving a global flood from literally every continent on this planet, with the exception of Antarctica, which I believe you all know my feelings on. Can you tell me Rock, what you know of the Great Flood?"

Rock stopped walking for a moment and brought up a meaty

fist holding a canteen. He gulped down a considerably large swig, replaced the cap and wiped a small runnel of water from his stubble covered chin. "Well, I suppose I know as much as the next guy...learned most of it in Sunday school as a kid. Ya know, God told Noah to build him an arky arky...," he sang as out of tune as a human being possibly could, eliciting a small laugh from those around him, "then he went and got two animals of every kind and put them on the boat and sailed around while the earth flooded, eventually they hit a mountain...then there's something about a dove, and he and his family repopulate the world...like I said, about as far-fetched a story as I ever heard. I mean, I seen the boat, and it is freaking huge for a boat...but two of every animal...come on...?"

Graham smiled, and Erich could tell that he was enjoying this exchange. There was little that Graham enjoyed more than opening people's eyes to what he believed the real history of the world was. "Well, I will get to that matter shortly..." he said, his eyes sparkling, "but first to the story of the flood. You do have the basics correct, but did you know that the story of Noah is not the only, or even the oldest, story to follow this same plotline? For instance, the Epic of Gilgamesh, which predates the story of Genesis, states that God spoke to Utnapishtim, 'Tear down your house and build a boat, abandon all possessions and look for life, despise worldly goods and save your soul...Tear down your house, I say, and build a boat with her dimensions in proportion – her width and length in harmony. Put aboard the seed of all living things, into the boat.' Utnapishtim and his family ride out the storm in their boat and eventually come to rest on the mountains of Nisir at which time Utnapishtim releases a dove, who, finding no resting place, returns. He then releases a raven who does not return, signifying to him that it is safe to exit the boat. After exiting the boat, Utnapishtim, and his family make an offering to the gods and repopulate the earth. Pretty similar wouldn't you say old chap?" Graham said with a small smile as he continued to speak. "An almost identical story was told in the Valley of Mexico, far before the arrival of the Spanish, in an area isolated from Judeo-Christian influences. The Aztecs of this region told of a deluge, 'Destruction came in the form of torrential rain and floods. The mountains disappeared...' According to this legend, only two humans survived: a man, Coxcoxtli, and his wife, Xochiquetzal, who had been forewarned of the flood by a god. The god instructed them to build a boat, which they did, and then it came to ground on the peak of a mountain. The dove again appears in this myth and, as with Noah, two people repopulate the earth. The Mechoacanesecs also tell of a great flood. They tell the story of a man named Tezpi who was warned by the God Tezcatlipoca that the world was soon to be destroyed by a flood. Tezpi and his family embarked on a boat with a large number of animals, birds, seeds, and supplies and eventually came to rest on a mountaintop. After the waters had begun to recede, Tezpi sent out a vulture which fed on the carcasses on the land and did not return. He then sent out a number of other birds until the time that a hummingbird returned carrying a branch in his beak, just as the dove in the story of Noah and the Epic of Gilgamesh had, and Tezpi and his family left the vessel and began to repopulate the earth. Stories just like these exist in China, North America, Alaska, Australia, Africa.... Almost every civilization in history tells the story of a Great Flood, and many contain the elements of a select few being forewarned by a god, gathering animals and plants into a large boat, and landing on a mountain, followed by those select few repopulating a devastated planet and saving the human race."

They had all stopped walking and were now gathered around Graham as he spoke, his passion was infectious and hard to turn away from. "Many of the people that told these myths were isolated from one another by hundreds of years and thousands of miles...and it is not difficult to begin to see that some shared truth flows among them. I believe that the similarities in these stories are not coincidence...it is my belief that one group of people visited all of these lands that tell the tale of the giant boat with the select few, and that their legend grew. I also believe that these select few shared amazing things with the people they met that helped to shape the world as we know it...things like agriculture and architecture, religion and myth, science and technology. I believe that this ancient, advanced society planted the seeds of civilization that seemed to sprout all around the globe at basically the same time. Let's not forget that science and history have no adequate answer for how, in such a short amount of time, relatively speaking, the world went from primarily being small bands of nomadic hunters and gatherers to large societies of farmers and some of the greatest builders the world has ever known...but that is a matter for another time. You asked about how I can be so sure that there even was a global flood, and so I will continue in that vein. I am not purporting that these myths alone prove anything at all, but they are not our only evidence."

Before Graham could begin speaking again, a soft chuffing noise arose from the jungle ahead of them. Everyone turned to see Raja stalk back out of the forest, eyes focused on Erich. She opened her mouth, letting out a soft growling sound and turned to continue on her trek through the forest. Erich looked at the group gathered around Graham and took a small drink of water before saying, "Come on guys, we need to move faster. Raja seems on to something."

"Not to mention we will need to make camp soon," Mitchell said looking up into the canopy and trying to gauge the time of day. "I'm gonna guess we have an hour or so of daylight left, so let's get as far as we can. No more hiking after nightfall, we need to start being more careful."

"Careful of what, exactly?" Rock said.

Mitchell shook her head, "I haven't said anything yet...," she began, "but Graham came to me a couple of days ago and let me know that the twins believe that we are being followed. They said they can smell that the jungle has been disturbed."

Rock looked skeptical, "I haven't smelled a damn thing...," he growled.

"The twins know the jungle better than any of us, they have lived here their entire lives. If they say we are being followed, then I would tend to agree with them. Any idea who it could be?"

Mitchell looked around and shook her head slightly, "I don't really know, but it could be anyone. Someone from Malik's group, a member of a guerrilla war party, there are several of those in this jungle, or it could be a tribe that we spooked that has decided to keep tabs on us, to make sure we aren't dangerous."

"You really think it could be a tribe?" Erich asked, "Should we be worried?"

"Worried about what?" Rock said dismissively, "what are they gonna do, shoot us with their bows and arrows? Besides, they see all of our guns, they would have to know they are outmatched."

Graham interjected, "I wouldn't be so certain of that Rock. First off, they may use any manner of weapons, bow and arrow, yes, but blowguns are also a popular choice, as are spears. And don't forget that they have a deep knowledge of the forest around them and would probably have any one of those weapons coated with any number of potentially deadly toxins found in the jungle. As far as the guns, if they are an uncontacted tribe, the sight of the guns will be meaningless to them as they won't know what they are, and therefore, won't be fearful of them. And if they do attack, it is pretty difficult to shoot what you cannot see, and these warriors will not be attacking from a visible location, I'm certain of this."

Rock shouldered his automatic rifle and with a grunt said, "Well then we should let the little bastards see what one of these bad boys can do. I could mow down a tree at seventy-five yards with this thing."

"That's enough Rock," Erich said exasperated, "just put it down, okay? Let's just keep watchful. They haven't done anything to hurt us yet, maybe they are just curious. That's my guess. I can't imagine that Malik's men could have remained unnoticed for very long."

Mitchell nodded in agreement and said, "Agreed, everyone just be aware of your surroundings, okay?"

"Alright, then let's go," Erich said, and they turned to enter the jungle, Raja still leading the way.

"Now then, on to the enlightenment...," Graham said, looking over at Rock. "So...where did we leave off?"

"Basically, you were trying to teach me that a bunch of old stories that are sort of alike proves that there was a great flood." Rock said, and then smiled slightly, "And I wasn't really buying it, I mean maybe the myths are the same because, like you said, the same people told them to everyone. I think that is more likely than a flood that covered the entire earth."

"Alright then, the striking similarities in the universal flood myths do not have you convinced, so how about we move to harder evidence, shall we? For hundreds of years, archaeologists have been finding remains of marine life in places that it simply does not belong. Numerous whale skeletons have been found hundreds of miles from the coast and above sea level, a full skeleton was found north of Lake Ontario 440 feet above sea level, another in Vermont more than 500 feet above sea level, and yet another in Montreal, Quebec 600 feet above sea level. In 1981, an archeology team found walrus, seal, and at least five genera of whale in Canada at an elevation of over 4,000 feet."

Rock seemed to be taking all of this in, although he still looked skeptical. "I can see that you are still not convinced," Graham said with feigned exasperation, and Erich knew that his old friend was greatly enjoying this, "So, let us continue the lesson. When flooding has occurred and remains of plants and animals are left behind, there are signs that show the deposits could only result from flooding. Flood deposits are unique in the way that animal and plant remains are often tangled together and then covered with a sand, known as "flood mud." These deposits are found on every continent, except Antarctica, although I would wager that, at some point, they will be found there as well, and are most often a mixture of ice age animals and plants. While exploring Alaska, a famed archeologist by the name of F. Rainey, upon encountering a flood deposit stated, 'We found evidence of atmospheric disturbance of unparalleled violence...The animals were simply torn apart and scattered over the landscape like things of straw and string, even though some of them weighed several tons. Mixed with piles of bones are trees, also twisted and torn and piled in tangled groups; and the whole is covered with a fine sifting muck, then frozen solid' which I think allows us a pretty clear picture of the devastation that this flood caused."

Rock shook his head, seemingly trying to shake off the idea that Graham could be right. He raised a hand to swat at the ever-present bugs that hovered and bit his exposed skin and grumbled, "So, if all of this stuff is proof that it happened, why don't they teach us this in school? What would people have to gain by teaching the wrong stuff and...why do all the other scientists call you a quack?"

At this, Graham laughed a little bit, "Well let's not forget that at one time the mainstream scientific community believed that anyone who thought the earth was not flat was a quack. This is the same mainstream scientific community that tried to kill Copernicus for stating that it was the sun that was the center of the solar system and not the earth. Science by its very nature is flawed, and will always be only as right as the current methods of testing allow it to be, and each time a significant discovery is made, there is bound to be resistance. For one thing, many men and women have staked their reputation on the previous truth, so when someone proposes that they are wrong, it does not typically sit well with the establishment, hence my label as a quack." Graham said with a mock bow, "They say quack, I say revolutionary free-thinker..."

"Potato, potata..." Rock said with a small laugh.

"Precisely," Graham said, "and to answer your question, I would say that the reason the scientific community's at large has failed to embrace any of these alternate ideas of our history is that they choose to continue to work with blinders on, blinders in the name of Plate Tectonic theory."

This statement caught Rock completely off guard, "What the hell does plate tectonics have to do with anything?"

"Well nothing to be precise, but the blind adherence to an obviously flawed theory has caused most scientists to discount the idea of a global flood because they feel there would be no force great enough to cause a disturbance of the magnitude required to flood the entire earth, which is true if one is to accept plate tectonic theory. As you probably know, plate tectonics suggests that the earth's crust sits on a series of plates that slowly relocate over millions of years. This theory refined the previous theory of continental drift and has been the favorite of the general scientific community for the last forty or so years. There are multiple problems that neither of these theories can explain, and in response to this, Charles Hapgood wrote a book titled, Earth's Shifting Crust, a Key to Some Basic Problems of Earth Science. Hapgood was a professor and member of Franklin Roosevelt's cabinet, and in his book, he developed an alternate theory to how our earth works that he named Earth Crust Displacement Theory or ECD. In Hapgood's mind, there were too many things that continental drift, which would eventually become plate tectonics, did not address. Hapgood believed that the earth's crust had gone through many rapid, and drastic, shifts, moving the entire surface of the earth thousands of miles in a matter of years."

"So, you're going to try and prove to me that you aren't a quack by quoting the theory of a different quack...," Rock said with a chuckle, "you see any problem with this Doc?"

"There was one notable contemporary of Hapgood's that happened to believe so strongly in the theory that he wrote the foreword to Hapgood's book, stating, among other things, 'I find your arguments very impressive and have the impression that your hypothesis is correct. One can hardly doubt that significant shifts of the crust of the earth have taken place repeatedly and within a short time.' Does that help convince you?"

"I guess that depends on who this contemporary was because it could just be a quack, advocating for the quack, that you, also an avowed quack, are advocating for."

This garnered a big smile from Graham, "Well, the quack in question happens to be Albert Einstein...is his opinion valid enough for you my dear boy?"

Rock stared at Graham, "Albert freakin' Einstein, ya, I suppose that'll do. Tell me about this theory and how it could cause your great flood."

Graham stopped walking and took a drink of water from his canteen and then offered it to Rock and Erich, who both declined. "Well, Hapgood states that an ECD would result in mass melting of polar ice caps, as the poles will have shifted to much warmer climates. Earthquakes would devastate the land and cause tidal waves and tsunamis. Much of the surface of the earth would become submerged by flood waters and animals would be forced to move to higher ground to survive, which sounds familiar, doesn't it? The result of a displacement would be widespread devastation, as once temperate lands were thrust into Polar Regions and Polar Regions were changed to warmer climates." Graham paused momentarily before continuing, "There is substantial evidence that supports Hapgood's theory. One of the most convincing arguments for ECD is the rapid deglaciation seen at the end of the last ice age. At the peak of the ice age, around 19,000 BC, there were approximately 6 million cubic miles of ice in the Northern Hemisphere and extensive glaciation of the Southern Hemisphere as well. Although this ice cap is estimated to have taken 40,000 years to develop, it disappeared for the most part in 2,000 years. Modern-day geologists have no convincing theory on how this rapid deglaciation took place. Currently, it is believed to have been the work of global warming, although other than the ice melting there is absolutely no known cause, or any proof, that climate change took place. This ice melt would have caused a rise in sea levels of over 350 feet causing the vast majority of coastal lands to be covered in water and allowing tidal waves to reach much farther inland. So, with Hapgood's theory, the cause of the ice caps melting was that the Polar Regions themselves were thrust very quickly into a temperate zone. The evidence that led Hapgood to believe that this event took place can be found in Siberia. Hapgood maintains that prior to the ECD, Siberia was not at the pole and that it moved rapidly to its current arctic location. Vast numbers of large mammals found buried in the Siberian permafrost led Hapgood to propose ECD. By far, the most plentiful mammal buried in this frozen wasteland is the wooly mammoth. There are so many mammoths buried in the permafrost of the New Siberian Islands that an early explorer of them described them as 'Being composed more of the bones and tusks of mammoth than of dirt and rock.' In fact, Siberia has been exporting mammoth ivory at an estimated rate of over 20,000 tusks per decade for over 500 years. As of this time, nothing grows in this area of Siberia, except for some scrub brush and a one-inch tall willow tree. And no, I did not misspeak, a one-inch tall willow tree. There would have been no way for the overwhelming number of mammoths that have been unearthed to have survived in a climate that was not lush with vegetation. If you think of the demands of food that an elephant herd requires, you can get an idea of the amount of vegetation that these incredibly large herds of even larger animals would have needed. Many of the mammoths and other mammals found frozen in the perma-frost do not exhibit signs of a slow death from climate change or starvation, in fact, a large number of the mammoths that have been unearthed still have undigested food in their stomachs and mouths, suggesting that death came swiftly and rapidly to these great beasts. Along with the mammoths that have been found are at least thirty-four other species of mammals, of these, only six were adapted to arctic conditions, the other twenty-eight needing a temperate climate to survive. Plate tectonics theory suggests that it would have taken this area millions of years to shift from a temperate climate to the arctic wasteland that it has become, but the animals buried in the permafrost tell a different story. The perplexing array of warm weather adapted animals found en-tombed in the ice of Siberia and Alaska, many with their last meals still in their mouth, speak more of a tragedy that took place devastatingly quickly."

Rock scratched at the stubble on his chin and spoke, "And so you think that what happened to those mammoths in Siberia hap-pened to an entire civilization in Antarctica...only it didn't use to be Antarctica, it used to be more like South America, at least cli-mate-wise...and was turned into an arctic wasteland and buried in ice after a flood covered the earth..."

Graham nodded his head approvingly, "That, my dear boy, is exactly what I think."

CHAPTER THIRTY-FOUR

"This is far enough for today, we better set up camp here." Mitchell barked as the group came to a small clearing beside the great Amazon River. The twins and Nagato spread out into the surrounding jungle, as had become their habit each time the team made camp, to search for food.

"I'm gonna go and gather some firewood, anyone want to join me?" Erich asked to no one in particular. At the sound of his voice, Raja came sauntering into the camp and rubbed against Erich's legs, purring with satisfaction. Erich looked down at his companion and said, "Well, I was thinking more like anyone that could help carry it, but you can definitely come along too, Raja."

"Ya, I wouldn't say no to her if I were you," Rock grumbled, "I'll come along too, Padre."

"As will I," Graham said nodding toward Rock, "It will give me a chance to enlighten our friend here further as to why it is I am so certain that we are on the right path."

"Sounds good to me," Erich said turning to Mitchell, "Are you and Paulus ok here by yourselves?"

"Ya, I think we can handle the excitement," Mitchell said sarcastically.

As they walked off into the jungle, Rock said, "So, let's just say that you're right about all of it...about displacement, about the flood, Atlantis buried in the ice...it still doesn't make sense to me that it would be these same people. How would they have gotten so far inland with these giant boats for one thing?"

Graham smiled and nodded, "That's an easy question to answer...they came up the river."

"In boats the size of the one that Erich found in Indonesia?" Rock asked flatly.

"Yes of course," Graham said, "the Amazon is no typical river. Did you know that it is the largest river by volume in the world, and by water discharge? In fact, it discharges more water than the next seven largest rivers combined. At the mouth of the Amazon it is over one hundred and fifty miles wide, and even in the dry season, it is up to ninety feet deep, sometimes deeper. Even in modern day, large ocean boats have managed to make it two-thirds or more of the way up its entire length. It really isn't hard to assume that the survivors of this great civilization could have made it up the river, especially if they possessed the types of powers that Paulus has alluded to."

"Well, don't get me started on that," Rock said with a snort, "I don't believe all of that magic stuff."

Erich chimed in for the first time now, "You know I saw Paulus rip a door from a wall with his mind, right?"

"At least that's what you think you saw...," Rock said, letting his statement hang in the air.

"And what do make of Raja?" Erich asked.

"How the hell should I know?" Rock said with a small laugh, "Maybe she's an escaped pet...or a former circus animal...that makes more sense than magic."

"If that's what you truly think then why did you agree to follow her, to allow all of us to follow her, into the jungle?" Erich said.

"Because we got nothing better," Rock grunted, "and who knows, maybe she knows something we don't. Look, I'm not saying you're wrong Erich, I wasn't there, I don't know what you saw. I've just never seen anything like that with my own eyes, so it's pretty hard for me to believe it."

"Maybe it isn't magic...think of it more like technology we don't understand."

"I'm not following ya," Rock said, a quizzical look on his face.

"Ok, think of going back in time, even just one or two hundred years ago, and trying to show the people of that time a cell phone and what it is capable of. Take video chatting as an example. They would have no basis in the technology of your day, so how would you describe what it does?" Graham asked.

"I would tell them that you turn the phone on, press a button and call the person you want to talk to, it's not that hard." Rock said flatly.

"Right," Graham said, "but they wouldn't understand what any of that meant because they don't know what a call is, they don't know what a video is, do you see the problem? To them, it would basically appear as though you had a piece of glass that allowed you to communicate with a piece of glass that someone else had. The two pieces of glass could connect to one another if you both look at it at the same time and you would be able to see and talk to the other person anytime from anywhere...and if you were in a situation that did not allow you the ability to speak out loud, you could simply write a message on your piece of glass and that message would appear simultaneously on the other person's piece of glass. Don't you think that this would seem like magic?"

Rock seemed to think about it for a moment before answering, "Well, I suppose so. But that's not really the same as moving things with your mind. A phone is technology...that stuff is just...well, magic..."

Graham smiled and said, "Well Rock, maybe magic is just technology that we don't understand yet. Arthur C. Clarke said that."

Erich listened, quite fascinated, to this debate. He had to admit that just a few weeks ago he would have fallen firmly on Rock's side of the argument, but things had definitely changed. Erich knew what he had seen Paulus do, and he knew that somehow Raja was here trying to lead them to their goal. He couldn't even really say how he knew it, but he did. Thinking of Raja, he looked around to see where she was now and realized that she was nowhere to be seen. "Hey guys," he said interrupting Rock and Graham's continuing conversation, "Did either of you notice where Raja went?"

"I am sure that she just ran off to do a little hunting...," Graham said, although he didn't sound all that sure. Rock, on the other hand, cupped his hands to his mouth, preparing to yell out her name, when Erich noticed a trickle of smoke further into the forest. He placed his hand up in front of Rock's face and silently shushed the big man. Obviously, they were not alone in the forest, and considering that they had been trying to intercept Malik's group, Erich assumed they better move forward with great caution.

"Listen," he whispered, "There's some smoke up there, I want to go check it out and see what I can find, but I think you two should just wait here for me. If something is up, I will come back and get you and we can regroup, I just don't want to take the chance of making extra noise with all three of us going through the jungle." Rock looked unsure, but Erich didn't wait for him to agree, with a small smile, he turned and sprinted into the jungle.

After running through the jungle towards the smoke for about ten minutes, he was rejoined by Raja, which definitely brought Erich some comfort knowing that the big cat would be there if he needed help. He had a fleeting moment of elation thinking that the source of the fire could be the lost village, and they would be that much closer to Gema, but he did not allow himself to get his hopes up. More than likely, it was just one of the many different Amazonian tribes that lived in this massive jungle, but it was better to be safe than sorry.

As Erich drew nearer to the source of the fire, Raja began to act strangely, *Well, strange for a giant black jaguar who has decided to befriend me and lead me through the jungle,* he thought to himself. She started by getting in front of Erich, making a soft mewling sound and trying to push him forward with her head. It was clear that she wanted him to continue to move forward through the jungle, but even with her prompting, he felt caution was the best approach. He decided to climb up a tree to see if he could get a better look at the source of the fire.

What Erich saw shocked him...it was not the lost city, it was instead a camp with several small tents and hammocks covered with mosquito netting. There must have been forty or fifty men wandering around the camp, most of them wearing military fatigues, and all of them carrying weapons. Not that he needed the confirmation, but as he watched, a man stepped out of one of the tents. Erich could make out Malik's bald head as he spoke with the other man, pointing in the direction away from Erich's camp and saying something animatedly.

Erich was too far away to hear what the men said to one another so he tried to crawl out further on a branch to see if he could make it out. As he looked down from his perch in the tree, he saw Raja stalking back and forth at the edge of the small camp. She looked agitated. Erich turned to see if he could tell what had the cat so worked up, and when he did, his hand grasped a weak branch that snapped under his weight. Instantly, forty guns were pointed in the direction of the tree. Erich froze and awaited the barrage of bullets, but before the men opened fire, Erich heard shouting from the camp.

The shouting grew louder he heard the sound of automatic rifle chatter, but the leaves around him did not shake with the passing of bullets. He ventured a look below and saw that Raja had burst into the camp when he broke the limb, so all of the men in the camp were focused on the giant black jaguar who had sprung into their midst. There were two men lying on the ground, clearly dead from wounds that Raja had inflicted. The men continued to fire at her, but she sprang back into the jungle, letting loose a deafening roar.

While the men all focused their attention on Raja, Erich quickly climbed down out of the tree. He wanted to get back to the camp and let Mitchell know what he had found, formulate a plan to come and rescue Gema; but he didn't want to leave Raja behind in the hands of these monsters. If there was any way that he could help, he knew that he should. As he tried to make his way closer to the clearing, Raja burst out from the undergrowth, knocking him down and landing on top of him. Her enormous feline head just inches from Erich's face. "Good job, girl," Erich whispered as he scratched behind her ears, "you saved my life, we need to go back and get the others, we need to save Gema."

CHAPTER THIRTY-FIVE

Rashan stood at the edge of the clearing and he could not believe his eyes. There was a man dressed in robes of red and gold standing in the midst of dozens of other men dressed in all black. The man in red held his hand in front of him, and it seemed he somehow was controlling Rashan's father, paralyzing him in place. Rashan knew of the immense power that his father could wield, and could not begin to contemplate the power that it would take to hold him motionless like this. A thousand thoughts ran through his mind at the same time. *Who was this man? Where had he come from? Was he somehow an Atlan? What did he want?* All of those thoughts went silent as Rashan saw two more men emerge from the jungle holding his mother between them. He unleashed a primordial scream and ran from the cover of the jungle towards the gathered men.

Jakon heard the yell and turned his head just in time to see Rashan running across the clearing, sword still in hand. The sight of the young boy running towards him, ready to fight seemed to amuse Jakon, who simply made a small motion with his head and two men split off from the pack and went to intercept Rashan. As they approached, both men split their staffs to reveal the black, glass-like blades hidden within them. They brandished their swords menacingly as their RaSheen took up positions on their sides, crouching, ready to pounce.

Rashan was not intimidated and continued his headlong dash. As he came nearer to the men, one of the RaSheen, a smaller mountain lion, took two bounding steps and leaped at Rashan. The boy quickly dove to the ground, tucking into a roll and avoiding the attacking cat's claws by mere inches. As he rolled under the beast, he spun and lashed out with his sword, catching the RaSheen with a direct blow to the chest. He felt his blade make solid contact and pulled it free, rolling to his feet without missing a single step.

The blow to the RaSheen proved to be fatal, and the cat fell to the ground in a heap, his Mul'Ki stumbled in response to the pain he felt from his companion. As the man fell to one knee, Rashan lashed out with his sword, slicing the man across the neck. Using his momentum, Rashan placed one foot on the man's back and leapt forward towards the other man, who seemed to be so caught off guard by the flurry of violence unleashed by this mere child that he hadn't moved at all. As Rashan flew through the air, he spotted movement on his left and turned to see the remaining man's RaSheen springing towards him. Undeterred, Rashan swung his sword in a high arc, bringing it down on the top of the man's head. The blow was so strong that the sword buried itself into the thick bone of the man's skull, the RaSheen collapsing from the air in mid-spring as its life force was extinguished alongside its Mul'ki's.

Rashan did not stop to retrieve his sword from the man's head, in which it was stuck, choosing instead to go into another roll when he hit the ground. As he rolled, he reached his hand to his back and pulled out the small curved dagger that he kept tucked there at all times. He sprang to his feet mere inches from the man in red and placed the razor-sharp blade across the man's throat. Sweat glistened on his arms as he tensed his muscles, barely able to restrain himself from finishing the deed and spoke in a low, threatening whisper, "Let my mother go, or you will die."

Jakon's lip curled as he spoke, "I do not take orders from children," he spat as hc lifted his other hand and using his Ari lifted Rashan into the air and hurled him backward. The boy hit a tree that stood at the clearing edge and crumpled to the ground. As Jakon returned his attention to Noah, he realized he had made a mistake. The boy's intention was not to actually try and harm him. Instead, it was meant only as a distraction. Jakon sensed more, then saw the dark shadow close in on him, and braced himself. The impact was much greater than he had anticipated and he was knocked to the ground, the full weight of Karok landing on his back, his massive claws digging deeply into his flesh.

Noahim and Jikar were released from the magic that held them. Noah looked into Namaah's eyes and found resolve there. Namaah gave a slight nod with her head in the direction that Rashan had flown when he hit the tree. Noah knew that she was right, he would come back for her, Rashan may have sustained grave injuries that required his attention. He sprinted towards his fallen son, turning just long enough to see Jikar battling with ten of the men from Jakon's force, their RaSheen all stalking around him, trying to find a way past his blade. Jikar used a mixture of outstanding swordsmanship and his Ari' to stave off the hungry pack of cats while he advanced on the men that he once called brothers.

Noah feared for his friend's safety but knew that he must focus on Rashan, first and foremost. Jikar had learned much from Noah since the group had fled Atla, and Noahim was certain that his power matched, if not exceeded, every man on the plain, save he and Jakon. As Noah slid to a stop at the forest edge, a small sob escaped his throat, Rashan was lying at on add angle, blood pooling from a wound on his head. "Rashan, my son, please speak to me...," Noahim pleaded.

Rashan's eyelids flickered once, then again, and slowly his eyes opened to half-slits. He looked up at his father through a tangle of blood-soaked hair and a small smile crept onto his face. "I guess it worked?" he croaked, "I knew Karok would know what I was doing. Does that man still have my mother?"

"Do not worry about that now son, your mother will be fine. Just lie still while I heal you," he said as he extended his palms towards the wound on his only son's head. Noah's hands began to glow, and he felt his power surge through him and into Rashan. The wound began to close itself, and as Noah watched, color came back to Rashan's skin and his breathing leveled out from the harsh rasping that it had been. Rashan struggled to sit up, but his father held a hand on his chest. "Wait here son, you will be fine now. I am going to go and save your mother." With that, Noah turned and left Rashan lying at the edge of the clearing and ran back into the heart of the fight.

Things had gone from bad to worse for Jikar. Noahim could see that he had a severe wound on one arm, it looked as though the cut was so deep his arm would fall off at any moment, but still, he held his own. Scattered all around Jikar's beaten and bloodied form were men and great cats lying dead. Noahim could not even count how many there were, although it looked as though only four men remained. Nuni could be seen bouncing in and out of the melee, screaming with anger and trying to blind the men by gouging their eyes or using his superior agility to trip them.

Noah searched the area for Namaah but did not see her anywhere. It was just then that he realized he also did not see Jakon. He ran towards Jikar and the men left fighting, drawing his sword as he did, and leapt into the midst of them. As he landed, he swung his sword straight down, planting it into the ground. A blast of power emanated from the spot where he landed and threw all four men and their RaSheen to the ground. Noah straddled one of the men and screamed at him, "Where did Jakon take my wife?!" Spit flew from his mouth as he screamed at the man, who simply smiled and brought up a small dagger from his belt. Before Noah even had time to react the man had plunged it into his own heart, his leopard RaSheen collapsing beside him.

Jikar looked at Noah, stunned, ready to ask the next man, when they heard a deafening roar from the jungle beyond the clearing. "That was Karok," Noah said to Jikar, "He must be on their trail. Go and ensure everyone else is safe, take Rashan with you, I will meet you back at the temple."
"Of course, brother," Jikar said and clapped Noah on the back, "Be careful, he is more powerful than he used to be." Noahim said nothing. He simply nodded at Jikar and ran into the depths of the jungle, determined to save Namaah...and kill Jakon.

CHAPTER THIRTY-SIX

Paulus looked to his left and saw the twins both crouched in the shadows. To his right, Rock lay in a prone position, pointing a small sub-machine gun towards Malik's camp. Mitchell, Nagato, and Erich should all be in position on the opposite side of the camp now, along with Raja. Graham sat crouched behind a tree beside Rock, using both hands to hold tightly to a small pistol. Erich had wanted Graham to stay behind, but he had insisted on coming. It was a starless night under the canopy of the great rainforest, and the plan was to get in and out with Gema and Sophia without alerting Malik and his men, although, as Mitchell had said, things don't often go as planned, so they had come heavily armed.

They had been watching the camp for the better part of the day, trying to discern where Gema and Sophia were being held, as well as doing recon on the enemy forces and armaments. Malik's men outnumbered them ten to one and were better equipped, which is why they had chosen stealth as their best option. In a firefight, Erich was almost certain they would lose. Rock, on the other hand, had been all for going in guns blazing, and he was certain that, while there were more men in the other camp, they could not match the skill of the fighters that stood with Erich. Mitchell had been quick to point out that a battle between Malik and his men not only risked the lives of Erich and the others, but also of Gema and Sophia, and it would be incredibly easy for them to be caught in the crossfire, and with that, Rock reluctantly agreed to this more subdued approach.

The camp was laid out in a circle. In the innermost section of the circle were two large cabin style tents. The one that held Gema and Sophia was guarded by five men with machine guns; the other belonged to Malik and had a single man posted by the door. The outer area of the circle was lined with ten sets of hammocks covered in mosquito netting. Small campfires dotted the interior in multiple places, although most of them had been reduced to small piles of glowing embers at this point, which served Erich and his team well. Paulus turned to look at the twins beside him one more time and gave a single, small nod of his head. The two men in unison nodded back and slid from the jungle's edge into the camp, crouched low, and gliding like spirits in the night.

From the opposite side of the camp, Erich's heart leapt into his throat as he watched the twins silently pick their way through the camp. When the twins reached the outer edge of hammocks, Erich reached down and placed one hand on Raja's back. She was tensed, ready to pounce, her head low to the ground and her back raised, muscles quivering beneath Erich's hand. Erich gave her a gentle nudge which was all that she needed, and she stalked into the camp, head low, eyes glowing green.

Unlike the twins, Erich and Mitchell hung in the shadows, as Raja strode directly into the center of the camp. After seeing Malik's men's reactions to the giant cat earlier in the day, the plan had been to use Raja to lure the majority of the forces to the outer edge of the camp, while the twins dispatched the guards at the tent...and anyone else who didn't follow after Raja. During the ensuing chaos, Erich and Mitchell would free Gema and Sophia. Paulus, Nagato, and Graham would all stay to the edge of the camp, ready to spring into action if there was any trouble, that way the entire group wouldn't be surrounded if Malik's men found them out.

Erich exhaled the breath he was holding in and turned his attention to Mitchell who simply gave him a half smile, a quick wink, and ran in a crouch to the nearest row of hammocks, pausing only momentarily to give Erich an all-clear hand signal and proceed closer to the tents in the center of camp.

Erich broke from the jungle cover and picked his way to where Mitchell was now crouched, her back against one of the large cabin tents, gun held at the ready. Raja had made her way to the far side of the camp now, and Erich watched as she turned and planted both front paws firmly in the dirt, arching her back and letting out a roar that seemed to shake the earth. Two men that had been standing close to Raja when she roared opened fire. Erich could see clumps of dirt flying as the two men strafed the area with reckless abandon. He could not see Raja any longer, which he assumed was a good thing, it should also mean that the men couldn't see her either.

As more men ran towards the area of the gunfire, the twins quickly swept in from the shadows. Staying low to the ground and not making a sound, they each jumped onto the back of one of the men guarding Gema and Sophia's tent. The twins placed a hand over the men's mouths and an arm around their neck, using the weight of their bodies to pull down and force the flow of air in the men to shut off. After several seconds, the men both stumbled to a knee and then collapsed all the way to the ground. The twins pulled the men into the shadows of the tents and prepared to take care of the three guards that remained on the other side of the tent.

These men were still distracted by the gunfight on the other side of the camp and did not hear as the twins drew their swords. They carried two curved swords, slung across their backs in an X. The twins flung themselves into the midst of the three men, spinning and slashing with both hands. It was as though the twins were one, and they had but one mission, bring swift, silent death. It was a chilling sight. In a matter of seconds the twins stopped moving, and the men that had been guarding the tent all lay in growing pools of blood, slashed through their throats and missing various appendages.

Mitchell turned with wide eyes to Erich, she also hadn't anticipated the damage the twins could inflict in such a short amount of time. She gave a quick nod and held her hand up, using it to motion to Erich that she would lead the way into the tent, and

Erich should follow, covering their backs. The twins stood beside the front of the tent now, swords back in their sheaths, neither of them even breathing hard from the violence they had just unleashed on the men. One of them gave Erich a subtle nod and turned, continuing to watch for any men that may be coming back. Erich now realized that the gunfire had stopped, and he feared that meant that the men had shot and killed Raja, but he had no time to worry about that now as he ran forward towards the tent that his love was in.

Mitchell lifted the mosquito netting that covered the entire tent above her head and reached up to untie the string keeping the flap of the tent together. She locked eyes with Erich one last time, and they both rushed into the tent. The scene inside the tent made such little sense to Erich that he, at first, couldn't quite realize what he was looking at. There, in the center of the floor, sat Sophia, her hands held in front of her, a small glass diamond-shaped object floating a foot above the floor and spinning much like a top. From its core, light emanated and, all around the tent, it appeared as though Erich were looking at the night sky, although this was like no sky that he had ever before seen, there were many more stars, and they were much brighter than he could remember ever seeing.

As he and Mitchell entered the room, Gema, who had been laying on a cot off to the side of the tent, jumped up and threw her arms protectively around the small girl. The diamond dropped to the floor, the night sky disappearing and light filling the room from a lantern that had not been visible when they first entered. "Please," she said, her voice like music to Erich, "do not hurt us..." she whispered.

"Gema," Erich stammered in a low voice, "It's me...it's Erich." He looked directly at her as he spoke and slowly she lifted her eyes to meet his gaze. As soon as their eyes met, the fear in her face melted and she leapt forward, throwing her arms around him with such force that he almost fell backward out of the tent. She kissed him hard as he brought his hands up to her face, holding her there, kissing her back, his heart exploding with love. Finally, after several seconds they broke from their embrace, and as they did, Erich noted the bruising all over her face and several large cuts that appeared to be from being struck with something. "You're hurt Gem...," he said.

She slid her hand into his and spoke, her voice wavering at first but growing stronger with each word, "I have never felt better...you came for me...for us...I love you, Erich. I have always loved you...," she paused and took a steadying breath as she turned to face Sophia, who still sat silently in the center of the tent. "Sophie," she whispered, "this is Erich...he is your father."

Erich's eyes went wide. His head swam and he felt as though he might black out. Mitchell's voice brought him back to reality, "Plot twist..." she said with a soft chuckle.

"Gem...are...are you sure?," Erich asked, still holding her.

"You are the only man I have ever been with Erich, I am sure, she is your daughter, she has your eyes..."

Erich turned to Sophia, and saw the steely resolve on the small girls face. "We must leave," she whispered in a small voice, "This man will stop at nothing. I have learned much from the book he had me translate, things that no one has known for countless generations...it is our duty to protect this information. We must leave."

Erich looked at Sophia, it was hard to rectify the child that stood before him with the words that she spoke. "Sophia has always had a way with words," Gema said smiling, "for one so young, she can sometimes be very wise."

"Well, I agree with the kid," Mitchell said, "we've been in here for too long, we need to get out of here before all hell breaks loose...pardon the language...," she said as she shot Sophia a glance. The child simply smiled and grasped her mother's hand, as Erich and Mitchell each stood to one side of the tent opening, weapons held firm. Mitchell leaned her head through the opening and made the all-clear sign, ducking through and motioning for the others to follow. Erich reached back and took Gema's hand, looking her in the eye and letting her know that he would never lose her again, and the three ran through the tent opening and into the night.

CHAPTER THIRTY-SEVEN

Noahim ran through the trees, using his Ari to aid his flight. He could hear Karok's distant roars and followed the sound, trying to catch up to the men that had his wife. Branches tore at his face and clothes leaving a small trail of blood, but he did not slow. The forest beside him was a blur, he was sure he had never moved so fast in all of his life. Ahead, he could see the giant stretch of the river where the Atlans had built their new home.

He continued his reckless pursuit, straining to hear the roar of Karok, but no sound reached him. He reached out to Karok with his mind, to speak to his RaSheen, but found that was not necessary as Karok came bounding out of the jungle.

He came to a stop in front of Noah, blocking his path. Noahim stopped and put his hands on his knees, breathing heavily. He looked up at Karok and through his ragged breath said, "Is she gone, old friend?" the only response he received was the great cat lowering his head and walking forward, nuzzling his head into his hand. Noah broke, sinking to his knees, he wrapped his arms around Karok. He had failed, Jakon had escaped with his love. As he sat sobbing on the ground, he heard a noise from behind and spun around ready to defend himself. Behind him stood Rashan, a look of terror in the boy's eyes.

Rashan slowly sank beside his father and put his arm around him, "It will be alright father. We will find this man, together."

Noah turned his eyes toward his son and saw the look of determination on his face, and in his weakened state, grew strong.

He picked himself up off the ground and took a deep breath, turning to face Rashan, "You are right my son, we will find her, this much I promise you. We need to go and speak with Jikar, we have work to do before we leave." The two of them made their way through the jungle and back to the temple in the center of the new Atla, where Jikar was waiting for them.

Upon seeing the two of them Jikar began to smile, but when Namaah did not appear with them, his smile quickly faded. "He escaped?" Jikar asked, "How is that possible?"

Noahim looked between Jikar, Rashan, and Amare and said simply, "I do not know. Jakon has learned much about the gift while they have been gone, and it is obvious that his gift has grown stronger. He must have used his new-found powers to hide from my sight, and my gift, I do not know how, though. For now, all that matters is that we find Jakon and Namaah before it is too late."

"Well, of course, that is all that matters, but where do we even begin?" Jikar asked, "We have no idea where Jakon is going..."

"Actually, I think we may," Noahim interrupted, "before Rashan charged from the jungle and attacked Jakon I had just begun to tell him that the secret to the Ari'Yet was not here, that it, in fact, was hidden at multiple places spread far across the globe. I had done this fearing that, at some point, Jakon would return, and he must never possess the true Ari'Yet. If he does, there will be no stopping him. With that information, I believe he will try to torture...," Noahim paused and swallowed hard as he said the last word, "Namaah, in hopes that she will reveal where he can find the secrets. My only hope is that Namaah knows that I will stop at nothing to find them. So, I hope that she will go along with Jakon and tell him where he can find the other books, knowing that we will intercept them at some point on this journey. This will not be an easy task. Jakon has had years to amass an army and has clearly spent his time learning more about his gift and how to harness greater power, but I believe that we can win. We must stop him!"

Jikar, Rashan, and Amare all stated their agreement, Jikar being the first to speak, "I will go and tell my wife that I must leave...will we be leaving tonight?"

Noahim looked at his oldest and closest friend and placed a hand on his shoulder, "Jikar you are my most trusted ally, and I have come to rely on you for more than you know, but you cannot make this journey with me. I need you to stay here and protect the people of Atla, to continue the training of the children in the ways of the Mul'Ki, and to keep a watchful eye on the skies so that we will be ready to use the machines when we must. We have given up so much to build the machines, and now that they are ready, I need someone with your gifts to stay here and take care of the people and the machines. I hope that you understand."

Jikar looked at his friend and embraced him, "Noah, you are my dearest friend, you are a brother to me, and I cannot imagine allowing you to go on this journey alone, but you are my high priest, and I will respect your wishes."

"He will not be going alone," Rashan whispered, a look of anger in his eyes, "I will be lending my sword and my gift to this fight."

"As will I!" stated Amare loudly.

"Boys, I understand your desire to help, but I cannot permit you to come with me on this journey, it will be far too dangerous," Noah said.

"I am sorry, father," Rashan said, his voice growing stronger, "but this man took my mother, and I will not allow him to take my father too, not without a fight. I am coming with you." As Rashan finished speaking, one of Karok's cubs that had become particularly fond of Rashan came and sat beside him, nuzzling his head into the boy's hand, the same way that Karok had done for so many years to Noah, and let out a small roar. Rashan looked down at the small cat and gave him a smile, "And you can come too, Ali'Ra..."

"Ali'Ra?" Noahim asked, "I did not realize you had given this little one a name...you named him after the Star God of destruction..."

"Yes, I did...because she will bring destruction to all those that stand in our way," Rashan said. "She is my RaSheen."

"Indeed, she is," Noahim said, "and it is a fitting name. If she is anything like her father, she will be a greatly feared warrior," and with this, Karok let out a roar. "That still leaves you, Amare. I am certain your mother and father will not agree to you coming on this dangerous journey."

"If you will not allow me to go, brother," Jikar said, "nothing would please me more than to lend my son's sword to your journey. After all, he is already better with steel than any of us. I trust that he can handle himself."

Noahim looked between Jikar and Amare and shook his head, "Then I gladly accept your sword Amare, go and tell your mother goodbye...we leave by nightfall. Jakon has an advantage of more men and the ability to block us from seeing him with our Ari, but I know where he will be heading. I do not know where he will go first, so we must hurry and try to beat him to the sites where I have left the pages. If we can get there before him, we may yet still be able to stop him. Jikar, help me ready one of the boats, and I need a crew of forty men and provisions to last us as long as possible. I fear this will be a long journey."

"Right away high priest, but before you go speak to your mother Amare, I have something to say." Jikar paused to clear his throat, "I cannot in good conscience send you into battle alone. I know that you will have Noah and Rashan, but a Mul'Ki is not fully prepared without a RaSheen. I want you to take Nuni, he will protect you. Have Noah teach you how to communicate with him, how to understand the ways that he tries to communicate with you. It is the greatest gift I can give you. Nuni has saved my life more times than I can count, I give his service to you until your return." Upon hearing this, the little monkey scurried onto Jikar's shoulder and placed his tiny hands one on each side of his face, looking intently into Jikar's eyes for a few seconds, and then he jumped through the air and landed lightly on Amare's shoulder, chattering into the boy's ear and tousling his hair.

"So, it is settled then," Noahim said with conviction, "The three of us will leave before nightfall. Jikar, I promise to bring your son home safely...along with my wife and son. Jakon will pay for what he has done here."

"I know that you will Noah," Jikar said as he embraced his oldest friend, "May Ratam light your path and bring you all home safe."

CHAPTER THIRTY-EIGHT

Erich, Gema, and Sophia made their way from the tent and out into the night. The glow from the few remaining embers of the campfires cast small pools of light in the darkness. Erich could just make out Mitchell ahead of them, making hand motions to the twins, both of them drew their swords again and prepared to head out. Erich took another look around the camp and couldn't believe that they were going to make it, they had done it. They had decided that if they were able to reach Gema and Sophia, they would try to go straight through the center of the camp with them and past the place where Paulus and Graham were still waiting in hiding. This would be a much faster escape, and there would be less chance of making noise than in the surrounding jungle.

As they crouched and walked, Erich's every sense was on high alert. He could hear all of the insects in the surrounding jungle, the crunch of a military-booted foot of one of the mercenaries, the wind rustling leaves in the canopy far above. He could smell the musty earth, the everlasting cycle of decomposition and growth from the jungle beyond, the smoke from the fires. He could taste the fear that they would be caught. As they moved further throughout the camp, he found that he was holding his breath, too wary of making any noise. He slowly released the air from his lungs and drew in a deep, calming breath. *Halfway there,* he thought to himself.

He thought that he was just able to make out Paulus sitting at the edge of the camp, staring intently at them, but it could have just been a shadow. The darkness of night made it easy for his eyes to play tricks on him. As they inched slowly forward, Erich noticed that many of the men that had gone after Raja were returning, all of them speaking to each other in the same strange language that he had heard at the Ark. There was something familiar about that language, but this was definitely not the time to figure it out. Right now, Erich's only thought was of getting everyone to safety, and he felt like that opportunity was closing with each passing second as the guards drew nearer.

They were just ten yards from the edge of the camp and Erich was certain that they were all now holding their breath. His legs were shaking and burning from their slow crouching crawl to the forest, and his lungs ached to take a deep breath. He felt like a swimmer that had dived to the very edge of his abilities and was now desperately trying to stay alive until he could reach the surface. Five yards now, the distance seemed to be an eternity away. Erich had never wanted anything in his life as badly as he wanted to make it safely to the forest edge with Gema and his daughter.

A pair of guards, apparently on perimeter patrol, had made it dangerously close to the group now, so close that Erich could smell the bug spray they had used. They still hadn't spotted the group because a mosquito net hammock stood between them, but Erich could tell that their patrol route would run them directly into the path of his group. He tried, somehow, to silently get Mitchell's attention. He was certain that no one else had seen the pair of guards yet, and knew that he must alert Mitchell. They had to alter their course, or they would be found. As Erich scrambled for a way to get Mitchell's attention, the wind shifted and caused a stream of smoke from a nearby pile of embers to flow across the group. Erich held his breath again, and then the smallest cough escaped from Sophia...and as Mitchell had feared, all hell broke loose.

CHAPTER THIRTY-NINE

As soon as that small cough had escaped Sophia's lips, flashlight beams lanced through the air and settled on the group. They began to make a break for it, but the flashlights were attached to submachine guns, and one of the men opened fire, spraying the dirt in front of them. Gema dove to cover Sophia, Erich spun with his weapon opening fire in the direction that he had seen the two guards, he saw one guard drop, the other diving to the ground. Mitchell stood and lobbed a stun grenade towards the center of the camp yelling for all of her people to get down and cover their eyes. Even through his hands, Erich could see the blinding flash, and the concussive blast was so loud that it took a moment for his hearing to return.

Erich stood up, trying to shake the effects of the stun grenade from his head. Floodlights from all around the camp had now been turned on, changing night to day in an instant. Erich blinked his eyes and shook his head again, and watched as some otherworldly form gathered behind the clearing smoke from the grenade. He couldn't tell if it was just an illusion from the smoke and the lights, or if it was an effect from the fogginess the grenade had caused to settle over his mind, but it seemed that shadows deep within the depths of the smoke were swirling, coming to claim them all. As Erich stood transfixed by the site, a shout drew his attention back to the present.

The guard that Erich had missed was standing mere feet from him pointing a snub-nosed machine gun at his chest, shouting in that strange language. Erich watched in horror as the man tightened his finger on the trigger, he tried to think of any escape but nothing came...but just then the shadows that had been swirling through the smoke burst forth and with a roar, Raja sliced the man across the throat with a massive paw. The man fell to the ground, dead before his body landed. The jaguar seemed to give some of the other men pause as they advanced on the group and that hesitation was enough time for the twins to erupt in a flurry of devastation. The two of them danced through the guards, blades swinging, inflicting damage with every single movement.

Paulus and Nagato had also now joined the fray, going immediately to the aid of Gema and Sophia, each of them flanking the two to ensure that no damage came to them. Paulus stood in the center of the glaring lights, bare-chested, the tattoo on his back seemingly alive with energy. As the twins rolled through the guards, Raja made a beeline for the smallest figure in the clearing. Erich watched in horror as the great cat leapt over Paulus, knocking Gema down in the process and slammed into Sophia, knocking her to the ground, attacking her face. Erich had leveled his gun and was preparing to pull the trigger when he realized that the girl was laughing. The sounds were so foreign in this landscape of death and destruction that he almost didn't know what it was, that is when he noticed that Raja wasn't attacking the child, she was licking her face. Sophia struggled beneath the weight of the beast, laughing and trying to push her off. Erich had no idea what to make of it, and as he turned back to continue the fight his blood ran cold.

Malik stood mere feet from Erich, a gun leveled at his chest, a look of pure hatred on his face. "Enough!" he shouted and shot, missing Erich's head by such a small fraction of an inch that Erich felt the top of his ear torn off and blood running down his cheek. "Bring me back the girl or I will kill this man. This is the only offer you will get. Any other choice will result in the death of all of you. I only want the girl; I need her...the rest of you, I do not. Bring her to me now!"

Erich faced the man who had taken his daughter, taken the

love of his life, and who clearly planned to take his life, and shouted defiantly, "Paulus take Sophia, escape into the forest, and don't look back!"

Malik simply sneered as he spoke, "So be it...," he said and pulled the trigger.

For a moment, everything seemed to move in slow motion. Erich heard Gema scream behind him, saw Mitchell raise her gun towards Malik. He watched the puff of smoke and flame shoot from the end of the gun, braced himself for the impact, the cold bolt of lead and steel that would end his life. He thought about everything that he had missed. He would never again hold Gema in his arms, never watch his daughter grow, never hold his grandchildren. In that split second, Erich contemplated the seeming futility of it all. He had done his best and Malik still won. He would still lose his family; this man would still stop at nothing to gain power. An overwhelming sadness gripped Erich as he prepared to meet his end.

And then...he felt something strange, it started as a tingle in his back and surged through him, it felt as though a bolt of pure energy had passed through Erich, illuminating the night, bringing with it the promise of hope. He felt the unbelievable power surge all around him and heard the smallest voice say forcefully, "NO!" Erich could not imagine where the voice had come from. It seemed to fill his ears from all directions, to come from everywhere and nowhere at the same time. He watched as Malik's face changed from one of sneering confidence to one of abject terror. He felt a tiny hand close on his and looked down into the storm blue eyes of Sophia.

Sophia stood, holding her father's hand, her other hand stretched out before her. There was an energy visibly pulsing from her open palm. It struck the incoming bullet, and the projectile disintegrated as though it were made of sand, falling harmlessly to the ground. Malik stared at the child. The jungle had fallen silent, the girl stood, her long hair lit by the mysterious light eminating from her hand. The energy ceased pulsing and Sophia lowered her hand and spoke, her voice strong and defiant, "There will be no more bloodshed here tonight. Take your men and go."

Everyone in the clearing simply stared at the small girl, the giant black jaguar standing at her side. Malik looked as though he wanted to say something, but he simply lowered his gun and turned away. Erich looked at his daughter in awe and spoke in a hushed voice, "You saved my life, Sophia. How did you do that?"

Sophia seemed to think about the answer to the question for a moment and then she simply stated, in the way only a child could, "I'm not really sure..." And turned to walk away. As Erich turned to follow his daughter he heard a noise and turned. Malik stood with his gun pointing at Erich once more and said, "She can't save you this time." As his finger tightened once again on the trigger, an ululating cry from the treetops above them could be heard. Malik did not pull the trigger. Instead, he looked up, trying to place the strange whistling sound he heard, and just as he realized what the sound was, three arrows fletched with bright red feathers buried into his chest.

Two men ran toward Malik, shouting to the others who all raised their weapons and fired towards the treetops. The men grabbed their fallen leader and lifted him, carrying him into the jungle beyond the clearing. As they did, there was a whoomping sound from overhead, the sound of fuel being lit, and blooms of fire erupted all throughout the treetops. There were clearly several dozen men in the trees now armed with flaming arrows. Another war cry broke out, and several of the archers let their arrows fly. Flaming arrows struck the tents in the center of camp, setting them on fire. Several men fell, arrows sticking from their chests. The rest of the men turned and ran, disappearing into the jungle.

Erich and his group stood in shock, too afraid to move, not wanting to draw the attention of the archers. Erich, Gema, and Raja protectively circled Sophia while Mitchell and Rock held their weapons at the ready, aiming high up into the trees. The branches rustled as the hidden archers gave chase to Malik and his men, and their war cries could be heard growing more and more distant. Rock, not surprisingly, was the first to speak, "Well what the hell do you suppose that was?"

"I would venture to say that was salvation, my dear boy."

Graham said.

"By the way," Rock said turning to Erich, "how many more times you figure you're gonna need your ass saved today? I'd love to see that disintegrating bullet trick your kid did again." And with that, he reached down and tousled Sophia's hair, earning a half-hearted growl from Raja in the process. "And, she seems to be over you, huh Padre?" Rock said pointing to Raja.

"It looks like she was after Sophia all along," Erich said, wonder filling his voice. "She led us straight here, I don't know how or why...but she found you..."

Sophia placed her hand atop the giant cat's shoulder, "I don't know why either...did I hear you call her Raja?" she asked Erich.

"Ya, we don't really know what her real name is, but she doesn't seem to mind being called Raja, I think you can probably call her whatever you want." He smiled down at the girl.

"Raja is a good name, I think it suits her," Sophia said stroking the cat's fur, Raja, purring loudly, was obviously enjoying this contact with the child.

Graham spoke again, "That still doesn't answer who saved us just now, and do you think that we should go after Malik?"

"I think Malik has his hands full," Mitchell said with a smile, "As for who saved us, it has to be the tribe that's been following us. My guess is that they saw that Malik was hurting a child, something that most of these tribes won't stand for, and so they came to our rescue."

Graham nodded his head, "And I would wager that Sophia's little...well, whatever that was that she did...convinced them to help. These groups tend to be superstitious and magic-based, and a sight like that would win their loyalty more times than not."

"Ya, but who are they?" Erich asked.

Almost in answer to the question, a man dressed in a simple loincloth, red paint smeared under his eyes, carrying a bow and a quiver of arrows fletched with bright red feathers, dropped from the treetop canopy into their midst. Rock quickly held his gun up, prepared to fight the stranger, but Mitchell placed her hand on the barrel of the gun and pushed it back to the ground. "This fella and his friends saved our lives Rock," she said calmly, "I don't think a gun in the face is a proper reception. Who are you? Do you speak English?"

The man simply stared at them and spoke a few words in a language that Erich had not heard before. He spoke the words again and turned to walk away. Sophia spoke up, "He wants us to follow him, he says he is a friend and has something to show us..."

"How can you know that?" Graham asked.

"I...don't know...but I can understand him...," the girl said with an awkward smile.

"How do we know that we can trust him?" Erich asked.

"Well, if he wanted us dead, he and his friends could have just left that to Malik...," Mitchell said.

"Good point," Erich said, "Sophia, could you ask him why they saved us?"

Sophia spoke quietly with the man for several seconds, Erich was in awe of the fact that it sounded like she was completely fluent in this new language. The archer spoke for a few more seconds and pointed to Paulus.

"He said the tattoo on his back," Sophia said pointing to Paulus, "is what made them realize that we are friends. He said that symbol is sacred to his people."

"Well, then let's see where our new friend is taking us, it seemed to work out well before," Erich said pointing to Raja. He then slipped his hand into Gema's and reached his other hand out to Sophia, and the group followed the strange archer into the jungle.

CHAPTER FORTY

Tarrin walked slowly down the steps of the rocking boat into the area where they held the prisoners. The smell from down there always made him feel slightly sick, but he pressed on. He had come down almost every day since they had left Noah and his people to bring Namaah water and something small to eat. Jakon had not been pleased, had said that this showed weakness and that she would comply if she were starving to death, but Tarrin had convinced him otherwise. There was nothing that would make Namaah go against Noahim, of this Tarrin was certain. He had tried to take the information himself from her, to read her mind, but Noah must have taught her to protect herself against this type of invasion, and no one had been able to penetrate it. His hope was that his mercy would weaken her defenses enough to allow him entrance into her mind. Then they would have the information that they needed.

As Tarrin entered the room, he heard a deep, guttural voice talking and saw a large man, one of the tattooed brutes from the desert, standing inches away from Namaah. His hand was firmly holding her between the legs, and he was hissing at her, "Maybe I can get you to talk," he spat, "I know that I can get you to scream...you are quite a beautiful woman..."

Namaah said nothing.

This only seemed to excite the man. He leaned in even closer and licked her cheek. Namaah struggled against the chains that held her arms above her head and bound her feet together, swaying slightly as she tried to get away from the huge man. "Please..." was all she said.

"You will beg me for more once I am done with you...I saw your pathetic husband...he could not stop us from stealing you away from him...a man so weak clearly cannot please a woman. I will be sure to tell him how much more you enjoy my company as I slit his throat." This elicited a small laugh from the other three men in the room.

The man moved in to kiss Namaah, she spit in his face, seething. The big man raised a fist and slammed it into her gut. She gasped for breath, tears gathering at the corners of her eyes as the man pulled a knife from a sheath at his waist and pushed the rusty blade into her cheek.

"For that," he said, "I will make it last even longer."

"Enough!" Tarrin shouted as he walked up behind the man. "None of you are to touch this woman again, is that understood?"

"Leave us be, boy," the huge man said sneering and flexing his muscles, looking down at Tarrin, "This does not concern you."

"If I say it concerns me, it does," Tarrin said violently, "Maybe you are too new to know who I am. I am Tarrin, leader of the Army of the Gods, second in command only to Jakon." As he said this, Nala stalked in from behind him and bared her teeth menacingly to the men, emitting a ferocious growl.

The man looked between Nala, Tarrin, and Namaah, and then looked over at the other three men, each equally as large as him that stood at the side of the room. He gave a small nod and the three men all drew swords from their sides and began to advance on Tarrin. The big man momentarily smiled at Tarrin and was preparing to say something when Tarrin held up his hand, palm facing the advancing men. All three of the men froze in place as Tarrin lazily turned his attention back to the big man, "You dare attack me?" He gave a small, almost evil grin and pushed his open palm toward the three men that were frozen in place. All three shot backward at inhuman speed and slammed into the wall of the boat. Blood filled the air as their skulls collapsed on impact. The men crumpled to the floor...dead.

"Now," Tarrin said as he advanced on the big man, who was staring with wide eyes at his fallen comrades, "as for you." Tarrin lifted his hand and pushed out toward the big man, who fell to his knees as though a weight were pressing on him. "I want you to tell everyone on this ship, every man that came from your army, that if they disobey my words, they will cease to exist. Do you understand me?" The man nodded his head as Tarrin continued, "Good, and as a small reminder for you...," he said as he took the knife from the man's hand and cut a deep gash in each cheek. "Now go, before I change my mind and send you to be with your friends. And know this, if any more harm befalls this prisoner, by any hand...even those not your own...I will cut your heart out."

The man stood, eyes wide with fear, and ran up the stairs and out of sight. Tarrin turned to Namaah and sighed. "I am sorry that happened to you," he said, in an odd, friendly way. The tears had made tracks through the dirt on her face, and a small line of blood was trickling from the wound the man had inflicted with his knife. "Here, let me get that...," Tarrin said holding his hands up to heal her cheek.

She turned abruptly away and said savagely, "Do not touch me, with your hands or your gift."

"I am trying to be your friend," he said, sounding wounded, "Do you have any idea what those men would have done to you? I have seen their handy work myself many times...trust me, you would be better dead than left to the whims of men like these."

"Then kill me," she said, "I will never give you what you want."

Tarrin stared at her for a moment and said, "Why do you love him? Why would you choose to die, rather than just give Jakon what he wants?"

Namaah seemed caught off guard by the question and looked as though she were about to answer, but changed her mind, staying silent.

"I brought you some food and water," Tarrin said. "If I unlock your chains, will you try to attack me?"

Namaah actually laughed at this, "And do what? I have no gift; do you mean to tell me that you are afraid of me? What could I possibly do to you Tarrin? You are a coward."

Tarrin did not get angry. Instead, he held a hand up and the shackles binding Namaah fell to the floor. Her arms came down, and she sank, rubbing her wrists and ankles. The feeling of relief was so great that she thought she might burst into joyous laughter. "Thank you, Tarrin," she said meekly after several moments, "thank you."

Tarrin regarded her curiously and then stood to leave, but as he walked away she said, "Why do you follow Jakon?"

Tarrin stopped and without turning around said, "Because, like your feelings for your husband, I believe that Jakon is the one."

"It is not too late for you," Namaah said, a note of pleading in her voice. "You have mercy in you, that is why you stopped those men, you can still rejoin the side of good. Help me escape, come with me to the new Atla...please..."

Tarrin still stood facing away from Namaah and said nothing for several seconds before responding, kindness in his voice, "I already stand on the side of good Namaah, it is you and your people that are evil. I have no desire to live in the new Atla...we will make the entire globe our new Atla...and Jakon will rule it all. I will not help you escape. You will give us what we want, eventually...and know that if you try to starve yourself, Jakon has ways of keeping you alive...painful ways...but they work. There is no escape from this...help us or this torturous existence is your life. I will see you soon," he said and, without a glance back, he continued towards the stairs. As he climbed the first one, Namaah saw his hand at his side raise slightly and gasped as the chains from the floor sprung back up and around her ankles, the other chain flying through the air and back through the rusted metal eye hanging from the ceiling hoisting her back into her standing position...tied up and helpless. A choked cry escaped her as a tear ran down her cheek, the salt stinging the place where the man had stabbed the knife.

CHAPTER FORTY-ONE

Erich and his group continued following their guide for many miles. It seemed that they were going higher into the mountains, but it could just feel that way because they were all so tired. It had now been almost forty-eight hours since they had slept, and they had spent the entire time trekking through the roughest terrain on the planet or trying desperately not to die in a firefight with a madman. Erich thought he had never needed sleep more in his entire life, but when he saw Gema his spirits lifted.

They were together again, and they had a daughter...an amazing daughter. So much had changed in the last several days; Erich knew his life would never be the same. He looked in front of him as Raja and Sophia climbed a slight rise in the ground and were momentarily framed in golden light from the rising sun. *This small girl saved us all,* he thought, as the hill that they were climbing crested and sloped gently back down. When Paulus had come to him with the insane story of magic people, and good and evil, and someone out to destroy the earth, Erich hadn't really believed a word of it, and now he had no choice but to believe. *What other explanation was there for Raja? For Sophia being able to stop that bullet? For everything that I have witnessed in the past few days?*

As he thought about this, he turned to look at the jungle around him and was shocked to see what appeared to be the same pool that was safely covered by a giant glass dome halfway across the world. The pool that Paulus had said was called the Jala'Kim, although this one was much larger than the one he had found with the Ark, almost three times as large to be exact. Erich heard a gasp and turned to see Paulus gaping at the pool, a look of pure awe on his face. "Do you know what this means Erich?" he said, "this is the lost city of the Sala'Ma. This man and his archer friends must live here in the ruins of that once great society. We have found it..."

Erich watched as a golden fish swam close to the surface and then dove back towards the depth of the pool. Paulus was right, somehow this strange archer that they were following had led them to the very place that they had been trying to find. As they continued to move through the jungle, Erich started to notice other buildings and structures hidden everywhere amongst the trees. It seems that these people had somehow crafted their city to blend in so naturally with the surrounding jungle that, often times, it was hard to tell where the houses ended and the jungle began. Erich was in awe as he surveyed the lush green vegetation of the jungle, seeing faces peering out at him from inside the homes. Men, women, and children all seemed to be observing the newcomers from a safe distance.

Then suddenly, they were in a central courtyard. A huge clearing dominated the space, although Erich noticed right away as he looked up, that the trees at the top of the clearing still covered everything completely; you would get no view of this city from the sky. It seemed like even the trees in the canopy had been made to grow closed in such a way as to allow some sunlight in but still keep this jungle city invisible. As he was looking up at the trees, he felt Gema's hand tighten on his, and it brought his gaze back to the ground. They had continued walking as Erich had been staring up, contemplating the trees, and he had missed what everyone else had already seen.

There in the center of the clearing stood three gleaming white pyramids. Each was not very large, he guessed only twenty-five feet tall, but he felt that they were laid out exactly like the pyramids of Giza; the only difference being that these pyramids were much smaller and looked to be made out of white marble. Their beauty was astounding, and Erich had a hard time tearing his eyes away from them. There was a bit of commotion at the front of the group now as their guide began speaking animatedly. Sophia listened and then shook her head, the guide disappeared around the corner of the center pyramid.

"What did he say?" Erich asked.

Sophia seemed transfixed by the pyramids, and didn't take her gaze from them as she answered Erich, "He said that we must wait here...he said that there is someone we have to meet."

"Someone we have to meet...," Erich said slowly.

"Probably getting the chief or something...," Rock said.

As the group stood debating this new development, the man strode back around the corner of the pyramid, although he seemed to be alone. "Well, I guess we're about to find out," Mitchell said under her breath.

The man approached them slowly, and as he turned, the group could see that another, much older man followed behind him. As he approached, the archer turned and took up a position beside the front of the group, making room for this elder. The man that stood before them was incredibly old, Erich could not even hazard a guess as to his age. His long gray hair almost touched the ground at his feet, and his beard hung well past his knees. He had the gaunt, haunted look of someone who had spent too long living on this earth, and his back was bowed with the weight of his years. He shifted his eyes slowly, took in the group around him, and then he smiled. It was a smile so joyous that it made Erich want to throw his head back and laugh.

"After all of these years," the man croaked out, "you have come. I did not believe that you would ever be here, but you have come to save us all."

He bowed slightly to Sophia and took her by the hand, "Come, I have so much to show you. All of you may come; to accomplish this task, the child will need your help."

CHAPTER FORTY-TWO

Sophia, Gema, and Erich sat across an ornately carved table from the old man. Mitchell and Paulus stood behind them, Rock and Graham leaned against the wall on the opposite side of the room, and the twins sat on the floor by the doorway. The old man was lighting a long ivory pipe as all of them sat staring at him. Everyone looked silently at one another until Rock spoke slowly, "So...you speak English?" he asked.

Suddenly, it was if the old man realized what was going on and he began to speak in a voice that creaked with age, "Yes, yes, of course, I speak English, I speak many languages. I am so sorry for my rudeness...I have not even introduced myself yet. My name is Jikar... I have been waiting for over 10,000 years for this day, this joyous day."

"10,000 years?" Erich said flatly, "You mean that your people have been waiting that long I assume..."

"Yes, yes, of course, they have been waiting that long for this," running his hand through his beard, "but as I said, so have I. There is much to explain, and I fear very little time so let me speak and ask questions of me when I am done. I am the last remaining survivor of a group of people from a land called Atla. We fled a great catastrophe many years ago, so many, in fact, that I have lost count. As you may someday find, years lose meaning the more of them you live through. For much of this time I have been here, awaiting the arrival of the one. You see, shortly after coming to rest here and completing the building of the machines that will make the Gods' Noise, our high priest Noahim left and embarked on a journey to...well...that can wait. The point is that Noah, his son Rashan, and my son Amare left, and that was the last day that I saw them. So, I stayed here, trying to protect our order; preparing for the day that the machines would need to be activated. I continued on in this same way for almost one thousand years but by that time, my health started failing me. After all, I am not invincible...not in the slightest. I began to have trouble moving up and down throughout the temple, so I had my things brought inside where I could simply stay and continue my teaching, and then a wondrous thing happened. The temple itself amplified my gift, when I was inside the temple I could feel the power being strengthened, I felt like a much younger man." Jikar paused momentarily while he coughed several times loudly, "Alas, I know not how much time we have as the Ra'Naset has once again opened, I will leave history to history and focus on what I must tell you...what is your name child?"

"My name is Sophia," she said, holding Jikar's gaze.

"Sophia, what a beautifully perfect name for you, wisdom indeed..." Jikar said, seemingly lost in his own thoughts momentarily before coming back to reality with a shake of his head. "Well Sophia, I was told of what you did in the jungle, about the power emanating from your body...I wish that I could have seen it with my own eyes, do you think you could do it again now?"

"I...I don't know how I did it, I just knew that I wanted to save...my dad...and that I didn't want anyone else to get hurt and it just happened. It felt amazing, like I could feel every living thing, does that make sense to you?" she asked.

"It does indeed make sense to me. I have never been able to harness that type of energy, I am not sure that anyone ever has before, although I know that Noahim once felt that power, but when he tried to touch it, he said that it dissipated. I think there is something very special about you indeed, Sophia." Jikar said with a smile, "Well moving on then, I am sure that you are the one that our prophecies spoke of. You are the one that can turn on the machines that will make the Gods' Noise. You must, or the earth will be destroyed yet again..."

"I'm sorry...destroyed again?" Erich interrupted, "and what machines are you talking about exactly?"

"Yes, yes, destroyed again...how much clearer could I be? Noah and I, along with the other survivors of Atla, built the machines, the ones I have been living in to prevent the same catastrophe that destroyed our homeland, but only the one can activate them. I used to believe that Noah was the one the prophecy spoke of...but after reading the words of the ancients, I believe that Noahim's obsession with finding and killing Jakon corrupted him, and so we were forced to wait for the one to come. Forced to wait for over ten thousand years...but now you are here; you can find the machines...and make them create the Gods' Noise, and the world will be spared..." Jikar smiled as if this should all make perfect sense, "You see, this is the cycle...man builds up...nature destroys...man builds up...nature destroys. What happened to Atla was not the first or last time that it will happen. This is the way of the planet, although thanks to the machines, we can stop it this time, we must so that the earth is not destroyed again...so that civilization does not have to start over once more."

Erich began to speak, but Sophia held up a hand, cutting him off, "And how do I turn the machines on?" she asked.

Jikar looked absolutely flabbergasted for a moment, stuttering and stammering he exclaimed, "How do you turn them on? How do you turn them on?! Well, how should I know? I am not the one. By RaAlla, how do you turn them on she says...the Ra'Naset has opened, it has displayed its beauty...after that, RaAlla will fall from its place in the sky, and then the disaster will be upon us...and this little one wants to know how to turn on the machines...'"

Erich spoke quickly, fearing the man would die in front of them, "What is the Ra'Naset...you mentioned that before...What is RaAlla? These things don't make sense to us..."

Jikar slowly stood and walked to the window of the room,

grabbing a flower and setting it down in front of them all. "This is the Ra'Naset. It has only opened one other time in my incredibly long life...six months before the sky fell...six months before everything was destroyed."

Erich interrupted Jikar at the sight of the flower, "I saw this flower by the pool with the other ark, this exact same flower, the dots on the petals reminded me of something I couldn't quite place."

Jikar squinted his eyes, "Other ark...do you mean that you found where Jakon and his followers built their city?"

"Yes, I found it, although I didn't know who's ship it was until now. No one was there, they had all been dead for a very long time." Erich said.

"That is good...Jakon is a foe that you do not need...you also asked about RaAlla, that is the star god that these machines are a map of...there will be time to discuss all of this later..." Jikar said weakly. "For now, will you go, will you find the machines and turn them on..."

Erich looked around the room trying to gauge each person's reaction. Graham was the first to speak, "As the resident quack of this group, I say that I believe what this man is saying, and I for one...am in."

Rock grunted and clapped Graham on the back, "Well if the doc is going, I gotta go, he still has a series of lectures he wants to bore me with." This elicited a small laugh from the group.

Mitchell spoke next, "Sounds like I better come too...just to make sure you guys don't get yourselves in any trouble."

Paulus looked at Nagato and the twins and said in a strong voice, "As descendants of the great Noahim we will join this crusade."

Erich looked at Gema, deep into her eyes and leaned in and kissed her, "I am going wherever Gema and Sophia go," he said to everyone, and then leaning closer to Gema he whispered, "I am never letting you out of my sight again."

Sophia looked around at all of these people she had just met, and she knew that somehow, they would save the world. "You say I am the one," she said, "I am not sure what this means, but I know that if there is a chance that I can stop the suffering and death of millions, if not billions of people...I must also go...," at this final statement Raja burst into the room with a loud roar and lay her head on Sophia's shoulder. Jikar looked as though he had seen a ghost.

"Karok...," he whispered reverently.

"Is that her name?" Sophia asked, "Do you know her...she found me in the jungle...she seems to like me...I call her Raja..."

"Raja...," Jikar let the name flow on his tongue, "I think that is a perfect name. Karok was Noahim's RaSheen, and he was the most fearsome beast in all of the world. Raja is the spitting image of Karok, although now I can see that she is maybe a little bigger than even he was! Raja is your RaSheen, Sophia, she will keep you safe, she will protect you. She is the Bala'Ra."

"What is a RaSheen...and what is the Bala'Ra?" Sophia asked sheepishly.

"Oh, little one, there is so much that I need to teach you. I do not know how many days I have left on this earth, but I plan on spending each of them giving you as much wisdom as I can. Also, I had these books prepared in case you arrived after my death, please take them now, they will be a good start on your teaching. They will not teach you everything, but they will introduce the ways of the Mul'Ki to you. They will help you understand the special bond you have with your RaSheen and how to cultivate that bond...," Jikar paused as the coughing came again, "they will help you harness your gift. They will help you become the greatest Mul'Ki that ever lived."

Sophia looked around at everyone gathered in the room and then turned her eyes back to Jikar, "What is a Mul'Ki?" she asked in no more than a whisper.

Jikar reached out and put his leathery hand over the much smaller hand of the girl, and said in low, gentle voice, "You are Sophia...you are."

Keep reading for a preview of the second book in the covenant series...

Covenant: Genesis

Available summer 2021 from Story Well.

CHAPTER ONE

Erich Lawrence sat on the ground, his legs stretched out in front of him and his back leaning against the massive trunk of a strangler fig tree. He tilted his head back and stared at the trunk that seemed to extend into infinity. Gema sat on the ground beside him, her long brown hair falling over his chest, her head resting on his shoulder. He turned to look at her and smiled, a feeling of warmth and contentment that he had not felt for a very long time spreading through him. *This is real,* he thought, *Gema is here. I have a daughter.* He slowly exhaled the breath he had unconsciously been holding while he stared into Gema's mocha eyes and turned to look at his daughter, Sophia, who was sitting cross legged twenty yards away.

Sophia was nine years old. She had the same dark hair and olive skin as her mother, but she had her father's eyes. Growing up in a small village in the rain forest of Indonesia, her blue eyes had always set her apart, although they weren't the only thing that made Sophia different. Erich watched as the girl reached down and plucked a small, round stone from the ground in front of her. She held the stone flat in her out-stretched palm and squinting her eyes in concentration stared at it, as she quietly mouthed two words that Erich could not make out and as she did, the stone rose into the air several inches and hovered above her hand. A small smile tugged at the edges of her mouth, giving her a mischievous look, and with a thought she sent the rock hurtling into the surrounding jungle. Raja, the gigantic black jaguar that had been laying lazily at her feet, sprung up and chased after the flying stone, eliciting a small laugh from the girl.

"That is quite impressive young one," a voice croaked from behind them. Erich, Gema, and Sophia all turned to see Jikar hobbling towards them leaning on a cane made of polished wood. A small monkey ran around his legs chattering.

"Thank you Jala'Ona," Sophia said in a quiet voice, using an Atlan word that Jikar had taught her that meant wise one. Jikar, amazingly, was over ten thousand years old. He had come to the Amazon rain forest thousands of years ago as he and his people sought refuge from a great flood that had destroyed their homeland. They had traveled for many years, seeking the places where a great book, Ratam Ra'Ava, had instructed them to build machines that would prevent the catastrophe from befalling the people of earth again. When the survivors from Atla, led by a man named Noahim, had first settled in the rain forest, it had the added benefit of helping hide them from a man named Jakon. He had led a group of men that wished to gain power at all costs. Even though Jakon had been dead for thousands of years, the thought of his name still ran a shiver up Jikar's spine.

Jikar looked down at the small girl that sat on the ground in front of him and beamed. He had been waiting for so long. He had so much to teach Sophia, but unfortunately her training would only last three more days, at which time Sophia and the others would leave to fulfill their mission of turning on the machines that would prevent the same catastrophe that had destroyed Atla all those years ago from happening again. "Well, that is enough playing around, come...come we have much to do." Jikar said in the rushed whisper of a man who had too much to do and too little time.

"Where are we going?" Sophia asked, looking out into the jungle, straining to see Raja.

"Where are we going she says...where indeed..." Jikar mumbled. "Reach out to your RaSheen and tell her to come to the Jala'Kim. You have much to learn before you must leave..."

Sophia nodded her head and closed her eyes, silently communicating the directive to Raja. Raja was Sophia's RaSheen, a word that Jikar had taught them that meant Star Companion. "So you still say we need to leave soon then?" Erich asked, standing up and brushing the dust from his pants.

Jikar looked over as though he hadn't noticed Erich sitting in the clearing at all and shook his head, "Of course you need to leave soon," he said as loudly as he could, "The Ra'Naset has opened, has it not? Would you have us wait until it is once again too late? How many times must I tell you, once the Ra'Naset has opened, RaAlla will fall from his place in the sky and then disaster will be upon us. It may indeed already be too late…"

Erich watched as Jikar seemed to become more and more agitated. He still didn't fully understand what the old man was so upset about. From what he had learned so far he knew that the Ra'Naset was a flower that somehow only opened as an indicator of an impending disaster. Erich had now witnessed the flower in two locations. The first was in the museum that had been built to house the Ark, the discovery that Erich had made in the Indonesian rainforest. It turned out that had been the boat that had belonged to Jakon and his people. The second time was upon entering Jikar's chambers inside the pyramid that he now stood in front of in the heart of the Amazon rainforest, and although Erich did think that the flower was quite beautiful with its black petals dotted with white in what almost appeared as a pattern of some type, he could not in any way understand the significance of it. Adding to his confusion, Jikar had told him that RaAlla was a star in the constellation known as Orion's belt that according to an ancient prophecy would fall from the sky prior to the beginning of the catastrophe.

"What I still don't get," Erich said to Jikar as the old man was turning to leave, "Is that if the prophecy said that RaAlla would fall from the sky as a harbinger of the coming catastrophe, and you said that is exactly what happened before Atla was destroyed, then how is the star still in the sky now?"

Jikar looked at Erich as though he were an idiot before rasping out his response, "I never said that if fell from the sky, nor did the prophecy. I said that it fell from its place in the sky, which it did, as did all of the other stars."

"The day the sky fell," came a voice with a strong English accent from surrounding jungle, "That's what you are talking about, correct?"

Erich and Jikar turned to see Graham Reynolds, Erich's good friend and the team's mythology and archaelogy expert making his way from the edge of the forest with Rock, the giant boulder of a man who comprised half of the security detail for the team. Graham's unruly gray hair poked out at odd angles from under his khaki colored hat. He removed the hat and pulling a white handkerchief from his shirt pocket wiped the sweat from his brow. Jikar glanced over at him, clearly puzzled, and responded as he hobbled towards Sophia, "Yes...the day the sky fell...how could you know that is what many of the survivors had named that day?..."

"Because," Graham began, pausing long enough to catch the canteen Rock had just tossed to him and take a large swig, "Your people are not the only ones that experienced that fateful day. Myths from all around the world reference the day the sky fell, hundreds of them. It's quite probable that many more myths have been lost over the years...and that many still dwell with people in places like this one, hidden away from the rest of the world."

Jikar nodded and muttered, seemingly to himself, "Of course there would be other legends...there were many others that survived the fall...why would they not know it as the day the sky fell?...For that is indeed what happened..."

Erich stood up shaking his head and offered a hand to Gema to help her to her feet, "I still don't understand the term the sky fell, what does that mean exactly?"

"Well there are differing theories," Graham began but was interrupted by Jikar.

"You may discuss your theories another time. Sophia's training cannot wait; the very fate of the world depends on the things that I need to teach this girl. Please, allow us to be on our way," Jikar paused as a fit of coughing overtook him, "Gema if you would be so kind as to go and tell Amaro that I am taking Sophia to the Jala'Kim and that I may need help back to the temple, every second that I am outside of its walls I grow weaker. And Stone, if you could find Miss Mitchell and ask her to meet me in the temple in one hour I would appreciate it."

"It's Rock," the big man growled under his breath, shaking his head.

"Stone...Rock...I see no difference..." Jikar said with the hint of a smile as he placed an arm around Sophia and leaning heavily on his cane walked with the small girl towards the jungle. Gema pecked Erich on the cheek and gave him a smile before heading off towards the village to find Amaro. Erich smiled and watched her leave, a look of longing in his eyes, and then he turned to look at Jikar and Sophia, who were already deep in conversation on their way towards the Jala'Kim.

Rock grunted out a small laugh and clapped Graham on the shoulder, "Well looks like it's the three of us. I think Mitch is out with the twins, but who knows where they could be. You two up for some adventure?" he said glancing between Erich and Graham.

Graham winced as he rubbed his shoulder where Rock's catcher's mitt sized hand had landed, "I'm getting a little too old for adventure, but I would love to sit here for a few moments and finish filling you both in on the myths of when the sky fell."

"No need," Rock stated matter-of-factly in his east coast accent, "I already pretty much got it. Acorn hits a chicken on top of the head, he freaks out, thinks the sky is falling, tells a duck and a fox, and then the fox eats them all. Moral of the story, don't be a chicken. So come on Doc, adventure awaits." He said sweeping his hand toward the jungle.

Erich laughed at the look on Graham's face and said, "Lead the way Stone."

The rain pounded against the glass of the observation windows as the waves rocked the massive boat. Noahim sat at a small table overflowing with books and scrolls, a small lantern hung beside him, feebly attempting to chase away the darkness of the oppressive night. Thunder crashed as a bolt of lightning lit the room momentarily, causing Noahim to blink several times, the light temporarily burning an image of the piled books into his eyes. He raised a hand and pushed back a strand of his hair, which had now grown to his shoulders and he closed his eyes, leaning back and exhaling a pent up breath. "It has been too long old friend, we cannot find them..." he said to the seemingly empty room.

As he spoke a shadow at his feet began to stir and the massive bulk of Karok rose into view. The giant cat blinked his green eyes slowly as he stood appraising his Mul'Ki, and as he did he moved his head to push it into the hand that Noah had absentmindedly dropped to his side. A low purring sound eminated from the black jaguar as he nuzzled his head into his companion's hand, silently reassuring his Mul'Ki that they would accomplish their goal, they would find Namaah and Jakon. The silence stretched, only broken by relentless pounding of the waves against the side of the ark.

"If you have any ideas now is the time old friend," Noah said with a weak smile, shaking his head as he looked down at his Rasheen. It had been over six months since the day that Jakon had returned and taken Namaah from him. It had taken the first three months to find even a trace of Jakon and his men. Noah, his son Rashan, and his best friend Jikar's son Amare had set out with a group of men from Atla on one of the Arks to find Jakon, although the boat had not been prepared to leave, nor had the men and so Jakon had an almost five day lead by the time they were able to begin pursuing him. To add to the difficulty it seemed that Jakon had learned to hide his mind and the minds of those around him from Noahim, a skill that Noahim did not know existed.

The Mul'Ki possessed many gifts, each man having his own strengths and weaknesses, but almost all of them could locate and communicate with one another telepathically, the distance that a Mul'Ki could achieve this feat was dependent on how powerful their gift was, but Noahim had never been too far away to at least feel the minds of all of the other Mul'Ki, but Jakon had now twice surprised him by appearing seemingly out of thin air, and neither time could Noah sense Jakon or the many men that he brought with him. It was this hiding of their minds that had allowed Jakon to ambush Noah and his people and kidnap Namaah...and now she was lost to him. He fought back the tears that threatened to come and shook his head. *Not lost.* He thought to himself, *Not forever. I will find you Namaah, this I promise you.*

Noahim pushed himself back from the desk and stood, walking to the window that overlooked the turbulent sea. He could hear men on the deck of the ship shouting and looked out to see them struggling with what appeared to be a broken mast. As he watched the men racing around trying to secure the mast before it completely snapped a profound anger settled over him. These men had not come to tell him of this impending disaster. A broken mast would slow their progress terribly and this was something that he could not afford. He walked to the door of the observation room and flung it open, striding purposefully into the rain swept night. As he walked into the fray on the deck the air around him seemed to crackle with electricity. He turned to one of the men that was trying desperately to throw a rope over the mast to leverage it back into place. Noah held his hand up and pushed out towards the man, who was knocked from his feet, sliding backward toward the edge of the deck. As he slid Noah deftly flipped his palm up, the rope the men had been holding seemed to react to the movement like a snake that was being charmed and rose into the air. Noah moved his hand until the rope was positioned on the mast and then with another small flick of this wrist the rope wrapped itself around the mast and flew down to loop itself through a ring in the deck.

The men all simply stared at Noahim as he concentrated on the rope, using his mind to secure it to the ring. He then turned his attention to the broken mast, searching up its incredible height for the reason that it had failed. About two thirds of the way up he saw the break. It appeared that lightning had struck the mast, causing the fracture. The damage was extensive but Noah was certain that he could repair it. Holding his hands out to his side and turning his palms up he whispered three words in the old language and slowly began to rise into the stormy sky. Once he had risen to the point where the mast was broken he turned his hands out, whispered another phrase and a golden glow filled the air around his hands. The strands of the damaged wood began to pull together, just as when he had healed Jikar all those years ago in Atla on the day that Jakon had attacked the temple. Noahim lost himself to the memories of that day, the memories of all that happened since. The catastrophe, the journey to find suitable places to build the machines, all of the people they had met along the way, their new home in the jungle, Jakon coming back...taking Namaah to aid him in his quest for ultimate power. Noahim came back to himself just in time to see the final strands of the wood repairing themselves. He closed his eyes and balled his hands into fists and instantly he was falling through the blackness towards the deck.

He hurled towards the deck at impossible speed. Even though the break was only two thirds of the way up he still must have been over one hundred and fifty feet above the deck. The men all stood frozen, fearing that something was wrong as their leader fell through the sky. Noah opened his eyes and watched the deck as it rushed to meet him, and seconds before he crashed into it he again flicked his palms up and alighted softly atop the wood planks. A cheer erupted from the men but was short lived as

Noahim walked over to the man that he had thrown across the deck with his Ari and pulled him to his feet. The man was named Vallin. He was a short man, but built like an ox. His large brown beard obscured almost all of his face. Noahim had known him since he was a child. Vallin's father had been the captain of one of the original arks when Noah and his people had fled Atla. He had been a good man. Vallin had been born on the journey, raised at sea, and had instantly taken to the boats. The men here trusted him above all others when it came to matters of sailing. Noah had always gotten along with the man, trusted his instincts as a sailor. He knew that Vallin was a good man, but at this moment none of that mattered to him. *Vallin should have come and alerted me to this, had the break completed I would not have been able to repair it, and then where would we be,* he thought, *where would Namaah be if we were stuck here in the middle of this god forsaken ocean because this fool was too proud to come and ask for help.*

Vallin stared up at Noahim as he held him up, he had never before seen Noahim look this angry. He prepared himself for the high-priests wrath. When Noah did finally speak he did not yell as Vallin had expected, instead he leaned in close to Vallin's ear and spoke in a whisper that Vallin thought was too quiet to actually be heard, but each and every word that Noah spoke rang through the cacophony of the stormy night. "If you ever fail to alert me to a problem again I will throw you over board and leave you to your beloved sea, is that understood?" he whispered.

Vallin swallowed hard and glanced to each side, seeing his men standing there, staring. "It all happened so f-f-fast Noahim," he said with a slight stutter, "there was no time to alert you. I believed that I could f-f-fix the problem."

Noahim looked even angrier as he released Vallin's shirt and took a step back, his voice rising in anger, "Fix the problem! How did you intend to fix the mast, you have no gift! Had that mast broke I would not have been able to fix it, and we would have been as good as dead out here, and more importantly Namaah would have been as good as dead..." he trailed off, the thought of Namaah causing him to lose some of the anger that was welling inside of him, threating to instead over come him with grief.

"I could have fixed it with rope, like sailors have done for years." Vallin said somewhat defiantly, his confidence growing, "the gift is not the only way to accomplish such things."

"The gift may not be the only way, but it is the best way." Noahim said, sounding dangerous now, "and when it comes to finding my wife I demand to be told of anything that could delay us. You are not in charge here Vallin, I am."

"You know nothing of sailing," Vallin said angrily, "and I think that it is time that we turn around and head home. It has been many months with no sign of Jakon and the others. The have probably themselves been lost to this sea..." his voice softened somewhat as he continued, "I am sorry Noah, but you must know that if Jakon and his men are still alive it is not likely that Nama....."

Noahim turned, fire blazing in his eyes and lifted his hand, putting all of the power of his Ari behind it and thrust forward. Vallin was thrown through the air, hurtling towards the edge of the great boat. All of the men simply stood and stared, no one dared to even breath as Noahim stood, rain drenched in the center of the ship, Karok circling his legs. A shout came from the stairs that led down to the sleeping quarters, "Father!" Rashan shouted as he lept onto the deck. He quickly took in the situation, saw the men standing silently staring at Noah, Noahim and Karok agitated in the center of the boat, and he turned just in time to see Vallin's feet disappear over the edge of the deck as he tumbled into the darkness. He quickly lifted his hand and shouted a phrase in the old language and a rope that was coiled on the deck sprang to life and much as it had for Noahim seemingly acted of its own accord. One end of the rope flew towards where Vallin had just fell from the edge of the deck, the other into Rashan's hand. Rashan could no longer see Vallin, he trusted that his gift would find him and was reassured when the rope jerked and he was pulled several inches forward.

"Help me," Rashan shouted to the dumb founded men all around, who quickly sprang into action. Several men grabbed the rope and began to pull, heaving Vallin back onto the deck. The man crumpled to the floor and lay there in a pile, breathing shallowly. Rashan ran to him and placed a hand over his chest, whispering the words of healing, feeling that the man had several broken ribs from the power of his father's Ari. "You are fine," he whispered to Vallin, "I will heal you."

Vallin opened his eyes slightly and smiled feebly, "Thank you Rashan, you saved my life."

Rashan smiled back and nodded, continuing to allow his Ari to flow into the man's wounds, relieving his pain. Rashan was not near the healer that his father was though and he knew that Vallin would need several weeks to fully recover. As he ended the flow of energy and stood he turned to see his father and Karok still standing in the same place in the center of the deck. Both of them were completely soaked, Karok looked angry but when Noahim met Rashan's gaze he saw the regret and hurt in his eyes. "Please, everyone, keep sailing," Noahim said in a voice that was difficult to hear over the pounding of the rain, "We must find Jakon. We must find my wife." And then he turned and walked back to the observation deck, leaving the men still standing in silence.

Author's Note

Writing Covenant has been one of the most challenging and rewarding endeavors that I have undertaken, and I sincerely hope that you enjoyed reading it as much as I enjoyed writing it. If you did please reach out to me through the Story Well website and let me know. I've been working on this book for about 5 years, although a lot of that work was doing the research behind the fiction. Being inspired by guys like James Rollins and Dan Brown I hoped to craft a story that was entertaining but would make people stop and question what was real and what wasn't. If you want to know what parts of the story are based in fact or just take a deeper dive into the world of Covenant please visit www.covenantbookseries.com.

I would also to take a moment to thank a few people. First to my beautiful and amazing wife Jessie, who helped my craft this story and was my inspiration for Namaah. Truly this book would not have happened without her unwavering support of me, her belief in me astounds me on a daily basis. To my kids for inspiring me every single day by just being themselves. To Amy Davison for all her hard work editing and to Marty for giving me his input and constantly giving me enough shit to keep me motivated to finish this first book. To Keith Davison for waiting patiently for 5 years to be able to finish reading it, and continuing to ask Marty almost every time they talked if the book was done. To Amanda Hudson for her feedback and support. Sean Browning for all the late night talks that leave my inspired...and a little exhausted. My good friend Kurt Lohse for listening to me rant about all of the topics of this book for endless hours and always being supportive, and to Troy Koch for bringing Covenant to life with his voice.

Finally I would like to thank all of you for reading! I truly hope that you are as excited as I am to see what happens to, Noah, Erich, Sophia and everyone else, they are constantly surprising me! I thank you so much for taking this journey with me and I can't wait to see where this all ends up, and on the way may Ra'Alla watch over us all!!